The TRUTH ABOUT MR. DARCY

SUSAN ADRIANI

sourcebooks landmark

Published by Sourcebooks Landmark, an imprint of Sourcebooks, Inc.
P.O. Box 4410, Naperville, Illinois 60567-4410
(630) 961-3900
FAX: (630) 961-2168
www.sourcebooks.com

Library of Congress Cataloging-in-Publication Data

Adriani, Susan.
The truth about Mr. Darcy / by Susan Adriani.
p. cm.
1. Darcy, Fitzwilliam (Fictitious character)—Fiction. 2. Bennet, Elizabeth (Fictitious character)—Fiction. 3. England—Social life and customs—19th century—Fiction. 4. Gentry—England—Fiction. 5. Families—England—Fiction. I. Title.
PS3601.D75T78 2011
813'.6--dc22

2010049268

Printed and bound in Canada

WC 10 9 8 7 6 5 4 3 2 1

For my family,
whose encouragement and
support has made
all the difference.

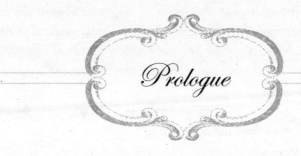

Prologue

SHE CAME TO HIM LATE ONE NIGHT AS HE SAT READING IN THE QUIET solitude of Netherfield's library, the delicate scent of lavender preceding her lovely form. He closed his eyes as he leaned his head back and inhaled her heady fragrance, a feeling of intoxication washing over his senses.

Without pause, she settled herself upon his lap and slid her arms across his chest to his shoulders, her slender fingers wandering to the edge of his cravat to tease the skin of his neck. He swallowed hard, struggling to regain the stoic composure she always managed to rob him of whenever she was near. Tonight, with her dark hair falling past her shoulders in silken curls, she was nothing short of breathtaking.

He looked upon her in wonder as the hint of a smile played seductively upon her rosy lips. She pressed her soft body firmly against his, her curves rendering him utterly powerless, her eyes sparkling with an invitation. Every fiber of his being ached to touch her, to tell her of his ardent—almost painful—desire for her, to finally claim her as his own after so many weeks of fantasies and sleepless nights.

Slowly, she began to feather her lips along his jaw, her hands blazing a path of fire over his chest before moving to unbutton his waistcoat. As her lips came to rest lightly against his own, so lightly they barely touched, she spoke, her voice low and sultry.

"Have you been waiting long?" Her breath was hot against his flesh.

With a throb of longing that could no longer be denied, the last fragments of his resolve crashed around him as he surrendered to her, claiming her lips in a desperate kiss and tangling his hands possessively into her hair. When they parted, their breathing was ragged, and their cheeks flushed.

"You have not answered my question, sir," she said on a breath. "How long have you been waiting for me?"

His voice was hoarse, and he whispered with feeling, "My entire life, Elizabeth…"

Fitzwilliam Darcy's eyes flew open. He was thoroughly appalled to discover himself in a leather chair in Netherfield's library, rather than the privacy of his own rooms. To make matters infinitely worse, he was aroused, and Elizabeth Bennet was staring at him from the next chair with a mixture of astonishment and impertinence written upon her face. He quickly averted his eyes, crossed his legs, and groaned inwardly. *Oh, good God!* he thought with rising panic. *Why is she staring at me like that? Surely she cannot possibly be aware of…?*

With as much aplomb as he could muster, Darcy took a shaky breath and returned his gaze to the book he had been holding in his hands. Perhaps if he simply ignored her and pretended nothing was amiss, all would turn out well. After a few moments of this, he hazarded a glance in her direction, only to catch her observing him out of the corner of her eye. He quickly averted his eyes and shifted his weight self-consciously in his chair, willing his inflamed ardor to cool.

"Are you feeling unwell, Mr. Darcy?" she inquired with a slightly raised brow.

He felt the heat of his blush and, without raising his eyes from his book, said as calmly as possible, "Perfectly well, Miss Bennet. I thank you for your concern."

"It is nothing, sir. I am relieved to hear it." There was a hint of amusement in her voice that caused his head to snap in her direction. She had returned to her reading but seemed to be struggling to repress a smile. Darcy's ire rose at her ability to laugh at his discomfiture, but rather than having a cooling effect on his lower body, for some reason he could not explain, he found himself becoming even more aroused. It was disconcerting, and he wracked his brain for anything that might afford him an opportunity to compose himself enough to be able to flee from her company.

Think, man, think! Something to repulse… something to repulse. He drummed his fingers upon the arm of his chair. He repressed a shudder. *Of course, Caroline Bingley. Caroline Bingley in one of those hideous orange frocks she favors. Hmm… and feathers. I must not forget feathers.* Darcy repeated his mantra, inhaling deeply. *Ah, yes, much better… much better, indeed.*

After several minutes, he felt in complete control of himself once again and, as though to prove a point to himself, allowed his gaze to flicker toward Elizabeth. She was reading, her bottom lip caught between her teeth as she wound a stray curl around one finger in an absent fashion. She presented a delightful picture, and Darcy found himself enchanted. His mind drifted from Caroline Bingley in her hideous orange frock to musings of a far more pleasant nature. *Elizabeth… my very own, lovely Elizabeth, just arrived at Netherfield, her hem six inches deep in mud, her hair disheveled, her creamy skin glowing. Oh, yes…*

Darcy began to feel a familiar tightness in his breeches. "No! Oh, no," he moaned aloud.

"Is something the matter, Mr. Darcy?" Elizabeth asked, raising her head.

"No, not at all, Miss Bennet," he stammered in a strained voice. "I was merely taken unaware by something I had just… read. I apologize for disturbing you."

With a frown, Elizabeth laid aside her book and rose, averting her eyes as she smoothed her gown. "If you will excuse me, sir, I fear my poor sister must be wondering what has become of me."

"Of course," he muttered. Darcy didn't dare rise. He would rather break with correct etiquette and appear rude at this point than risk exposing himself, quite literally, to any further mortification in front of Elizabeth. Turning his full attention back to his book, he proceeded to give the illusion of engrossing himself thoroughly in its text. Darcy did not move until he heard the click of the door as it closed soundly behind her. Throwing his head back with relief, he expelled a long, slow breath, ran his hands over his face and through his hair, and cursed himself for being so susceptible to her charms.

Chapter 1

ELIZABETH HAD NEVER BEEN SO HAPPY TO LEAVE A PLACE IN HER entire life. Surely she would always remember with fondness the rewarding occupation of nursing her dearest Jane back to health. Bingley, of course, had been nothing but his gracious, amiable, and generous self. He was an excellent host, forever solicitous of both her welfare and that of her sister. *His* sisters, however, had been everything that was *un*gracious and condescending, and the proud and haughty Mr. Darcy, in her opinion, had been little better.

It had not escaped Elizabeth's notice that the man seemed to materialize everywhere she had happened to venture during the few moments she was able to leave Jane for any length of time. She had met him quite by accident in the library on countless occasions—and also in the conservatory, in the music room, in the morning room, in the garden, and on the grounds. If Elizabeth had not known better, she would have sworn he was deliberately throwing himself in her way, but she *did* know better. Whenever they were in company together, Darcy was usually cool and aloof, yet he chose to stare at her constantly and with a level of intensity that had begun to make her uncomfortable. Surely such a handsome, wealthy, and intelligent man, who was used to nothing but the very finest society, could not deign to look upon a woman of her inferior station and circumstances in life unless it was to find fault, and indeed, she knew he *had* found fault with her, almost from the very first moment of their acquaintance at the assembly in Meryton some weeks ago.

Elizabeth laughed as she recalled his disdainful comment. *"She is tolerable, I suppose, but not handsome enough to tempt me."* Yet, while she was at Netherfield, Darcy had paid her no insignificant degree of attention, even going so far as to engage her in several heated intellectual and philosophical debates while in company with the rest of their party, none of whom he had included in their almost-private verbal sparring. To Elizabeth's amusement, such pointed notice of her often resulted in Miss Bingley becoming angered, and Elizabeth had found herself banished to the far end of the table during family dinners, with only the inebriated Mr. Hurst for companionship, while Miss Bingley fawned over Darcy and tried to monopolize his notice. Yet, even at these times, Darcy's dark, penetrating eyes continued to seek *her* out. Whatever could it mean?

Charlotte Lucas had often told Elizabeth she believed Darcy admired her a great deal, but Elizabeth could not agree with such a notion. Her usual reply was to laugh it off and tell her, "That is simply not possible, Charlotte, for I know he dislikes me as much as I do him," before steering the conversation to some other topic. After a while, Charlotte no longer commented on such observations, but she did raise a speculative brow and cast a knowing look at Elizabeth each time she caught Darcy observing her friend, which was almost constantly whenever they were thrown into company together. Elizabeth found this occurred quite often.

The two gentlemen from Netherfield had just entered Meryton

on their way to Longbourn when they chanced to notice the very ladies whom they were, indeed, intending to call upon, standing on the opposite side of the street. With great eagerness, Bingley urged his mount toward the object of his affection, Miss Jane Bennet, while Darcy remained several paces behind, struggling against the turmoil incited in his breast by the pleasing form and fine eyes of Jane's sister Elizabeth.

It had been happening for many weeks now and, no matter how many times Darcy reminded himself of the unsuitability of her situation and the lowness of her connections, the lively intelligence, clever wit, and graceful yet unassuming manners of the lady never failed to impress upon him the very great danger he faced in spite of his disapprobation.

He had tried every method within his power to rid himself of his overwhelming—and rather disconcerting—feelings for her, but the bewitching Elizabeth Bennet would not grant him reprieve. When Darcy was awake, she invaded his thoughts constantly, and in the late hours of the night, she ruled his subconscious, leading him to forbidden imaginings of passionate splendor.

Darcy reined in his horse, his eyes fixed firmly upon Elizabeth. She was engaged in conversation with an unidentified gentleman who appeared to be paying her rapt attention. After a few moments, their conversation waned, and in the next instant, she looked up to see Darcy staring at her. She acknowledged him with a small, polite inclination of her head, which caused the gentleman she had been talking with to turn.

Immediately, Darcy felt the color drain from his face as his mind reeled with painful recollections of Ramsgate and his sister, Georgiana… and Wickham! *Good God! What the devil is George Wickham doing here?* Anger spread like wildfire through his entire body, leaving him fighting to master his emotions. It was not a feat easily accomplished in the midst of Meryton. He was seething as Wickham touched his fingertips to the brim of his hat, his mouth curling into a smirk as he acknowledged Darcy's glare. Darcy forced himself to look away toward Bingley, who was shrouded in happy oblivion as he smiled down from his horse at Jane Bennet. He had clearly missed the exchange between the two men.

This was not the case with Elizabeth, who had been appraising their interaction with some degree of concern on her face. Her gaze darted from Darcy to Wickham and back again. Without meaning to, Darcy's gaze came to rest upon her just as a particularly severe look of displeasure spread over his handsome features. Elizabeth started at this, and Darcy, instantly regretting it, softened his expression, perhaps more so than he would have wished, providing Wickham with a private bit of information—information Darcy would never have wanted him to have at his disposal. Turning from Darcy with a sneer, Wickham focused all his charm on Elizabeth and proceeded to engage her, once again, in conversation.

Darcy's blood grew cold. The idea of George Wickham gaining Elizabeth's good opinion was more than he could stomach, but what could he do about it? Nothing! Absolutely nothing without laying his personal business open for all the world to scorn. He could not bear to put Georgiana through such humiliation and censure. But what of countless other young ladies? What of *their* honor? What of *their* respectability? And what of his Elizabeth? Darcy suddenly felt all the frustration of his position anew as a familiar ache in his breast reminded him she was not rightfully his to protect.

Lydia Bennet's wild laughter echoed through the street. Wickham's easy manners and handsome countenance had most likely already recommended him to Elizabeth's youngest sisters. Darcy watched with resentment and alarm as Wickham conversed easily with Elizabeth. After several agonizing moments, her eyes turned up to meet his own tortured ones, and in their depths, Darcy could easily discern surprise, confusion, and curiosity. Surely, the witty and intelligent Elizabeth Bennet would not be taken in by the likes of George Wickham!

But what if he was in error? Wickham was charismatic and dangerous. Yes, she had no fortune to tempt him, but knowing Wickham as intimately as he did, would her relative poverty be enough to ensure her safety? She was certainly one of the handsomest women of Darcy's acquaintance, and she had a multitude of charms to recommend her to any man. Darcy was agonizingly aware of each of them. Another alarming thought occurred to him then—should Wickham happen to succeed in imposing upon Elizabeth, what slanderous falsehoods might he fill her head with about *him?*

Darcy's relationship with Elizabeth had always held an underlying level of anxiety. Even now, after nearly six weeks of being acquainted, including living under the same roof at Netherfield while she nursed her sister, it seemed tenuous at best, but any lies Wickham might now see fit to tell her could very easily cause irreparable harm to his suit. *But why?* he demanded in exasperation. *Why should that be of tantamount concern? As deep a desire as I feel for her, could I ever sanction myself to act upon those feelings? Could I ever truly allow myself to form any real design on her?*

He fought to repress the attraction he had felt toward her since the very first moments of their acquaintance. It had been a constant struggle, one he knew he was losing. *Bloody hell!* It was simply no use! Even the merest possibility of Elizabeth Bennet thinking the worst of him—and at Wickham's hands—made Darcy's present agitation all the greater. He could not leave his desire for her esteem to chance, and with an impulsiveness few who knew him in Hertfordshire would recognize, he leapt from his horse.

This action finally succeeded in rousing Bingley from his unabashed admiration of Jane, and he followed Darcy's lead with enthusiasm. Blissfully unaware of the hostility radiating from his friend, Bingley greeted the assembled group, then turned his attention back to Jane. "It is a pleasure to see you this morning, Miss Bennet, and all your sisters! We were just on our way to Longbourn to call upon you when we happened to see you here. It is certainly an exceptionally fine day, is it not?"

Jane blushed becomingly before replying that, indeed, it was. Denny, one of the officers under Colonel Forster's command, stepped forward then to introduce Wickham to Bingley's acquaintance, informing him that his friend was to take a lieutenant's commission with their regiment, now quartered in Meryton. Bingley received him with his usual unaffected good humor and, though he gazed at Jane every few seconds, somehow managed to maintain an intelligent discourse with the gentlemen.

Darcy silently noted Elizabeth's continued observation of his thinly veiled hostility toward Wickham. He knew he must speak, or she would certainly think the worst of him for such animosity. With nothing short of a supreme effort of will, he forced himself to assume a semblance of composure and inquire after the health of her parents.

She met him with civility as she replied, "They are both in excellent health, I thank you," and fell into silence.

"Um, do you often walk into Meryton, Miss Bennet?" he asked, failing to suppress a scowl at his adversary who, at that moment, dared to be smiling at *his* Elizabeth while attempting to speak convincingly with Bingley.

"Why, yes, Mr. Darcy. It is a pleasant enough walk, and as you can see, there are always an abundance of acquaintances to be met with." Here, she glanced boldly at Wickham. Darcy wrestled most fervently to hide his displeasure. Elizabeth continued calmly, "What think you of the village, Mr. Darcy?"

"Charming," he muttered, his answer perfunctory.

"And have you had an opportunity to acquaint yourself with the various establishments, sir?"

"What? No, not well. I have been too much engaged since my arrival to have had that privilege."

Though Wickham's eyes appeared to be focused most diligently on the rest of their party, Darcy knew with certainty Wickham was paying very close attention to his conversation with Elizabeth. The master of Pemberley desperately wished to say something—anything—that would communicate an appropriate warning to her in some small way, but he knew it to be impossible under the circumstances. His frustration was extreme. Relief, however, came from a most welcome quarter.

"As it so happens, Mr. Darcy, there is a particular item I was hoping to procure this morning in one of the shoppes, just there, at the end of the street. If you feel you can bear my company, sir, I would be quite willing to assist you in familiarizing yourself with all the attractions Meryton holds."

Though Elizabeth's offer took Darcy by surprise, the benefit of such a proposal registered immediately. He tore his gaze from Wickham's profile long enough to offer her his arm, which she took after a slight hesitation. "Thank you, Miss Bennet," he said sedately, "I am most obliged to you."

He led her away from the group at a restrained pace, and Elizabeth nonchalantly pointed out various aspects of the town and certain shoppes.

Darcy offered distracted responses, contemplating how best to address her on the unsavory subject of Wickham. After walking far enough to avoid being overheard, Elizabeth startled him once again by inquiring, in a somewhat direct manner, how long he had been acquainted with Mr. Wickham.

Darcy overlooked her boldness and stated, "I have known him practically my entire life, Miss Bennet. His father was my father's steward, and a very respectable man. We played together as boys, grew up together on my father's estate, and, at one time, even looked upon each other almost as brothers." He paused to observe her startled reaction before blurting out, in spite of his better judgment, "You seem to take an eager interest in that gentleman's relationship with me, Miss Bennet. Why is that? Is it merely curiosity on your part, or something more?"

"Why, Mr. Darcy, I was concerned only for the gravity of your countenance. It appeared to me even more serious than usual, and I merely thought you could use a diversion. Seeing as you do so enjoy staring out of windows whenever something greatly displeases you, I thought, perhaps, you might appreciate the opportunity to stare *into* them instead."

Darcy, who under normal circumstances and with any other lady would have deemed such impertinence offensive, found it, instead—and when coming from *this* particular lady—to be nothing short of enchanting. Oh, how he dearly loved it when she took it upon herself to tease him! The corners of his mouth turned up ever so slightly as he said, "Yes, well, I thank you for your concern, Miss Bennet."

He then cleared his throat and continued, "After the passing of Mr. Wickham's father, my own excellent father supported him at Cambridge with the intention the church would be his profession, and a valuable family living would be his once it were to fall vacant. After my father's passing, which was but five years ago, Mr. Wickham professed a desire to study the law. Knowing by that time his habits deemed him quite ill suited for the life of a clergyman, I hoped rather than believed him to be sincere. He requested and was granted the sum of three thousand pounds in lieu of the living..."

If Elizabeth had not known exactly what to expect, Darcy surmised from her shocked expression it certainly was not this. Steadily and with no small degree of increasing agitation, he continued to give her a detailed account of Mr. Wickham's rather lengthy history of disreputable behavior.

When he came to the events of the previous summer at Ramsgate, however, the pain was still too fresh, and Darcy found his pride would not allow him to utter the name of his beloved sister. Instead, he revealed only the attempted seduction and elopement of an estimable young lady of his acquaintance. At last, he had done.

Elizabeth's gaze remained on Darcy's face. She was sickened to think she, who had always prided herself on her abilities of discernment, had been so ready to tease and insult the taciturn man before her—a man whom she had known for many weeks now—in favor of a complete stranger whom she had only just met and was, even now, for the most part, still unknown to her. Wickham's easy countenance and pleasing manners had, in the mere quarter of an hour she had spoken with him, managed to make quite a favorable impression upon her, but what a mistaken impression she had apparently formed! Elizabeth blushed with mortification. That it should have taken place in the presence of Darcy made her agitation all the more extreme. For some reason she could not quite explain or even fathom, Elizabeth could not abide Darcy thinking any less of her than he already did for having erred so greatly in her judgment of such a man as Mr. Wickham.

Elizabeth's anxiety was apparent, and Darcy felt all the responsibility of it as he stopped and, in a low voice full of heartfelt concern, said to her, "Miss Bennet, I am sorry, exceedingly sorry if what I have just related has caused you such distress. Please believe me, my purpose in doing so was solely to warn you and your sisters of the very great danger to yourselves from Mr. Wickham's society. It was not my intention to be malicious or to cause you pain, and I must beg your understanding and hope you will forgive me for having upset you."

Elizabeth looked away. "No, sir, I am perfectly well, and indeed, you are mistaken. There is nothing to forgive, but I find I must now confess to you how unprepared I was to hear such an infamous account of the same amiable gentleman with whom I have only just become acquainted. I find it almost beyond me to credit such dreadful accusations and such duplicitous behavior, yet, given what I have come to know of your character, and given it is also your intimate history with Mr. Wickham, I fear I must believe you and allow it is true."

Darcy uttered an audible sigh of relief and ran the back of his hand across his mouth. "Yes," he said quietly, "it pains me to insist it is true in every particular. Please believe my sincerity, Miss Bennet, when I say there is no one who wishes more than I that Mr. Wickham's gentlemanly appearance would ever be more than just an appearance."

By the time Darcy and Elizabeth returned to the rest of their party, Wickham and Denny had since taken their leave. Elizabeth went to Jane and requested they all return home without delay. Jane readily agreed. Bingley, who proclaimed he was not entirely prepared to part with the ladies so soon, begged leave to accompany them back to Longbourn—a proposal that was met with happy acceptance from Jane. Feeling the danger of spending more time than he ought in the disconcerting company of Elizabeth Bennet for one morning, Darcy declined to join them, saying he had some pressing correspondence he had long put off but now found required his immediate attention.

That evening, in the privacy of their room, Elizabeth disclosed to Jane the particulars of her conversation with Darcy. Never wanting to think ill of anyone, Jane insisted Wickham could not possibly be so very bad as Darcy's account of him made him seem.

"But, Lizzy, are you certain, absolutely certain, he has such designs at this time? Perhaps he has come to regret his past actions and is anxious to reestablish his character in the eyes of the world. He seems to possess such an expression of goodness in his addresses."

Elizabeth shook her head. "No, Jane. I would well wish to think as you do, but I cannot help but believe it unlikely. Though Mr. Darcy's countenance bespoke the most vehement dislike of Mr. Wickham, you did not notice the way Mr. Wickham looked at Mr. Darcy. His expression was one of such derision and insolence. No, I cannot so easily acquit him of the crimes Mr. Darcy has laid at his door. I feel most inclined to believe he is not a man to be trusted."

"By this account, then, Lizzy, he appears to feel as passionately for Mr. Darcy as Mr. Darcy does for him. Something very bad, perhaps even worse than what Mr. Darcy has related to you with regard to their association, must surely have occurred to promote such strong feelings of aversion."

"I confess I am of your opinion on this matter. Mr. Darcy was most disturbed, Jane. Even as he was speaking privately to me of Mr. Wickham, he remained visibly so. It is most out of character for him to reveal such emotions on any matter, and given this, I cannot help but wonder whether he may yet be keeping something further to himself."

Jane was thoughtful for a long moment before saying quietly, "Lizzy, I do believe Mr. Darcy must be in love with you."

Elizabeth stared at her and laughed. "Jane! Whatever makes you think such a thing? Surely Mr. Darcy feels nothing for me. You remember his comment at the assembly, do you not?"

"Indeed, it was very wrong of him to say such a thing at all, never mind in company, but, Lizzy, does it not strike you as incredible that a man of Mr. Darcy's notoriety—such a proud, private man of much significance in the world—would speak with you so willingly and openly about his dealings with such a man as Mr. Wickham? I can hardly credit it. No, it could only be a compliment to *you*, my dearest sister."

"Really, Jane, this is too absurd!" She laughed again. "You know just as well as I do, Mr. Darcy holds me in contempt for my decided opinions and my impertinent manner. He would never deign to pay his addresses to me, an unknown country miss with nothing more than fifty pounds and my charms to recommend me, not when he could have a fashionable woman with fifty *thousand* and a title."

Jane smiled. "I beg to differ."

Elizabeth made to protest, but Jane silenced her. "You forget, Lizzy, I, as well as Charlotte, have noticed the attention Mr. Darcy pays you, even if it is nothing more than staring at you from across the room. It cannot have escaped your keen observation that *you* are, indeed, the *only* lady he stares at." Jane shook her head. "No, there is no other explanation for it. Mr. Darcy *must* be in love with you." The discussion was continued in earnest, and half the night was spent in conversation.

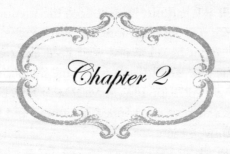

Chapter 2

THE NEXT DAY SAW THE ARRIVAL OF AN UNEXPECTED ADDITION to the family party at Longbourn: Mr. Bennet's cousin and heir, the Reverend William Collins. With the intention of making amends for an ongoing estrangement by his late father and the entail of Longbourn estate to himself upon Mr. Bennet's death, Mr. Collins journeyed from Kent to choose a wife from among Mr. Bennet's five daughters. If this did nothing to recommend Mr. Collins to the young ladies, it did at least add the promise of entertainment for their father, who was an enthusiastic admirer of the ridiculous. Mr. Collins did not disappoint.

Though none of Mr. Bennet's daughters, with the exception of Mary, could receive Mr. Collins's arrival or his attentions with genuine pleasure, the same could not be said for Mrs. Bennet, who welcomed him with open arms—as she would any gentleman of an eligible age and a good income. Mrs. Bennet introduced him to her girls with great cordiality and enthusiasm.

Being the most beautiful of the five sisters, Jane immediately caught his eye. Fortunately for Jane, however, her mother most dutifully pointed out to him that Bingley and his five thousand a year had preceded him. It was then only fitting for Mr. Collins to transfer his affections from Jane to Elizabeth—the next in age and beauty—and he did so with surprising alacrity.

"Lord, Lizzy!" her youngest sister, Lydia, laughed that evening after the gentlemen had withdrawn after supper. "I daresay you are becoming quite popular with all the pompous gentlemen in the neighborhood. First you are seen in Meryton talking *alone* with that dull Mr. Darcy, and now you have gone and caught Mr. Collins's eye, as well! What a good joke if Papa were actually to force you to marry one of them! I could not imagine being shackled to such wretched bores!"

"Oh, yes!" Kitty joined in. "But really, Lizzy, you are being selfish. Will you not leave *any* eligible prospects for the rest of us?" she admonished before bursting into a fit of giggles.

Elizabeth folded her arms and scowled. "Lydia! Kitty! I would remind you both not to talk of such things, particularly when you know nothing of the circumstances."

"Who shall be next then, do you think?" Lydia asked merrily. "Oh! I know! Mrs. Goulding has an old, incontinent relative visiting her. Perhaps he will do nicely for Lizzy, as well!"

Mrs. Bennet interjected. "Now, girls, that is quite enough. You know perfectly well Mr. Pritchard is far too elderly for your sister… although, he would likely leave her with a very pretty estate in Devonshire…" She frowned. "Now, Miss Lizzy, what is this I hear about your talking alone with that odious Mr. Darcy?"

Elizabeth blushed. "It is nothing, Mama. I was merely showing him some of the village. It was all quite innocent, I assure you. I have no interest in that particular gentleman, and I am quite certain Mr. Darcy has very little interest in me."

"I do not doubt that one bit," she agreed as she wrung her lace handkerchief. "I will admit there was a time when I would have been happy to see one of you girls so advantageously settled as mistress to that man's estate—goodness! *Ten thousand a year!*—but he has since shown himself to be such a proud, disagreeable man that I would not have him near any of you for all the gold in the Kingdom! No, Mr. Collins will do very nicely for you, Lizzy. Mark my words. You are very lucky to get such a man… so affable! So promising! So fortunate in his patroness, the great Lady Catherine de Bourgh!"

Elizabeth, for all her protests, could not convince her mother she would not suit Mr. Collins at all, nor would he suit her. In the end, she only retired to bed, determined to avoid Mr. Collins as much as possible and to also avoid doing anything in the future that might incite any unwelcome speculation about her and Mr. Darcy.

Over the course of the next few days, Elizabeth found herself often in the presence of Darcy. Though that gentleman continued to stare at her just as steadily as he always had, Elizabeth was startled on several occasions to have him approach her as well, with the obvious intention of engaging her in conversation. Elizabeth did everything in her power to quickly extract herself from his company and to avoid him whenever possible, making a point to speak politely with every officer or gentleman, save Lieutenant Wickham, who paid her even the slightest attention. She had no intention of speaking with Darcy, either alone or in the company of others.

Each evening Darcy now passed in Elizabeth's society, saw him become brooding and withdrawn. He could hardly like her friendly attentions to others, not when he wished for nothing more than her eyes, her lively teasing, and her smiles to be directed at him. He could not understand what could have occurred to make her wish to avoid him now, for it was quite clear to him Elizabeth *was* avoiding him. Though Darcy felt a great deal of pain over her inexplicable actions, he could at least rejoice in the fact she did seem to take his warning about Wickham to heart. She avoided prolonged contact with that gentleman, as well.

The following evening, the Bennets were all to dine at the home of their Aunt and Uncle Phillips in Meryton. Mr. Collins was delighted to find himself included in the invitation. He had been loath to part from Elizabeth, to whom he had been attentive since he had decided upon her several days earlier. Mrs. Bennet wasted no time by publicly proclaiming her immense delight with the match and encouraging it in whatever way she could.

To Kitty and Lydia, this continued to be a ceaseless source of amusement, especially since they considered themselves most fortunate to have escaped any such notice by the stodgy Mr. Collins. After all, in the opinion of Mrs. Bennet's two youngest daughters, what woman could ever be bothered to give two straws about a droll clergyman when there were far more satisfying prospects to be had parading themselves about the countryside of Hertfordshire in regimentals? They delighted in making their sentiments known.

With immense relief, Elizabeth managed to slip away from Mr. Collins's attentive and somewhat overbearing society while he spoke with great enthusiasm to her Aunt Phillips about the grandeur of Rosings Park and the condescension and affability of his patroness, Lady Catherine de Bourgh. In her aunt, Mr. Collins was sure to find a most obliging listener and, in Mrs. Phillips's guests, an audience eager to hear his raptures on his favorite topics for the greater part of the evening.

She soon found herself uneasy, however, as she recognized Mr. Wickham standing slightly apart from the other officers and guests in her aunt's home, an insincere smile gracing his face, and his gaze resting upon her. She had not spoken with him at any length since their first meeting in Meryton, when Darcy had cautioned her not to be taken in by his easy manners. Elizabeth had imagined any association with Darcy would have been enough to deter Wickham from wishing to renew their slight acquaintance, but in that she had been mistaken. He had taken every opportunity, on the few occasions when their paths did cross, to attempt to engage her in conversation. She could see by the determined look in his eyes that tonight would be no different, and indeed, no sooner had she left Mr. Collins than Elizabeth found herself being addressed with a low bow and an ingratiating smile.

"Good evening, Miss Elizabeth. I must say you are looking lovely this evening."

She returned his compliment with guarded civility. Wickham was far from discouraged. "I must confess I had hoped to have become better acquainted with you by now, but alas, I have not had the pleasure of seeing you in Meryton with your sisters these six days at least. I can only imagine this is due to some far more rewarding pursuit of yours, which must, undoubtedly, have a prior claim on your time."

Elizabeth did not know whether or not she trusted his words and, with a raised brow, replied, "I engage in many pursuits I find to be rewarding, Mr. Wickham."

"Do you indulge yourself in these rewarding pursuits daily, then?"

"Yes, I suppose I do, whenever I find I am at leisure."

"I see. And which pursuit, if you do not mind my asking, brings you the most pleasure, Miss Elizabeth?" Wickham inquired.

Elizabeth hesitated. "I am partial to any form of exercise that might afford me an opportunity to be out-of-doors, particularly when the weather is fine."

"You enjoy taking your exercise out-of-doors, do you? How interesting. Tell me, Miss Elizabeth, would I be correct to assume you also enjoy taking your pleasure *indoors* whenever you can?"

Elizabeth observed him with a puzzled expression. "Indoors, Mr. Wickham? I am not certain whether I understand your meaning. Certainly, when the weather is uncooperative, one will find pleasure in one's needlework, at the pianoforte, or in a good book, but you must own that one can hardly compare taking a turn in a stuffy drawing room to the satisfaction of a leisurely ramble in the fresh air of a wooded path."

Wickham's voice took on a tone she could not like. "Oh, come now, Miss Elizabeth, there is no need to be coy. I have noticed your intimacy with a certain gentleman from Derbyshire… or, to be more accurate, his marked preference for you. I can imagine it must be rather gratifying for a young lady such as yourself to be singled out by such a wealthy and distinguished man who has lived very much in the world."

Elizabeth gasped as comprehension dawned on her. Wickham lowered his voice in a disturbing manner and said in a throaty whisper, "Does his… society satisfy you, Miss Elizabeth? Because I, for one, would be most obliged to step in and instruct you myself whenever you may feel the urge for far more superior *companionship*. I assure you, I have never been known to disappoint a beautiful woman." He took a step closer while his gaze roamed over her form. A smirk began to tug at the corners of Wickham's mouth, and the same insolent sneer he had worn for Darcy appeared for her.

Elizabeth was appalled and sickened by the vulgarity of this man, and before she could stop herself or recall where she was, she raised her hand to slap him hard across his face. To her further horror, Wickham caught her hand roughly in his and forced it, instead, to his lips as he let out a soft, derisive laugh.

"Of course, I knew you and I would soon come to an understanding of sorts."

Elizabeth struggled to pull her hand from his grasp, but he gripped it tightly—almost painfully—his gaze boring into her in a most offensive manner before he finally released her, but not before muttering in her ear, "He is a very lucky man, Miss Elizabeth. Please be sure to give him my best compliments when you are next with him. And if you should ever change your mind…"

In alarm and disgust, Elizabeth broke away and fled from Wickham. If there had been any doubt in her mind about the credibility of Darcy's information regarding Wickham's character, the offensiveness of his address and his repulsive behavior had just removed it completely. She saw Jane in avid conversation with Charlotte Lucas on the other side of the room. Bingley, she was certain, had very likely been attending them, though at this moment he was moving quickly and deliberately in her direction with a frowning countenance. Elizabeth found herself extremely grateful that, for once, Jane had not succeeded in monopolizing his attention. When he reached her, Bingley drew her quietly aside into an unoccupied corner and addressed her with great concern. "Miss Elizabeth, are you well? Forgive me, but I could not fail to notice your distress as you were speaking with Mr. Wickham. Did he impose himself upon you in any way? Did he insult you?"

Elizabeth struggled to regain her composure. After a minute, she was able to find her voice and said shakily and with revulsion,

"I believe, Mr. Bingley, were you to reveal to me at this very moment prior knowledge of Mr. Wickham's intent to come here with the express purpose of insulting me in a most vulgar and offensive manner, I would not be at all surprised to hear it."

Grimly, Bingley then asked her to relate to him the entirety of her conversation with that gentleman, but Elizabeth, feeling far too mortified to think upon all that had been said, let alone repeat it to Bingley, adamantly refused. Wickham's disgusting manner and offensive implications of an intimacy between her and Darcy made her agitation extreme.

Offering Elizabeth his arm, Bingley scanned the room. Wickham had been observing them before sauntering over to Mrs. Phillips to take his leave. Once he was out of the house, Elizabeth visibly relaxed. Bingley was most solicitous as he steered her to Jane's side before politely excusing himself to speak privately with Colonel Forster.

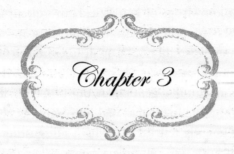

Chapter 3

When Bingley arrived home that evening, Darcy was engrossed in a book in Netherfield's library. "How was your evening, Bingley?" he asked absently as he turned a page. "I hope Mrs. Phillips's society was to your liking."

"An excellent question, Darcy," he responded heatedly as he threw himself into a chair by the fire, "but perhaps you might do better to inquire after the pleasure of Miss Elizabeth Bennet's evening, of which I can most heartily assure you there was none."

Darcy closed his book immediately. "Miss Elizabeth Bennet? To what do you refer, Bingley?"

"I refer, Darcy, to the disturbing and insulting behavior I witnessed toward her this evening at the hands of your so-called *friend* George Wickham!" Darcy's blood ran cold. Had he heard Bingley correctly? *His* Elizabeth accosted by Wickham? Bingley's expression told him all. Darcy leapt to his feet as his anger took a firm hold over his senses. "What in God's name did he do to her? Damn it, Bingley! You must tell me you protected her! Please tell me she is unharmed!"

Darcy was incensed and, in his rashness, took several threatening steps toward Bingley, a maneuver that caused his friend to jump from his seat and retreat several paces. Raising both hands to Darcy's chest, he replied in earnest, "Yes, she is safe! She is safe, Darcy! Calm yourself, man! She was only in conversation with him and not long, though I must tell you it was most distressing to watch. I believe he must have said such things to her that would never bear repeating in polite company, for she refused even to tell Jane—er, I mean Miss Bennet—what they were. At one point, she actually attempted to strike the libertine."

Darcy looked at Bingley with incredulity. "Elizabeth struck Wickham?" His unguarded use of her Christian name was lost on his friend.

"No," Bingley stammered. "He caught her hand before she could make contact, and that scoundrel kissed it, not at all inclined to release her, I might add. It was then when I went to her."

Darcy raked his hands through his hair, utterly sickened by the prospect of Wickham touching any part of Elizabeth's person. He began pacing the length of the room, praying for some modicum of control to return. "And what of her father? What of her uncle? Colonel Forster and the other officers? Did no one else do anything in her defense? Surely, you could not have been the only person to go to her aid? I find it impossible to accept an entire house full of people, including members of her own family, could be blind to such a scene!"

Bingley shook his head. "I could hardly believe it myself, but I was absolutely the only person aware of the nature of the exchange between them. Mr. Bennet was not present, her mother and sisters were engaged, and not even that half-wit of a clergyman, who has all but glued himself to her for the last five days, had any knowledge of the insult. I did happen to speak to Colonel Forster, though. He was most disturbed when I informed him of the incident and has promised most faithfully to personally look into the matter. I plan on riding to Longbourn tomorrow to speak to Mr. Bennet. I feel he should be made aware of the events that have transpired." He hesitated a moment. "I have been thinking, Darcy, perhaps it would be best if you were to accompany me, given your past dealings with Wickham and your insight into his character. I believe Miss Elizabeth's father has a right to know of what he is truly capable."

Darcy strode to the window and leaned his forearm against the casement, staring out into the night. Several minutes passed in silence before he finally spoke, his voice ragged with feeling. "I should have been there with her. This never should have been allowed to happen. She would not have left my sight for a moment."

Bingley shook his head. "Darcy, it was only by chance I caught the exchange between Miss Elizabeth and Wickham. I fail to see how you could have prevented what you may not have noticed yourself."

It was simply too much. All the frustration he felt from his endless struggle against his overpowering feelings for Elizabeth caused Darcy to explode. "I would have been *aware* of it, Bingley! I, who am most excruciatingly conscious of her every movement when I am in her company! I see every smile she bestows, every expression of tenderness, every breath that fills her lungs—none of which is *ever* for me!" He swallowed hard and tried desperately to compose himself.

Bingley's mouth dropped open. After a moment, he closed it and said, "I must confess I am at a loss. I had no idea you had tender feelings for Miss Elizabeth. Pray, how long have you felt this way?"

Striving to collect himself, Darcy muttered, "Forgive me. It has been so for many weeks now. I am only surprised you failed to notice it, because it was most easily discerned the other day in very little time by George Wickham." He let his forehead rest against the glass, allowing its coolness to soothe him.

"Does Miss Elizabeth know?"

Darcy sighed. "That I am in love with her? No, and I would be most grateful if it were to remain that way."

"But surely you *mean* to tell her?"

"No, Bingley, I assure you I do not."

"But why, Darcy? Why would you endeavor to keep such extraordinary feelings hidden from her? What could ever be gained by it? Do you not think Miss Elizabeth would welcome your addresses?"

"No," he said evenly, "she would not. She does not return my regard, and I would be lying to myself if I believed differently. Even if, by some stroke of exquisite good fortune, Miss Elizabeth were to love me, it would in no way change our circumstances. I cannot make a fortuneless country beauty the mistress of Pemberley, no matter how desperately I may desire it. Duty to my family—to my position in society—strictly forbids such a union between us."

"Duty to your *position*?" Bingley cried. "Duty to your position be hanged! What about your duty to yourself, Darcy? Would it not bring you incredible joy and comfort to make Miss Elizabeth your wife and to see your children running through the halls of Pemberley? Would you not truly be content to grow old with her by your side? Do you honestly expect me to believe your family and your friends—all those who most desire to see you happy in life—would wish instead for you to spend your days alone and in misery, or worse, married to another in a loveless union, simply because the one woman you happened to fall in love with does not move in the same social circles as they do? I cannot accept it. Elizabeth Bennet is the daughter of a gentleman, and she is in every way a lady. You are equals; no one can deny that."

Darcy turned away from the window and faced him. "But what of her mother, Bingley? What of her younger sisters, her aunts and uncles? Certainly you must recognize their behavior and low connections must materially lessen the chances of one's marital felicity. Anyone who chooses to align themselves with such a family would be shunned in London society. Her family would never even be acknowledged, never mind accepted. I would not wish that upon Miss Elizabeth. I would not wish it upon anyone whom I hold dear."

"And this should be of significant consequence? The insipid opinions of the London *ton,* whose favor and disfavor, approval and censure, are so easily bought and sold like tradeable goods? No one who conducts themselves in such a manner could ever esteem a man of your impeccable character and intellect in the first place, Darcy! And, surely, your family would not be so insensible and unfeeling as to follow their example. Would you have *me* act in such an irrational manner? Would you have me make myself unhappy—expect me to give up my Miss Bennet—for no better reason other than Caroline's and Louisa's selfish disdain for the connection?"

Darcy did not respond.

"Do you not approve of my relationship with Miss Bennet, Darcy?"

Darcy winced. He had not wanted it to come to this, especially tonight. "I am sorry, Bingley, but I cannot. You clearly do not understand the consequences and the disgrace you will suffer should you continue in your endeavor to align yourself with such a family. It would be your ruin. I cannot speak any plainer than this."

Bingley was angry; Darcy had never seen him more so. "You are correct, Darcy, I do not understand anything of the sort! I do, however, comprehend the wretchedness Miss Bennet and I would suffer were I to allow myself to be so *disgracefully* persuaded from following the counsel of my own heart on such a matter! No, Darcy. That is a consequence I am most unwilling to suffer for any person, be they relation or friend, and most *especially* for any damned, misguided notion of duty!" He turned then and stormed from the room, leaving Darcy alone with much to consider.

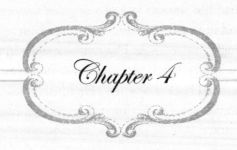

Chapter 4

Elizabeth had been disturbed by Wickham's behavior toward her the previous evening, more particularly so because they had not been alone together, but in public, among her family and friends. What she found even more distressing was his vulgar allusion to a clandestine arrangement between Darcy and herself. She was completely baffled as to where Wickham could have gotten such a notion. Thoughts of it plagued her for hours before she finally succumbed to fatigue and was able to sleep.

Her slumber was fitful at best, filled with disturbing dreams where Darcy sat staring intently at her, much in the same manner he had when she had stayed at Netherfield to nurse Jane. But rather than the usual haughtiness and criticism, his dark eyes held a burning desire that penetrated every fiber of her being and left her body aching in anticipation of she knew not what. The sensation remained with her long after she awoke.

When Elizabeth arrived downstairs for breakfast, she was disconcerted to learn Bingley and Darcy were locked in conference with her father in his library. She could only imagine one reason for it—the events of the night before. She sat heavily, suddenly feeling not at all hungry. She had hoped Bingley would have kept the mortification of such an encounter between her, Bingley, and Jane. She had not wanted him to worry her father unduly, and she certainly had not wanted him to bring Darcy into the fold. She was now thoroughly relieved she had not yielded to Bingley's demands that she tell him all Wickham had said to her. How would she ever be able to face Darcy today if he had been made aware of it, as well? The recollection of Wickham's disrespectful behavior, coupled with the distracting tingles from her dreams, brought a deep flush of mortification to her face.

Halfway through breakfast, the gentlemen joined them. Her father's expression was grave, as was Darcy's. As they sipped their coffee, both men silently appraised Elizabeth—Mr. Bennet with a father's concern, Darcy with something much more unnerving. His eyes had been troubled, almost fierce when he had first entered the room, yet there was an immediate softening and a warmth that occurred the moment he settled his gaze upon Elizabeth. The intensity of that gaze aroused sudden stirrings within her and made Elizabeth feel far more vulnerable than she ever had at the mercy of Mr. Wickham. She could not recall seeing that fire in his looks before, yet there was something notably familiar about the way his eyes seemed to penetrate her. Could it always have been there, and she had simply failed to recognize it for what it was? She found the idea most distressing.

As the morning was particularly fine, Mrs. Bennet encouraged the young people to walk out together. Though Mary had proclaimed she would much rather stay at home, as there was a particular passage in a book she wished to meditate upon and would not be swayed, the rest set out directly. The two youngest girls were bent on going into Meryton but, given the likelihood of meeting Wickham there, Jane and Elizabeth were not eager to sanction such a scheme.

"But why can we not go, Lizzy?" demanded Kitty. "We promised Mrs. Forster most faithfully to call on her this morning."

"Yes, Lizzy, you and Jane cannot tell us we are not to go!" Lydia crowed. "You would not have us disappoint the wife of the colonel of the regiment, would you? Mama would be quite angry with you, for Harriet and I have become such particular friends. Besides, we were hoping to look at some new fabric and ribbon for Mr. Bingley's ball. It is to be held in three weeks, you know, and we cannot possibly wear the same tired old gowns in front of all the officers. Lord, how would we ever get husbands?"

"Lydia, please!" Jane hissed, blushing.

Darcy rolled his eyes.

"Well, I daresay we shall go without you, then," Lydia insisted. "Just because you do not wish to go, it shall not keep us from going by ourselves. What fun we shall have!" This declaration was seconded immediately by Kitty.

"Miss Lydia," said Bingley, "I see no reason why we should not continue on to Meryton together." He fixed Darcy with a significant look before he turned to Mr. Collins. "Gentleman, what say you to this? Would it not give you great pleasure to accompany these lovely ladies into Meryton on such a fine day? It would be unpardonable for us to allow them to continue on without our solicitous escort."

Here, Mr. Collins proceeded to simper and smirk about the delicate constitution of elegant females, while Darcy, who looked as though he would rather ride his horse backward to London while blindfolded, managed to mutter that he could think of nothing else he would rather do than shop for ribbons in Meryton.

Hence, they continued on—Kitty and Lydia running ahead, followed more sedately by Jane and Bingley, Darcy and Elizabeth, and Mr. Collins, who, with a nauseating show of condescension, proclaimed himself to be at the particular disposal of his fair cousin Elizabeth.

There were enough officers swaggering about the streets of Meryton in their regimentals to sufficiently distract Kitty and Lydia from their purpose, and Bingley did an admirable job of corralling the younger Miss Bennets away from mischief and off toward the milliner's shoppe. Inside, the ladies separated from the gentlemen to admire ribbons and bonnets, and to talk of gowns and gloves. Before long, Bingley moved to take his place at Jane's side as she stood holding two spools of silk ribbon in apparent indecision.

Left only with Mr. Collins for company, Darcy quietly slipped outside to wait for the ladies. To endure that insipid man's addresses while watching him fawn over Elizabeth in such a fashion was insupportable. The morning was, in every way, a punishment to him. He could not believe he had voluntarily placed himself at the disposal of Lydia Bennet. *What in God's name is becoming of me?* he demanded of himself in irritation.

It was then that he glimpsed Elizabeth through the shoppe window, and his breath caught in his throat. She was a vision of loveliness as she ran her fingers along a length of velvet ribbon the color of sunlight. She was so graceful and unassuming in her movements that he became completely entranced. He longed to discover how it would feel to have those fingers caress him with such exquisite tenderness. Unconsciously, Darcy raised one hand so it rested against the glass as his eyes continued to drink in her beauty. At that moment, he wanted desperately to open his heart to her, to take her in his arms—and to his bed—and never let her go.

A cold, mocking voice invaded his wistful thoughts. "Shopping, Darcy?"

He spun around to see George Wickham's insincere gaze leering in a most offensive manner at Elizabeth. Not trusting himself to speak, he fixed Wickham with a glare of pure loathing. Wickham was unperturbed. "I daresay Georgiana would enjoy having her for a sister, but who among us would not enjoy *having* her?" Wickham turned his eyes upon Darcy. "Come now, Darcy. Such coldness. Is this any way to greet an old friend?"

"You dare to call yourself my friend, Wickham?" he spat in a dangerous voice.

Wickham laughed derisively. "Perhaps I was presumptuous. Old habits die hard, you know. Speaking of which, you were absent last evening from the Phillips's. I was rather expecting to see you there, but I suppose the society in Hertfordshire does not agree with you, save for that of one."

Darcy's jaw set in a hard line as he struggled to contain his anger. A malicious smile flickered across Wickham's mouth, and their eyes locked in challenge. Wickham lowered his voice. "I had the good fortune of finding Miss Elizabeth Bennet without a proper escort and looking absolutely fetching. We had a very satisfying conversation, she and I, though I must confess I could not see any indication she returns your regard. But I suppose that is an inconsequential matter."

Wickham turned his gaze back to Elizabeth. "All that beauty before you—all that temptation—and none of it waiting for you. Tell me, Darcy, how can you stand it? Her lush body, her coy smiles. It must drive you positively mad to be so denied… you, who have never been denied anything." His voice was barely above a whisper. "Don't you just long for once to damn propriety and take her? I daresay many men of far less consequence would be more than willing to pay a very heavy price to lay claim to such an exceptional creature, and indeed, I have no doubt Miss Elizabeth Bennet would make any man a most *spirited* conquest."

He had finally gone too far, and before Wickham even saw it coming, Darcy had driven his fist into his sneering mouth with such force that Wickham was brought to his knees. Darcy was upon him again in the next heartbeat, closing his hands around Wickham's throat and dragging him to his feet. Bingley, accompanied by Jane, Elizabeth, and Mr. Collins, emerged from the shoppe just as Darcy slammed Wickham against the side of the building, his hands squeezing the breath from Wickham's body.

Darcy spoke through gritted teeth, his tone venomous. "You will not *touch* her! You will not *look* at her! You will not *think* of her! And you will never, *ever* insult her in my presence again as long as you live, or so help me *God*, Wickham, I will hunt you down like the animal you are and run you through! *Do. I. Make. Myself. Clear?*"

"Darcy!" Bingley yelled. "Good God, man! You will kill him! *Darcy!*" He tried to tear his friend from Wickham, but Darcy was beyond reason, rendering Bingley's battle utterly in vain. It was not until Elizabeth laid her hands upon his arm and began begging most fervently for Wickham's release that Bingley was able to successfully pry Darcy's shaking hands from Wickham's neck and drag him away. Wickham collapsed to the ground, massaging his throat as he gasped for air.

The magnitude of the situation suddenly hit Darcy with full force, and it was sobering. His breathing was as ragged as Wickham's, and in his heart he harbored not a single doubt he surely would have killed Wickham had Elizabeth and Bingley not stopped him when they had. *Elizabeth!* His lips formed the syllables of her name. What evil demon had taken possession of his senses to incite such behavior at the slightest provocation? *No,* Darcy recalled, *there was nothing slight about it!*

His eyes searched frantically for Elizabeth. She was staring at him, clearly horrified by his loss of control… and she was trembling. Darcy's eyes felt suddenly full, and he ran shaking hands over his face in shame. He did not trust himself to speak or even to look at her. He could not bear to be near her while she looked at him in such a way. Without a word, he turned away and began walking quickly toward Netherfield Park.

Elizabeth had watched, paralyzed with horror, while Bingley tore Darcy's hands from Wickham's flailing form. Her ears had caught every word Darcy uttered in his rage, just as her eyes had registered every tortured expression that contorted his features into something monstrous.

Why? she demanded in shocked desperation as she leaned against the wall for support, fighting back hot tears. The words Darcy had spoken as he blindly choked Wickham to within an inch of his life resounded in her mind. *Would some vulgar insult leveled at me by Mr. Wickham have moved him to commit such a disturbing assault? He, who has looked at me before only to find fault?* It was inconceivable to her, but then Elizabeth recalled the shock and pain etched on his face as he turned away from her, and the fire and warmth that had appeared in his eyes earlier at breakfast, and she gasped, wondering again and again, *Could Jane be correct? Could Mr. Darcy actually care for me?*

With concern, Bingley watched Darcy leave. He had an excellent notion as to his friend's feelings at the moment, and he was worried. In any other situation, he would have gone after him without a second thought, but now... Bingley looked from Jane to Elizabeth to Wickham, only to realize Darcy had left him in a most distasteful predicament. To make matters worse, a crowd had gathered in eager anticipation of gleaning enough information to kindle idle talk into a roaring blaze of scandalous gossip.

Though Wickham appeared no worse for wear, Lydia and Kitty exclaimed and fussed over him as though he were a hero wounded in battle by Napoleon himself. Bingley cursed softly under his breath in exasperation, quickly moving to support Jane as she swayed dangerously. Elizabeth, in contrast, stood as still as a statue, staring after Darcy. Tears spilled down her cheeks while Mr. Collins prowled around her like a caged beast, ranting about the mortification to be suffered by his noble patroness should the report of her nephew's behavior ever reach Rosings. It was insufferable.

Wickham pulled himself to his feet, to the voiced relief of Kitty and Lydia, and proceeded to dust off his regimentals. Bingley could hardly believe Wickham's audacity as he sauntered past Mr. Collins and addressed Elizabeth directly. She turned her head away with an expression of anger and revulsion.

Bowing low, he said stiffly and with a sneer he could not completely repress, "Apparently, Miss Elizabeth, you are, indeed, the one person to whom Darcy will refuse nothing. I daresay he would have killed me with very little regret if you had not stopped him. I thank you for taking mercy on me, and I will take this opportunity to apologize for any *ungentlemanly* conduct that may have offended you, *madam.*" He quickly swept his gaze over her form, bowed once again, and took his leave.

Elizabeth's legs shook as she watched him go.

Colonel Forster arrived then, and after dispersing the crowd and ascertaining the situation, he requested permission to see the ladies safely back to Longbourn. Bingley was grateful to have another gentleman join their ranks, as Mr. Collins had been of very little comfort and no assistance whatsoever.

Upon their arrival home, Elizabeth retreated immediately to the sanctuary of her room, and Colonel Forster and Bingley entered directly into conference with Mr. Bennet, apprising him of the events that unfolded in Meryton. They had not been in the house above a quarter of an hour before they made their excuses and hastily removed to Netherfield to speak with Darcy.

Chapter 5

Though Bingley was by now almost a daily visitor at Longbourn, no one in residence had either seen or heard anything from Darcy since the day of their fateful walk into Meryton. Five days had passed, and still, Elizabeth could not but recall—with striking clarity—the stricken expression upon his face as he had turned a tortured gaze upon her, his lips silently pronouncing her Christian name. Nor could she forget the shock she had felt at his completely forgetting himself in such a manner.

Though Darcy's uncharacteristically violent behavior had managed to stun and upset Elizabeth, in actuality, it was his addressing her with such an intimate familiarity that had ultimately succeeded in making such an overwhelming and lasting impact upon her sensibilities. As a result, Elizabeth's concern for what he might be suffering continued to increase over the days that followed. Again and again she continually turned the events of the past week over in her mind. It had taken much out of her.

She had always believed Darcy to be of a taciturn, disagreeable disposition, but she had now grown doubtful of her initial assessment of the nature of his character and found herself forced to rethink her opinion of him several times. Though she had told herself the slights Darcy had dealt her at the Meryton Assembly several months ago had not meant much to her, on further reflection, she discovered, in fact, they had. His thoughtless comments had wounded her vanity, as had his refusal to dance with her. Elizabeth had found herself so much affected by his rejection that, once Darcy had eventually come to express a desire for her society, she had returned his insult and slighted him, not once, but repeatedly, and in a most impertinent manner. She had held his bad behavior against him these several months and repaid him with worse. Elizabeth had always considered herself to be a fair and accurate judge of character, but in this case, she found herself slowly forced to concede she had erred greatly. She had clearly not known Darcy at all, for if she had, she would have recognized long ago his opinion of her had not been at all the same as her opinion of him. She was heartily ashamed of herself.

Jane had approached her the night before, and they had, once again, stayed up late discussing the incident in Meryton and, more particularly, Darcy, and Elizabeth's new insights into his character.

Jane had finally seen him earlier that day at Netherfield, as she had been invited to dine with Bingley and his sisters. She could not fail to see he was clearly not himself. He was uncharacteristically sullen, distracted, and unbearably, almost painfully, quiet. It had always been Darcy's habit to be out-of-doors as often as possible, but Bingley had confided to Jane that he had not left the house once since the day he had walked back from Meryton alone.

Well knowing it would be Elizabeth's fervent wish to keep any public speculation and scrutiny regarding the true origins of his disgraceful altercation at bay, Darcy had chosen to keep to himself most of the painful and compromising details of his disturbing conversation with Wickham. After hearing Darcy's abridged account of the events, corroborated explicitly by Bingley, Colonel Forster reassured Darcy his actions, though not exactly praiseworthy, were also not a cause for serious reproach, especially given the general nature of the circumstances. Darcy also admitted to having had some private dealings with Wickham in the past, which had been far from pleasant.

Though appreciated, Colonel Forster's exoneration did very little to alleviate the shame and distress Darcy felt every time he closed his eyes and saw Elizabeth's lovely face staring back at him in horror. As penance, Darcy sequestered himself within the confines of Netherfield's library, spending his days avoiding the unwanted company of Bingley's two sisters and his brother-in-law, who were also staying at Netherfield, and staring at the floor. He suspected it was obvious from the dark circles beneath his eyes that his nights were spent in much the same manner.

Bingley had a very good idea as to the deeper cause of Darcy's sleeplessness but was at a loss as to what he should do about it, if anything. After Bingley consulted with Jane, who confided to him Elizabeth's increasing concern for Darcy, the two of them decided the best course of action would be to invite Elizabeth to Netherfield as soon as possible, particularly since it seemed highly unlikely Darcy would be persuaded to leave the sanctuary of Netherfield to travel to Longbourn. Though Elizabeth showed initial reluctance to accept his invitation, when Bingley returned from Longbourn the following day, both sisters accompanied him.

With a ragged breath, Darcy slumped forward in his chair by the fire, his eyes closed as he held his head in his hands. For countless weeks he had struggled against his ardent feelings for Elizabeth.

His mind, so full of society's prejudices and misguided expectations, constantly fought an ever-losing battle with his heart.

It was on the very first night of their acquaintance, Darcy remembered, that he had so arrogantly dismissed her as entirely unsuitable; yet it had taken only one further encounter for him to find her eyes and pleasing figure had captured his full attention. The potent physical attraction he had begun to feel for her—far more powerful than any he had ever experienced toward any other woman—soon possessed him, and the demanding, insistent passion he experienced every time he so much as thought of her rendered him incapable of focusing his attention on anything other than the bewitching woman who held him completely mesmerized by her charms.

Having been repeatedly thrown together at assemblies and private gatherings only made his delirious desire for her grow, for countless hours of attentive observation soon made it clear to Darcy that Elizabeth Bennet was not one of the insipid young women of the London *ton*. Her beauty, which he had very early withstood but which had fast become an object of his deepest admiration, almost paled in comparison to her quick wit and her lively intelligence. Darcy had begun to understand, far too late, that his house in Town, his grand estate of Pemberley, and his extensive fortune would not aid him in securing her affections. Indeed, he knew that, to Elizabeth, none of his worldly assets and, most particularly, his prominent position in the first circles of society would ever prove inducement enough to tempt her into accepting him.

He was so full of love for her, yet the ache in his breast—the wretched knowledge that his love was unrequited—consumed him. Along with the painful acknowledgment of this torture came a sobering epiphany: he needed Elizabeth Bennet. He needed her laughter, her love, and her passion for life more than he suspected he needed to draw breath. No matter what society would say or how they would censure him, Darcy now knew in his mind, as he always had in his heart, that he could no longer willingly sacrifice the sheer joy and complete fulfillment he knew only she was capable of bringing him—not for duty nor honor nor family nor friends.

He knew Elizabeth did not love him—Wickham had been right about that—and that knowledge alone was enough to leave a desolate ache of despair in his heart. He was devastated by her indifference to him, but, when he was forced to consider what she must certainly feel for him after witnessing his savage loss of control in the streets of Meryton, it made him want to weep with regret for what his shameful, rash actions had most assuredly cost him. So tortured was he by his thoughts, he failed to hear Elizabeth when she entered the room.

For several long minutes, Elizabeth quietly observed him, overwhelmed by the look of vulnerability about him and greatly distressed by his obvious misery. Never had she seen him thus, and it pained her to know *she* could likely be the cause of such acute suffering. With a pang of disappointment and regret, it suddenly occurred to her that, perhaps, her intrusion into such an intimate moment would not be met by Darcy with any degree of welcome.

Then, after detecting a faint scent of lavender, Darcy opened his eyes and looked up to see her standing before him, a vision of beauty bathed in the last rays of the afternoon sun. It took his breath away, until he finally collected himself enough to realize he was being rude by remaining seated. He quickly made to stand, but Elizabeth stopped him with a touch of her hand on his arm, which, in his current state of misery and confusion, threatened to discompose him completely. He was stunned when she knelt before him on the carpet and gave him a small, hesitant smile.

"I believe I owe you my thanks, Mr. Darcy, for your ardent defense of my good name." Her voice was soft, yet with a tenderness in her tone, which, were she broaching any other topic, would have given him great pleasure to hear.

He looked away from her, ashamed to hear any reference to that horrible day. When he finally forced himself to speak, his voice was hoarse, both from the emotion he felt and from lack of use. "You owe me nothing, Miss Bennet, most particularly your thanks. My behavior was utterly barbaric. You cannot possibly know how it torments me, and I owe you my deepest apologies for behaving in such a reprehensible manner. Truly, it should be I sitting at your feet to beg your forgiveness for *all* my offenses, not merely for those of the last week, but those throughout our entire acquaintance."

Elizabeth was surprised and more than a little saddened by his harsh admonishment of himself and his allusion to the awkwardness in their past. "I think, Mr. Darcy, you are far too severe upon yourself," she said gently. "You have done nothing that is so unforgivable in my eyes that you should seek my absolution, and, as you are well aware, sir, Mr. Wickham is anything but a gentleman. Perhaps your actions in this case may have been impulsive and rash. Your purpose, though you may now deny it, was and will always be an honorable one. I must be permitted to commend you for that, at least, if for nothing else." A smile of appreciation tugged at the corners of her mouth as she then said, "And if I may be allowed to say so, sir, I can think of no other method of persuasion than the one you employed, nor any other man beside yourself who would have been as successful in his endeavor of carrying his point with the likes of Mr. Wickham."

"Do you make light of the fact I nearly strangled a man to death, Miss Bennet? Even one so worthless as Mr. Wickham?" he asked solemnly, his voice barely above a murmur.

Elizabeth's mouth formed into a serious line. "No. I could never do that, nor would it ever be within my power to commend any action of such a nature. Indeed, I was very distressed by it, perhaps even more so after its occurrence. However, I have been very concerned about you and what you must now be suffering as a result of it. Truly, I cannot but be moved by the esteem you must have for me, Mr. Darcy, in order to do such an awful thing in defense of my honor."

Upon her declaration of concern for him, he stared at her, surprise on his face. Indeed, after all that transpired, how could he not?

Seeing his astonishment and wishing to put him at ease, if only a little, Elizabeth extended her hand and laid it boldly upon his cheek. She heard his sharp intake of breath and then watched in awe as he closed his eyes and melted into her touch. After a moment, seemingly unable to resist such a temptation, Darcy covered her hand with his and slowly turned his head to place a kiss upon her palm. Elizabeth gasped as the sweet sensations from his lips, as well as the gesture itself, completely overwhelmed her senses.

"Mr. Darcy," she whispered. She had intended her quiet words to serve as an admonishment, but discovered too late she was far from equal to such a task. In confusion and taking a shaky breath, she carefully withdrew her hand and rose.

The place where Elizabeth had touched him felt tantalizingly warm, and the sensation soon spread throughout his entire body. Darcy did not want her to remove her hand, to retreat from him, to leave him alone again—not now, not ever. Boldly, as he rose from his chair, he reached out to her and gently caught her hand.

To his immense relief, Elizabeth did not pull away but remained frozen where she stood, her breathing as rapid as his heartbeat. Darcy drew closer to her, and she turned her lovely face upon him. Her eyes were dark and expressive, and in their depths, he saw something that made his heart swell with hope—a flicker of passion that had never before been present.

Pushing aside all rational thought, he proceeded to close the distance between their bodies with agonizing slowness, their fingers intimately intertwined, just as he had so fervently wished their hearts and lives someday to be. "Elizabeth," he breathed in an almost inaudible whisper, "dearest Elizabeth…"

She closed her eyes. The surprising intimacy of hearing him utter her Christian name sent an ache of desire pulsing through her body. Darcy tilted his face down to hers, and his lips caressed with exquisite tenderness her cheek, her jaw, and, daringly, the curve of her neck. Elizabeth found his gentle ministrations intoxicating, and though well knowing such actions were highly improper, she soon found herself wanting nothing more than for him to do it again.

Darcy was equally affected by the intimacy of their encounter. He did not dare trust himself any further and reluctantly began to release her. At the last moment, however, he could not resist the urge to reclaim her hands and draw close to her once more. As he lifted her fingers to his lips, she drew an unsteady breath.

"Please," he whispered, his voice quivering with the strength of his emotions, "please tell me I am not dreaming this." His words caught in his throat, and he fought against an overwhelming yearning to enfold her in his arms and bury his face in her hair.

Darcy felt her hands gingerly squeeze his, a gesture he wanted desperately to interpret as one of affection and encouragement. Elizabeth's reaction to him was, by far, more than he had ever dared to dream possible just an hour earlier, and he craved more—so much more—but his fear of alarming her with the fervency of his affections was great. She had not spoken since he had kissed her, and he was desperate to know her mind and her heart. He ached to have her for his own, even more so now that the gentle pressure her fingers were exerting against his continued to increase, and he silently prayed she would not reject him outright. He knew not how he would ever survive a future without her.

To Elizabeth, it was truly beyond her, the vast array of feelings and emotions this one man was able to elicit from her body with only the slightest of touches. Until a week ago, she had never even suspected the proud and haughty master of Pemberley could ever be so humbled by the depth of his feelings about anything, most especially, feelings for her. Even though, she suddenly recalled, Jane and Charlotte had long since believed Darcy to be enamored of her.

She had been shocked by the sensations that coursed through her when his lips had first met her flesh, and she had reveled in the contentment and warmth she felt as he reached for her a second time. Though it was now apparent—to her—that Darcy seemed to know *his* desires quite well, Elizabeth still remained confused and doubtful as to her own.

There was most definitely an attraction between them; she could no longer deny that. But how much of it was purely physical, especially on her part? In a relatively short amount of time—for, to her, it seemed a very short amount of time—Darcy had somehow come to feel a great deal for her, and in light of her recent insights into his character, Elizabeth suddenly found herself wondering how difficult it might be to put all her ill-appointed past prejudices and misgivings aside, and get to know Darcy on a far more personal level, perhaps even intimately. Could she ever grow to love him? Did she even wish it? Her head was clouded with endless questions as her body traitorously cried out, *Yes,* to each and every one.

The possible answer to one particular question, however, disconcerted Elizabeth greatly, for if she *were* to allow herself to fall in love with a man like Darcy, could her heart survive the disappointment she suspected she would experience should he ever change his mind about his feelings for her? She needed to think coherently and knew she could not expect to do so while in such close proximity to him, especially while his large, gentle hands held fast to hers, his thumbs tracing circles upon the backs of them. While such a tender action felt heavenly and reassuring, it was not at all conducive to inspiring rational thought, and in an effort to put some distance between them, she gently tugged her fingers from his grasp and turned away.

Darcy felt the loss acutely and could not repress a moment of alarm when Elizabeth withdrew from him and walked quickly toward the fire. His throat felt so tight and his mouth so parched, he was unable to speak, and as he had on so many occasions, so many he could no longer count, he simply swallowed his pride and watched her, drinking in her beauty, his love for her, he suspected, brimming in his eyes. With hesitant steps, he came forward to stand just behind her.

In spite of the blazing fire, Elizabeth was wholly conscious of the heat radiating from Darcy's body, and she felt a deep blush spread across her face, her torso, and all her most intimate places. Daringly, he placed his hand upon her shoulder. When she did not object, he slid unsteady fingers along the muslin of her gown until he reached her delicate skin. His heart beat wildly, and his breath caressed her cheek. There was no mistaking her gasp, but he had to strain to hear her voice over the pounding of blood rushing through his ears.

"What exactly is it you would like from me, Mr. Darcy?"

His voice was hoarse as he answered honestly, "Everything. Anything."

Elizabeth turned to face him, and he recaptured her hands and looked at her with a penetrating gaze full of love and anguish.

"Do not turn me away," he said. "I beg you. Say you will allow me the chance to love you as you deserve to be loved—as I have already loved you these many, many weeks—most ardently and with a passionate admiration and regard I can no longer conceal from the rest of the world."

She stared at him in astonishment, but he had not done. "If you will consent to be my wife, I promise I will do everything within my power to make you happy. Marry me, dearest, loveliest Elizabeth. Relieve my suffering, and grant me the opportunity to know what it is to be content every day of my life, for without you, I fear I shall never truly know."

Elizabeth could not immediately speak, so startled and moved was she by his heartfelt and unexpected declaration. *How am I to answer him? How can he expect me to accept a proposal of marriage when, until now, ours has been such a tenuous acquaintance? Certainly, even he must see such a union between us at this point would simply be nonsensical, to say the least? But, oh! To be held in those strong arms for the rest of my days and kissed by those lips each night!* She took several deep breaths to calm herself.

When she finally spoke, it was quietly, but not without proper feeling. "You honor me, sir, with such a beautiful proposal, but I am afraid you will think me the greatest simpleton when I confess you have caught me quite off guard. I am moved, flattered, stunned that you have come to hold me in such a tender regard, and honored beyond words by your offer. As much as I do not wish to be the cause of any further distress to you, I am very sorry, Mr. Darcy, but I am afraid I cannot possibly give you the answer you wish to hear, at least not at this time. To be completely honest, sir, after spending so many weeks in your company, I am ashamed to say it has been only very recently I have begun to develop a better understanding of, and a true appreciation for, your admirable character, and it pains me to now say that, until a few days ago, I truly had no inkling of your deep regard for me."

"I see." His disappointment was extreme, but Darcy would not be so easily dissuaded after such an honest speech—or such a positive physical response to his caresses. "Will you allow me, then, the honor of courting you, Miss Bennet?" he asked in a painfully quiet voice. "It will give you an opportunity to know me better. It will be a chance for both of us to know each other on a far more personal level. I promise I will not press for anything more in the near future, but please, if you cannot at this time agree to be my wife, I fervently hope you can, at least, find it within your heart to allow me this much."

Elizabeth could not see any polite way to refuse such a reasonable request, especially given her difficulty in resisting the look of hopeful longing in his eyes as he gazed upon her. It obviously meant a great deal to him, and once she had begun to consider the idea, she had to agree that knowing him better could only serve to benefit them both. Finally, she gave him a small, almost shy smile and said, "I will agree to a courtship, Mr. Darcy. I do believe the prospect of knowing you better, sir, is one I shall welcome wholeheartedly."

His smile was nothing short of radiant, and Elizabeth realized then she had never before seen him smile as he did at that moment, with his full self, as though illuminated from within. Though her answer to his proposal was not what he could have hoped for, the sheer pleasure her concession brought him was apparent, and it made her smile warmly in return. "Thank you," he breathed as he gazed at her, his features full of rapture and love.

His expression was soon to grow serious, however. In the next moment, before either of them could possibly know what they were about, Elizabeth found Darcy leaning in to brush her lips so tenderly with his. She could not have prevented the shiver of pleasure she received even had she tried. Placing her hands against his chest, she became distracted by the gentle pressure of his lips as his fingertips lingered along the neckline at the back of her gown, caressing her shoulders and the nape of her neck in the most tantalizing manner.

As he noted Elizabeth's continued responsiveness to his ministrations, Darcy felt an unadulterated thrill travel through his body and, with it, the last fragments of his self-control. With a wrenching determination, he pulled away and caressed the softness of her cheek with an unsteady hand, one thought predominant in his mind: *If it is the last thing I do, I shall win her heart and make her my wife!*

That evening at Netherfield there was a noticeable difference in Darcy. The sullenness and despair that had consumed him for the past week now seemed to be nothing more than an unpleasant memory. Hope reigned in his heart with the pure elation he felt since kissing Elizabeth. Each time Darcy's gaze fell upon her lovely face, he was flooded with a warmth that truly became him, which brought relief and joy to Jane and Bingley, and a flush of feeling to Elizabeth.

To Miss Bingley, who was hardly blind to his marked preference for Elizabeth, it was nothing short of infuriating. She had tried for days to draw him out—and for years to interest him. *Damn Charles for ever coming into Hertfordshire! What could have inspired him to settle in such an odious place?* All her efforts would be for naught if Darcy ended up paying his addresses to Elizabeth Bennet.

Miss Bingley glared as Darcy's gaze followed Elizabeth to the pianoforte with a half-drugged look of desire in his eyes. *Intolerable! How could he even think of throwing himself away over an impertinent little nobody? And Charles is no better, following Jane Bennet around the countryside like a lap dog.* Something needed to be done before any more time elapsed. Perhaps they could remove to Town before Christmas? London was far enough away from the charms and allurements of the Bennet sisters, and though she and Darcy would no longer share the distinction of residing together in the same house, the trip to Town would at least provide the relief of far more superior society for her brother.

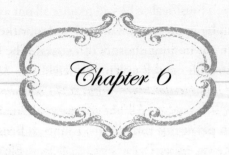

Chapter 6

ONCE JANE AND ELIZABETH HAD TAKEN THEIR LEAVE OF THE Netherfield party and were on their way back to Longbourn, Miss Bingley allowed herself to breathe easier, eagerly anticipating the restoration of Darcy's full attention to the members of his own party—namely, herself. The entire evening, however, seemed calculated to disappoint and vex her at every turn. When Bingley and Darcy finally returned from seeing the ladies to their carriage, which, as far as Miss Bingley was concerned, had taken far longer than civility required, the two gentlemen quickly excused themselves and retired to the billiard room, where they passed the rest of their evening.

With a disdainful huff, Miss Bingley swallowed her irritation and approached her sister with the purpose of soliciting her support for her scheme to remove their entire party to London as soon as possible. She had felt fairly certain she would meet with success on this front; however, to her increasing vexation, she soon found herself facing disappointment once again.

"Though I do long to be in Town, Caroline," said Mrs. Hurst distractedly as she examined the elegant gold bangles adorning her wrists, "I hardly think it would be prudent to travel there now, when our brother is planning to hold a ball within a matter of a few weeks. Surely you must realize he will require all our assistance, and Christmas shall be upon us soon after. No doubt the local gentry will expect him to do *some* measure of entertaining, you know, if he wishes to establish himself well in the neighborhood. It shall not be all *that* bad, I suppose. Hertfordshire, I do hear, is uniformly charming once it snows, even if the society itself leaves something to be desired. A sleigh ride through the countryside might be quite pleasant, you know, Sister."

"My dear Louisa," Miss Bingley said with disdain, "we could enjoy a sleigh ride just as well in London, but *that* is hardly the point. I was thinking only of poor Charles when I devised this plan. Do you honestly think it wise to permit him to stay on here in this savage society and carry on as he has with Jane Bennet? He has all but proposed to her, and I am convinced it is only a matter of time before all hope will be lost for us."

"Certainly you do not think Jane Bennet would refuse our brother?"

Miss Bingley was incensed. "Refuse him? I should say not!"

"Well, then I do not understand what you can be about, Caroline. Though you are well aware I, too, had my reservations in the beginning, I confess I do not remember ever having seen Charles so much in love. Certainly her connections are not what one would have hoped for—*Ugh! Her mother!*—but Jane Bennet is a sweet girl; not even you can deny it, Sister, and I believe she will make him very happy. He could do far worse, as you well know."

"Louisa, all that is immaterial!" Miss Bingley hissed as she clenched her fists upon her lap. "He is our brother! What will our acquaintance in Town say should they hear of this infatuation of his? No. It is not to be borne. His judgment has obviously been impaired by Jane Bennet's figure and her serene smile. Charles needs our protection from these scheming country people. They are not so artless and simple as they would have us believe."

She was fuming. This was not at all going to her liking. "And what about poor Mr. Darcy, Louisa? Since we have arrived in this odious part of the country, he has not been at all himself. Surely he can no longer be in his right mind, for if he was, you must know he would never have approved of Charles's forming such an unsuitable connection. It would be a punishment for him. He is used to only the very best and most refined society, and I strongly believe the savagery here has managed, in some grievous way, to unhinge him. Why, you must have seen Elizabeth Bennet tonight, Sister! She all but threw herself at him. It was most shocking. She is attempting to ensnare him with her arts and allurements. Her behavior is almost scandalous!"

Mrs. Hurst, whose attention was now focused on her rings, merely shrugged. "Mmm..."

Miss Bingley threw back her head in frustration and exhaled loudly. Her gaze soon came to rest upon Mr. Hurst, and she decided to try another approach. "Come, Mr. Hurst," she cooed in what she perceived was a persuasive tone, "certainly we must hear your opinion of this wretched business, sir!"

Mr. Hurst's eyes suddenly flew open, and he expelled a loud grunt of surprise. If Miss Bingley had been more astute in her observation, she would have recognized that her brother-in-law had no opinion prepared for her to hear; he had been dozing upon the settee for the last half hour, at least. "What was that?" he grumbled in irritation. Upon seeing Miss Bingley smirking at him, he rolled his eyes and muttered, "Damn tedious waste," before promptly shutting them again.

Miss Bingley turned to her sister with a smug look of triumph. "Oh, I quite agree! You see, Louisa, Mr. Hurst and I are of exactly the same opinion. We cannot allow the dear man to be placed in such a compromising position—to be further subjected to the machinations of such a penniless and impertinent little upstart who behaves in the most reprehensible and unfashionable manner I have ever seen. It is deplorable."

Mr. Hurst blinked at her in confusion and struggled to pull himself to a sitting position. "What the blazes are you prattling on about now?" he asked gruffly as he reached past her and began to refill his empty glass with wine.

"As I was saying, Mr. Hurst, we must do everything in our power to protect our Mr. Darcy from that mercenary little chit, Elizabeth Bennet."

"*Our* Mr. Darcy, eh? You think he needs *your* protection, do you? Huh!" he snorted. "That is rich, indeed! If you want my opinion, you should leave the pair of them to themselves. In case you have not noticed, Caroline, the man has been hiding himself away in bloody misery for the last week, and tonight he finally snapped out of it. It can hardly be construed as a coincidence that it was after Elizabeth Bennet came to call. I say, if it took a few smiles from a little country lass to do… *whatever* it is she did to him, then let Darcy have her, and be done with it. There can be no harm in a man indulging in a little sport every now and then."

Miss Bingley sat with her mouth hanging open in shock at his forgetting himself in such a vulgar manner.

"Oh, come now, Caroline," her brother-in-law said with a smirk as he drained his glass and set it upon the table next to the settee, "the way Darcy's eyes were devouring that woman tonight, I would not have been surprised if he had forgotten we were even in the room. If I did not know better, he looked as though he would have taken her right there in the middle of the first course had the opportunity presented itself." And with that, he removed himself to join the other two gentlemen in the billiard room, chuckling over his sister-in-law's pale complexion and her scandalized look of alarm.

"Hurst, come in and have a drink," Darcy said with uncharacteristic cheerfulness. "I was just thrashing Bingley at billiards."

Grateful for an opportunity to lay aside his cue, Bingley poured a healthy glass of port for his brother-in-law and refilled Darcy's and his own. As Mr. Hurst accepted his drink, he fixed Bingley with a level look that belied his inebriated state, and said, "By God, Bingley, that sister of yours will be your ruin." Then he raised his glass in Darcy's direction. "And she won't do you any favors either, I might add." He took several satisfying gulps of the contents as Darcy stared at him with a furrowed brow.

"Come, Hurst," said Bingley with his usual good humor, "I grant you that Caroline may be difficult, but I hardly think it will lead me to ruin. And as for Darcy"—he laughed—"well, I doubt there is any woman in all of England who is prepared to do more for him!"

Darcy shrugged his shoulders, simultaneously rolling his eyes with distaste.

"Bloody right about that one! If I were you, Darcy, I'd think twice before courting Elizabeth Bennet again in Caroline's company. Damned jealous of that one, she is, and rightly so. Come now, man, you must know Caroline has been determined to get you since the day she laid her eyes on Pemberley, and she is pretty blasted angry right about now." Mr. Hurst took another drink and laughed. "What the devil ever possessed you to stare at Elizabeth Bennet like that all night in decent company? Caroline would have sold herself to the devil for half a glance, never mind what went on between the two of you tonight. Now she wants to drag us all the way to Town just to be rid of her. She may as well remove us all to the Continent for all the good that would do her."

Bingley sighed and shook his head in exasperation. "Yes, that does sound like our Caroline."

Mr. Hurst noticed Darcy's frown. "Now do not go and take offense, Darcy. Though he only manages to gawk at her like a lovesick puppy, I suspect my sister-in-law has similar plans to dispose of Bingley's Miss Bennet as well."

Bingley sputtered and choked on his port.

"If you have any thoughts of proposing, Bingley, I would get to it, if I were you. There is no telling what Caroline is capable of when she sets her mind to it." He threw back the rest of his drink and bid them both a good night.

Earlier that evening, after Darcy and Elizabeth had abandoned the relative privacy of Netherfield's library to rejoin the rest of their party, the couple had found very little opportunity to be alone. Toward the end of the night, however, they managed to steal a few moments of privacy, where they wasted no time orchestrating a plan that would enable them to meet discreetly.

It was quickly decided Darcy would ride out early each morning, as was his wont, to meet with Elizabeth at Oakham Mount. As she habitually indulged in early morning rambles, it seemed a logical plan, so long as the weather was conducive to exercise out-of-doors. From there, they would walk out together, spending at least an hour in each other's company before parting and returning to their respective households. Darcy would have far preferred to visit with her at Longbourn and openly declare himself to her father, but she had requested he refrain from doing so for the time being. Though he did not like it, Darcy was hesitant to do anything that might cause Elizabeth to withdraw her acceptance of his courtship. He agreed to the scheme only to appease her.

Though Elizabeth was not completely at ease with the idea of keeping their courtship a secret from her father, she *was* determined to conceal it *completely* from her mother, whose rampant effusions and scheming, she well knew, had the potential to drive away even the most determined suitor. It would not do to subject either Darcy or herself to her mother's high-handed machinations just yet. There was much she felt she needed to learn about Darcy, and she was determined to discover it away from the prying eyes and embarrassing scrutiny of her nearest relations.

The late November morning was a particularly fine one. Elizabeth, now well past the pale to the entrance of her father's estate, broke into a run as she hurried toward Oakham Mount. She should have set out a full quarter of an hour earlier but had found herself unhappily detained by Mr. Collins, of all people. To her growing irritation, with the passing of each week he spent in Hertfordshire—and, indeed, his initial plan had been to spend only one—the odious parson somehow managed to extend his stay. How his patroness could possibly spare him for so long baffled Elizabeth exceedingly; though, if Lady Catherine found her clergyman's ingratiating attentions half as offensive and tiresome as the young ladies of Longbourn did, it was no wonder she would encourage his absence. *Thank Heaven for dear Jane and her unending patience with that man!* Elizabeth sent up a silent prayer of gratitude for her angelic elder sister, all the while hoping Darcy would still be waiting when she arrived.

Elizabeth was surprised to admit the last fortnight had been one of the most enjoyable she had ever spent. She had faithfully—and secretly—managed to meet with Darcy every morning, and on many occasions, they found themselves reunited again in the afternoon or evening, either at small, informal gatherings or at dinners given by one neighbor or another.

At first, Darcy was hesitant to approach her when in company and reluctantly resigned himself to the possibility that he would be forced to find consolation in the form of his old standby—staring at the woman he loved with undisguised longing from across the room—but, to his immense delight, Elizabeth no longer seemed to be of a mind to stay away.

Having gained a better understanding of Darcy's taciturn disposition and his haughty composure when in company, Elizabeth made every effort to draw him into conversation with her friends, her neighbors, and the few truly intelligent members of her family.

Much to Darcy's surprise, he discovered that under Elizabeth's keen and solicitous guidance he was beginning to relax his stoic mien and even enjoy himself with the people of Hertfordshire. But Darcy found he was never so much at ease—he had never felt so accepted nor so valued for his own merits and contributions—as when he was alone with Elizabeth on their early morning rambles.

Elizabeth turned onto the path leading to Oakham Mount and immediately discerned the familiar figure whose presence she had come to welcome, even anticipate, as he leaned against a tree. She took a moment to study him while he twirled a strand of dried hay between his fingers, seemingly lost in thought. Even in such an informal setting—or perhaps in spite of it—Darcy presented a striking picture. Elizabeth raised her hands to her hair, smoothing any stray curls that may have escaped the confines of her bonnet. She struggled to calm her breathing and then, repressing a smile of pleasure, made her way toward Darcy.

A wide smile overspread his face as he beheld her—her cheeks aglow from the exertion of her morning exercise. It took less than an instant for his mind to begin contemplating how she might look after having partaken of another form of exercise—that of writhing beneath him in ecstasy as he plundered her lips and pleasured her body, claiming her as he so fervently wished to do, forever as his own.

She extended her gloved hand to him as she approached, and he took it, lifting it to his lips and bestowing upon it a kiss. His eyes never left her lovely face.

Elizabeth found herself blushing as his ardent gaze almost seemed to reach inside to caress her very soul. After several long minutes of silence, she managed to find her voice. "Good morning, Mr. Darcy. I trust you are well today?" she asked with a touch of her usual archness.

Darcy did not relinquish her hand and quietly replied, "I find I am very well this morning, Miss Bennet… now that you are come."

She broke into a beautiful smile. "Why, Mr. Darcy, I remember a time when I had not believed you capable of such pretty compliments."

He was immensely pleased by her teasing and so answered honestly, "There was a time, Miss Bennet, when I will admit I had not the proper inducement, nor the desire, to bestow such heartfelt sentiments, but it seems my existence needed only the addition of a particular lady of my acquaintance, whose intelligent eyes have bewitched me, along with her wit, her vivacity, and her unrivalled beauty."

A lovely blush colored Elizabeth's cheeks, and she said merrily, "Well then, sir, I should very much like some day to meet this lady of whom you speak. Certainly she must be a rather remarkable creature to inspire such a proper gentleman as you to boldly profess such feelings!"

Darcy's eyes gleamed, and he said in a low voice, "Truly, for it is she, and she alone, who has taught me how to be alive and not just merely to endure. Now I know such a woman exists for me, here, on this earth, and not just in my dreams; I shall never again be the same as I once was, nor would I ever wish it. I wish only for her… always for her." His voice was now hardly more than a whisper. "Elizabeth, what you have done to me?"

Elizabeth could not help but be affected by his words and his emotion, and stood entranced, unable to tear her gaze from his. As Darcy held her in thrall, drawing ever closer, one hand sliding up her arm to rest upon her shoulder, the other still grasping her hand, she felt his warm breath against the coolness of her skin and shivered in anticipation of what she knew was surely to follow. Her eyelids fluttered closed, and her lips parted. Her heart beat rapidly in her chest. It was but a moment later when she felt the exquisite sensation of his lips as they tenderly pressed upon her own. She returned the gentle pressure with feeling, and Darcy deepened the kiss. Elizabeth could not prevent the soft sigh of pleasure she breathed into his mouth as Darcy's fingers made their way from her shoulder to the delicate flesh of her neck. She felt her knees begin to grow weak, and before she knew what she was about, she found her hands slipping to his broad shoulders. She was beginning to understand what he meant.

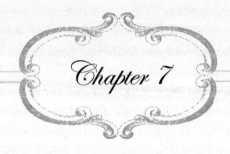

Chapter 7

THE TWO UNMARRIED GENTLEMEN FROM NETHERFIELD WERE prevented from meeting with the two eldest Miss Bennets until the very evening of the Netherfield ball. In addition to a seemingly endless succession of cold rain, which had lasted a full four days, both households were thrown into somewhat of an uproar—Netherfield with final preparations for food and flowers, decorations and dancing; and Longbourn with the preoccupation of gowns and gloves, slippers and silk.

Darcy, who had long been in the habit of riding out nearly every morning for the sheer enjoyment of the exercise and, lately, to meet with Elizabeth—to say nothing of the added means of escaping Caroline Bingley's effusive attentions—instead found himself imprisoned by the inclement weather. Unable to take any pleasure while indoors at Netherfield so long as Elizabeth was, likewise, confined to Longbourn, he spent the bulk of his time avoiding his friend's shamefully persistent sister, seeking refuge in the library or the billiard room, where he was able to commiserate with Bingley in relative safety.

Elizabeth had never derived enjoyment from remaining indoors for prolonged periods of time, particularly in the trying company of her mother and younger sisters, and found herself longing for the solitude and opportunity for quiet reflection her early morning rambles often afforded her. She sighed with frustration every time her mother scolded her for hiding herself away in her room, insisting, instead, she spend her time more productively by sitting with Mr. Collins and encouraging his unwanted attentions.

At times like these, Elizabeth could not help but think wistfully of Darcy, with his soft lips, his penetrating eyes, and his intelligent discourse, knowing full well she would much rather be encouraging *his* attentions. With no hope of escape, she endured her confinement with such forbearance as she could manage under the circumstances, though her patience was certainly pushed beyond its limits when a simpering Mr. Collins solicited the honor of her hand for the first two dances the following evening.

Happily, the morning of the Netherfield Ball dawned clear and crisp, promising an evening very much the same. Carriage after carriage rolled up to Netherfield's front entrance, which had been illuminated by torchlight, to deposit several hundred elegantly attired guests with great efficiency. Nearly the last of the parties to arrive, the Bennets were greeted graciously by Bingley and less so by his sisters. Positively beaming, their host wasted no time offering one arm to Jane and the other to Elizabeth. Without further ceremony, he ushered them into the ballroom.

As a guest in Bingley's home, Darcy felt it would have been inappropriate to stand with the members of the family as they greeted each of their arrivals in turn, and so chose instead to await Elizabeth's arrival in the ballroom. Though he had been learning to mix more agreeably in the somewhat smaller drawing rooms of Hertfordshire Society, he still found it difficult to move easily among larger crowds. Darcy had never felt completely at ease in a ballroom, and as such, he reverted, however unconsciously, back into his more reserved and haughty self, taking up a station in the farthest recesses of the room, where he hoped he might garner the least amount of notice.

When Darcy saw Elizabeth finally enter on Bingley's arm, he froze. Wearing a low-cut gown of creamy silk that seemed to cling to her inviting curves in a most flattering manner, Elizabeth was breathtaking. Her hair was arranged in a far more elaborate style than she usually wore, and intertwined throughout the mass of dark curls piled high upon her head, there were silk roses that had obviously been fashioned with great care to complement her gown.

Darcy felt he would be content simply to gaze upon her all night, but as Bingley approached and presented her to him, he somehow managed to shake off his stupor and step forward to receive her, applying a gentle pressure to her gloved hand as he raised it to his lips.

"Good evening, Mr. Darcy," she said quietly, with a small, enigmatic smile.

"Miss Bennet," he murmured, unable to tear his gaze from the vision of loveliness she presented, "you look absolutely stunning this evening."

Elizabeth felt a familiar pull deep within as she returned his admiring gaze with equal feeling. "Thank you. You look very handsome, as well." She spoke the words softly, her throat suddenly dry.

Bingley, grinning with satisfaction, left Elizabeth staring at his friend while he escorted Jane to the middle of the room to open the ball.

The first half of the evening, save for Elizabeth's obligatory dance with an incompetent and overzealous Mr. Collins, afforded the couples much pleasure.

Bingley, who was far more captivated by Jane than he was by his role as host, threw caution to the wind by dancing as many dances with his angel as the space of one evening would allow, while trying not to cause overt offense to any of the other young ladies in attendance.

Darcy, who was not normally inclined to dance, found immense pleasure in the act so long as Elizabeth was his partner. He found himself soliciting her hand repeatedly just to be close to her until, after their third dance partnered together, which had caused many a curious eye to turn upon them, Elizabeth finally laughed and teasingly chided him for his total disregard for ballroom propriety.

He reluctantly danced the next set with Jane while Elizabeth partnered with an attractive officer who clearly admired her. Darcy found himself watching them with increasing displeasure until his jealous glare was met by Elizabeth, whose sparkling eyes gave him such a look of chastisement that he actually blushed. Jane, apparently far from offended by Darcy's preoccupation with her most beloved sister, smiled gently at his contrition and engaged him in conversation. To the relief of all, Wickham was reported to have been sent to London on business for Colonel Forster and, therefore, was not in attendance.

When supper was announced, Darcy steered Elizabeth past a perspiring and genuflecting Mr. Collins, taking care to settle her between Jane and himself, and at some distance from the rest of her family. The two sisters were flushed from the exertion of having danced every dance, but the exercise only succeeded in brightening their eyes and adding a healthy glow to their complexions, which the gentlemen greatly admired.

During the first course, the buzz of constant conversation filled the room, but to Elizabeth's mortification, she was able to distinguish her mother's shrill voice as she spoke loudly to one of their neighbors of Mr. Collins. "Ah, yes! He is a most agreeable young man! He first admired Jane, you know, but Bingley was there before him. He has since taken quite a fancy to Lizzy, though, and has been *excessively* attentive to her, paying her every courtesy." She then leaned closer to her companion and said smugly, "We are expecting him to make her an offer of marriage any day now! Of course, Mr. Collins does not have *five thousand a year* like Bingley, but I must say *his* income shall do well enough for Lizzy, for you know she is not half so handsome as Jane, nor such a favorite among the officers as my dearest Lydia!"

Catching the entirety of this conversation and having just taken a mouthful of wine, Darcy nearly choked himself. He recovered quickly, however, and wasted no time turning his gaze severely upon Mrs. Bennet.

Bingley, as well, could not help but stare, his eyes wide and his mouth hanging open in shock.

Jane sat stiffly at his side, conversing with Charlotte Lucas while struggling to maintain her serene composure.

Elizabeth was beyond mortified. In fact, she wanted nothing more than to escape. Darcy's reaction to her mother's ill-bred comments had not been lost on her. With a sudden stab of alarm, she wondered how enthusiastic he would be to continue their courtship after bearing witness to such a display of vulgarity. At the thought of the possibility of Darcy withdrawing his suit after the enjoyable fortnight they had shared, Elizabeth felt a sudden, insurmountable pang of regret. She felt her eyes suddenly grow moist, and while his attention was still fixed firmly upon her mother, she silently slipped away.

Shivering on the balcony just off the ballroom, Elizabeth stood alone as silent tears rolled down her cheeks. She chided herself for not having thought to bring her wrap, when she heard the soft click of the French doors. She looked up in surprise to see Darcy striding purposefully toward her, holding the very article she had been wanting just moments before. As he draped it across her shoulders, she noticed how his hands seemed to linger over the act. *Surely he must be thinking this will be the last time he will touch me so,* she thought with no small degree of bitterness and a heavy heart, *for how could he ever willingly seek my society after such an outrageous display?* She murmured her thanks and quickly turned away to blink back a fresh set of tears that threatened to fall. How would she be able to bear it when he finally withdrew his affection? For it was now becoming frighteningly clear to her that her heart was no longer untouched.

"Miss Bennet, will you not look at me?" he asked, his voice soft and full of concern. To Elizabeth, his tenderness only served to make their imminent parting all the more painful, and she walked several paces from him to stand by the railing, struggling for the ability to project some small semblance of composure.

Darcy was confused by her withdrawal, and it was not long before a sinking sensation began to invade his body. He forced his suddenly leaden legs to move in her direction so he could stand behind her. When he spoke, his voice betrayed his anxiety. "Miss Bennet—*Elizabeth*—have I done something tonight to cause you offense?"

Elizabeth gave a soft, rueful laugh and answered him. "No,

Mr. Darcy. Not at all. You have been a perfect gentleman and a delightful companion all evening. As a matter of fact, I have very much enjoyed your company, sir, though I cannot help but wonder whether you might still find *my* society quite so acceptable?"

He was surprised. "Of course. Why ever would you think otherwise?"

She took a deep breath and said with some bitterness, "I am certain it has not escaped your notice, sir, that my mother is not the most tactful, nor the most discreet conversationalist."

A small smile of comprehension turned up the corners of Darcy's mouth. "Ah. No. I must agree with you that she is most decidedly *not.* Nor, may I add, is she the most observant." He paused to press himself closer, and she felt his warm breath upon her neck and shivered. "I was actually rather offended by one comment she made in particular."

"Only *one*, sir?" she asked, feeling slightly overwhelmed by his proximity.

His voice was soft and caressing. "Yes, only one. Can you not guess, Elizabeth, which remark might have caused me such offense as to prevent my acknowledging any others?" Elizabeth shook her head, not trusting herself to speak, and Darcy continued: "It was when your mother voiced her opinion that you are not half so handsome as your sister Jane. In this she is gravely in error, because anyone with eyes can clearly see, my *loveliest* Elizabeth, you are ten times more beautiful than any of your sisters. As a matter of fact, I have long since considered you to be the handsomest woman of my acquaintance."

He placed his hands upon her shoulders and turned her around so she faced him. He was startled to see her tears and the look of absolute surprise upon her face. Gently, he raised his thumb to dry her cheek. *Is it possible she doubts my steadfastness, my utter devotion to her?* he wondered with incredulity. Darcy searched her eyes and soon found his answer. Quietly, he said, "I have been in agony for many weeks over the strength of my feelings for you, Elizabeth—feelings that run so deep I can honestly say I have never before experienced anything even remotely similar for any other woman. You have seen me at my very worst, yet in spite of my reprehensible actions, you have found it in your heart to give me a chance to hope. It is you, and you alone, who have been responsible for *any* happiness I now have. After bearing witness to such, how can you come to doubt the depth of my attachment? Do you have so little faith in me as to believe my most fervent emotions and desires so alterable, and over some ridiculous blunder of your mother's?"

She opened her mouth with the intention of speaking, but Darcy raised two fingers to her lips in an effort to silence her. "Two weeks ago I asked you to become my *wife*, Elizabeth, and I would gladly drop to my knees before you now and ask again if I thought there was any possibility you would say yes. You have no idea, no idea at all, what you do to me. I will never change my mind about my feelings for you… *never.*" Darcy tilted her chin so he could search her eyes, which were still glistening with emotion. "But I do fervently pray every day I will soon be able to change your mind about becoming my wife."

His eyes were so deep and expressive, and Elizabeth found herself wondering how she ever could have once mistaken such an ardent look of love and longing for one of cold disdain and indifference. She reached out to him, moved by his words and his devotion to her, and found herself questioning what she had ever done to deserve such admiration from an exceptional man. How could he, even after bearing witness to her mother's disgusting declarations, continue to want her? Yet, somehow, he did. Elizabeth's heart flooded with warmth at such a realization.

Resting her gloved hands on either side of his face, she began to trace her fingers over the line of his jaw and the curve of his lips. Darcy closed his eyes and sighed, his breathing becoming shallow. At that moment, she finally realized how extremely fortunate she was—far more fortunate even than Jane. *Perhaps*, she thought with a sudden revelation, *the risks of surrendering my heart to the keeping of such a worthy man would be well worth the rewards to be gained from knowing—and accepting—such an unfathomable love.*

Slowly, Darcy opened his eyes and placed a kiss upon her gloved fingers.

"What is your Christian name, Mr. Darcy?" Elizabeth asked.

His mouth felt suddenly dry. "Fitzwilliam," he said in a hoarse whisper as he looked at her with undisguised longing.

"Fitzwilliam," she murmured. "May I call you Fitzwilliam when we are alone together?"

Swallowing, he said, "You could call me anything you wish, Elizabeth, and I would think it wonderful so long as it came from your lips." In a seemingly unconscious gesture, she ran her tongue lightly along her own lips as he watched, utterly transfixed. "May I?" he whispered.

She had barely nodded her acquiescence when he leaned in to capture her mouth in a slow, seductive kiss, his arms slipping around her waist to draw her body firmly against his as he caressed the small of her back with soothing strokes. Her hands, still lingering upon his face, soon coiled themselves into his dark curls, brushing the skin of his scalp with her gloved fingertips. She sighed against his lips, once again marveling at the way Darcy was able to take control of her body and awaken such delicious sensations of pleasure within her. She felt surprisingly complete, as though she had been waiting her entire lifetime for his touch. Elizabeth shivered from more than just the cold.

Darcy, though well on his way to losing himself in her expressive mouth, felt it acutely as an extension of his own body. His hands wandered to caress her hips, and a moan rose from Elizabeth's throat. With concern, he suddenly recalled their somewhat prominent location on Bingley's balcony and reluctantly broke the kiss. He touched his forehead to hers and held her close for a brief moment before once more brushing her lips and releasing her. Their hands immediately joined, and they held on for a few moments longer as their breathing evened.

"Though it is by no means what I would rather do, I am afraid we ought to return. I would not wish to risk your reputation, though, now that I come to think of it"—he smiled—"it would, undoubtedly, prove to be invaluable in my endeavor to convince you to accept me."

She flashed him an arch smile filled with warmth and amusement. "I believe you are correct, Fitzwilliam, as well as incorrigible. But, by all means, let us return now to the house."

Darcy's pleasure upon hearing Elizabeth speak his name as she teased him could only be described as transparent. He raised both her hands to his lips and lingered over them while his gaze caressed her, touching her inner core with a flood of warmth she hardly knew how she contained.

As he tucked her hand into the crook of his arm and covered it, she heard his voice, low and soothing, say, "Come. I will take you back to your sister before I find myself tempted to do something—nay, *several things*—which I ought not."

Contrary to popular opinion, Mr. Collins was not an ignorant man. It is true he did think rather well of himself, for how could he not, having had the exquisite good fortune of finding himself, at the age of five and twenty, on the receiving end of a valuable living from the illustrious Lady Catherine de Bourgh?

To say he merely worshiped her ladyship would be a gross injustice, for there was nothing in the world the obsequious clergyman would not do to pay her the proper respect and reverence he believed was her due as his esteemed patroness, and it was this, and only this, that had kept him from stepping in and tearing his fair cousin Elizabeth from Darcy's side throughout the course of the evening.

With no small degree of pride, Mr. Collins had enjoyed the dubious distinction of opening the ball with a woman as handsome as Elizabeth, which, in his opinion, should have been enough to ensure an animated evening of dancing, wholesome conversation, and perhaps, if he was truly fortunate, at the end of the evening, a stolen kiss with his coveted future partner. He was effusive in his admiration of his cousin's feminine charms and smugly congratulated himself for having selected for his intended bride a woman who was, undoubtedly, held in the highest regard by Lady Catherine's own nephew.

Though more than willing to relinquish Elizabeth's hand for a few inconsequential dances, save for the opening set, for the express purpose of indulging and flattering Darcy, suffice to say by the time the guests had been called in to supper, Mr. Collins was no longer feeling quite so honored by that gentleman's particular attentions to the object of his own future happiness.

He had been extremely gratified to hear Mrs. Bennet's enthusiastic though wholly improper compliments to himself, not finding it offensive in the least when she stated her expectations of an impending marriage between her second-eldest daughter and him. To be perfectly honest, Mr. Collins had viewed the entire situation as a blessing in disguise, for, surely, after hearing his intentions being thus spoken of in so favorable a light by her own dear mother and in such a public forum, Darcy could not possibly continue his marked attentions to Elizabeth in any honorable way. Therefore, it was with shocked indignation he later watched the gentleman in question escort his fair cousin back into the ballroom from the balcony, where they had been alone together for some time.

When he observed Darcy standing close to Elizabeth and reaching around from behind her slender figure to unclasp the closures of her wrap, Mr. Collins's jaw nearly fell to the floor. The manner in which Darcy eased the garment from Elizabeth's shoulders and then handed it to a waiting servant while he whispered intimately in Elizabeth's ear, all the while keeping his eyes fixed upon the bewitching woman in front of him, was almost indecent to see—and seen it was by several in attendance, including both of her parents.

So intoxicated was Darcy by Elizabeth's presence, and so overwhelmed was he by the intimacy of the words they had exchanged on the balcony, he did not even realize the liberties he was taking with her—and in full view of Bingley's guests, no less. Indeed, he could think of nothing beyond the beautiful woman in front of him, of how she had looked at him only moments before with such heartfelt delight and tenderness in her eyes, and of how very much he longed to be alone with her once more so he could continue to reassure her, in a most ardent fashion, of his devotion. With such sentiments, Darcy could no more stop himself at that moment from reaching around to unclasp her wrap and whisper words of adoration to her than he could stop the rise of the sun in the east.

Mrs. Bennet was the first to reach them, nearly tripping herself in her efforts to remove Elizabeth from the overly solicitous company of the *wrong* man before steering her toward the *correct* one, leaving Darcy gaping after her in shock as he found himself suddenly jolted back to reality. Unsurprisingly, her voice carried to half the room.

"What do you think you are doing, Miss Lizzy, leaving Mr. Collins alone while you scamper about? Why, if I were Mr. Collins, I would begin to think you did not care for me at all, and I would be quite put out by your ungenerous, unfeeling behavior, no matter *how* rich and disagreeable a man Mr. Darcy has shown himself to be!"

"Mama, please," Elizabeth murmured most uncomfortably. "He is not at all disagreeable, and he will hear you."

"And what should you care if he does?" her mother replied with indignation. "Mark my words; there is nothing for you in *that* quarter, so you had better concentrate your efforts for the rest of the night on securing Mr. Collins. Oh, selfish child! You have no compassion for my poor nerves!"

Elizabeth could do nothing but allow her mother to hand her over to the keeping of Mr. Collins and look miserably at Darcy from across the room as her father approached him.

"Well, well, Mr. Darcy, you look exactly like a young boy who has just had his favorite toy taken away from him."

Darcy had no idea how to respond to such a statement by Elizabeth's father, and so he wisely chose to remain silent.

"I have noticed your admiration for my daughter on several occasions, sir, but I must confess I was rather startled by your marked attentions to Elizabeth in such a public setting as this. I trust you have not failed to realize you were observed in your attentions by others, as well?" he asked.

Darcy swallowed. "No, sir. It has, by no means, escaped my notice."

"I also trust I have been in company with you often enough to understand you are not the kind of man to trifle with a gentleman's daughter, so I can only assume your intentions toward Elizabeth are honorable."

"Yes, they are. You have my word, Mr. Bennet, as a gentleman."

"Come see me tomorrow morning, Mr. Darcy, and we shall continue this discussion in a more appropriate environment."

Chapter 8

THE MORNING THAT FOLLOWED THE NETHERFIELD BALL WOULD be a leisurely one for the five inhabitants of Netherfield Park and the four-and-twenty country families who had been their guests well into its early hours. As it was unlikely that calling at the usual time upon one's neighbors would be expected after such a late night of stimulating company, joyous dancing, excellent food, and overconsumption of wine, it could only follow that more sedentary pursuits close to home would be the order of the day.

Though the Bingleys and the Hursts slept well past noon, Darcy rose at his usual hour, just after dawn. He had much on his mind—foremost, his conversation with Elizabeth's father. Mr. Bennet had been generous with him by not demanding immediate satisfaction for the familiarity Darcy had been exercising with his favorite daughter in public. Darcy did not doubt he would probably do so once he reached Longbourn later that morning, but he was more than willing to comply with any demand in that quarter.

One of his greatest fears, however, was Elizabeth's reaction to being forced into a marriage with him after she had turned him down just over a fortnight ago. His other fear was that his aunt's sycophantic parson would somehow manage to manipulate a union between himself and Elizabeth before Darcy could manage to plead his own case.

Then there was the issue of what had led to Darcy's overly familiar manner with Elizabeth in the first place. He knew he had no right to touch her—or to take *any* liberties with her at all, for that matter—but he could not for the life of him imagine how he was ever going to completely curb his ardor when he was in her company. True, he had been quite adept at the practice for several agonizing months, but that was before he had fully come to terms with his feelings for her. Now that Elizabeth was actually allowing him to court her, and knowing at last what it was to hold her in his arms and feel her lips upon his—not to mention the exquisite sensations that accompanied these tender exploits—how would he ever survive her intoxicating presence and maintain an appearance of composure?

Darcy breakfasted alone, thankful for the silence the unconscious household afforded. Within a quarter of an hour, he was out the door and astride his horse, ready for a good ride to clear his head and ease the tension that had settled in his body. There was a decided chill in the air, and the surrounding landscape was blanketed by frost. He breathed deeply, filling his lungs with fresh air. It was invigorating. With no particular destination in mind, he urged his horse into a full gallop. Leaning low over his mount, Darcy guided his beast across the surrounding fields and far beyond, determined to lose himself temporarily in the thrill of a hard ride.

Like Darcy, Elizabeth had also risen early, and to a mercifully empty breakfast parlor. She sat sipping a cup of hot tea, pleased to see that the day promised to be especially clear. After donning her spencer and gloves and securing her bonnet, she set off at a brisk pace to enjoy her morning walk.

The crisp November air assaulted her senses, making her feel alive and rejuvenated. Elizabeth continued her energetic pace and soon found herself traveling through one of the many fields bordering her father's estate. She stopped at the edge of a thicket to catch her breath, enjoying the magical, frosty transformation of the landscape. She discerned the pounding of approaching hooves and soon glimpsed a lone rider galloping toward her. As he neared, Elizabeth recognized his form, and a smile spread across her face.

Darcy reined in his horse and, in one fluid movement, leapt from the saddle to stand before her with one of his rare, devastating smiles. He labored to catch his breath, his chest heaving from the exertion of his long, hard ride, and brought her gloved hand to his lips. "Good morning, Elizabeth," he said.

"Good morning, Fitzwilliam." Her voice was warm, and she painted a tantalizing picture, her cheeks a most becoming shade of pink from her exposure to the morning chill. "You are certainly up early, considering the lateness of the hour we kept last night."

"I could easily say the same for you," Darcy quipped. He had not bothered to relinquish her hand. "I am often an early riser, but I confess I did not sleep very well last night."

"Oh? And pray, why was that, sir?" she asked in a teasing voice.

"Something particular weighed heavily upon my mind, and I missed you terribly after our evening ended. I am afraid such a combination made repose impossible."

A sympathetic smile played across Elizabeth's mouth as a blush appeared on her face. She, too, had found it difficult to fall asleep once she had returned to Longbourn, her head overflowing with images of Darcy and memories of his lips upon hers and the warmth of his hands upon her body. *What on earth is this hold he has over me?* she wondered for what must have been the hundredth time. Elizabeth could hardly credit it. When Elizabeth was with him, she could think of very little beyond the exquisite pleasure his company afforded her—to say nothing of his touch, his mouth, even a penetrating look from his dark, expressive eyes. Even when alone, her thoughts were filled with Darcy.

But what distressed her most was how she could possibly feel such a powerful urge to abandon propriety, for that was very much what Elizabeth found herself wishing every time she observed Darcy's intense gaze settle upon her. And Darcy's gaze *always* came to rest upon her. This enigmatic power he seemed to have over her sensibilities disconcerted her greatly. It seemed so easy to surrender her body, but was she truly equal to completely surrendering her heart to such an overwhelming passion? Was she even worthy of such a love as he claimed to possess for her?

It had been far easier than Elizabeth had ever anticipated to come to like him. And, indeed, she now had to admit she liked him very much. Darcy had shown himself to be an excellent man, intelligent, insightful, fair-minded, and honorable, with a dry, clever wit she could well appreciate. Yet, at the same time he could be tender and caring—passionate, even—and vulnerable. *But surely I cannot be falling in love with him so soon!* she attempted to reason with herself. *What if I am mistaken in this? My Lord… how am I ever to be certain of anything?!*

Something in Darcy's eyes caught her attention then, and Elizabeth found herself drawing closer. She could see just by looking at him that whatever unpleasant preoccupation had been weighing upon his mind the previous night tormented him still. She felt an overwhelming urge to comfort him, and almost without thought, she moved to place her free hand upon his face. "Would you care to speak of what bothers you?" she asked quietly.

The heat from her touch and the delicate lavender scent of her fragrance flooded his senses. Darcy closed his eyes briefly and shook his head. "I would rather not. Not at this time. Forgive me, Elizabeth."

"There is nothing to forgive."

The urge to bring him comfort did not abate. Elizabeth traced the line of his jaw, brushing her thumb across his bottom lip while his breathing deepened. She kept her voice as soft and caressing as her touch. "Is there, perhaps, another way, then, that I might ease your troubled mind as effectively as you seem to be able to ease mine, dearest?" She tilted up her face to his and parted her lips in an invitation.

It was the first time Elizabeth had ever referred to Darcy by such an endearment, and the fact that she was the one initiating the physical intimacy between them caused an unbearable source of emotion to surge through his breast. His body grew heated with undeniable passion, and before he could master himself, Darcy pulled Elizabeth against him in a tight embrace, kissing her passionately and with unwonted abandon.

He had caught her completely off guard. His way was usually more tender and less demanding, but apparently Elizabeth found this exchange to be far from unpleasant. So loving was her response, that his hunger for her threatened to overpower him.

They continued thus for what seemed an eternity, Darcy holding her as he ran his hands down her back and over her hips, reveling in the utter intoxication of losing himself in the woman he loved. He suddenly felt himself desiring her so much, he found himself vocalizing his fervent wish that she was already his.

Elizabeth gasped at the boldness of such a declaration, as well as the path of his hands as they traveled upward from her hips to caress the softness of her breasts. She froze, held captive by the many delectable shocks of desire coursing through her from this new intimacy.

It took Darcy a moment to comprehend, that Elizabeth was no longer returning his ardent kisses, and realizing with sudden horror the liberties he had been taking, he tore himself from her and stepped away.

"Forgive me, forgive me," was all he could manage, but he repeated it over and over again in a whisper as he sank to his knees and ran his hands over his face. He was appalled he had taken advantage of Elizabeth in such a way—*his* Elizabeth, whom he loved and respected beyond measure—even beyond reason. He knew he had no right to do what he had done, just as he had no right to wrap his arms around her waist to draw comfort from her presence, but when she quietly moved to stand before him, he could not resist doing just that.

Darcy clung to her, burying his face in her spencer and the soft folds of her gown while she removed his hat and entwined her fingers through his curls. It had a soothing effect on him. He could not cease marveling at her generous capacity to continually overlook his offenses. *How can she still be so tender and caring toward me? How can she even permit me to hold her after I have taken such liberties?* If anyone had come upon them, Elizabeth's reputation would have been in tatters; yet, here she was comforting *him*. He was overwhelmed.

"Fitzwilliam?" Her voice was soft and gentle, with no hint of admonishment in her tone, only concern.

Shaking his head, he said, "You have placed your trust in me, enough to offer yourself in such a way, and yet I have taken advantage of your generosity and tenderness in a manner that can only be described as completely reprehensible. I do not deserve you."

Elizabeth recognized the self-loathing in his voice and stared at him for a moment in confusion. "Why would you think that? Surely, you must have noticed the pleasure I receive from your attentions?"

He remained silent.

She lowered herself to the ground and held his hands. "Fitzwilliam, look at me. Do you truly think I would not welcome such a natural progression of intimacy between us? If this is the case, I can assure you that you are mistaken. I welcome it, very much. If I did not, I would never encourage you to kiss me or permit you to take me in your arms as I do. You must know that."

He sighed before saying, "Yes. I do. I also know you would never have allowed the liberties I have taken in the first place if you did not feel some degree of tenderness for me. It is just that the regard I know you now have for me is not yet equal to the strength of my feelings for you. I do not wish to ask too much of you, Elizabeth. I would never be able to live with myself if my... affections for you were to drive you away from me. I cannot tell you how much I fear losing you, losing what I have found with you." His voice was suddenly hoarse. "You know not how much I—"

"Shh, dearest, shh," she said as she stroked a curl from his brow, "there is no need to think of such things."

Needing very much to feel her reassurance, Darcy pulled her onto his lap, and they held each other in silence for some time before he finally allowed himself to voice a concern that had been tormenting him since the previous evening. "Elizabeth, you must promise me you will not allow your mother to persuade you to marry that... *man*. I could not bear it."

She could not help but laugh. "By '*that man*,' I suppose you refer to my cousin, sir? No"—she smiled—"have no worries on that account. Heaven forbid, even if I were to be found with Mr. Collins in a compromising situation, and the chance of that is practically nonexistent, I can safely promise you I would *never* consent to marry *him*."

"And what if you were found in a compromising situation with me?" he asked softly and with complete seriousness. "Would you continue to refuse me, as well? Or might I be successful by employing some particular manner of persuasion that might entice you to accept me?"

"I believe, Fitzwilliam," she said with an impish smile as she caressed his jaw, "that in a matter of only a few weeks, you have already had far more success on that score than my poor cousin could ever hope for in the course of his entire life!"

Darcy's eyes flared. "Truly?"

She bowed her head and looked up at him through her lashes. "Truly. But I believe I am not yet prepared to formalize more than a courtship between us at this time. I hope you understand and are not terribly discouraged. You see, sir, I have only just now come to learn I do not enjoy being the cause of any disappointment to you."

He traced her cheek with his finger as his eyes devoured her. "Then why do you continue to refuse me the one thing that would most assuredly *not* disappoint me?"

She raised her brow in admonishment.

"Forgive me," he said. "I should not have asked it. Of course, I would never wish for you to consent to anything I ask of you before you are ready to do so with your whole heart."

"I know, and I thank you," she whispered as she leaned in to kiss him with warmth and feeling. *If I cannot yet agree to say what I know will make him happy, at least I can show him how much happiness he brings to me.*

Not until some time later, Darcy and Elizabeth managed to find their way back to Longbourn, where they were met at the end of the walkway by Mrs. Bennet, her nerves in an obvious dither.

"Good gracious! Mr. Darcy, you are certainly out early this morning. And how kind of you to condescend to escort such an impertinent, headstrong girl home from her wild ramblings about the countryside. You are very welcome to breakfast, sir, for we are all just sitting down now, but I am afraid Lizzy will be prevented from joining us. Mr. Collins has something very particular he wishes to speak to her about." She snatched Elizabeth away before either could raise any objection, and propelled her into the house.

Darcy was horrified. *Good, God! It can only mean my aunt's half-witted parson intends to propose to her!* He experienced a sudden, desperate urge to run after Elizabeth and tear her away from her mother's grasp, to put her upon the back of his horse and carry her off to London without delay, where he would marry her immediately. The scandal that would surely follow them would demand they marry in any case. Knowing, however, that Elizabeth would be displeased by his taking such a rash measure, he swallowed hard, passed his hand over his eyes, and considered his other options. Darcy was forced to admit that, other than publicly declaring the very particular manner in which he had just compromised her in the middle of the field, he was left with very little else but to present his suit and try his luck at reasoning with Mr. Bennet.

Squaring his shoulders, Darcy strode into the house, and seeing no one else about, he knocked upon the door to Mr. Bennet's sanctuary. He heard a faint, "Enter," issued from within the confines of the library, and breathed a sigh of relief before pushing open the door, hoping to find the elder gentleman alone.

"Ah, yes. Mr. Darcy. I have been expecting you, sir. Come in, come in. It is early yet for anything stronger than coffee, but I will not discourage you if, under the circumstances, you are feeling so inclined." Mr. Bennet's mouth was turned up in a wry smile, not unlike the one he had often seen upon Elizabeth's pert lips, Darcy observed.

"Thank you, no, sir."

"Very well. Let us get to it, then," he said as he leaned back in his chair. "Am I correct in supposing you have come to ask me something particular about my Lizzy?"

"Yes, sir, I have, but I hesitate to tell you there appears to be a slight… impediment." Darcy watched uneasily as Mr. Bennet's eyebrows retreated into his hairline.

"An *impediment*, did you say? I do not suppose you would care to enlighten me, Mr. Darcy, by telling me precisely what this *impediment* is and why it should affect your making my daughter an offer of marriage this morning?"

"It is precisely that, Mr. Bennet. I have already made Miss Elizabeth an offer of marriage not more than a fortnight ago, and she has refused me. She has, however, granted her consent to allow me the privilege of courting her, and I now respectfully ask you for yours until such a time as I am able to persuade her to reconsider."

Mr. Bennet leaned forward. "Let me rightly understand you, Mr. Darcy. You proposed to Elizabeth *two weeks* ago?"

"Yes."

"And she has refused you?"

"Yes."

"And, in spite of her refusal of your hand, she is willing to allow you to pay court to her in the meantime?"

"Yes."

"Extraordinary!" Mr. Bennet steepled his fingers and sat silently in thought for several minutes before addressing Darcy with a stern look. "Can you give me one reason, after the display I witnessed at the Netherfield ball, why I should not force Elizabeth to accept you today, regardless of what her current wishes might be? Before you answer me, I will remind you that your conduct was not witnessed only by me, but also by her mother, her elder sister, her cousin, Mr. Bingley, *and* his family, and God only knows how many of our other well-intentioned, gossiping neighbors."

"I do not wish for Miss Elizabeth to be *forced* to marry me. It is not what she wants, nor is it what I would wish for her."

Elizabeth's father was incredulous. "Not what *she wants*? Not what *you would wish for her*? That is not good enough for *me*, Mr. Darcy! Both of you should have been responsible enough to have taken the consequences of such actions into account *before* you chose to behave so in public! You can think whatever you like, sir, but it is obvious from what I saw that my daughter is far from averse to your attentions. As a matter of fact, she seems to favor you with an astonishing familiarity I cannot help but find disturbing under the circumstances. So I am sure that, in light of this pointed observation, neither of you will remain unhappy for very long after you have entered into matrimony as soon as possible."

Darcy was at a loss. He knew not what to do nor how to convince this man he could not possibly marry his favorite daughter without *her* declaration of love. He soon realized, however, any further assurances of the vehemence of *his* love for Elizabeth and *his* desire for the preservation of her happiness and her wishes would not aid him in the least. He clearly needed another approach. Deep in thought, he ran the back of his hand across his lips. "Sir, may I speak plainly?"

Mr. Bennet sighed and nodded curtly.

Darcy strode to the window and back several times before he finally said, "I *will* marry Miss Elizabeth, you have my word, both as a gentleman and as the master of Pemberley, Mr. Bennet, but I do ask that you reconsider and indulge your daughter's desire for a formal courtship. Announcing an impending wedding between us at this time would succeed only in adding fuel to any local gossip that may arise. However, should it, instead, become publicly known that there already exists between us a prior courtship—which there most certainly does—then, perhaps continuing in this vein for several months or so might be a better option than announcing an engagement. It will give Miss Elizabeth the time she desires to come to better know her heart, not to mention it will very likely provide ample time for any idle talk and speculation to die down, as well."

Mr. Bennet glared at him as Darcy placed his hands upon the desk. "Mr. Bennet, because I am not unacquainted with the fervency of your attachment to your daughter and her very great affection for you, I must now ask you to consider whether forcing such a life-altering, permanent arrangement upon her in such a manner could truly prove to be beneficial. Miss Elizabeth will surely feel resentment toward both you and me over such a course of action. And I feel I need not point out that resentment is hardly an element that can be construed as conducive, either to marital felicity or to familial harmony. Forgive me, sir, but I find it very difficult to believe you would truly wish to force such an unwelcome fate upon your favorite daughter."

Mr. Bennet observed Darcy in irritated silence. *Touché, Mr. Darcy,* he thought bitterly and with no little resentment of his own. As much as he hated to admit it, this arrogant young man had known precisely how to carry his point with him. No, Mr. Bennet would certainly not wish to be the one to cause his Lizzy any unhappiness in life. Indeed, bringing misery to his favorite daughter had always been something he had studiously avoided, although, with such a woman as Mrs. Bennet for a mother, sometimes some measure of misery could not be helped. Mr. Bennet thought long and hard about his own unequal marriage and ran his hand over his tired eyes. *If Darcy's conjectures are correct, then perhaps I might, even yet, be able to spare Lizzy this displeasure… if only for a little while longer.*

Mr. Bennet had had enough dealings with Darcy to know he was an intelligent, honorable man, but that did not mean he was happy about this turn of events. Drumming his fingers upon his desk, he finally sighed in resignation. "Very well," he grumbled.

Darcy exhaled and took a seat in one of the two chairs across the desk from Elizabeth's father. "Thank you, sir."

"Yes, well, what else can I say? I fear I am only too familiar with the consequences of marrying in haste. I would not wish that upon my Lizzy or her future children, not even with a man I know to be as honorable and intelligent as you. I yield to you, sir. Elizabeth shall have two months in which to become better acquainted with you, but I must caution you not to misinterpret my ruling, Mr. Darcy. Should *any* scandalous gossip result from your unguarded behavior, stemming either from the ball or from some future incident, I will be forced to take action and insist upon my daughter accepting you whether or not she has acquired the feelings you desire for her to have."

Darcy extended his hand to Mr. Bennet, who clasped it firmly in his. It was at that moment that Mrs. Bennet burst into the room.

"Oh, Mr. Bennet! We are all in an uproar! You must come immediately and make Lizzy marry Mr. Collins!"

Darcy visibly paled. "In God's name, whatever for?" he demanded.

Mr. Bennet looked in astonishment, first at his guest, then at his wife. It was short-lived, however, as expectancy intervened. Without a doubt, the situation promised some unanticipated amusement for him, and he settled in comfortably. "Forgive me, Mrs. Bennet, but I do not have the pleasure of understanding you. To what are you referring?"

Mrs. Bennet was clearly exasperated. "To Mr. Collins and Lizzy! Lizzy has declared she will not have Mr. Collins, and Mr. Collins begins to say he will not have Lizzy!"

"Thank God for that!" Darcy muttered under his breath and, with relief, fell back into his chair.

Mr. Bennet looked thoughtfully at his wife. "Let me rightly understand you, Mrs. Bennet. Am I correct it is your wish that Lizzy accept Mr. Collins?"

"Yes. I insist you make her marry him."

"Very well." Here, Mr. Bennet turned to Darcy. "I am afraid, Mr. Darcy, we seem to have stumbled upon yet another impediment, so to speak." He enjoyed seeing the look of alarm that had transformed Darcy's usual calm demeanor into one of absolute horror.

Darcy could hardly believe what he was hearing, his shock apparent as he protested loudly, "An impediment! Mr. Bennet, you cannot seriously be considering—?"

"For Heaven's sake!" exclaimed Mrs. Bennet. "What does Mr. Darcy have to do with Mr. Collins and Lizzy?"

"Well, nothing with Mr. Collins, to be sure," replied her husband evenly, "but, as I have just granted Mr. Darcy my consent to court Lizzy for the purpose of marriage, I would imagine he might have a few words he would like to interject on the subject." Mr. Bennet looked back at his wife, quite pleased with himself.

So stunned was Mrs. Bennet by this declaration, she could not speak for a full five minutes. After only two, however, her husband took pity upon his agitated guest. "In light of this recent information, Mrs. Bennet, do you still wish for me to prevail upon Lizzy to accept Mr. Collins, or would you prefer to remain forever silent on the subject?" Seeing his wife did, indeed, plan to remain silent on the subject, he addressed Darcy. "If I am not mistaken, Mr. Darcy, Lizzy should be extremely pleased to have you join her at this time. That is, if your wishes remain unchanged."

I believe, Mr. Bennet, there is nothing anyone could say or do that would ever change my mind regarding your daughter, he mused, but aloud said, "I see no reason for any alteration at present." The corners of Darcy's mouth turned upward as he bowed and made to leave. Mr. Bennet, having had enough diversion for one morning, waved him on his way.

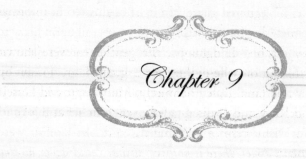

Chapter 9

THE FOLLOWING MORNING SAW BINGLEY AND DARCY OUT OF the house and on their way to Longbourn before the rest of the Netherfield party had even come down to breakfast. After several weeks of careful meditation about Caroline and her plans to separate him from his angel, Bingley was determined not to waste another day dawdling about in courtship. Today he would ask Jane Bennet to become his wife, and if all went well, he would return to Netherfield that evening engaged and the happiest of men.

Though enticing thoughts of matrimony pervaded Darcy's mind as well, he knew to act upon such would be jumping too far ahead of the good fortune he had so recently found with Elizabeth. He was more than willing to take her as his wife without the delay of an additional heartbeat, but he was also well aware of the fact that any tender regard she now felt toward him was still quite new.

But Elizabeth did desire him. The reality of it was enough to cause his heart to soar with pleasure, but that she did not yet feel love for him left much still to be accomplished. He would take his time and go slowly—well, as slowly as their passion for each other would permit. With a wry grin, Darcy struggled to push the delicious image of Elizabeth as his wife from his mind. For today and, he supposed, countless weeks to follow, he would have to content himself with the pleasures of courting her. *At least I am now at liberty to do so with her father's blessing.*

When they reached Longbourn, the gentlemen were shown into a cheerful parlor where they were greeted graciously by Mrs. Bennet while Jane smiled demurely, Mary engrossed herself in a book, and Kitty and Lydia giggled over some private joke of their own. To Darcy's concern, Elizabeth and Mr. Collins were noticeably absent. After exchanging the usual pleasantries, Darcy mumbled an excuse about checking on his horse and went on a quest to find Elizabeth.

After searching for some time, he finally discovered her in one of the gardens toward the rear of the house. Elizabeth was so preoccupied with her feelings of disgust over Mr. Collins's continued perseverance in his pursuit of her, despite her pointed refusal of his offer of marriage and Darcy's prior interest, that she failed to hear Darcy's approach.

Standing much closer than propriety would ever allow, he said, "When I did not find you in the drawing room with the rest of your family, I feared Mr. Collins had carried you off to Gretna Green."

Elizabeth turned to look at him with an arch smile Darcy had come to recognize well. "I would not yet put it past him, sir; however, you will be happy to know I am prodigiously capable of defending myself against any such attempt."

He took her gloved hand in his and raised it to his lips to bestow a lingering kiss. Rather than releasing it, however, Darcy yielded to temptation, allowing his gloveless fingers to trace the skin of her exposed wrist while he gave her the barest hint of a teasing smile. "I am very relieved to hear it. Otherwise, I would certainly find myself in the uncomfortable position of having to call out my aunt's clergyman. I am a very possessive man, Elizabeth, when it comes to you."

"Are you, Mr. Darcy?" Her voice quivered from his ministrations. He nodded almost imperceptibly, his fingers continuing to caress her wrist in a most delightful manner. Elizabeth felt weak from his touch. Striving to lighten the mood, she smiled unsteadily and said, "Then you must tell me, sir, how I might reassure you of my fervent desire for your society."

The hunger in Darcy's eyes was tangible.

"I should have thought that by now, such an answer would have been obvious," he whispered as he leaned in to press his lips against hers, lightly at first, but her responsiveness to him soon spurred him to deepen his kisses. Slowly, his arm began to encircle her waist as he drew her against him, his other hand cradling the back of her head.

Her knees became suddenly weak, and Elizabeth slid her hands to Darcy's shoulders to steady herself, rejoicing in the sensations he was able to stir within her. She knew she should not be permitting him to take such liberties with her within full view of the house, but his mouth, then traveling down her neck, was exquisite in its distraction. Elizabeth soon found it impossible to think of anything beyond him. She was, therefore, at a loss when she felt Darcy suddenly release her and step quickly away. Her eyes met his briefly with a look of bereft longing before Jane and Mr. Bingley were upon them.

With a smile, Jane left Bingley's side and went directly to her sister. Lost in her own joy, she had not seemed to notice Elizabeth's discomposure.

"It is too much! I do not deserve it! Oh, Lizzy, why is not everyone as happy?"

Elizabeth followed her gaze to Bingley, who was receiving Darcy's heartfelt congratulations with obvious pleasure, and smiled. "Oh, Jane! Certainly, if you do not deserve such happiness, I cannot think who does. I am so very pleased for you." Elizabeth embraced her sister with warmth. They were immediately joined by the gentlemen so Darcy could kiss Jane's hand while Bingley joyfully shook Elizabeth's, claiming the right of a brother.

The foursome wandered for some minutes together in happy conversation until they were joined by Charlotte Lucas, who had come to visit with Elizabeth. Bingley, who was most anxious to call upon Mr. Bennet, and Jane, to go to her mother, left Charlotte with Elizabeth and Darcy. It wasn't long before they, too, returned to the house for some refreshment, where Charlotte heard Mrs. Bennet's effusive raptures over Jane's betrothal to Bingley, Elizabeth's courtship with Darcy, and, more discreetly, Elizabeth's refusal of Mr. Collins.

To that unfortunate gentleman, residing in the same house with Elizabeth, Mrs. Bennet's pronouncements were nothing short of a punishment. Mrs. Bennet, who had until only very recently been so encouraging and supportive of his suit with his fair cousin, was now fawning over the other gentlemen in the parlor with unabashed enthusiasm, Mr. Collins all but forgotten. Bingley's smiling face and obvious success with Jane only served to remind him of where he had so recently failed. He could not like it one bit.

Mr. Collins looked resentfully toward Elizabeth, who was engaged in conversation with Charlotte while Darcy observed her with undisguised admiration, and a bitter taste rose in the back of his throat. On the other side of the room, Lydia and Kitty burst out in raucous laughter, their mirth-filled eyes fixed upon him. Mortified, Mr. Collins abruptly stood, readying his escape.

In the very next moment, he was startled to see Elizabeth making her way toward him with her friend. While she said very little, Mr. Collins found Miss Lucas to be a most amiable lady, readily engaging the clergyman in pleasant conversation for nearly a quarter of an hour. As she rose to take her leave, she extended an invitation to dine with her family that afternoon. This was most fortuitous, indeed, as it provided an immediate reprieve from the company of his fair cousin and his esteemed patroness's nephew. With great eagerness, he accompanied Charlotte to Lucas Lodge.

Much to Mrs. Bennet's vexation, as she still had three perfectly good daughters yet to be spoken for, Mr. Collins did not return to Longbourn that evening until very late, just as the family was retiring for the night. He was gone shortly after breakfast the following morning, much to everyone's surprise and, once again, not to return until the Bennets were on their way to bed. When the third day afforded much the same routine, the inhabitants of Longbourn were at a loss as to where Mr. Collins could possibly be spending his time. Not until Elizabeth paid a visit to Charlotte at Lucas Lodge several days later, was light shed upon the subject.

"Engaged! To Mr. Collins?" Elizabeth stared at her friend in shock.

"Why, does it surprise you, Elizabeth, that Mr. Collins should manage to procure any woman's good opinion simply because he was not so happy as to succeed in procuring your own?"

Elizabeth hardly knew how to answer her.

"I see what you must be feeling," her friend continued, "especially since Mr. Collins was only lately paying his addresses to you, Elizabeth." Charlotte sighed. "I am not romantic, you know. I never was. I ask for only a comfortable home, and considering Mr. Collins's character, connections, and situation in life, I am convinced my chances of happiness with him are as fair as most people can boast upon entering the marriage state."

Elizabeth was at a loss. "Undoubtedly," was all she could manage. She had always known Charlotte's views of matrimony did not necessarily coincide with her own, but to accept Mr. Collins—to pass the rest of her life in his company and as his *wife*—was incredible to her. She could not imagine enduring such humiliation and sacrifice simply to secure such a future for herself, yet it was an opportunity Charlotte seemed eager to embrace. How could her friend, whom she had always valued for her good sense, sentence herself to such a fate with a man whom she could never completely esteem?

As Elizabeth walked back to Longbourn, her thoughts gradually drifted from Charlotte and Mr. Collins to Darcy and herself. How fortunate she was to have engaged the affections and admiration of such an intelligent and worthy man! He had cared for her, ardently, these many weeks, and yet, she had been blind to it until only recently.

Elizabeth found herself wondering what a future with him might be like. No doubt, much more palatable than a future in Mr. Collins's society! Her mind wandered to the intensity of Darcy's penetrating eyes and the way he could evoke a passionate response from her body without ever having touched her. It made her shiver.

Though she found such intimate interactions with Darcy to be more exquisite than anything she had ever dared to imagine possible between a man and a woman, there were other aspects of their relationship that also brought her unparalleled gratification. She had found a source of immeasurable satisfaction in Darcy's insightful discourse, and in his keen interest and knowledge of world affairs. Indeed, in the last month they had passed many enjoyable afternoons and evenings in one another's society, discussing books and music, philosophy and history—even travel. And, though Elizabeth had not yet been given much opportunity to venture farther than London, she had still managed to impress Darcy considerably with her extensive knowledge of America and its lucrative investment opportunities, information she had gleaned from extensive reading and from conversations held with her father and her Aunt and Uncle Gardiner in London.

The more time she spent with Darcy, the more Elizabeth was forced to admit she would, most likely and quite soon, be in very great danger of finding herself in love with him. It unnerved her. She had always relied upon her own liveliness of mind and independence of spirit to provide her with ample sources of enjoyment, but now she found herself coming to depend more and more upon one very particular man, whose society, she happened to find, was far superior to that of every other gentleman of her acquaintance.

Chapter 10

THE PASSING OF ANOTHER TWO DAYS FINALLY BROUGHT A CLOSE to Mr. Collins's rather lengthy stay at Longbourn, but as he was, by no means, ready to take his leave of his dear Charlotte after having so recently discovered her, Lady Catherine de Bourgh had, yet *again*, graciously condescended to grant him her permission to extend his stay until the following Friday. This did nothing to appease Elizabeth, who, in spite of his engagement to her good friend and her own understanding with Darcy, continued to be an object of that gentleman's interest, though she was hard-pressed as to understand why.

To Darcy, her cousin's actions were far from acceptable. He did not at all like the way the clergyman's eyes followed Elizabeth when he was in company with her. It was not exactly a look of admiration or even lust the man bestowed upon her, but more an expression of scrutiny and bitterness, as though Mr. Collins wished to discover something to criticize in her behavior toward him.

As far as his treatment of Darcy was concerned, however, Mr. Collins continued to take pains, however grudgingly, to maintain his abject attentions toward the master of Pemberley—but only out of reverence for Lady Catherine and his exalted position as her most humble servant.

On one particular morning, Darcy, after bearing witness to Elizabeth's agitation and discomfort while in the presence of her cousin, requested they walk out together with Jane and Bingley. She readily agreed.

As the ladies went to their room to fetch some warmer attire for their outing, Mr. Collins, who was lingering just outside in the hall, happened to overhear Darcy remark in a low, disgusted voice to Bingley about his very great displeasure with the clergyman for his continued interest and scrutiny of Elizabeth. A few other choice words of observation on the subject were exchanged between the two gentlemen before they were finally rejoined by Elizabeth and Jane. Exchanging warm smiles, the foursome then removed themselves from the house.

Mr. Collins was incensed. Was it not enough Darcy had managed to rob him of the connubial felicity he felt sure would have resulted from an alliance with his pretty cousin? Now he had also seen fit to publicly censure him, as well—and after all the condescension and preference he had continued to show him as the nephew of his patroness! *No, I am not deserving of this infamous treatment, even though Mr. Darcy is such a wealthy man and the favored nephew of Lady Catherine de Bourgh!* A smile then overspread his indignant face as he suddenly imagined the reaction his patroness would have upon learning she was likely to gain an untitled niece who was clearly without fortune or connections. *Yes, Lady Catherine will have much to say on that subject, but first…* It was with alacrity that Mr. Collins quitted the room and went in search of Mr. Bennet.

It was not until several hours later that the professed lovers finally wandered back to Longbourn—Bingley and Jane smiling, Darcy and Elizabeth laughing, and all four in obvious high spirits. Darcy had barely removed his greatcoat and hat when Mr. Bennet approached him with a grim countenance and ushered Elizabeth and him into his library, where they were surprised to find Mr. Collins sitting smugly in one of the chairs near the fire. Elizabeth's father took his usual position behind his desk and began without preamble. "Mr. Darcy," he said severely, "I am afraid Mr. Collins has recently brought to my attention a matter of some import regarding your intentions toward Elizabeth."

Darcy fixed the clergyman with an icy glare before replying, "And precisely what, may I ask, is this matter of great import that would so prompt Mr. Collins to dare to question my intentions toward Miss Elizabeth?"

Before another word could be spoken, Mr. Collins inclined his head and began addressing Elizabeth. "My dear young cousin," he said with his usual haughty flourish, "I know not how the nephew of my esteemed patroness, Lady Catherine de Bourgh, has imposed upon you, and far be it from me to rejoice in being the bearer of such grievous news that will, no doubt, mortify you while leaving nothing but pain and disgrace in its wake. I feel, however, that my very respectability as a clergyman qualifies me to assume the unhappy role of apprising unfortunate young ladies such as yourself of certain events that you must have brought to your attention for your own very great benefit, and with all due haste.

"Though your charms are numerous, fair Cousin Elizabeth, I see no cause at this time to lay any blame *directly* upon you, per se, for even I, a man of such humility and condescension in the eyes of God, have found myself recently under the spell of your feminine arts and allurements…"

Mr. Bennet cast Mr. Collins a look of warning.

Darcy could hardly believe this ridiculous man had not only failed to arrive at his point but had actually managed to insult Elizabeth with his offensive accusations. "Good God, man, have you anything of even marginal sense to impart?" he demanded with irritation. "As of this moment, you have done nothing but ramble on in a completely reprehensible manner and insult a lady. I will not have it. Either come to your point or have done."

Catching Mr. Bennet's eye, which had been fixed firmly upon him with a look of displeasure—and misinterpreting it entirely—Mr. Collins contorted himself into a bow of capitulation. "Yes, of course, my dear Mr. Darcy! Please allow me to take this opportunity to offer you my most humble apologies for my unforgivable failure to properly apprise my patient young cousin of the important news I have yet to impart on behalf of you and your aunt, the most affable and generous Lady Catherine de Bourgh, a woman of the highest condescension…" and on he went as anxiety began to intrude upon Darcy, for he had suddenly realized what it was his aunt's clergyman wished to tell Elizabeth and had probably already told her father.

He was furious but somehow managed to convey nothing stronger than contempt. "Yes, thank you, Mr. Collins. We all know how much you admire my aunt, but I have reached the end of my patience. I now feel with absolute confidence I can guess precisely what it is you are trying so inarticulately to convey to Miss Elizabeth, and you can rest assured, sir, it is a matter that does not concern you."

Mr. Bennet spoke then, his voice harsh. "Perhaps not, Mr. Darcy, but I believe you might agree that, as Elizabeth's father, it most certainly does concern *me*."

Elizabeth did not know what to think; she had not been able to make sense of anything that had been said thus far.

Seeing her confusion, Mr. Collins addressed her yet again.

"My poor, naïve cousin, forgive me for saying so, but you have been most injuriously deceived, for I am certain beyond a doubt Mr. Darcy could never have been serious in his attentions to you, no matter how marked they appeared to have been. I have it on excellent authority, from Lady Catherine de Bourgh herself, he is engaged to be married to her very own daughter, Miss Anne de Bourgh of Rosings Park in Kent."

Elizabeth started at this declaration. Her eyes met Darcy's with disbelief. "No," she whispered, shaking her head with vehemence. "No. Everything you have said to me—everything that has passed between us—it is not true. What Mr. Collins says cannot possibly be true."

Darcy moved immediately to her side and, against propriety, took both her hands. "You are quite right, it is most definitely *not* true," he said with feeling, and then, so softly only Elizabeth would hear his words, he added, "my dearest love."

Still retaining her hands, he fixed her father with a level stare and proclaimed, "Mr. Bennet, any rumor of a pending alliance with my Cousin Anne is precisely that and nothing more. I can heartily assure you, sir, neither she nor I have ever desired such a union between us, nor will such a union ever take place. For many years now it has been solely the wish of my aunt, whom you may readily imagine is not used to brooking opposition on matters she has long ago arranged in her mind to suit none but her own purpose. I do not answer to her, Mr. Bennet, and I believe you are well acquainted with my wishes and intentions regarding your daughter."

Mr. Bennet visibly relaxed. "Yes, Mr. Darcy, that I am. I hope you can understand why I felt moved to question you regarding your intentions toward Lizzy in such a situation. Indeed, it could not be avoided."

Darcy nodded curtly, and both men glanced at a nearly apoplectic Mr. Collins.

Elizabeth's eyes suddenly filled with tears. No matter what anyone else might be persuaded to believe, she was absolutely certain her cousin's intentions were motivated by malice. Without even so much as a glance toward any of the gentlemen, she pulled her hands from between Darcy's, ripped open the library door, and fled from the room.

Darcy immediately made to follow her, his concern propelling him, but found himself prevented from crossing the threshold to the main foyer by Mr. Bennet's firm voice. "Let her go, Mr. Darcy. If I know my daughter, she is only in need of some time to herself. I believe all will be well, but for now, I suggest you indulge her. She will return to us in due time."

Elizabeth lay upon her bed, a stream of tears flowing across her cheeks and onto the embroidery of her pillow. So consumed was she by her roiling emotions and her fear of the loss she had very nearly incurred, they now eclipsed even her hostility toward Mr. Collins for his perverse machinations. After her cousin's display, she could no longer deny that what she felt for Darcy was far more than simple warmth or excessive fondness. No, after the conversation that had taken place in her father's library and her powerful reaction to it, Elizabeth knew in her heart she was far beyond mere friendship. She was in love with him. She was in love with Fitzwilliam Darcy.

Should Mr. Collins's words have been true, the disappointment Elizabeth would surely have suffered would have been beyond painful. She now knew that, had Darcy actually been engaged to his Cousin Anne—bound to her by honor and by duty—she would never have recovered from such a loss. The thought of living the rest of her life without him, without his searing touch, his ardent looks, or his superior society suddenly made the insistent pounding in her head increase to an almost unbearable level.

Jane's concerned voice called to her from the other side of the door, but feeling unequal to facing anyone at the moment, Elizabeth choked back the hot lump that had lodged in her throat and ignored her. It was not long, however, before the last fragments of her composure crumbled completely. With a muffled sob, she shed bitter, resentful tears for what had nearly been taken from her—the only future she could now envision for herself—a future with Darcy. A future as his wife. Collapsing under the strain of the morning's events, she soon cried herself to sleep.

Elizabeth did not return for several hours. When she did finally make an appearance, however, it was obvious to all in attendance that she had been crying. Darcy felt a new surge of contempt for Mr. Collins, but, if only for the sake of Elizabeth's serenity, he swallowed the bile that had risen in his throat, and held his tongue.

Understanding their need to discuss what had occurred, Mr. Bennet decided to bend the boundaries of strict propriety and allow Darcy a private interview with his daughter in one of the smaller parlors in the rear of the house. The room was light and airy, and the last rays of the setting sun could be seen filtering through the sheer curtains. It was a room Elizabeth favored on those cold, wet days when she would find herself confined to the house for extended periods of time. It was, in a sense, a sanctuary for her, a refuge from the constant badgering of her mother and the tittering and arguing of her youngest sisters. She was grateful to her father for his unexpected gesture.

Leaving the door open, Darcy guided her to a sofa near the fire. To his surprise, she did not take a seat beside him but settled herself upon his lap and wrapped her arms about his neck, holding him close. He closed his eyes and enfolded her in his embrace, more than happy to breathe in her heady lavender scent and feel the warmth of her body pressing against his own. After several minutes of silence, however, Darcy felt compelled to speak and, in a low voice, said, "I am so very sorry you had to bear witness to such a ridiculous display earlier."

His apology was cut short by Elizabeth's firm voice. "There is no need to say anything, Fitzwilliam, and there was certainly nothing ridiculous about what transpired. I am afraid everything that was said today was uttered in a vindictive spirit and was aimed to harm us, perhaps irreparably. Wretched, hateful man! I cannot forgive his interference." She drew away from him, but only far enough to gaze upon his face and brush an unruly curl from his forehead. "My love," she whispered, "if you had truly been promised to your cousin, however could I have learned to live without you?"

Darcy's breath caught in his throat as he stared at her. "Elizabeth!" he whispered urgently, "Please, dearest, will you not say it again?"

"Say what again, Fitzwilliam?" she asked as she proceeded to kiss his jaw, her hands leaving a delightful path of fire across his shoulders.

He closed his eyes briefly as he reached out his hands to still the movement of hers. "You called me your *love*, Elizabeth," he said with a hitch in his voice. "I have dreamed of hearing those words fall from your lips for so very long. I have prayed every day to be granted the privilege of knowing such sweetness as it flows from your beloved mouth. Elizabeth, I beg of you, please tell me this is not merely another dream from which I will again awaken to disappointment."

"Oh, Fitzwilliam," she whispered, "after all we have shared, after all that has passed between us, how could you doubt it? How could you not feel it? Indeed, I love you with all my heart." After all she had allowed him, the idea that Darcy might need verbal confirmation of her love seemed incredible.

He reached for her, and she wrapped him tightly in her arms. Breathing deeply, Darcy buried his face against the curve of her neck and murmured, "I have loved you for what seems to me an eternity, Elizabeth. Indeed, I have long been in need of you, even before I came to know of your existence. You can have no idea how much it means to me, after months of despair and weeks of uncertainty, to hear you say you love me. You have made me so happy. Indeed, I could wish for nothing more, nothing more except…" The words died on his lips as he realized it was probably too soon to broach the subject of marriage once again.

"Except for what, my love?" she entreated, her voice soft and filled with tenderness.

Darcy raised his head, brushing her cheek with his. Their eyes met and then closed as he rested his forehead against hers. "More than anything, you know I wish to have you for my wife, yet I dare not ask again for fear of your rejection."

Elizabeth stroked his cheek as she feathered her lips against his. Darcy inhaled sharply when he heard her whisper, "I assure you, Fitzwilliam, your fears are entirely unfounded."

A burning hope suddenly flowed unchecked through Darcy's veins. He forced himself to take several deep, calming breaths before saying, "Dearest, loveliest Elizabeth, will you do me the very great honor of becoming my wife?"

Tears of love and emotion burned in her eyes as she drew her head just far enough away to look into his eyes once more. He loved her almost beyond reason, and only now did she truly understand what it was to be able to return such a love. "Fitzwilliam, I love you now so very dearly. Nothing would give me greater pleasure than to have you for my husband. I am only sorry it has taken me so long to commit myself to you. You are truly the best man I have ever known. It will be an honor for me to become your wife."

The remainder of the day passed without further incident, aside from Darcy's joyful application to Mr. Bennet for Elizabeth's hand, which he was not denied. The happy couple spent the last hour or so of the waning afternoon pleasantly with Bingley and Jane, much to the consternation of Mr. Collins, who had stubbornly declined an invitation to dine with Charlotte at Lucas Lodge. After witnessing Darcy's denial of familial duty to Miss de Bourgh, the clergyman was convinced, more than ever, that the master of Pemberley had been infamously drawn in.

Chagrined by his cousin's unwarranted accusation toward his future son-in-law, and his own recently inflicted injustice in the same quarter, Mr. Bennet was resolved to give the lovers one more day of peace by delaying the announcement of Elizabeth's engagement until the following evening, thus insulating Darcy against further insult from having to bear witness to the endless raptures of his future mother-in-law.

Just before dinner, in an effort to defuse some of his mounting anger toward Mr. Collins's persistent and offensive scrutiny, Darcy asked Elizabeth to take a turn with him in the garden. The night was clear, the moon was full, and stars twinkled in the heavens.

As they made their way toward a little copse on the far side of the garden, Elizabeth shivered from the chill of the night air.

The spot was a pleasant one and had become a favorite of theirs, as it afforded them some degree of privacy from several sets of prying eyes that might be observing them surreptitiously from the house. Settling himself upon an intricately carved bench, Darcy pulled the woman he loved into an embrace upon his lap.

"How I have longed these past hours to kiss those tempting lips of yours, my lovely Elizabeth!" His voice was soft and filled with urgency, and before she could respond, Darcy had captured her mouth with his in a gentle yet thorough kiss that bespoke all the emotion of the day. When his lips finally released hers, both lovers were breathless.

Darcy gazed with love upon the woman before him. He wanted to touch her, to feel her, to know every inch of her, and impatiently tugged his gloves from his hands so he could delight in the softness of her skin. With a contented sigh, Elizabeth leaned into his caress and, tilting her head, placed her lips slowly and firmly upon his warm palm.

Darcy was mesmerized as she cradled his hand in her own and proceeded to dust kisses from the tips of his fingers to the sensitive skin on the inside of his wrist. Her eyes were closed, her breasts rising and falling rapidly with each breath. His own breath was beginning to come faster, and he hardly knew how he had willed himself to remain so still when such a lovely sight was before him, tantalizing him with her sweet lips.

No longer able to remain passive, Darcy nuzzled her neck, then feathered his lips slowly, seductively along the contour of her jaw, down to the hollow of her throat, and back again to reclaim her mouth in an ardent kiss.

To Elizabeth, his ministrations were heavenly, and this time, when his hands wandered ever so sensuously past her waist to caress her hips, she arched herself against him in an unspoken invitation.

With measured deliberation, Darcy dared his hands to move upward to her full breasts, where he stroked her with his fingertips, eliciting from Elizabeth a soft moan. It was almost more than he could stand, and he pulled his head just far enough away to look upon her beauty illuminated by the moonlight.

"My love, does this please you?" he asked, still caressing her through the velvety fabric of her spencer.

Elizabeth was almost beyond herself with desire. "Yes." Her voice was barely audible, her breathing ragged as she leaned into his touch.

"Good." Darcy worked several buttons on her spencer free and slipped his hand inside. Her body was warm, welcoming, and unbelievably responsive as his fingers grazed the flesh at the neckline of her gown, his thumb applying the slightest circular pressure to her nipple through the soft fabric. Again, Elizabeth moaned as though with delighted ecstasy, and with a surge of burning desire, Darcy parted her lips and drank from her mouth.

Elizabeth was lost to everything around her except Darcy and the exquisite heat his caresses ignited deep within her body. She could feel the tension of the morning melting further away with every teasing stroke of his fingers and every embrace from his lips. She was desirous of more; every fiber of her being cried out for him.

It was Darcy who, through the haze of his own passion, finally realized the danger of their situation. Her passionate responsiveness to him, her unprecedented generosity in permitting him such liberties with her body, her obvious desire, all brought an acute pang of warning that finally forced him to rein in his passion. Gradually, he lightened his kisses and withdrew his hands, which shook as he refastened the buttons of Elizabeth's spencer. He drew her head down to rest upon his shoulder, unbuttoning his greatcoat and wrapping it around them to further warm her trembling body with the heat of his own.

There they sat in the middle of her father's garden, in the dark and most likely facing an engagement of at least three or four months. Their actions were more than unwise—they were dangerous. *How on earth am I ever to survive months of this blissful torture before I can make her truly mine in every way?*

Elizabeth's thoughts, unsurprisingly, were very much along the same lines.

They remained thus for a long while, holding one another in the crisp silence of the evening, lost to all else. Then there was a sound just behind them—the snapping of a twig beneath stumbling feet—and Darcy stiffened. Elizabeth raised her head and, scanning the darkness, suggested they return to the house. It was just as well, as they espied, not half a minute later, the meddling Mr. Collins, who, judging by the appalled look upon his portly face, had very likely observed Darcy brushing Elizabeth's lips with a lingering kiss as she secured the last several buttons on his greatcoat, her fingers dancing over his chest while he proceeded to pull on his discarded gloves.

Dinner that night at Longbourn was an interesting, strained affair, to say the least. Elizabeth was mortified and angry that Mr. Collins had witnessed the intimate exchange between her and Darcy. Darcy was furious that his aunt's insufferable clergyman had the audacity to forget himself so far as to dare to meddle in his personal affairs. Mr. Collins was absolutely indignant on behalf of himself and her ladyship for the unscrupulous and scandalous behavior of Darcy and his Cousin Elizabeth.

Jane felt for Elizabeth; Bingley felt for Darcy; Mary felt for Mr. Collins and busied herself by wracking her memory for a few appropriate words of reflection from *Fordyce's Sermons*; Kitty and Lydia bickered for the duration of the first course; and Mrs. Bennet could be heard above it all, talking away in her shrill voice about trousseaux, new carriages, and frippery for Jane's upcoming nuptials. Mr. Bennet observed them all with amusement.

By the time the gentlemen retired to Mr. Bennet's library after the meal, there was an almost tangible air of tension. As could be expected, a healthier amount of port than was usually offered seemed to be in order. Aside from Mr. Collins's sermon on morality and familial duty, there was little conversation to be had. It was all Darcy could do to keep his temper in check, especially after struggling against the uncharacteristic inclination he felt to lay claim to a substantial portion of the decanter.

As they rejoined the ladies, Mr. Collins succeeded in further astonishing those around him by approaching Darcy and requesting a private conference with him.

"You cannot be serious, Mr. Collins. I have nothing further to say to you tonight on any subject." His reply was barely civil and his features filled with a cold disdain that would have easily deterred a more discerning man. Darcy quickly turned his attention back to Elizabeth, but Mr. Collins stood his ground and continued his assault.

"But my dear Mr. Darcy," he continued in an urgent, slightly amplified voice, "as a clergyman, and particularly one who has pledged my undying bond of allegiance to your own, most respectable aunt, I feel it is my holy duty to point out to you the particular evils of such lustful pursuits as you have so recently engaged in, for it has been my keen observation that you, sir, have not been the first illustrious gentleman to have been led astray by the wiles of a woman. My heart, in any case, goes out to you, for your lamentable weakness in succumbing, and most unconsciously I might add, to the forbidden lures of the flesh."

There were horrified gasps, and then the entire room fell into uncomfortable silence. The void was filled again, and quickly, by Mr. Collins. "Furthermore," he continued, "though my fair cousin does have innumerable temptations at her disposal, which have, undoubtedly, served to benefit her most advantageously in this nefarious ensnarement, I feel, and am certain, beyond any doubt, my most generous and condescending patroness will agree with me when I say that, as an unsuspecting victim of this cruel and artful ploy to capture your favor, not only, Mr. Darcy, are you truly not at fault for indulging in such a natural indiscretion such as this, but you are most certainly to be pitied and prayed for to our merciful God in Heaven and not to be held accountable in the least for any breach of faith in your otherwise honorable and dutiful intentions toward your cousin, Miss Anne de Bourgh of Rosings Park." He finished this speech with what he apparently believed to be a subservient smile before bowing.

It was, by far, too much. "You forget yourself, sir!" Darcy's furious voice filled the quiet drawing room, resonating off the walls and causing Mr. Collins to cringe. Raising himself to his full height, he took several threatening steps toward the clergyman, who, it appeared, had finally acquired sense enough to retreat several faltering steps in the opposite direction.

"Until now," Darcy said in a dangerous voice, "I have endured your preposterous impositions, your tiresome meddling, your baseless slander, and your outrageous insults! You flatter yourself,

Mr. Collins, with your gross assumptions, not only in presuming yourself superior enough in situation and rank to dare to speak on behalf of my aunt and my cousin, but by your insufferable presumption that you could possibly have any knowledge of my heart, my mind, and my desires. There is but one other person aside from myself, and one person only, who is privy to such information, sir, and you have unjustly insulted her at every turn and in a most offensive manner in her own father's home. You will take the opportunity now to apologize to my future *wife*, and if I ever learn of your leveling another insult at her for any reason, make no mistake, Mr. Collins, it will become my mission in life to see you live to regret it."

Mr. Collins was not remiss in his apology to Elizabeth, making use of all the eloquence in his possession as he groveled before her, begging her forgiveness for his crimes. Whether he truly meant it was another matter entirely.

By this time Darcy had long since had enough, and making his apologies to Mr. and Mrs. Bennet for losing his temper in their drawing room, he took his leave, but not before exchanging a private, lengthy, and somewhat emotional good-night talk with Elizabeth.

It was not until Darcy was safely removed from Longbourn that Mrs. Bennet happened to recall several words from the heated exchange with Mr. Collins in which Darcy had referred, most definitely, to Elizabeth as his future wife. Upon receiving confirmation of this, both from her husband and her daughter, she reacted in very much the only way she was accustomed to responding to such happy news. Her raptures were so effusive that none in attendance were in any doubt of her joy of the impending event, which could be heard all the way to Meryton and, very likely, well beyond.

Chapter 11

AFTER RECEIVING SUCH A SET-DOWN FROM DARCY, AND AFTER indulging in a fair amount of reflection, Mr. Collins was finally forced to concede what had become painfully obvious to everyone else in the house—he could no longer expect to receive the proper distinction and respect he believed his due by remaining any longer at Longbourn; thus, he quitted his cousin's house at first light the following morning and hastened to Lucas Lodge, where he would remain until his departure for Hunsford several days hence.

Rather than riding over to Longbourn and braving the effusions of Mrs. Bennet after spending what he had deemed to be an exceptionally trying day in that house not twelve hours earlier, Darcy suggested to Bingley that they extend an invitation to the two eldest Miss Bennets, entreating them to spend the afternoon and evening at Netherfield instead. Declaring it an excellent idea, and quite wishing they had thought of it a good deal sooner, Bingley wasted no time dispatching a footman with his carriage and a note to Jane.

Just as the ladies were making ready to leave, Charlotte arrived. "Lizzy!" she called out as she hurried toward them.

"Charlotte! It is good to see you," she said with a smile and an affectionate embrace. "We are to dine today at Netherfield and were just about to depart."

Charlotte's expression, which her friend had thought appeared somewhat troubled, became even more so. "I am glad, then, to have caught you, Elizabeth. I am afraid I have some rather distressing news to relate that I would not wish you to hear from another source. Indeed, it cannot wait."

Elizabeth and Jane looked at her quizzically. Taking Elizabeth's hands, Charlotte revealed that it concerned Elizabeth and Mr. Darcy.

"Me and Mr. Darcy? Charlotte, I cannot possibly imagine what could be so distressing about any news concerning us."

"I am sure you are aware of Mr. Collins's hasty removal this morning to Lucas Lodge?"

Elizabeth and Jane nodded their assent.

"You must also be well acquainted, then, with his immense displeasure on the subject of Mr. Darcy and the strength of that gentleman's attachment to you."

Again, both sisters nodded.

"Elizabeth, Mr. Collins is extremely indignant. He has claimed Mr. Darcy has gone against the express wishes of his aunt, Lady Catherine de Bourgh—and, perhaps—his entire family by entering into an engagement with you. From what I have been told, Mr. Darcy has a prior understanding with Lady Catherine's daughter."

Jane gasped, and though she felt a moment of panic at the mention of Darcy's family, Elizabeth only scowled and said in a bitter voice, "Yes, that is what Mr. Collins has *accused* him of, Charlotte, but I can assure you any claim of that sort is untrue. There was *never* any understanding between Mr. Darcy and Miss de Bourgh. Mr. Darcy informed me himself that it was merely the fanciful whim of Lady Catherine and nothing more."

"I confess I am relieved to hear it. Please understand I do not doubt you, Elizabeth, nor do I doubt Mr. Darcy's integrity as a gentleman, but Mr. Collins has taken the liberty of relating all the particulars as he is acquainted with them, not only to myself, but to my father, my mother, and my entire family—and all within earshot of the servants. Tomorrow morning he means to leave for Kent to inform Lady Catherine of Mr. Darcy's engagement, and that is not all, I fear. I hesitate to mention the rest."

"Charlotte, please," she entreated, "did you not just say you would not wish for me to learn of anything from idle gossips?"

By now, all three ladies had grown decidedly agitated.

Charlotte drew a deep breath and exhaled fully before she next spoke. "Very well, Elizabeth, I will tell you all, but please know it gives me great pain to do so." She tightened her grip on her friend's hands and continued, "Mr. Collins has spoken quite explicitly of a moment of shocking intimacy he claims to have witnessed between you and Mr. Darcy last night in your father's garden. I believe it is his intention to inform Mr. Darcy's aunt you have somehow drawn him in—*seduced* him, even—thus, forcing him to offer you his hand under duress. Oh, Elizabeth, I am so very, very sorry! Mr. Collins seems quite confident Lady Catherine will insist upon Mr. Darcy breaking his engagement to you, and, as he has told me Lady Catherine is one of Mr. Darcy's few living relations and very nearly the head of his family, he is certain her wishes shall be carried out."

It was Elizabeth's turn to gasp as she felt the blood drain from her face and swayed.

Jane, though feeling rather unwell herself, moved to help Charlotte support her. There was concern written plainly on the faces of both.

"Lizzy," said Jane urgently, "you must come into the house, and we will inform our father at once of all we have just learnt. Certainly, he will know what is best to be done."

For several moments, Elizabeth was capable of nothing beyond a blank look of incomprehension and, when she had finally recovered her voice enough to speak, sounded so very much unlike herself—so faint and distressed—that Jane and Charlotte found themselves fearing for her. "No. I must go to Netherfield. I must speak to Mr. Darcy at once."

Jane attempted to dissuade her, but on this, Elizabeth was adamant: she would speak with Darcy. Seeing her sister's distress only continue to increase, she finally consented, though with great reluctance, and all three ladies soon found themselves settled in Bingley's carriage and on their way to Netherfield. Charlotte accompanied them only as far as the lane to Lucas Lodge.

When the carriage arrived at its destination, both gentlemen were waiting to greet the ladies from Longbourn. Bingley hurried forward and handed Jane down with a smile, which faltered upon seeing her troubled expression. When Darcy stepped forward to extend his hand to assist Elizabeth, she remained in the far corner of the carriage, her naturally rosy complexion decidedly pale, and looking as though she would burst into tears at any moment.

"Good God!" he exclaimed. "Whatever is the matter? Truly, Elizabeth, you look extremely ill!" Unable to elicit from her any response beyond a look of utter despair and complete wretchedness, he turned toward Jane with no small amount of concern.

"I am afraid, sir," she began unsteadily, "we have just had a visit from the future Mrs. Collins, in which she has imparted to us some most distressing news. I am afraid it concerns Lizzy and you, and, I am sorry to say, is of a most disturbing nature."

"What news? What in God's name has that odious man to accuse me of now?" he demanded indignantly.

Eying the driver and footman, Jane quietly addressed Bingley. "Cannot we all go into the house, Charles? I believe we should discuss this unfortunate development with Mr. Darcy in private."

Bingley understood her perfectly. "Yes. Yes, of course. Darcy, I am certain Miss Elizabeth would benefit from a few moments in which to collect herself. Perhaps you can join us in my study when she is feeling better?"

Darcy nodded distractedly, and after Bingley had dismissed the driver and footman and escorted Jane into the house, he took a seat in the carriage beside Elizabeth and closed the door. No words were uttered, but Darcy was able to read her anguish as clearly as if she had spoken it aloud. Suddenly, Elizabeth reached for him, burying her face in his lapel. He enfolded her in his embrace, one arm wrapping around her shoulders while his other hand moved to cradle the back of her head. He held her while she wept.

It seemed as though an eternity had passed before Elizabeth was once again in control of herself. Darcy produced his handkerchief from his waistcoat and wiped her tears with unexampled affection. When he had done, he drew her back against his chest, his tone soft and filled with concern. "Elizabeth, dearest, please. Will you not speak to me of it?"

Her head was pounding, and at first, she was unequal to saying anything, but after several moments she managed to speak in a low, angry voice, the words nearly choking her. "He *saw* us, Fitzwilliam. My *hateful* cousin. He actually watched us last night for some time when we were together in the garden… while you and I… when you were… *touching me*. He saw it all! I am disgraced! My reputation, my family, all my sisters! We are all sullied because of this!

He means to tell your aunt and put an end to our engagement!" Elizabeth fought to control her agony, to prevent more tears of anguish from falling, but it proved a hopeless business.

Darcy continued to hold her close, kissing her hair and stroking her back. He could not stop himself from shaking with the rage rising within his breast at the persistent, unwarranted, and malicious interference of Mr. Collins. Try as he would, Darcy's anger did not abate. At long last, Elizabeth quieted, giving way almost completely to exhaustion.

When she finally felt well enough to leave the carriage and enter the house, it was to discover her sister had already apprised Bingley of their conversation with Charlotte. After repeating the particulars for Darcy and watching his anger continue to swell to a quiet fury as he paced the length of the room, Bingley rang for a servant to prepare a room for Elizabeth, so she might rest for a few hours. Pausing to take a long, thoughtful look at the woman he had long since given his heart to, Darcy excused himself and strode stiffly from the room.

It was many hours later that Elizabeth opened her eyes to vaguely familiar surroundings. Casting her gaze about her, she was startled to find herself still occupying the elegant bedchamber that Mr. Bingley's housekeeper, Mrs. Blakely, prepared for her that afternoon, along with a strong cup of medicinal tea the elderly woman insisted would ease the throbbing in her head and allow her to sleep. As her headache now appeared to have gone, and the delicate floral pattern upon the walls was bathed in nothing but the soft glow of a low-burning fire, she could only assume the tea must have worked its magic. She yawned and attempted to pull herself to a sitting position, only to discover she appeared to be restrained by something warm and heavy pressing upon her body.

Panic flowed through her, and she began to struggle against the weight that seemed to be pinning her. Then she heard a muffled voice and felt a warm breath upon her neck, which made her freeze. "Shh, Elizabeth, it is late. Go back to sleep, my love."

"Fitzwilliam!" she gasped. "What are you doing here? Why are we sleeping in the same bed?" She could not begin to account for his presence there, for such a complete breach of propriety—and under his friend's own roof!

Darcy tightened his hold on her and, nuzzling her neck, replied in a sleepy voice, "You have nothing to fear from me, dearest. Go back to sleep, or you will surely wake the house."

Despite Darcy's reassurance, Elizabeth could not help but worry. "But why has no one bothered to wake me? Where are the Bingleys and Mr. and Mrs. Hurst? And where is Jane? She must be terribly worried about me." She stopped then, placed her hand over her eyes, and groaned. "Fitzwilliam, please tell me I have not slept all afternoon. Poor Mr. Bingley must think me unpardonably rude."

At this, Darcy released her and, raising himself upon one elbow, fixed her with a steady gaze full of love and longing. He was lying beneath the counterpane, clad only in his fine linen shirt and, Elizabeth fervently hoped, his breeches. Her gaze traveled over his handsome features, and she inhaled sharply as she beheld the beauty of his neck for the first time, completely unencumbered by a cravat.

Darcy chuckled at her reaction and took pity on her. "As I said, you need not have any fear of me, Elizabeth. Your sister is sleeping just down the hall, and a note has long since been dispatched to Longbourn, informing your family you had taken ill upon your arrival. I am sorry to inform you, however, you have indeed slept, not only through luncheon, but through supper, as well. By the time your sister and Bingley became aware of the lateness of the hour, the weather had taken such a turn as to make it necessary for both of you to spend the night. You are now, and quite to my satisfaction, I might add, stranded by a rather unrelenting storm."

More than a little mortified by his account of her current circumstances, not to mention most reluctant to credit it, Elizabeth threw back the counterpane and made her way toward the window, muttering irritated words under her breath about Mrs. Blakely and the strength of her tea. Sure enough, upon peering through the curtains, her sight was instantly assailed by a blinding torrent of thick snow.

Turning back to Darcy in astonishment, she found his eyes lingering on her form with a look she had come to know well. It was at that moment she recalled she was wearing only a low-cut night shift she had borrowed from Mrs. Hurst, which clung to her body. Judging from his passionate gaze, he had noticed as well.

"Are you going to continue there all night in the cold, or will you come back to me where I can resume keeping you warm?" Darcy patted the empty space beside him on the bed.

Elizabeth moved to cover herself, but finding nothing near at hand to suit her purpose, she was forced to settle for wrapping her arms securely about her chest. This only served to make Darcy erupt in silent laughter. Elizabeth failed to see the humor in her situation. "I… well… exactly *what*, pray, are you doing in my bed, Mr. Darcy? I *am* correct in my assumption this is, indeed, *my* bed, sir, am I not?" She finished with a raised brow and an arch look.

"Indeed, it is, *Miss Bennet*," he said in a voice full of mirth as he rose from the bed to join her by the window. "But I far prefer to think of it as *our* bed."

"*Our bed?* Really, Mr. Darcy." She was taken aback by his boldness, but not wholly intimidated. "And are you not afraid someone will discover you here, sir, in *our* bed?" she asked rather impudently.

Darcy was standing directly before her, his body so close Elizabeth could feel the heat radiating from him. "Not at all," he said in a low voice. "I have taken the liberty of locking the doors."

Elizabeth swallowed hard at this declaration but found her voice again quickly. "Ah, such foresight, sir, but it seems you have forgotten you will have to return eventually to your own chamber before morning. So how, pray, do you propose you will manage that feat without calling attention to our current, scandalous situation?"

"That, my love, is simple." He directed her attention to a door she had not noticed, next to the chaise. "Our rooms are adjoined. I need only open that door to return to my own apartment quite undetected."

Her mouth formed a silent "O," and her eyes widened.

"Yes, it is most convenient." He took a deep, steady breath and, with a small smile, trailed his hands down the length of her arms.

Elizabeth closed her eyes and sighed. "I am surprised Mr. Bingley and my sister approved of such an arrangement. You must admit it is highly improper."

"Yes," he murmured, "highly improper. If I am not mistaken though, your sister is quite unaware of the close proximity of our chambers. Bingley, on the other hand, would very much like to believe the orchestration of this arrangement to have been an oversight by a careless servant."

"I see," she whispered, her pulse quickening. "Yet, it was not an oversight, was it?"

"No," he agreed, "it most definitely was not."

They stood in silence for some time, the eyes of each searching the depths of the other, before Darcy spoke again. "Truly, I intended this only for the purpose of slipping into your room undetected to provide comfort to you should you be in need of it, but, forgive me, Elizabeth, once I laid my eyes upon you as you slept so peacefully, I could not bring myself to leave you. I know it was very wrong of me, and indeed, I have no excuse to offer you for my behavior other than a sincere, heartfelt concern for what I know you to have suffered."

Elizabeth stared at him, her eyes sparkling in the waning light of the fire. She reached out to him then, placing her hands upon his chest. Darcy swallowed, his throat suddenly parched as he forced himself to say, "I believe the time has come for me to return to my own rooms. If you are truly feeling better, my love, I would not wish to put your reputation at risk any more than I already have."

He placed a chaste kiss upon her forehead and made to leave, but was stopped by Elizabeth as she laid her hands upon his arm. "You do bring me comfort," she whispered. "Please do not go. Stay with me. No one need ever learn of it."

Darcy could hardly believe what he was hearing and so closed his eyes, willing himself to remain in control of his senses. Elizabeth's fingers had begun to move over his chest in the most exquisite manner, robbing him of all coherent thought. He took several deep breaths before finally managing to summon the strength required to remove her hands from his body. She gave him a puzzled look as he released her and took a step backward. "I cannot. You know I cannot."

She was hurt; he could read as much in her expressive eyes. "You do not wish to lie with me, then?" she inquired, her voice pained.

"No," he said hoarsely. "It is because I want nothing more right now than to lie with you that leads me to refuse you. Surely you are not so naïve as to believe you would awaken in the morning a maiden still if I were to lie with you tonight? My self-control when I am with you, and especially at this moment, I am afraid, is sadly lacking. I cannot consent to such a thing, my love. Not before you are truly my wife."

Elizabeth raised her eyes. "My own self-possession, I fear, where you are concerned, also leaves something to be desired. So as you can see, sir, I believe it is a hopeless case."

"Elizabeth," he whispered, "you know not what you say. It is not right. You should be my wife."

"Then make me your wife, Fitzwilliam. Make me your wife tonight."

Darcy silently stared at her for some time, struggling against the overwhelming urge to surrender his body and soul to the intoxicating woman before him. His heart was already in her possession; it had been so for many months now, from almost the very first moment he had laid his eyes on her.

Elizabeth was gazing up at him, an unmistakable look of love in her eyes, and Darcy felt a searing pang of longing shoot through his breast. Suddenly, such temptation, when presented to him in the irresistible form of the woman he not only loved, but desired above any other, was simply too much. With a shaky breath, he indulged one of his favorite fantasies—that of entwining his hands possessively within her hair.

Elizabeth ran her tongue over her parched lips and quivered in anticipation, unable to deny the desire pulsing through her veins.

"My Elizabeth, I love you so," he whispered, his voice hoarse. "Are you certain, absolutely certain, this is what you truly wish?"

Elizabeth nodded, her eyes never leaving his, and Darcy pressed his body against her own and claimed her lips in a kiss that conveyed the depth of his desire. He deepened the kiss, and Elizabeth parted her lips, welcoming his tongue as it explored her mouth. His hands disengaged her curls to roam freely over her curves, tantalizing her body with firm strokes, his fingers pausing only to loosen the bodice of her night shift before resuming their previous ministrations.

Elizabeth was utterly lost to everything around her save for the man before her, and seemingly without warning, the thin fabric of her shift slid from her shoulders and down to the floor in a cascade of creamy silk, exposing her breasts and hips to his adept touch. It left her gasping as the chill of the room and Darcy's skilled hands assaulted her bare flesh.

He withdrew just far enough to allow his gaze to devour the vision before him. Elizabeth's mouth was parted in anticipation of his kisses, her full breasts with their pert nipples heaving, her hips—he dared not think of her hips—so smooth and inviting, waiting for him to draw forth all the undeniable passion burning within her. In the wake of his increasing ardor, Darcy struggled to regain his senses and, so softly he could barely hear his own words, murmured, "My dearest love, you are exquisite beyond my wildest dreams."

Elizabeth slowly opened her eyes. She had always imagined being completely unclothed before a man would have been, at the very least, disconcerting, to say nothing of embarrassing, but on this night with Darcy, she found it surprisingly natural, utterly pleasurable. His ragged breathing felt hot against the side of her face as he stared at her with a smoldering look in his eyes that she returned with equal emotion. Elizabeth encircled his neck with her arms, burying her fingers in his tousled hair and, standing on the tips of her toes, teased the exposed skin of his neck with her lips and the velvet of her tongue.

A groan rose from the back of his throat, and she felt him shiver as she pressed her naked body against his solid, clothed form. He recaptured her mouth in an urgent kiss, holding her against him with one hand as the other slid along the curve of her spine and around the swell of her hip to insinuate itself between her thighs in the most intimate of caresses. It took her by surprise, and Elizabeth found her senses overwrought by an entirely new sensation. As the tension within her continued to build, her knees weakened, and she found herself moaning her pleasure against his lips.

Darcy could hardly contain his desire as he held her. She was beyond magnificent, a woman surrendering herself completely to her desires, a willing, active participant in his lovemaking. His own arousal was fierce, and he longed to possess her, to bring her to the pinnacle of satisfaction, to make all his dreams a reality. Her breath was coming in fast, shallow pants, and when Elizabeth uttered his name with longing, he begged her for the honor of making her his at last.

She answered him with a smoldering kiss and a breathy "Yes," and with an inarticulate sound, Darcy lifted the woman he loved in his arms and carried her to the bed, where he made quick work of removing his shirt and breeches before taking his rightful place beside her. Instantly, his lips resumed their ministrations, burning a trail of kisses across her shoulders and neck and the small, sensitive spot behind her ear. All the while, his hands explored her curves in the most insistent manner.

He moved lower, running his wet tongue over her breasts until she could stand it no longer and, with the gentlest touch, barely grazed her nipple with his teeth. Elizabeth cried out as delicious sensations traveled throughout her body.

In an effort to silence her, Darcy returned his mouth to hers while his hands continued to pleasure her body. He ran his fingers lightly along her breasts, over her ribs, her waist, her hips, her thighs, and when her legs parted to allow him entrance to her most private place, he felt a new surge of desire for her and heard her gasp with pleasure as his fingers slid into her moist folds.

As Darcy began to stroke her most sensitive flesh in small, slow circles, Elizabeth lost all sense of everything else, surrendered herself to his fiery touch, and approached the height of her passion.

Darcy lifted his head to look at her. She was beyond exquisite with her hair strewn across the pillows, her eyes closed, her breathing labored, her back arching as he teased her with his finger. When she began to writhe from the ecstasy of his touch, he took her breast in his mouth and suckled her until she cried out for him, as though she were delirious with desire. At last he felt her release. Her body convulsed as wave upon wave of spasms washed over her.

Darcy's eyes searched hers. In their liquid depths he saw no fear of what was yet to come—only love, fulfillment, and trust. "My dearest, are you quite certain this is truly what you want?" he asked softly, his voice hoarse, all the while praying her answer would be in the affirmative.

Elizabeth reached out to him. Her voice caught in her throat, and she whispered, "Fitzwilliam, make me yours."

He placed a lingering kiss on her swollen lips, and as he parted her legs with his own, he was very nearly overcome by his desire for her, his arousal hard and insistent as it strained against her warmth. Darcy entered her with care, his eyes never leaving hers, desperately wishing he could gauge her thoughts and emotions. Elizabeth was gloriously tight, lush, and welcoming, and it took every ounce of inner strength he possessed to remind himself to go slowly, so as not to cause her any undue distress. When he met her resistance, he whispered in a strained voice, "My love, this may be painful, but only for a minute," and in the next moment he thrust deeply, penetrating her last barrier. A small cry of pain escaped her; it could not be helped. He took a great deal of time to kiss her until he felt her body begin to relax around his.

Darcy wrapped her legs around his hips and began moving with slow, deliberate strokes, feeling the delicious heat quickly building to an almost intolerable pitch. He was overwhelmed with the feelings she inspired in him and could not help but marvel at the wonder of her and the tremendous intensity of their love. His need for her increased almost violently, and his motions accelerated to match his insatiable desire.

Elizabeth soon found her initial discomfort replaced by a hot, tingling sensation at her innermost core, and she began to move her body in time to Darcy's rhythm until, with one final, deep thrust, he sent them both cresting over the edge of their passion, shuddering in a dizzying crescendo of ultimate pleasure.

They lay spent, their breathing erratic, their bodies glistening with perspiration in the waning light of the fire. At length, fearing his weight had become too much, Darcy withdrew to lie beside Elizabeth, pulling the counterpane around them. It was with great tenderness that his lips lingered over hers as his hand played with her curls. "Are you well, Elizabeth?" His voice was filled with love.

She snuggled against him, relishing the communion they had just shared. "Mmm… very well, Fitzwilliam."

"I am relieved to hear it." He kissed her again with feeling and whispered, "I adore you."

Elizabeth smiled contentedly against his shoulder. "I would hope so, after sharing such a profound intimacy."

Darcy's voice filled with emotion. "You know not how long I have dreamt of making you mine. Visions of your beauty have haunted my thoughts for months, but none so breathtaking as the vision now before me. Truly, tonight was a gift beyond any I ever imagined."

Elizabeth allowed her fingers to caress his chest. "Yes. It was very beautiful. I feel as though I am bound to you for all eternity."

"And I to you, though you must realize my love for you already bound me to you months ago. But I agree. We have become even more, so much more. Nothing can ever tear you from me now, my sweetest Elizabeth." Their lips met again as they held each other close, their bodies eager to repeat the intricate motions of a dance as old as time.

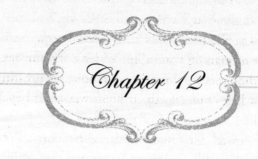

Chapter 12

It was not surprising that the next morning Elizabeth awoke somewhat later than usual. She reached across the bed for Darcy, whom she knew to have spent the entire night in her arms, only to find him now gone. It was just as well, for discovery would only add to their current difficulties. She gazed out the window and saw the storm had not abated during the night, and with a contented smile, she snuggled deeper beneath the counterpane, recalling the many hours she had passed in blissful occupation with Darcy, a deep blush overspreading her cheeks.

Last night Darcy had made love to her with a tenderness that had left Elizabeth in no doubt of the depth of his feelings for her. Indeed, she had found the entire experience to be overwhelmingly intimate, profoundly beautiful, and immeasurably satisfying. Even afterward, as they lay spent in each other's arms, Darcy's concern for her comfort and her well-being remained great, as was his concern for the preservation of her reputation.

Without bothering to dress himself, Darcy had taken his discarded cravat and, walking to the washbasin, dipped it in the clean water. He then returned to her and, gently spreading her legs, had proceeded to cleanse all evidence of her maiden blood from her body, using the coolness of the water to soothe any physical discomfort she may have experienced. He had then checked the condition of the bed linens and, thanking the heavens there seemed to be no sign of a stain, tossed his soiled cravat onto the fire and returned to her. When she had questioned the necessity of such actions, he had explained he did not wish to leave any evidence behind to give one of the maids any cause, either for alarm or for gossip. Grateful for his solicitation, as well as his reassuring presence, Elizabeth had very soon drifted off to sleep, enveloped in his arms.

With a sigh and a strong desire to see Darcy, Elizabeth threw back the counterpane and rose, dressing herself in her discarded shift. She then rang for a maid and ordered her bath. She had just laid aside her wet towel and had wrapped a robe around herself when she heard a soft knock upon the door to her chamber.

"Lizzy?" Jane's concerned voice called to her from the other side. Elizabeth bid her enter, and she soon saw her sister was carrying a fresh gown for her, most likely on loan from either Miss Bingley or Mrs. Hurst. She held it up and wondered how she would ever manage to fit into it, for Miss Bingley was rather taller than she and both ladies significantly less endowed.

"You look tired, Lizzy. I hope you have not slept ill."

"No, not at all. I am fine, Jane. I am only a little distracted this morning; that is all."

"I cannot say I am surprised to hear it. Oh, Lizzy, would but Mr. Collins had only minded his own business and never concerned himself with your affairs with Mr. Darcy. He cannot know what pain he gives us."

"I beg your pardon, Jane," she said with some distaste, "but I believe he knows precisely what he is about. Has it never occurred to you that in the wake of his disappointment, our cousin may harbor some degree of resentment toward me for having refused his suit? And, of course, he would be indignant on behalf of Lady Catherine and her daughter. Mr. Darcy is her favorite nephew, and I have accepted him, so it should only follow he should also suffer for having succeeded where Mr. Collins, himself, has failed."

Jane was thoughtful for a moment. "I confess I had not considered that."

"No, of course you did not. It is not in your nature to entertain such unscrupulous possibilities. You are far too good, Jane. I envy you your faith in the world." They joined hands and sat companionably upon the bed for some time.

"Truly, you look pale, Lizzy. Are you certain you are well? You were not at all yourself yesterday."

"I assure you, I am recovered enough now from the initial shock of Charlotte's intelligence. Please do not worry yourself over me. My concern now is not so much for myself but for the rest of our family. You and I have had the good fortune to have made prudent matches with respectable gentlemen who happen to value and esteem us, but Mary, Kitty, and Lydia have yet to find husbands. I cannot help berating myself for acting so carelessly. I should have anticipated the very great possibility Mr. Darcy and I could easily have been discovered in a moment of… vulnerability. That it was Mr. Collins who came upon us only makes it all the more wretched."

Jane hesitated. "Then it is true? You have permitted Mr. Darcy to take liberties with you?"

Elizabeth found it difficult to repress a mischievous smile at her sister's unease. "Yes, I am afraid Charlotte's report is accurate, in *that* respect at least. But please do not misunderstand me, Jane.

It is not my intimacy with Mr. Darcy I regret, for I can never have any lamentation on that score. My only remorse stems from our unguarded behavior in a fairly public setting. We gave very little thought to any repercussions from our actions and even less to the possibility of discovery. I am afraid we have both been rather irresponsible." *If she only knew of what took place last night!*

A blush spread across both their cheeks, and Jane asked in a whisper, "Was it *very* intimate, what you and Mr. Darcy shared? Was it… more than kissing?"

Elizabeth averted her eyes, unsure of what she should relate—certainly not their lovemaking from the previous night. "I… it was more, yes. To be honest, much more." She dared a glance at Jane. "Are you terribly shocked?"

"No, not *terribly*, I suppose. I always suspected with your liveliness and your passion for life, you might *be* inclined to act far more impetuously than I ever could, Lizzy. Oh dear! Please, forgive me. I certainly did not mean to imply such a thing!"

Elizabeth only laughed. "Jane, please. You have said nothing at all that has caused me any offense. You are correct, though. I have never been, with regard to many matters, as conventional and reserved as our parents could have wished, nor so concerned with following the dictates of proper propriety as you undoubtedly are, especially where Mr. Darcy is concerned. As a matter of fact, my behavior, if you were aware of the half of it, *would* certainly shock you. Yet, still, I cannot bring myself to repent any of it. In fact, I would happily repeat it many times over. There. That, I am sure, must certainly succeed in shocking you."

"Oh, Lizzy, it is not what I think nor what anyone else thinks that truly matters, but what you believe. Surely, if Mr. Darcy does not object to receiving your affections, then what business is it of the rest of the world? So dear as you are to me, you must know I would never judge you in such a manner. We are, both of us, very different in our own ways, yet in some ways we are similar."

Elizabeth was surprised. "Jane, do you mean to tell me you have allowed Mr. Bingley to take liberties with you?" she teased.

Jane looked down and examined her lap. "Not *so many*, Lizzy. We have held hands, and I have allowed him to kiss me. On several occasions in particular, his kisses were very… *expressive*. If Mr. Darcy's kisses are half so pleasant as Charles's kisses are, then I can certainly comprehend how it could easily lead to greater acts of intimacy between the two of you."

After such a bold declaration, Jane could not help blushing profusely, now more than eager to change the subject. "Enough. Now I will help you to dress, or you shall miss breakfast as well as supper." As she assisted Elizabeth with her toilette, however, she fixed her with a sly look. "I am sure Mr. Darcy is quite anxious to see you, Lizzy. I do believe he would have come himself to inquire after you this morning if it had not been at all improper."

Elizabeth only smiled as Jane fastened the buttons on her gown.

Darcy slipped his arms around Elizabeth's waist and pulled her into a sitting room just outside the breakfast parlor. "Forgive my boldness, Miss Bennet," he whispered as he kissed her neck, "but it has been my observation that Caroline Bingley has never managed to look half so fetching while wearing this gown."

"Well then, sir, I shall take that as a compliment, although I cannot say I am at all comfortable wearing it in company." Indeed, her décolletage was extremely revealing.

He looked at her then with some degree of concern. "Are you…

uncomfortable in any other way, Elizabeth? Last night… was I too rough with you, my love?"

Elizabeth gazed into his troubled eyes. She gave him a small, reassuring smile and shook her head, her curls bobbing. "Not at all, Fitzwilliam. I feel only some minor soreness from all the… *exercise* we engaged in last night. Aside from that, and being a little tired, I am fine; as for being too rough with me, I can assure you, sir, that was not the case, far from it. You were all that was gentle and considerate."

Darcy sighed. "I am thankful to hear it." He then looked away and, in a worried voice, said, "Are you… that is to say… do you at all…" He took a deep breath and exhaled slowly before finally saying, "Elizabeth, my love, do you now regret that we have anticipated our vows? Does it trouble you that you will no longer come to my bed as an innocent on our wedding night?" His agitation was extreme.

Elizabeth reached out and, caressing his jaw, said, "Indeed, I have *no* regrets. I love you, Fitzwilliam, and I cannot but treasure this new-found intimacy between us just as I treasure you—with my whole heart. The only regret I have is that you may, very soon after we are married, in fact, find me shirking my duties as the mistress of Pemberley in favor of the far more pleasurable duties I now know I will have when I am your wife."

"Elizabeth," he whispered, his eyes flaring as his gaze drifted from her lips to settle upon her ample bosom.

Seeing as they were in a public room, however, Elizabeth felt it best to keep their physical interaction somewhat more chaste. In an attempt to divert his present musings, she laughed quietly and said, "May I dare to hope, sir, that there will be very little chance of my appearing in a gown such as this one once I become the mistress of your great estate? I doubt very much you would wish for your wife to appear in society wearing such a garish creation!" Her teasing, however, had precisely the opposite effect.

Pressing her body more firmly against his, Darcy muttered, "Certainly not. However, I should have imagined you to be filled with nothing but gratitude today for having been spared the necessity of donning one of those dreadful orange horrors Miss Bingley seems to favor. Heaven knows she must have dozens at her disposal… though, I must confess, you would, no doubt, lend even the most unappealing garment in her wardrobe an air of complete allurement." With a rakish look, he lowered his head to allow his lips to graze the enticing swell of her breasts as his thumbs caressed her nipples through the fabric.

"Fitzwilliam, not *here*!" She pushed him away with an arch smile. Caroline Bingley's disdainful voice could be heard with relative ease as she abused one of the servants over the sparse selection of fruit on the sideboard.

"If not here, then where?" he whispered. "Elizabeth, take pity on me. You cannot expect me to conduct myself as a gentleman when you appear to such… advantage in this insidious dress." His lips claimed hers with a ferocity that caught her off guard while his hands roamed along her curves in the most intoxicating manner. When Darcy finally released her, he rested his forehead against hers and said, "Truly, I have no idea how I will ever survive this engagement after making love to you last night. I fear I will never be able to sleep again without you in my arms."

"Mmm… nor I," she murmured as she stroked his cheek. "When I awoke this morning, I was disappointed to find you gone, though I know I should not have been surprised. I realize the risk we took and how dangerous it would have been to be found together in such a compromising situation."

"It is perhaps more dangerous than we have considered. It has occurred to me there could be consequences from last night, Elizabeth, and perhaps from tonight, as well, should this storm continue as it does." He gave her a deep, penetrating look that caused her eyes to widen and her breath to quicken.

"I have been thinking that, perhaps, I should ride to London as soon as the weather clears to procure a special license, that is, if it is acceptable to you. I feel it would be for the best if we were to marry as soon as possible… for obvious reasons, though I cannot say I am anticipating the conversation I shall be forced to have with your father on this subject."

A blush heated Elizabeth's cheeks, and she looked away. "No, I would imagine not. He will not be pleased."

"And I cannot say I would blame him. I would not be inclined to look favorably upon any man who came to me to suggest such a thing in Georgiana's case." Darcy could not stop himself from exploring the low neckline of her gown with the tips of his fingers.

Elizabeth made a fair attempt to ignore him as she felt herself moved to confess certain concerns that had been preying upon her conscience. "What about my cousin? Our marrying so soon after becoming engaged will, no doubt, be seen as nothing short of scandalous, and it can only serve to help him carry his point with your aunt, as well, not to mention any gossips who may happen to hear the tales of our prior indiscretions." She found it difficult to conceal her bitter resentment toward the clergyman and his officious interference.

"And then there is the question of your sister. She will come out soon, and I would not wish to have society judge her unfairly based upon our sins any more than my own dear sisters. It pains me to think I may have brought such an injury upon her—I, whom she has never before so much as seen. Nor do I wish for the first report of me to reach her ears to be of my wanton behavior with her beloved brother. Whatever will she think of me, Fitzwilliam?"

"You underestimate Georgiana, Elizabeth; and me, for that matter. Do you imagine that I have never written of you to my sister, nor enumerated your merits and charms in nearly every letter I have addressed to her since my first entering Hertfordshire? Do you believe her ignorant of my initial struggles and my utter elation upon your acceptance of my suit? Dearest, she knows all—or she very soon will—most particularly that we are to be husband and wife and that I love you unreservedly. Though I confess I would far prefer to shield her from any rumors of our unrestrained behavior, I am certain Georgiana will take any idle talk at face value and be willing to overlook the fact that we may have been rather more expressive in our affections because I love you so very dearly and cannot do without you. Both she and I have been alone for so long, with only each other. Please trust me when I say Georgiana will feel nothing but joy for our union and very soon grow to love you as a sister."

Darcy paused to kiss her and then sighed. "As for my aunt, if there is one thing we can rely on in that quarter, it is Lady Catherine's absolute secrecy in this matter. As you may already have surmised, she is extremely concerned with appearances and familial duty. She would never wish to have my name or that of Pemberley linked with a scandal. It would only serve to taint my cousin Anne and, therefore, Rosings and her by association, since any rumor of a union between my cousin and me has long been purported exclusively by her own mouth for many years now.

Believe me, no matter how much my choice may displease her, and no matter how vehemently she may vocalize her disapprobation to my face, Lady Catherine will remain the soul of discretion when in company." He brushed a stray curl from Elizabeth's cheek as she nestled against his coat.

Elizabeth drew comfort from his closeness. "I hope you are correct. I will have to trust you in this, since I am not acquainted with either lady, but I cannot undervalue my own cousin's vindictive determination to expose us to censure and scorn. I believe, sir, where your aunt is concerned, Mr. Collins can be faithfully relied upon to do nothing by halves."

"We need not concern ourselves with Mr. Collins today. I doubt the weather will show any sign of improvement before nightfall; therefore, you may consider him every bit as stranded at Lucas Lodge as we are here at Netherfield. No word will reach my aunt for several days at least, and by then I will have obtained the license and made the proper arrangements. All will be well, my love. Until then, let us talk of more pleasant things." Darcy gave Elizabeth a warm look full of love and longing, which she could not but return with equal sincerity, and they did, indeed, proceed to engage their mouths in far more pleasant musings, though no conversation could be discerned by anyone happening to file out of the breakfast parlor.

Darcy had been correct in one particular aspect—the storm did not abate, and by the close of the evening, Jane and Elizabeth found themselves required to extend their stay at Netherfield one more night, much to the delight of Bingley and Darcy. All four lovers had to admit, however, their daytime activities would have been passed in a far more agreeable manner had Bingley's sister, Caroline, been stranded at his brother-in-law's house in Town rather than at Netherfield with them.

After experiencing countless days of continued frustration in which Miss Bingley could no longer ignore the fact that Darcy, much like her brother, now all but lived at Longbourn—as well as all the disturbing implications to be associated with such marked attentions—she had begun to grow agitated and distressed. Since witnessing Darcy's scandalous behavior toward Elizabeth at the ball, she had longed for an opportunity to be alone with the master of Pemberley without the overt interference of Elizabeth Bennet. When Darcy and her brother opted to spend the previous day at home rather than travel to Longbourn, Miss Bingley had believed providence had finally granted her just such an opportunity, but her hopes were soon dashed by the arrival of the two eldest Miss Bennets.

Though she was well able to tolerate Jane's society with some small degree of insincere civility, she had yet to master the art of extending such a courtesy to Elizabeth, and after having finally rid herself of one ailing Bennet not many weeks earlier, one could hardly have expected her to be anything less than incensed to learn of another—and her least favorite, at that—falling ill shortly after arriving at Netherfield. Her only consolation with such a repetition of history had come from the knowledge that even someone as reputedly impertinent as Elizabeth Bennet could hardly continue to influence Darcy with her charms from the confines of her guest chambers abovestairs. If she had only known how very wrong she was!

It was with great irritation that Miss Bingley forced herself to think back to the distasteful events of the previous day.

Shortly after Elizabeth had retired to rest herself, Miss Bingley had sought out Darcy, eventually tracking him down in the library, where he appeared to be pacing in agitation, a worried frown creasing his countenance. Immediately, she imagined him to be worrying over Elizabeth, which vexed her to no end. Consumed by her jealousy and a poorly directed ill humor, Miss Bingley soon found herself making disparaging remarks at the expense of the second-eldest Miss Bennet, a terribly unwise tactic to use on Darcy at such a moment.

"I certainly hope, Mr. Darcy, you are not troubling yourself unnecessarily over the indisposition of Elizabeth Bennet"—she smiled—"for I daresay her fine eyes will not long suffer the ill effects of having traveled a mere three miles in a coach."

Darcy pursed his lips, opting to say nothing in response, concentrating his efforts, instead, on holding his temper in check.

Heartened, Miss Bingley sniffed disdainfully. "I, for one, cannot see that it could possibly be anything of a serious nature. Elizabeth has always been of a healthy, robust constitution, not at all out of the common way for others in her station, mind you. Certainly, these country people have been bred to withstand such trifles as colds and indisposition. Of course, I would not be surprised in the least to hear she is not ill at all, but merely acting the part, no doubt to further ingratiate herself with my generous brother. Poor, naïve Charles! As if being taken in by the likes of Jane Bennet has not been punishment enough for all of us."

Though Darcy was obviously seething with anger by this time, Miss Bingley somehow managed to misinterpret his dangerous look, going so far as to lay her hand upon his arm in a rather forward manner as she cooed, "Mr. Darcy, allow me to give you some friendly, heartfelt advice, for it has been my experience, sir, that a wealthy gentleman such as yourself, who is sought after by every manner of society, can never be too careful when thrown into company with such scheming, mercenary people as one is sure to find in this part of the country."

Darcy fixed her with an icy look and said coldly, "No more so than one often finds in Town, as well, I daresay. Would *you* not agree?"

Miss Bingley felt the slight but was too stunned to credit it. Her smile faltered, however, and Darcy continued in the same vein. "Though I cannot pretend to be so presumptuous as to speak for your brother, Miss Bingley, in the future I would thank you not to speak ill of Miss Elizabeth Bennet or her family in my presence. I find it to be most offensive and ill-bred, and as I have just become engaged to be married to Miss Elizabeth, I am sure you can understand how I could very easily come to interpret such ill-mannered criticism of my future wife as a personal slight to me, as well."

Miss Bingley could only gape at him in outraged astonishment, to say nothing of her undisguised horror. With a small but satisfied smirk, Darcy firmly muttered, "Good day, Miss Bingley," and removed himself from her company, leaving his friend's sister quite alone to contemplate those of her actions that had succeeded in causing trouble and misery for no one but her.

On their second night together, though in a different room, as Bingley was certainly not of a mind to allow his friend the luxury of having his bedchamber adjoin with that of his betrothed for a second night, and well past the hour when the other occupants of the house had retired for the evening, Darcy lay in Elizabeth's bed. His body curled around hers from behind as he stroked the soft skin of her arm with his fingertips, their clothing long since discarded upon the carpet in front of the fire.

"I have been thinking, my love..." he began tentatively.

"Of what, my dearest?"

"Of what will happen when I remove to Town to obtain the license. I will have to be gone for several days at least, as I also have some business I should probably attend to with my steward once I am there, and then there is Georgiana. I really ought to spend some time with my sister."

Elizabeth rolled away from him and propped herself up on one elbow so she could search his troubled eyes. "What exactly are you trying to tell me, Fitzwilliam?" she asked, her concern evident in her voice.

"Come with me, Elizabeth. We can be married in London almost immediately, and then we shall not have to part again. You will be my wife; nothing will bring me more joy than to have you with me every day for the rest of my life."

Elizabeth could not immediately answer him. After a few moments of silent contemplation, she entwined her fingers in his and said, "Just like that, Fitzwilliam? Abandon everything and everyone whom I have ever known and loved without a care in the world as to what the consequences will surely cost us or our relations? Do you not think, my love, that we have already acted rashly enough without further adding to our current plight?"

Darcy lowered his eyes and looked away. "No. Of course not. You are correct. It was selfish of me to even suggest such a thing. But is there no other way, Elizabeth? I dread parting from you, especially if you should happen to become with child from our nights together. What if something unforeseen should happen to you because of it? What if you need me and I am unable to reach you due to the weather or some other unforeseen circumstance? I could not bear it. No, I wish for you to be with me. It is the only way I shall feel completely at ease."

Both were silent for a time, each deep in his or her thoughts. "Is it so important to you to be married so soon?" Elizabeth asked.

Darcy nodded and brushed her lips with his own. "You are important to me."

"And you to me." She hesitated another moment. "Fitzwilliam, I may know of a way that might enable us to marry very soon and without the need to disclose any of our actions to my father, as well as cause any further harm or anxiety to any of our relations, but I fear it could try your patience severely." Elizabeth bit her bottom lip.

"Elizabeth, the only thing that could possibly try my patience is to have to wait any longer for you than is absolutely necessary."

"Very well then," she said as a wry smile graced her mouth. "You could invite my family to Town for Christmas under the pretense of acquainting me with my future home. While we are there, we can arrange for an intimate ceremony and marry discreetly with both of our families present. I know my mother would not be opposed to such a scheme, especially since she will also see it as an opportunity to shop for wedding clothes for Jane and me. Perhaps Mr. Bingley could also join us. What do you think? Could you put up with my mother's effusiveness for a fortnight or two?"

A radiant smile overspread Darcy's face and he kissed her soundly. "Elizabeth, if it means that I shall have you for my wife within a few short weeks, and under my roof in the meantime, I believe I could put up with a great deal, including your mother, almost indefinitely."

Elizabeth laughed. "Be careful what you wish for, my dear! Remember, you are marrying *me*, and once *my* mother sees your comfortable house in Town, she may never wish to leave us!"

Darcy rolled his eyes and expelled a sardonic laugh. "Heaven forbid!" he exclaimed before pulling her body close and claiming her lips in a passionate kiss that went a long way in reassuring Elizabeth he was, indeed, quite serious about bringing her entire family to London as quickly as possible.

Chapter 13

Having been confined to Lucas Lodge while the storm raged and, ultimately, waned, Mr. Collins, though he was by no means ready to be separated from his betrothed, was finally seen departing Hertfordshire for Kent two days later, no doubt eager to relate the news of Darcy's unequal alliance to his esteemed patroness without further delay. It was with much relief that the report of his removal from the area reached Longbourn, though there were four persons at Netherfield who could not, in all good conscience, feel the restoration of their peace of mind once he had actually gone.

After ascertaining that, rather remarkably, there appeared to be no untoward gossip yet circulating in Meryton, Darcy left quickly for London to procure a special license from the archbishop and to alert his staff of the impending arrival of Elizabeth and her family. The Bennets, the Bingleys, and the Hursts were to follow at the end of the week—though it was only the former who would be staying in Grosvenor Square at Darcy House. Bingley and Miss Bingley would be staying with the Hursts, who had their own house a short distance away in Grosvenor Street.

Upon his arrival, Darcy was met with affectionate enthusiasm by his London housekeeper. Mrs. Hildebrandt was a plump, motherly sort of woman who had enjoyed the honor of doting on him since his adolescent years. "Welcome home, master!" she exclaimed as she relieved him of his greatcoat and hat. "I believe you will find everything to be in order. My, but you look a sight! Shall I have Mr. Stevens draw you a nice, hot bath, sir?"

Darcy laughed good-naturedly, pleased to see her, as well. "I thank you, yes, Mrs. Hildebrandt. A bath sounds like an excellent idea, but I am afraid I will have to do without Mr. Stevens for the time being. I rode on ahead of him this morning and do not expect to see him for another three hours, at least. Perhaps you could ring for Mr. Jackson in his stead in, say, half an hour?"

"Certainly, sir. I will tell him directly and arrange for lunch to be served in an hour, if that pleases you?"

"Yes, that is fine, but make it an hour and a half. I would like to see my sister in the meantime. Is she at home?"

Just then the delicate sound of a pianoforte being played with proficiency floated into the foyer. Darcy smiled. "Ah. I see she is. Excuse me, Mrs. Hildebrandt."

Darcy slowed his eager pace when he reached the open door of the music room, pausing to lean against the frame, his arms crossed over his chest. A young lady with features as fair as Darcy's were dark sat at the pianoforte, her normally reticent demeanor replaced by a passion for her music, which had only just begun to reassert itself since her ordeal the previous summer at Ramsgate.

She finished her piece, a movement by Mozart, and was met by soft applause. "Fitzwilliam!" she exclaimed as she rose and ran to him, "You are home at last! I am so happy to see you, Brother!"

Darcy enfolded her in his arms for a long embrace, placing a kiss upon her head. "And I you, dearest. Your playing was beautiful. I see you have been practicing a new piece."

"Yes. I have been spending a great deal of time on my music, actually. It has brought me much pleasure, but not nearly so much as seeing you affords me. Please say you will be staying in London for Christmas. Aunt Rebecca and Uncle Henry are sure to have their usual dinner parties and family gatherings, and I have no wish to attend by myself."

"By yourself? Is Richard not in London?" Darcy inquired, referring to the cousin who shared in Georgiana's guardianship.

Georgiana gave him a look filled with sisterly love and admiration. "Oh, yes, Richard has been in Town for nearly a fortnight. Please do not tell him I said so but, though I do love him dearly, Fitzwilliam, making due with Richard in your absence is by no means the same as having you here, Brother." Darcy smiled at her and kissed her cheek as she continued to press him for an answer. "So, will you be staying?"

"Yes. I will be remaining in London, I hope, for some months." Georgiana's eyes lit up with pleasure at the prospect of spending so much time with her brother. Darcy led her to one of the sofas and seated himself beside her. "I have invited some guests to join us—friends from Hertfordshire."

A frown darkened Georgiana's features. "Oh, no. You did not invite Caroline Bingley, did you?" Upon noticing her brother's stunned expression, she added, "I meant, how lovely. Of course, it will be delightful to see Mr. Bingley… and his sisters."

Darcy suppressed a smile. He had always suspected his sister's opinion of Miss Bingley coincided with that of his own, and was now gratified to see the proof it. "Yes, it is always an unparalleled experience to be in company with Bingley's sisters; however, *they* are not the guests I wished to allude to." Darcy chuckled. "Have no fear, Georgiana. Miss Bingley will be taking up residence in her brother-in-law's house, not here in ours, but tell me, Sister, what you would say to spending Christmas with Miss Elizabeth Bennet and her family?"

The change in Georgiana was instantaneous. "Oh, yes, Fitzwilliam! Truly? I have for so long wished to meet her. Is Miss Bennet really to come here, to London, to stay with us?"

Darcy smiled at her enthusiasm. "Yes, truly. But keep in mind her entire family is to come, as well. As you may well remember from some of my earlier letters, Elizabeth's mother can be somewhat… enthusiastic, not to mention extremely trying at times, and her family, as a whole, is often completely overwhelming, to say the least. Do you think you can bear their coming in order to gain such an excellent sister?"

"*Sister!* Has Miss Bennet accepted you, then?" Her eyes sparkled at the prospect as Darcy grinned.

"She has. We are to be married as soon as possible, hopefully within a month. I have no wish to wait longer than that. Does this please you, dearest?"

Georgiana squeezed his hands tightly in her own, positively beaming. "Oh, Fitzwilliam, if you are finally to know such happiness, then nothing could please me more than to receive such a sister."

Darcy could not have asked for a better response. "I daresay you will be gaining *five* sisters, dearest, and though they may not all be precisely what you may have imagined, I can promise you will be just as pleased with Elizabeth's eldest sister, Jane, as you will be with Elizabeth. She and Elizabeth are extremely close, and she has a sweet disposition, generous heart, and elegant manners, not unlike your own. She is to marry Charles Bingley."

"Oh, how wonderful! I do hope they will both grow to love me, as well."

Darcy kissed her forehead. "I daresay they will."

In the next instant, a wry smile could be seen crossing Georgiana's pretty face, and it was with no small degree of slyness that she said, "Fitzwilliam, do you not find it diverting that after all this time Caroline Bingley will finally be able to call herself my sister?"

Darcy could not help but laugh at her wit. "Yes, it is excessively diverting, is it not? But I hardly think *this* particular arrangement is quite what Miss Bingley had in mind these many years during her pursuit of such a notable alliance with you!"

"No!" she said and laughed. "I should say not! Poor Miss Bingley!"

The arrival of the Bennets was everything Darcy had feared it would be. Mrs. Bennet's effusive approbation for all the splendor and wealth before her could not be ignored as her voice rang shrilly throughout the many halls and corridors of Darcy House, seemingly without pause. Her boisterous enthusiasm, coupled with that of Kitty and Lydia, was, in turn, followed with the dignified dry humor of Mr. Bennet as he calmly exchanged pleasantries with his future son-in-law over the impossible din of his wife and two youngest daughters.

Though Georgiana was certainly shocked by such an outward display of energetic behavior—particularly from people whom she had only just met and was determined to think well of—she observed that Mr. Bennet appeared serenely unaffected by the actions of his wife and youngest daughters, treating it simply as though it were a perfectly natural occurrence. She noticed the same could not be said for her brother, however, who seemed to be struggling in order to maintain a calm demeanor. Elizabeth and Jane, she also observed, appeared to be equally mortified, and out of concern for the deepening distress of her two prospective sisters, Georgiana soon recovered herself enough to don a nervous smile, enacting the daunting role of hostess.

The sheer pleasure Darcy experienced upon being reunited with Elizabeth was evident to all who took the trouble of observing them together, mainly, those who loved them best—Jane, Georgiana, and Mr. Bennet. Elizabeth's happiness was by no means less than that of her future husband, and given Elizabeth's embarrassing lack of interest in nearly every aspect of her future home—with the noted exception of her betrothed—Georgiana was soon reassured beyond measure that theirs was most assuredly a love match.

By the time they had finished an ample lunch of cold meats and other savory fare, followed by cake, as well as various fruits of the season, Georgiana had become equally enamored of her future sister, and Elizabeth just as delighted with Miss Darcy. They passed the afternoon agreeably with a tour of the house, ending in the music room, where Darcy and Georgiana entreated Elizabeth to play for them on the pianoforte. Though she lacked the practiced proficiency and polish that can come only with constant dedication, such as Georgiana's, she played with a natural talent and much obvious enjoyment. When she finished her song, Elizabeth found her performance met with great enthusiasm by Miss Darcy, who remarked upon the delight she had received from the sensitivity and feeling Elizabeth expressed so effortlessly.

Later, after the tea things had been cleared away, Mrs. Bennet, Jane, and Mary retired to their rooms so they might rest themselves before dinner, while Kitty and Lydia disappeared to their own chambers, clutching the latest issue of *La Belle Assemblée* between them, overflowing with talk of London fashions and the number of officers they were certain to meet with while in Town.

Finally free of the incessant chatter that had accompanied him since his departure from Hertfordshire that morning, Mr. Bennet was entirely content to install himself in Darcy's library, the quietude of a good book and a glass of port being the only companions he desired.

Elizabeth and Georgiana spent the rest of the afternoon in companionable conversation. Darcy sat as near to Elizabeth as he could without violating propriety, but doing so in any case by brushing her thigh with his hand as he smiled at the sisterly bond that was already beginning to form between the two most important women in his life.

After he had seen his guests settled for the night in their respective chambers, Darcy, knowing sleep would not come easily, retired to his study. He found himself missing Elizabeth's physical presence so much he had begun to feel it as a dull, almost insistent ache. He very much wanted to go to her but was in a quandary over how she might wish for him to act in such a situation—her parents and all her sisters, not to mention his own sister, being under the same roof. He sighed and silently cursed the fact she was installed within such a close proximity to her family in the guest wing. If he had been less of a gentleman, he realized, then perhaps he could have summoned the necessary audacity to have ordered a servant to *accidentally* place Elizabeth nearer to the family wing instead. At least there, he mused, there would have been next to no one to bear witness to his slipping into her room late at night or to observe his leaving in the early hours of the morning.

It was with these particular thoughts that Darcy's mind was so agreeably engaged when he was joined, quite unexpectedly, by the lady in question.

"Fitzwilliam, why have you not yet retired, my love?"

Though she was still dressed in the gown she had worn at dinner, after sweeping his gaze over her form, Darcy noticed Elizabeth had removed her slippers and stockings. He found it strangely erotic to see Elizabeth's bare toes peeking from beneath the hem of her gown, burrowing into the thick carpet pile in his study. He swallowed hard and moistened his lips with his tongue, his mouth suddenly parched as he began to feel the familiar stirrings of arousal. At that moment, he could not decide whether he was more pleased by Elizabeth's appearing before him in such a state or worried someone might interrupt them should he choose to act upon the thoughts that seemed to come unbidden to his mind. He glanced at the clock upon the mantle and noted it was, indeed, very late—late enough for the entire house now to be abed.

Elizabeth slowly advanced, coming to stand just inches from him, her dark eyes sparkling with wit and intelligence… and more than a hint of passion. Darcy, breathing in her faint lavender scent, raised his hands to caress the curve of her neck and the skin of her shoulders.

Elizabeth closed her eyes, entreating him to lead her to a place where all else would soon fade into oblivion, where nothing mattered but their love.

Without uttering a word, Darcy brushed his lips against hers. He repeated the gesture, gradually deepening his kisses as she swayed before him. His hands continued to travel along the lines of her shoulders before wandering lower, down her arms to her hands, where he entwined his fingers with hers, wrapped his arms around her waist, and drew her body against his as they continued to kiss in a sweet, unhurried fashion.

When at last they stopped, they simply held each other. Darcy stroked her back with deliberate slowness, while Elizabeth caressed his hips beneath his tailcoat. Not wanting to start something he knew they could not likely continue, Darcy released her to move toward his desk. "I have something for you," he said in a low voice. "I had hoped to present it to you this afternoon, but I did not have the pleasure of a moment alone with you." He removed a small box from a locked drawer and handed it to Elizabeth.

Elizabeth smiled at him, touched that he would think to get her a gift, and removed the lid. Her breath caught as she beheld a beautiful ring set with a single, creamy pearl. It was large in diameter but by no means ostentatious, surrounded by many shimmering diamonds, which, though considerably smaller in comparison to the pearl, were exquisite all the same. "Fitzwilliam, it is truly lovely. Never in my life have I owned anything so beautiful."

Darcy simply gazed at her, the love he felt for her clearly written on his face. "Nor have I."

Elizabeth blushed, knowing full well he was not referring to the ring. "Thank you," she said, "for this exquisite ring, as well as your generous compliment. I do not think I deserve either, but I believe I am not in a position to argue with the master of Pemberley. As your sister kindly informed me this afternoon, sir, it appears you are never wrong."

Darcy took the ring from her and slipped it onto her finger. "No," he said as he raised her hand to his lips, "at least not on this matter. I will brook no opposition, Elizabeth. Though it was my mother's favorite, and her mother's before her, in the last few days it has become simply another ring to me, the same as any other piece of jewelry. It is *you* who is exquisite. I have always thought so, and so I shall until the end of my life."

Their eyes held for several long moments, speaking volumes without any words being uttered. Elizabeth finally broke the silence, her need evident in the quiet urgency of her voice. "Do you believe our chances of discovery here within the next several hours to be very great, Fitzwilliam?"

He only looked at her, surprised by the implication of her words.

"Will a servant intrude, do you think, if we were to renew our intimacy with one another?"

"Here?"

Elizabeth nodded.

Darcy slowly shook his head, his mouth feeling very much as though he had been chewing cotton. "No. I am often here late into the night going over matters of business. The servants know not to disturb me at such a late hour."

Elizabeth gave him an amorous smile and placed her hands upon his shoulders.

Darcy swallowed. "And what of your maid?" he asked hoarsely. "Will she not be waiting to assist you before you retire?"

Trailing her fingers along the edge of his cravat, she said, "That is one advantage of growing up in a house with four sisters. Having but one maid to share between us, I have grown quite accustomed to seeing to myself. In fact, I have long since dismissed Sonia for the night; however, if I later find I am in any particular need of assistance, then perhaps *you* can see to me personally, sir."

She kissed him then, a long, sensuous kiss that succeeded in melting away any remaining fragments of his reserve. After a moment, Elizabeth backed away from him, a mischievous smile playing upon her lips. Darcy watched, mesmerized, as she made her way to the door, her hips swaying, and turned the key in the lock. She then moved toward the fire and, reclining fully upon the large leather sofa before it, beckoned to him. "Will you not come to me, Fitzwilliam?" she asked, her voice soft and inviting. "Will you not make me yours once again?"

Darcy watched as Elizabeth slowly ran her hand from the elegant curve of her neck down to her full breasts. An inarticulate sound rose in the back of his throat.

"Come to me, my love," she whispered.

Who was he to argue?

Chapter 14

Mrs. Bennet's voice had increased to at least ten times her usual volume as she eagerly informed Jane and Elizabeth of her plans for the day. Much to his consternation, Darcy heard her even before he reached the bottom of the staircase in the main hall. Slowing his pace, he struggled against an inclination to seek refuge in his study. *Perhaps, I could say I have a pressing matter of business to attend to?* Then he thought of Elizabeth and sighed.

They had parted not five hours earlier, after passing some of the most tender moments of his life in front of the fire in his study. As he recalled those blissful hours with fondness, the need to gaze once more upon her face became overwhelming. Drawing himself up to his full height, Darcy steeled himself against his future mother-in-law's boisterous effusions and forced his legs to continue toward his original destination. After crossing the main hall and taking several deep breaths to subdue his annoyance, he nodded to the servant to open the door to the dining room. In the next moment, he entered and took his place at the head of the table. Another servant approached and began serving his breakfast.

"Do not be ridiculous, Lizzy," Mrs. Bennet proclaimed. "Of course, you will need new gowns. Six at the very least, and most likely more. Since you have been clever enough to catch yourself such a rich husband, I am sure your father will not mind the expense one bit, for he must realize that your marrying Mr. Darcy will certainly throw your sisters into the paths of other rich men."

Darcy took several swallows of tea in order to dislodge the toast he had choked on, then glanced sharply at Mrs. Bennet before allowing his gaze to dart toward Elizabeth. It was precisely as he had suspected—she appeared to be in misery.

Her cheeks blazing with mortification, Elizabeth muttered, "Mama, *please*," as she wished for the floor beneath her to open up and swallow her whole. Though she did not dare look at Darcy, she could feel the intensity of his penetrating eyes upon her. *He must be disgusted by my mother's lack of decorum!* she thought, feeling no small amount of shame. *For her to say such a thing in front of him—and while she is a guest in his own home, no less! Without a doubt, Fitzwilliam must be questioning the soundness of his decision to marry me, for how could he possibly believe the daughter of such a silly and vulgar woman could ever make a suitable mistress for Pemberley or a proper wife for him? I would not blame him in the least if he is, even at this very minute, regretting his rash decision!*

Seeing Elizabeth in distress pained Darcy, and he found himself wanting to do nothing more than offer her comfort, to go to her and wrap her in his embrace, but he knew he could not. He looked instead to Mr. Bennet, who, Darcy noted with a touch of irritation, was observing them all with an expression of repressed amusement. Seeing he was to have no ally in his future father-in-law, Darcy cleared his throat and said as amiably as he could, "I take it then, ladies, that a visit to the modiste is the order of the day?"

Georgiana was quick to answer. "Oh, yes, Fitzwilliam. I thought to take Miss Elizabeth to Mrs. Duval's in Bond Street." Then, turning to Elizabeth, she said, "Mrs. Duval has always been very accommodating whenever I have had the need for a special gown to be made in very little time. I am sure she will be delighted to design your trousseau, Miss Elizabeth. Her work is truly excellent and she currently has the most beautiful pale yellow silk in the window. I do believe the color would look lovely on you."

Elizabeth gave her future sister a warm, appreciative smile. "Thank you, Miss Darcy. I am looking forward to seeing it. Indeed, I am quite certain Mrs. Duval will have many beautiful things in her shoppe."

"Lizzy, have you not always said you longed to own a yellow ball gown?" chimed Kitty. "I daresay now that you are to become Mrs. Darcy, you shall most likely have twenty!"

"Kitty, I would hardly need twenty ball gowns," Elizabeth said. "Indeed, I have very little need even for one."

But her mother agreed with Kitty, proclaiming that Elizabeth would surely have twenty if she wanted them, for Mr. Darcy, as rich as he was, could certainly afford to buy her as many as forty such gowns and very likely more. Elizabeth felt her mortification increase.

All the ladies departed for Bond Street shortly after breakfast, the number of gowns Mrs. Bennet insisted they must purchase multiplying with the passing of every ten minutes. Jane and Elizabeth did all in their power to discourage their mother's thinking—*and speaking*—quietly stressing the impropriety of spending so much of their father's money on so many gowns, but to little avail. Georgiana, equally as uncomfortable with such talk, attended them in relative silence.

Before they had departed, Darcy had taken Georgiana aside.

Knowing Elizabeth would certainly not be of the same mind as her mother, who had appeared more than eager to overspend her father's limited funds, he had given his sister strict instructions to make certain she paid very close attention to each additional item Elizabeth favored and to secretly charge them all to her own account. This included the designs of certain gowns Elizabeth would not have the resources to purchase while she retained her maiden name. He was adamant that, as his wife, she would want for nothing, but, most especially, the pale yellow ball gown her sister had spoken of at breakfast. In fact, after learning that Elizabeth had always desired to own just such a gown, Darcy had become quite determined to see to it that her father would not absorb the cost of that particular item. He wanted to see her eyes light up with pleasure when *he* presented it to her after their marriage, just as her beauty and vivacity caused his heart to swell each and every time he so much as thought of her.

As soon as the ladies set foot in the modiste shoppe, their party was met by a young assistant who made her way to Georgiana.

"Good morning, Miss Darcy," she said. "How can I be of service to you today?"

Georgiana smiled. "Though there are several items I may wish to acquire, Miss Granby, we are here today to shop for a trousseau for my future sister." She linked her arm with Elizabeth's.

Miss Granby quickly—and rather openly—surveyed the Bennets, who were by no means dressed so fashionably nor so expensively as Miss Darcy, before offering Elizabeth a somewhat restrained smile. "Of course," she said. "Allow me to offer my congratulations, *Miss*…"

Elizabeth raised her brow. "Bennet. Thank you," she returned with equal coolness.

Miss Granby gave her another haughty look and said, "Well, Miss Bennet, please follow me, and we shall get you started."

Though Georgiana thought she had made it clear to Miss Granby they were there primarily to shop for Elizabeth's trousseau, she could not but notice with some distress it was she who received the solicitous attention of Mrs. Duval's staff, and not her future sister. The lengths to which the staff went to be of service to her while almost pointedly ignoring Elizabeth bordered on shocking to the privileged girl, who was quite accustomed to receiving the very best of service. Indeed, she could not comprehend how Miss Granby and the other assistants attending them could behave in such a cool, condescending manner to the Bennets and, especially, to the future Mrs. Darcy. She turned to Elizabeth several times with an expression of real concern and no small degree of embarrassment, only to see her respond to Miss Granby's rudeness by raising a brow and addressing the woman in an arch manner that appeared to express her total lack of intimidation. If Elizabeth *was* truly bothered by the staff's indifferent attitude toward her and their lack of basic courtesy, Georgiana was forced to concede she did a convincing job of hiding it.

Indeed, Elizabeth hid her distress very well. Though she could not admit to being surprised by Miss Granby's initial haughty attitude toward her, she was both startled and pained to see the contrasting deference so pointedly paid to Georgiana in her presence. No doubt her future sister was used to receiving preferential treatment wherever she went, but given the circumstances, Elizabeth had expected at least some form of conciliatory acceptance and civility toward herself, if not toward the members of her family.

Whether it was the elegance of the establishment or the elegance of the wealthy patrons in it who cast many not-so-surreptitious glances in the direction of their party, Elizabeth found her mother uncharacteristically reserved for such an occasion. Not even the vast array of lace, of which Mrs. Bennet had long held very decided opinions, could rouse her to her usual overzealous effusions. As a matter of fact, considering her two youngest sisters were also surrounded by the finest muslin and silk money could buy, they, too, seemed surprisingly subdued, exhibiting far better behavior than Elizabeth had ever imagined possible.

After sitting for so many hours in one attitude, examining patterns and selecting fabric and trim while being ignored by the staff, Elizabeth was in desperate need of a change of venue. Making her excuses, she rose and made her way to the other side of the shoppe. She was in the midst of admiring a beautifully embroidered pair of silk gloves when she happened to overhear two assistants engrossed in a rather animated conversation. Though they spoke in hushed tones, their voices carried easily to Elizabeth.

"But you must admit she gives every appearance of being a gentleman's daughter, even if the gown she wears is not of the finest muslin."

"She *is* the daughter of a gentleman, I hear, but he owns a rather meager estate—nothing to Mr. Darcy's—and she is rumored to have several relations in *trade*."

"In *trade*? My word! Are you certain?"

"Yes, and I cannot imagine why Fitzwilliam Darcy would lower himself to offer for a woman who is apparently so unconnected and penniless. She has a dowry of only *fifty* pounds per annum, I hear!"

"*Fifty pounds!* When, for years, he has had his pick of far more refined women with fifty *thousand*?"

"Precisely. It makes one wonder."

"Can there be any real affection on his part, do you think? You never know. Perhaps he lost his heart to this little country beauty."

The other assistant snorted. "His heart? You mean his head, more like! I overheard Caroline Bingley, whose brother is Mr. Darcy's oldest and dearest friend, tell her own very great friend, Cecelia Hayward, that Mr. Darcy was *drawn in* while he was a guest in her brother's house. It was all so shameful to watch, she said. And shocking! Why, whenever the two of them were in company together, *he* could not tear his eyes from Miss Bennet's well-featured *charms,* so to speak. Perhaps they were caught in a compromising position, and he is being *forced* to marry her. In any case, he certainly cannot go through with this marriage to such an unconnected woman."

"No, certainly not. Can you just imagine what his titled relations will say when they hear about the match? No doubt the earl will put an end to the engagement straight away!"

They tittered loudly. "Oh, yes. Knowing Lord Matlock, he will be outraged over the disgrace his nephew will bring upon their entire family. You mark my words, there is no chance we shall ever see poor little Miss Bennet return as Mrs. Darcy. She will be sent back to the country in shame, and he will be married within a fortnight to his well-dowered cousin or another woman of the *ton*, who is far more suitable."

Elizabeth had heard enough, and, shaking, she turned and walked out of the shoppe. Georgiana joined her only moments later, an expression of concern etched upon her face.

"Miss Elizabeth, are you well?" she asked.

Elizabeth swallowed down the hot lump that had lodged in her throat, and looked away.

"Pay them no mind," she continued as she placed her hand on Elizabeth's arm. "Anyone who has had the pleasure of seeing you and Fitzwilliam together can be left in no doubt of your love for each other. What those two women said inside was horrible, but it was nothing more than gossip, maliciously purported by *Caroline Bingley*, no less. She has always aspired to catch my brother, and now she is angered that all her scheming has come to nothing. And as for my uncle, I know he will love you. He is not so concerned with birth and connections as he would have the rest of London believe. The most important thing to him, and to my aunt, is that Fitzwilliam is happy, and they will be reassured of that the moment they see the way he looks at you."

Though Elizabeth was touched by the words her future sister offered, she could not soon forget the rude treatment she received, the unkind remarks and the hurtful gossip she overheard, nor the resulting pain associated with it all. That morning, the happy prospect of ordering new gowns for her trousseau had greatly appealed to Elizabeth, but considering the emotional cost she was required to pay, she no longer felt equal to the task. She was eager to be away from Mrs. Duval's shoppe as soon as possible and not at all looking forward to having to return.

While Mrs. Bennet, Jane, Mary, Kitty, and Lydia were eager to continue their shopping excursion in another part of London, Elizabeth and Georgiana chose to return to Darcy House. When they entered the foyer, it was nearly teatime, and Georgiana was informed that her brother was entertaining none other than Lord and Lady Matlock in the music room. Elizabeth, at Georgiana's urging, accompanied her future sister, and when they entered the room, she saw an elegant older lady and two finely dressed gentlemen engaged in easy conversation with Darcy.

Georgiana's eyes lit up with pleasure. "Aunt Rebecca, Uncle Henry. How wonderful to find you here." She kissed them both before turning to the other gentleman. He appeared to be no more than several years older than Darcy. "Hello, Cousin. Have you come to meet Miss Elizabeth, or are you here only to tease me mercilessly, just as you always do?"

He laughed and gave her a kiss on the cheek. "I am always eager to tease you, dearest, but I confess to being quite curious about the young lady who has finally managed to captivate my infamously imperturbable cousin."

Smiling wide enough to show his dimples, Darcy hastened to Elizabeth's side. "Elizabeth, please allow me to present my uncle and aunt, Lord and Lady Matlock, and my cousin, Colonel Richard Fitzwilliam. Aunt Rebecca, Uncle Henry, Richard, it is my very great pleasure to introduce Miss Elizabeth Bennet of Longbourn in Hertfordshire."

Lady Matlock smiled kindly. Her husband addressed Elizabeth stiffly. "Miss Bennet, allow me to offer my congratulations to you. My nephew has been rather negligent in his duty, I am afraid, and saw fit to inform us of his engagement to you only the other day. If you are truly all he claims, I daresay you will find much happiness in your union."

Elizabeth understood him. The earl did not yet know her, and despite whatever Darcy had told his family, his uncle would reserve judgment on her. She chose her reply carefully. "Thank you, Your Lordship. Your nephew and I have already shared much happiness. He is one of the most intelligent men I have ever had the pleasure of knowing, to say nothing of his kind and generous heart.

I consider myself extremely fortunate to have earned the affection and esteem of such an excellent man." She exchanged a look of affection with Darcy, who moved even closer to her and brushed her hand with his own.

The affectionate action was not lost on Colonel Fitzwilliam, who grinned at having caught his reserved cousin performing such an impropriety in front of his parents. Never before had he seen his cousin so besotted with a woman. Now that he thought of it, he could not remember *ever* having seen Darcy besotted with a woman. He observed Elizabeth with interest while his mother engaged her in conversation.

Though his cousin's fiancée had seemed somewhat reserved at first, she was now listening with rapt attention to Lady Matlock as she related some story about her own courtship with the earl. Elizabeth leaned in then and, smiling archly, said something that caused the older woman to laugh. The earl merely harrumphed, but his twitching lips indicated his amusement.

By the end of the visit, it was obvious to Darcy his relations were impressed by Elizabeth's wit, candor, and keen intelligence. It pleased him beyond measure to see that even the earl did not remain unaffected by her charms. The older gentleman had become more animated as the hour wore on; his eyes turned often upon Elizabeth with interest and, perhaps, even a touch of admiration.

Darcy saw them all to the door with regret. He kissed his aunt and slapped Richard on the shoulder. Before Lord Matlock quitted the house, he took his nephew aside and muttered, however grudgingly, "She'll do, she'll do." A small, satisfied grin played upon the earl's face as Darcy bid him a good evening.

Dinner that evening passed in much the same manner as breakfast. Mrs. Bennet and her youngest daughters talked of the success of their shopping trip and of the vast number of new gowns they had ordered, while Elizabeth sat in mortification, and Mr. Bennet silently laughed at their silliness. Darcy, as could be expected, could find nothing so humorous in the scenario at his table, especially given how Georgiana and Jane seemed to glance repeatedly at Elizabeth throughout the meal, with expressions of concern. It was not until the very last course was taken away that he discovered, through Mrs. Bennet's loud ranting, their trip to Mrs. Duval's shoppe had not gone at all as they had anticipated.

After the meal, while the Bennets retired to the music room, Darcy summoned Georgiana to his study under the pretense of discussing a minor household matter. In actuality, he was anxious to hear her own account of the visit to the modiste. It infuriated him to no end to learn of such an affront to his beloved Elizabeth, and it had, in fact, taken all of Georgiana's powers of persuasion to convince Darcy not to leave the house at that very moment for Mrs. Duval's residence in order to personally reprimand her for the outrage that had been perpetrated at the hands of her staff. Instead, he paced in his study for a full quarter of an hour, attempting to regulate his temper before rejoining his guests. By the time Darcy entered the music room, Georgiana was immersed in her playing on the pianoforte, entertaining the Bennets with a lovely piece by Handel.

Darcy searched the room for Elizabeth. He discovered her standing apart from her family at one of the large windows overlooking the street; her distress was obvious by the manner in which her hands twisted the material of her gown. Greatly affected, Darcy joined her. "You have been very quiet tonight, my love."

Elizabeth turned to him and gave him a half-hearted smile. "I am fine, Fitzwilliam. I am only a little tired. I was thinking of retiring soon. I am afraid I will not be suitable company tonight."

Darcy's brow furrowed. "I was hoping to have a moment alone with you, Elizabeth. We have not yet had any time to ourselves today, and I find myself desirous of your presence."

Elizabeth lowered her eyes. "And I am very much in need of yours," she murmured as she took his hand between both her own.

Darcy glanced about the room. All her family appeared to be well entertained for the moment. "Will you come to me tonight?" he whispered as he moved a curl from her face. "I have some matters of business I must see to in my study. I will be there until very late. Please say you will come."

His eyes beseeched her to agree, and without so much as a second thought, Elizabeth nodded.

It was just past one o'clock in the morning when Elizabeth finally joined Darcy in his study. She found him seated behind his mahogany desk, going over pages of documents. When his gaze lit on her, he laid them aside and smiled. She ran to him, and in the very next instant, Darcy pulled Elizabeth onto his lap and enveloped her in his arms, cradling her in his embrace. She sighed as some of the tension from her unpleasant day melted away.

"Fitzwilliam," she murmured as she circled her arms around his shoulders and buried her face in the fabric of his cravat. "I have missed you." She could not help but inhale his distinct, masculine scent. He smelled wonderful, like sandalwood and black pepper. How she loved the smell of him and the feel of his comforting presence!

"And I, you," he murmured as he placed a lingering kiss upon the curve of her neck. "May I take your hair down?"

She inclined her head, and Darcy removed the decorative pins from her dark locks. As he pulled out the last pin, Elizabeth's hair fell like a rich veil to well below the middle of her back. His breath caught, and he buried his fingers deep within the silken depths of her curls.

Elizabeth snuggled against him, breathing deeply as she enjoyed the feel of his fingers moving through her hair. She found it soothed her, just as it had when her maid would brush her hair many years before, when she was still but a girl. Before Elizabeth could stop herself, she almost shyly asked Darcy whether he would mind performing that same task for her now.

He was pleasantly surprised by her request and most eager to comply. He hastened to retrieve a beautiful silver-plated brush he had only recently purchased, engraved with an elegant, flowing *E.D.*, from a locked drawer in his desk. He took a seat closer to the fire and settled Elizabeth upon his lap, this time with her back to him, as he ran the brush through her curls with care.

Elizabeth relaxed under his tender ministrations, and her gaze began to roam over the many objects in Darcy's study. It occurred to her then that this was his inner sanctum, his refuge, much the same as her father's small library was to him. She could not help but admire the understated elegance of her future husband's good taste.

"You have a wonderful home, Fitzwilliam. It is tasteful and refined while being comfortable, and not the least bit ostentatious. I know I am going to enjoy living here very much, but only because you and Georgiana will be here, as well, and I shall be able to awake every morning in your arms. Apart from the theatre and the opera, I confess London society holds very little allure for me. I believe I will need to seek refuge in your excellent library quite often, sir, preferably with you to keep me company."

Darcy placed a lingering kiss upon her hair and said, "*Our* library, Elizabeth. It is now *your* home, as well, and you can change anything you wish in order to make yourself more comfortable."

She shook her head. "I have no wish to change anything, and until we are happily married, I shall be perfectly content with being no more than a guest in *your* home."

Darcy placed the brush upon an end table and shifted so he could look deeply into Elizabeth's eyes. He caressed the softness of her cheek, his voice tinged with emotion as he whispered, "In my heart, Elizabeth, you are already my wife. Surely, you know that?"

Her breath caught in her throat as tears pricked the corners of her eyes. Cradling his face in her hands, she drew his mouth slowly toward her own, stopping just short of their lips touching. "Thank you, Fitzwilliam," she whispered. "You can have no idea how very much I was in need of hearing you speak such words to me tonight."

Their lips met with a tenderness that soon threatened to overwhelm them both, and as Elizabeth felt her body begin to tremble from the strength of her emotions, Darcy lifted her in his arms and carried her toward the fire. He laid her with care upon the carpet, where he joined her after removing his waistcoat and his riding boots. Then he began to work the buttons on her gown free, his gaze never leaving her eyes, not even for a moment.

Once Elizabeth was fully unclothed, her curls framing her face as she lay before him upon the carpet, Darcy took his time to tease her body with his lips, his tongue, and his hands, lingering along those areas of her flesh he knew to be most receptive to his caresses. Not until after Darcy heard her soft cries and felt her body begin to writhe under his touch did he dare permit himself to give any thought to his own ardor.

Darcy traced her nipple with his tongue as he massaged the small, sensitive pearl between her thighs with his finger. She was slippery and wet, indicating her readiness just as much as the muffled sounds Elizabeth moaned against his lips. Darcy pulled his head back and stared at her, mesmerized, unable to tear his gaze from her beauty, longing to bring her over the edge and into the abyss of ultimate release. Suddenly, Elizabeth's back began to arch, and her lovely body shuddered violently as he brought her to her completion. When she stilled, Darcy returned his mouth to hers as she assisted him with the buttons on his shirt and breeches.

He entered her slowly and began to move with smooth, long strokes he knew would encourage Elizabeth's desire to build again quickly. As he increased his rhythm and felt the delicious heat begin to supplant every other awareness, Elizabeth matched his frenzied movements with her own, drawing small grunts of satisfaction from Darcy every time they met.

They pushed their passion for each other ever faster, ever deeper until, with one final thrust, they spiraled into a pulsating oblivion of insurmountable pleasure.

They lay spent, languid and content in each other's arms, their limbs entwined as they basked in the afterglow of their lovemaking. Elizabeth ran her fingertips over his bare chest as Darcy's hand played with her hair. She gazed up at him and noticed a distant look in his eyes. "Fitzwilliam?" she asked softly.

"Mmm?"

"You seem far away. Is everything well?"

Darcy placed a lingering kiss upon her swollen lips and stroked her arm. "Yes. I am very well, my love. There is nowhere else I would rather be." He tightened his hold on her and settled into silence once more.

Though Elizabeth did not doubt the sincerity of his words, she was still not convinced his mind was completely free from anxiety. They remained silent for a while. Finally, Elizabeth said, "Your family seemed very nice. I especially liked your aunt. She is a very clever woman, and I enjoyed talking with her very much."

"Yes, she is. I believe she liked you, as well, as did my uncle, though I doubt he is ready to admit as much." Darcy laughed. "I believe you impressed him far more than he ever anticipated. I was very proud of the way you handled yourself with him. He can sometimes be difficult."

Elizabeth smiled somewhat sadly. "I gathered as much by his speech today, but I can hardly blame him. It is obvious he loves you a great deal and is only trying to protect you. For all he knows, I could be a fortune hunter interested only in Pemberley, your annual income, and your position in society. He is right to be cautious. You know you would do no less for your sister."

Darcy's brow furrowed. After several minutes, he asked, somewhat hesitantly, "Did you enjoy your shopping excursion with your family and Georgiana today?"

Elizabeth grew pensive. "It was fine, Fitzwilliam. I very much enjoyed spending time with your sister. She is a remarkable young woman."

Though Darcy was pleased to hear she liked spending time with his sister, he was not convinced Elizabeth had enjoyed herself otherwise. In fact, he knew it to be quite the opposite, and he longed to speak to her of what had really taken place at Mrs. Duval's shoppe. Darcy had thought Elizabeth had seemed rather subdued when she and Georgiana had arrived back at Darcy House that afternoon, though she did appear to recover quickly enough, enchanting his relations with her wit, her vivacity, and her natural grace. After speaking with Georgiana after dinner, however, he had a much better understanding as to why she seemed out of sorts.

Throughout the rest of the evening, Darcy had watched her closely, looking for any further signs of distress or melancholy, but, if there were any, Elizabeth—whom he had never known to dwell upon the negative—endeavored, however unsuccessfully, to hide them. If given a moment alone, he had hoped she might open up to him, confide her feelings and her hurt, but, even now, she appeared to have little inclination to do so. If anything, she seemed to be taking comfort from his presence and his love, and for that, Darcy found himself ever grateful.

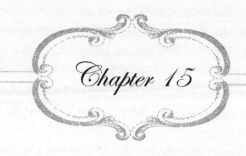

Chapter 15

THEY DINED THE FOLLOWING EVENING WITH ELIZABETH'S Aunt and Uncle Gardiner in Gracechurch Street, where they—the Bennets, the Gardiners, the Darcys, and Bingley—passed many happy hours in extremely pleasant company. Though their house was not half so large nor so grand as his own—being in Cheapside rather than the fashionable Grosvenor Square—Darcy found himself invariably impressed by the elegant manners and intelligent conversation of the Gardiners, who, to his complete surprise, turned out to be brother and sister-in-law to Mrs. Bennet.

When they arrived back at Darcy House, it was well past midnight, and everyone was anxious to retire for the night. While Elizabeth's parents and sisters went directly to their respective rooms to commence with their bedtime routines, Elizabeth and Miss Darcy stood together, finalizing plans they had made to visit Hyde Park in the morning. Darcy was seeing to some last-minute business in his study. Tired from their long day, the two ladies were just about to bid each other good night when the door to the drawing room was thrown open to reveal none other than Lady Catherine de Bourgh.

"Where is my nephew!" she demanded as her gaze swept through the room. As soon as her gaze came to rest on Elizabeth, her eyes narrowed with distaste. "And I suppose *you* are the insolent girl who has drawn him in!" It was not a question.

Georgiana gasped and looked on helplessly as her aunt advanced toward Elizabeth. She somehow forced herself to take a step forward and say, though somewhat meekly, "Aunt Catherine, may I present Miss Elizabeth Bennet of Hertfordshire?"

"I already know who she is!" she hollered in a voice that made her niece cringe. Then, turning to Elizabeth, she exclaimed, "I know it all, Miss Elizabeth Bennet! I know how you refused a perfectly good proposal of marriage from a respectable man whose prospects and station are far better suited to your meager situation in life in order to ensnare *my* nephew! Oh, yes! I have it on very good authority you have used your many charms and allurements in a shameful manner to seduce him—yes, *seduce him*, Miss Bennet!—into offering you marriage. Such disgraceful behavior will not be tolerated by his family. Whatever scheme you have been aspiring to will never take place. Mr. Darcy is engaged to *my* daughter. Now, what have you to say to *that*?"

Normally, Elizabeth would have found quite a bit to say, but she was currently so stunned to discover that any of Darcy's well-bred relations could possibly act in so deplorable a manner, it took her several moments to find her voice. Shaking only slightly, she spoke in as calm a manner as she was able. "If that is true, your ladyship, then Mr. Darcy certainly should never have made an offer to *me*; however, as I understand it, there is no prior commitment between your nephew and Miss de Bourgh. Mr. Darcy has denied the existence of such an arrangement, and therefore, as he has always been a man of his word, I must believe *him* over others who may feel far more of an inclination to be biased on this subject."

Lady Catherine gasped.

"As to the other charges you have laid at my door, they are disgraceful indeed, but I shall never dignify them with a response. You have insulted me at every turn, and I beg you would excuse me. You cannot possibly have anything further to say that I would wish to hear." She turned and made to leave, but Lady Catherine had not done. She reached out and actually caught Elizabeth's wrist to detain her.

"Not so hasty, Miss Bennet! You refuse to acknowledge the fact that your cousin, Mr. Collins—my very own trusted parson—witnessed you in a compromising position of the most offensive nature with my nephew, and still, you will not answer for it? Shall this be borne? No, it certainly shall not! You, Miss Bennet, have shown yourself to be a woman of the worst kind—wild, wanton, and totally unfeeling for all you shall make my poor nephew suffer! Perhaps you have managed to mislead *him*, but *I* am not so easily fooled. I see you for what you are—nothing but a fortune hunter who is no better than a common woman of the night!"

"*Enough!*" Darcy's voice rang loudly throughout the room as he stalked over to his aunt. By his expression, all present could tell he was furious, his body practically shaking with his contained rage. When he turned his gaze upon the two women who meant more to him than anything else, he was further angered to see Elizabeth's eyes swimming with unshed tears. He took his place beside her and moved to encircle her waist with his arm, but to his surprise, she pulled away and, without so much as a glance at him, walked swiftly from the room. Casting a wary look at her aunt, Georgiana followed her.

Darcy fixed his aunt with a look of loathing she would not soon forget and, through gritted teeth, demanded, "How dare you accuse my future wife of such a disgusting machination! What evil demon has robbed you of your senses and induced you to speak such vile filth in my home? Of what could you *possibly* be thinking?"

"Come, Nephew! You cannot possibly know of what you speak. Admit it. You have been taken in, duped, if you will, by this scheming little upstart. Can you not see that she cares nothing for you? It is only your money she wants. You have been blinded by her charms and her favors. When word gets out you intend to marry a woman you have taken as your mistress, we shall all be disgraced! Is such a woman to be sister to Georgiana? Are the shades of Pemberley to be thus polluted? Your parents would turn over in their graves to see you behaving thus!"

Never before had Darcy felt as though he could have struck a woman, but as he stared in disbelief at his aunt, he had to remind himself repeatedly to rein in his temper before it caused him to act in a way he would certainly come to regret. Breathing deeply, he paced the length of the drawing-room floor as her ladyship continued her tirade, mercilessly berating Elizabeth. At length, when she began to talk of his cousin Anne and how Darcy's own mother had planned their union to join their ancestral houses, it was absolutely the last straw.

His tone was venomous. "Lady Catherine, you would do well to remember you are still insulting my future wife with such outlandish insinuations! *Never* do so again, madam, and do not attempt to disillusion me with such ridiculous nonsense! I never heard my mother speak of her wish for a marriage between Anne and myself, nor have I ever heard it uttered by any member of my family other than you. As a matter of fact, it has been many years now I have believed such a scheme to be merely your own machination in order to lay claim to Pemberley and unite the Fitzwilliam fortune under one name. It was wrong of me to remain silent. Now I must insist you leave."

He rang then for a burly footman, who seemed to materialize out of thin air, and then he ushered his aunt out of the drawing room, into the foyer, and toward the door. Lady Catherine attempted to speak her mind, but Darcy would hear none of it. "You can have nothing further to say, Aunt. I will take this time to tell you, however, should you take it upon yourself to spread *any* of these vicious falsehoods—and they *are* falsehoods—against Elizabeth and myself, I will not be held accountable for my actions. This malicious slander has been fabricated and expounded upon by a sycophantic, small-minded man who is uncommonly bitter over the rejection of his own misdirected suit. That obsequious little parson of yours wasted no time, I might add, insinuating himself upon another respectable woman in the very same neighborhood, whom he managed to convince to accept him only three days later. *Three days!*" he bellowed, "Yet, still, he insists on being vindictive and spiteful. Worse still, he is *your clergyman*, Lady Catherine—hand-selected by you, though God only knows what for!"

They reached the door, and the footman yanked it open. "If you will not think of me, Aunt, then perhaps you will think of Anne and what she will likely suffer at the hands of society, should you and your faithful servant proceed in your endeavor to disgrace the future mistress of Pemberley. Imagine how Anne will be treated when the *ton* hears she has been thrown off by her cousin in favor of, how did you put it—oh, yes, by *'a woman I have taken as my mistress'*? You have purported the rumor of your daughter's impending engagement to me for many years now, and though

I have always had a familial affection for Anne, my first loyalty will always be to my wife. If you insist on destroying Miss Bennet's reputation, you will also be tainting that of your beloved daughter and all your relations. Remember that, Lady Catherine, before next you speak!"

Lady Catherine opened and closed her mouth, clearly outraged to have had no effect in swaying her stubborn nephew from his endeavor to marry the woman of his own choosing. Darcy simply glared at her and slammed the door in her face.

The burly footman's lips twitched.

"Not so much as one word of this is to be breathed, Tanner," Darcy warned. "Not so much as *one word*."

Georgiana knocked upon the door to Elizabeth's bedchamber and, although she received no answer, pushed it open and entered. Elizabeth was lying upon the bed, her shoulders shaking. Georgiana went to her and placed a hand upon her hair. "Oh, Elizabeth," she whispered, "please, do not take to heart anything my aunt has said. She can be truly unfeeling when she is moved to do so. You did nothing to deserve such wretched treatment from her. I am so sorry."

As Georgiana watched Elizabeth struggle to compose herself, her face burned with shame for her aunt's castigation of the woman who would very soon become her sister. Elizabeth sat up and managed a weak smile as she moved to dry her tears. "I am happy to finally hear you address me by my Christian name, Georgiana. Thank you. It brings me more pleasure than you might imagine."

Georgiana returned her smile. "My brother has rarely referred to you by any other. Only in his very first letters to me after he had gone to Hertfordshire, do I believe he ever called you, 'Miss

Bennet.' As wrong as it was, by the time I had received his fourth correspondence, I had already come to know you well as simply 'Elizabeth.' It was then when I realized he was probably in love with you, though I recall wondering at his being aware of it himself at the time."

"I can well believe he may not have been. I know I was quite oblivious to any partiality on his part. He kept his feelings so well concealed that by the time I finally realized the depth of his regard, it came as more of a sudden revelation." She became very quiet, and a nostalgic smile flickered across her lips. "Your brother is an exceptional man… the best man I have ever known. Truly, I do not know what I have ever done to deserve such love and devotion from him, but I do know I shall be forever grateful."

Georgiana reached for her hand. "My brother has very often said those same words in reference to you and your feelings for him. Truly, I believe there are no two people more deserving than you and Fitzwilliam. And from the way you faced my aunt, I know I am extremely fortunate to be gaining such an exceptional sister."

Elizabeth's smile faded, and she grew pensive, slowly shaking her head. "No, Georgiana. From what you have just heard of me from your aunt, I believe you would do far better than to associate with such a woman as I shall soon become in the eyes of society."

Georgiana gasped. "Certainly, you cannot mean that, Elizabeth! My aunt has been beyond cruel, and her words, heartless and wrong. She will say anything to wound when it serves her purpose. I know her too well to believe any of the appalling things she accused you of tonight." To Georgiana's surprise, however, rather than bringing her comfort, her words seemed only to have occasioned Elizabeth more pain. She watched in dismay as her future sister turned away from her, her hands covering her face.

There was a knock on the sitting room door then, and casting a glance from Elizabeth to the outer room, Georgiana rose. She had reached only as far as the door to the bedchamber, however, before Darcy entered. He took in the sight before him with a troubled frown and then, brushing past his sister, hastened to Elizabeth's side. Without preamble, he sat upon the bed, gathered Elizabeth into his arms, and settled her on his lap. She did not resist. Georgiana watched, transfixed, as her brother whispered words of comfort, punctuated by soft kisses on her hair. He stroked her back with one hand and cradled the back of her head with his other. Elizabeth simply clung to him, burying her face against his coat.

Several long minutes passed, and to Georgiana, it was as though they had completely forgotten she was even in the room. She heard her brother utter something to Elizabeth about his having no regrets regarding anything they had shared together. The implication of such words, when seen in the same light as his tender actions, suddenly hit her—hard. Had her brother been *intimate* with Elizabeth? The possibility of Darcy committing such an impropriety astounded her.

It seemed those same words also had an effect upon Elizabeth, for she suddenly withdrew from Darcy, a look of sadness and shame piercing her eyes. Darcy reached for her as she removed herself from his lap, but Elizabeth avoided his arms, twisting away from his embrace to stand with her back to him as she stared out of the nearest window.

Darcy gaped at her, panic settling into the pit of his stomach. The look in her eyes had been one of such desolation and grief… and resignation. *Resignation to what?* he wondered. *Surely Elizabeth would not break our engagement because of my aunt? Surely she would never leave me? No. She could not possibly leave me. She is mine! I have already made her mine!* He recalled the events of the previous day and Elizabeth's distress over the hurtful gossip she had overheard in Bond Street. Darcy was no longer convinced she would not act in a manner that would be of greater benefit to him in the eyes of society. It took some effort, but he managed to swallow the searing lump that had formed in his throat. Tears stung his eyes; then he recalled his sister was still in the room. Without taking his gaze from Elizabeth, he said in a strained voice, "Georgiana, leave us."

Georgiana gaped at him. How could her brother ask this of her? How could he expect her to comply with such a highly improper request—especially when Elizabeth was clearly in emotional distress and, therefore, most vulnerable? She hesitated and then heard Darcy's voice, more commanding this time, as he said again, "Leave us, Georgiana. I must speak privately with Elizabeth." When still she did not move, Darcy turned on her, his eyes flashing. "I said go!"

Georgiana flinched. She had not seen that particular look on her brother's face since last summer, at Ramsgate. She began backing slowly toward the door to the sitting room and, when she reached it, cast one last, reluctant look at the man who was more like a father to her than a brother, before finally fleeing the room.

Georgiana ran until she reached the family wing and then entered her own sitting room, pacing the length of it for nearly three-quarters of an hour. She was concerned for Elizabeth, but also for her brother. She had not missed the look in Elizabeth's eyes, nor misinterpreted it, any more than she had been blind to the panic and pain in Darcy's. Wondering if enough time had passed for the two to have resolved their differences, she decided to adjourn to her brother's sitting room to see if he had retired. When she reached his chambers, however, she was met by his valet, Mr. Stevens.

"I am sorry, Miss Darcy, but my master is not in his rooms."

Georgiana's brows furrowed. "Oh. Well, then I shall wait, Mr. Stevens. It is very late. I am sure he cannot be long."

Having known Miss Darcy since she was a small girl, the valet smiled, wishing to shield her from what he surely knew would bring her little pleasure. "Forgive me, miss, but I do believe my master may be quite a while yet. I know he would not wish you to wait up for him. The last several nights Mr. Darcy has had much to attend to and has retired very late."

Frowning, Georgiana uttered, "Of course. He must be in his study, then. I will just go to him there. I am certain he would not mind my bothering him."

A fleeting look of alarm passed over Mr. Stevens's face as he moved to detain her. "Miss Darcy," he said, his voice firm, "I would not disturb my master in his study."

"Why not, Mr. Stevens?" she asked.

Mr. Stevens sighed. "My dear girl, I beg your pardon, but I am not at liberty to speak without betraying my allegiance to Mr. Darcy; however, as I also know my master would not wish for you to come upon him unawares, I must entreat you to return to your room and to forget about speaking with him tonight. I regret to inform you that my master will not be available to anyone until the morning."

Georgiana stared at him. "But I know my brother to have been with Miss Bennet not an hour ago."

The valet averted his eyes and nodded. "Yes, miss."

Comprehension suddenly dawned upon her, and swallowing hard, she asked, "My brother has not slept in his rooms for several nights, has he, Mr. Stevens?" Seeing the man's obvious discomfort, Georgiana added, "Never mind. Good night, Mr. Stevens." She turned to go then, her heart heavy as she returned to her room.

Darcy had just closed the door and turned when a sudden movement in the shadowy corridor caught his eye. Clad only in his shirtsleeves, breeches, and boots, he froze as he watched Mr. Bennet approach, clutching a well-worn volume of Shakespeare's *Othello*, which Darcy recognized as one from his own collection. It was obvious by the elder gentleman's incredulous expression and pale complexion that he had witnessed him leaving Elizabeth's rooms. A multitude of possible explanations raced through Darcy's mind, yet he felt unequal to uttering any of them, knowing full well Elizabeth's father had already deduced the true purpose of his presence outside his daughter's bedchamber.

Oddly enough, it was Mr. Bennet who was the first to regain his composure, his voice strained and tired. "Shall we retire to your study for some of your excellent brandy, Darcy? I believe I am suddenly in great need of it." Darcy nodded almost imperceptibly and proceeded down the corridor to the staircase, Mr. Bennet following a few steps behind.

Elizabeth's father took a long, slow mouthful of brandy from his glass in a remarkably calm fashion, while Darcy roughly threw back the contents of his own and quickly poured himself another. He took a healthy swallow and ran an unsteady hand across his lips before stationing himself at the window to look out over the square, which was just beginning to emerge from darkness. After his aunt's visit, he had been hard-pressed to imagine his night getting any worse, yet here he was, caught red-handed by Elizabeth's father. He could hardly believe his misfortune.

Mr. Bennet's calm voice broke through the silence. "Am I mistaken in my assumption that the only formality that remains for your marriage to Elizabeth is the actual ceremony itself?"

Darcy was quiet for several moments. "No, sir," he finally answered in a tightly controlled voice without turning around, "you are not mistaken in that regard."

Mr. Bennet sat down in one of the leather chairs by the fire and ran his hands over his face, his voice unruffled. "When did this happen?"

Darcy ran his tongue over his lips, his mouth feeling like a desert. "Not quite a fortnight ago, when heavy snow kept her at Netherfield for two nights with Miss Bennet."

"At Netherfield," Mr. Bennet said tightly. He exhaled, clearly not pleased, but still trying to remain reasonable all the same. "And while we have been in London?"

Darcy did not respond.

"Darcy?"

He swallowed, cleared his throat, and managed to say, "She has been my wife."

"You mean your *mistress*!"

Darcy faced him, his expression icy. "Elizabeth is my *wife*!"

Mr. Bennet remained silent, knowing if he spoke now, he would no longer be able to control his temper.

Darcy strode to his desk and withdrew several documents from a locked drawer. "My reason for quitting Hertfordshire was to obtain a special license so we might marry as soon as possible. My main reason for inviting you and your family here is so we might marry quickly in London before any news of a scandal touches us, as I am sure it eventually would. Hopefully, our marrying now will prevent it from ever happening, though there is still no guarantee. As it is, I had an unpleasant visit from my aunt, Lady Catherine de Bourgh, tonight. Apparently," he said with undisguised contempt, "Mr. Collins has wasted no time informing her of my relationship with your daughter. To say she was less than pleased would be a gross understatement, but I shall not insult you by relating the particulars of my conversation."

He crossed to the other side of the room and offered the documents to Elizabeth's father, who took them. "I had my solicitor draw up the settlement for Elizabeth the other day. In the event of my death, she will be well provided for, even if she does not provide me with an heir. I arranged for ownership of the Pemberley estate to pass directly to her, as well as that of this house and all monetary assets. Though I trust you will inform me if you find anything insufficient, I believe I can say with complete confidence I know of no man who would *ever* be fool enough to make such a settlement upon a woman he considered only as his *mistress*."

Mr. Bennet pursed his lips, biting back a sarcastic retort, and began to read through the legalities. When he came to the amount Darcy was to settle upon his daughter after their marriage became official, he drew a sharp intake of breath and, after a few minutes, said, "I realize you have ten thousand a year, young man, but can you truly afford to be so generous as to settle forty thousand pounds on my Lizzy?"

A wry grin turned the corners of Darcy's mouth. "It appears the good people of Hertfordshire have been remiss in their speculation of my fortune. That they should think I have *only* ten thousand a year, I find excessively diverting. Pemberley, of course, takes in just over that, but if you were to include my other holdings and investments, both abroad and in Scotland, my net worth should be closer to twenty, perhaps a little more. I believe all the particulars are mentioned there in detail. And forgive my impertinence, Mr. Bennet, but *your Lizzy* is very soon to become *my wife*. Forty thousand pounds is no more than she deserves."

Massaging the bridge of his nose between his thumb and forefinger, Mr. Bennet could not but agree with him.

"I would like to marry Elizabeth by the end of the week."

Mr. Bennet sighed. "Yes. As well you should. I see no reason to put it off any longer than that, especially given the urgency of the current situation. I do believe it would be in everyone's best interest, however, if this conversation remained between the two of us." Mr. Bennet rested his elbows upon the arms of the chair and steepled his fingers. "Do you agree with this proposal, or would you prefer I bring my wife into our confidence? It is your call, Darcy."

Hoping, rather than assuming he had been joking, Darcy repressed a shudder as he imagined Mrs. Bennet learning he had been sharing a bed with her daughter. There was no doubt in his mind that news of the scandal would spread through the streets of London in a matter of hours. "No. On that we are in complete agreement. We need not distress Mrs. Bennet with any of the particulars."

"No, I thought as much." Mr. Bennet rose from his chair and made to leave. "If you will excuse me, I believe I will return to my room now for some much-needed repose."

Just as he was about to close the door, however, Mr. Bennet turned and fixed Darcy with a stern look. "Oh, and Darcy, if you cannot remain in your own bed for a mere five nights until your wedding day, and I happen to learn of it—and make no mistake, I *will* learn of it—I daresay you will not find me quite so forgiving as I have been tonight." And with that, Mr. Bennet stepped out into the hall, closing the door firmly behind him as Darcy fell back into the well-worn leather chair behind his desk.

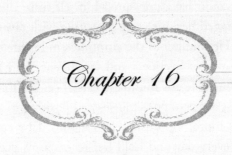

Chapter 16

Darcy did not go to bed the night of his aunt's visit. He did not consider having shared Elizabeth's bed as actually sleeping, particularly since those emotionally exhausting hours were mostly spent in earnest, yet painful conversation, and in reassuring her of his steadfastness, his devotion, and his ardent love. It was not a night he ever wished to repeat.

It was but a matter of moments after Georgiana had left them that Darcy's deepest fears had been realized. It had mattered not to Elizabeth that she had already given herself to him completely—that she had become his wife, both in heart and in body, if not yet in the eyes of God—for her sweet, unsteady voice had uttered the words he had dreaded to hear above any others: *"I am sorry, Mr. Darcy, but I am afraid I can no longer agree to be your wife. I hereby release you from our engagement."*

Hearing her refer to him in so stiff and formal a manner made him feel as though a knife had been driven into his heart. It had taken Darcy nearly half the night to convince Elizabeth to reconsider taking such a rash measure, and now, as he looked back upon those wretched hours, he was not the least bit ashamed to admit he had done everything within his power to hold on to her. He could no more have stopped the tears that had threatened to fall from his eyes than he could have prevented himself from dropping to his knees as he begged her, his voice quivering with raw emotion, not to leave him. He told her of the emptiness in his life before he had met her, of how her liveliness and intelligence had brought such joy and fulfillment to his mundane existence. He told her of how the tediousness of his responsibilities and position in society would become, once more, a punishment for him if he could not gaze into her eyes every day and hold her in his arms every night. He could not bear the thought of living without her, for a life without her would be no life for him at all.

It was not until the clock had struck half past four in the early hours of the morning that Elizabeth had finally accepted another proposal from him—*My third one*, Darcy had thought with some irony—and finally, through glistening eyes, she had proclaimed, and with a passion to rival his own, what Darcy had been praying all night long to hear—that she could no more bear the thought of living without him than he could bear contemplating a life without her.

They had not made love—both were far too emotionally and physically drained for that—but, by unspoken agreement, Darcy had stayed with her, cradling Elizabeth in his arms and caressing her hair long after she had finally succumbed to sleep. When he had finally forced himself to leave the comfortable warmth of her bed, it was only to be discovered in a most untenable position by Mr. Bennet.

By the time a rather displeased, but resigned, Mr. Bennet had left Darcy alone in his study, the sun had already begun to show over the horizon. Given it was now morning, Darcy had chosen to remain there, deep in reflection and tormenting himself with what

Elizabeth had been prepared to do to spare him further censure from people whose opinions he cared nothing for in the first place. *It matters not in any case, for she must marry me now that her father has discovered the extent of our intimacy.* Darcy stifled a yawn and closed his eyes, resting his head against the back of his chair. It was then that Lord and Lady Matlock were shown into his study—at far too early an hour for polite visitation—to find him far from being at his best.

"Goodness, Nephew," cried Lady Matlock as she took in Darcy's haggard appearance. "You look absolutely wretched. Did you not get any sleep at all?"

Darcy rose to his feet and raked his hand through his hair. "Forgive my appearance, Aunt Rebecca. I fear your visit this morning has taken me by surprise."

She gave him an appraising look and raised her brow. He was not wearing his tailcoat, waistcoat, or cravat. "That is apparent, Fitzwilliam."

Lord Matlock spoke in his usual gruff manner. "Well, I certainly hope your young lady is faring better than you look, Nephew."

Darcy averted his eyes. "I have yet to see Elizabeth this morning."

The earl raised his brows. "Hmm. Interesting… interesting. By the look of you, I would be willing to wager a great deal that you have."

Darcy's head snapped up; his lips tightly pursed.

"Henry, that is enough," Lady Matlock admonished. "We did not come here to make further accusations. We came to offer our support."

Darcy stared at her. "You did?"

Lord Matlock grumbled. "Yes, well, I suppose your aunt is correct. We did not come to upset you, Darcy. I imagine Catherine has already done that job admirably. No, no, we came to show our support for you and your Elizabeth. Fine girl, if I do say so myself. Beautiful features, excellent mind, and a tongue as sharp as a double-edged blade! Ha-ha! I daresay you could not expect to do better if you were to court every eligible lady in the first circles of society!"

Darcy raised his chin. "I have no intention of looking elsewhere, Uncle. There is no other woman who could ever make me happy. I am to take Elizabeth as my wife by the end of the week and not a day later. We have yet to finalize all the arrangements, but I hope very much you will both attend."

Lady Matlock smiled and moved to embrace him, placing a kiss upon his unshaven cheek. "Of course, we will be there, Fitzwilliam. We are very pleased for you, dear. I enjoyed Elizabeth's company immensely, as did Richard. She shall make an excellent addition to our family. I should like to see her now, if I may. Which room have you given her?" Darcy told her and, before he could move to accompany her, she had quit the room, leaving him very much alone with his uncle.

"Well, Darcy, I know it is early still, but I would like to partake in some brandy. Catherine always manages to have that effect on me. Even as a girl, she drove me to my wits' end. Meddlesome woman," he muttered. Darcy accommodated him, pouring a glass for himself, as well, though it was not generally his habit to imbibe so early in the day. They settled into silence, nursing their drinks.

At length, the earl fixed him with a serious look. "I would speak to you, Nephew. Keep in mind now, it is not my intention to judge you. But, ah, well… Catherine has thrown out some mighty offensive accusations regarding your engagement, some of them downright vulgar—foremost, the circumstances surrounding your interest in Miss Bennet."

Darcy opened his mouth to object, but the earl held up a hand and continued. "Save your breath, Nephew. You forget I have already seen you together. I know a love match when I see it. I had one myself with Rebecca and still do to this very day." Here, Lord Matlock gave Darcy a significant look. "And I am not such an old man not to remember how it once felt to be a young one. My Rebecca was always a stunning woman, as is your Elizabeth. From the moment we laid eyes on each other, I wanted nothing more than to make her my wife in every sense of the word. We loved one another with a passion that consumed us, so much so that, eventually, it did not much signify to us *how* the means were achieved—or when." Darcy quirked his brow at such an implication, and the earl cleared his throat. "However, much like your aunt, Elizabeth seems to be too much of a gentlewoman to have *initiated*… ah, well… let us just say I believe my sister is entirely in the wrong as far as your wife is concerned. You, Darcy, are another matter entirely."

Darcy bristled and demanded, "Am I? How?"

Lord Matlock chuckled. "For starters, the way you look at her. The way you touch her—yes, Darcy, I have seen you caress her hand, her arm, the small of her back. I have seen you *innocently* pretend to brush against her—repeatedly, I might add. You were in full company, and you fooled no one, including your aunt, and Elizabeth handled it all with grace and dignity, as a well-bred wife who has a true affection for her husband would." He gave Darcy another pointed look. "I say *wife*, Nephew, because I suspect you have already taken her as your own. Am I wrong to think it?"

Darcy stood and walked to the window. He placed his forearm against the casement, his other hand on his hip, and expelled a deep breath. Several minutes ticked by in silence before he admitted

"It is true." A moment later, however, he spun around and added, "And do not *dare* to call her my *mistress*!"

The earl considered his words with a grim countenance. "Has someone aside from your Aunt Catherine referred to her as such?"

Darcy turned away and said tightly, "Elizabeth's father, after he discovered me leaving her room just before dawn this morning."

Lord Matlock pursed his lips and let out a low whistle. "That could not have gone well for either of you."

Darcy laughed ruefully. "Believe me, it went far better than it would have with any other lady's father. Elizabeth has always been his particular favorite, and Mr. Bennet is a reasonable and, I daresay, extremely forgiving man, even under such circumstances. His daughter's happiness is his foremost concern. In short, he has not called me out nor demanded satisfaction in any way other than to ascertain that I hold Elizabeth in the highest regard and will restrain myself from any further *contact* with her until after we exchange our vows on Saturday. She has yet to learn of his knowledge of our situation. I would, of course, prefer she does not."

The earl nodded and asked, "And he is the only one you know of who has discovered this facet of your relationship, aside from Catherine and her parson?"

"I… after Lady Catherine left last night I went to Elizabeth in her room. Georgiana was with her. I confess myself to have been so furious with my aunt and so concerned for what Elizabeth was suffering, I gave very little thought to propriety. I soon became so caught up in offering my comfort to Elizabeth, I had completely forgotten Georgiana was present, witnessing my attentions. Though nothing scandalous took place between Elizabeth and me in her presence, per se, I believe she now suspects something of the truth. At one point"—and here Darcy hesitated, his voice becoming hoarse—"at one point Elizabeth withdrew from me. She had such a look of sorrow and hopelessness in her eyes. I was terrified she was going to break our engagement. I could not… I could not think, for the fear that gripped me. I demanded Georgiana leave us, which she reluctantly did, but only after I had lost my temper." He walked a few paces and slammed his fist against the wall. "Would to *God* that I had been more careful!"

Lord Matlock rose and went to Darcy, placing his hand upon his shoulder. "Darcy, what has been done is done. Unfortunately, you must now deal with the repercussions of your actions. Like I said, your aunt and I can be counted on to welcome Elizabeth into society, as can your cousins. Should any rumors get out, we will do all in our power to quell them. Once they have the pleasure of meeting your Elizabeth, I very much doubt many members of our circle will believe any of it anyway. It shall be dismissed as malicious gossip and die a quick death. Any reverberation will not be of a long duration, and neither of you will have to bear this alone, my boy. Therefore, do not worry yourself over it any further. All will be well." Lord Matlock embraced him, clapping him upon the back.

Darcy returned the gesture with no little emotion. "Thank you, Uncle."

Lady Matlock knocked upon the door to Elizabeth's rooms and waited. "Elizabeth?" she called. "It is Lady Matlock. I would very much like to speak with you, my dear."

The door opened, and Elizabeth appeared. Though she was dressed far more appropriately to receive visitors than Darcy had been, she happened to have the same worn, defeated look about her Darcy had exhibited when his aunt had first seen him earlier. It pained Lady Matlock no less to see it on Elizabeth's lovely features than it had to see it upon the face of her nephew. She smiled kindly and stepped into the room. "Well, my dear, I believe you have had a rather trying night, have you not?"

Elizabeth managed a weak smile and averted her eyes. "Will you not sit down, your ladyship?" she asked as she indicated a small sofa and several chairs in the sitting room.

Lady Matlock took a seat upon the sofa and indicated that Elizabeth should join her. Taking her hands in her own, she said, "It would please me very much if you would call me Aunt, Elizabeth, especially since I have just spoken with my nephew regarding your marriage. From what I understand, you are to become my niece sooner than we expected."

Elizabeth blushed and bowed her head.

Lady Matlock gave her hands a squeeze. "I know my saying so can be of little consolation after what has so recently occurred, but Lady Catherine can hardly lay claim to a reputation for affability and warmth. It was her dearest wish that Fitzwilliam marry her daughter, Anne, though, I must say it was by no means his wish any more than it was Anne's. Elizabeth, you must understand, my nephew could have chosen the most affluent, well-connected young lady in all of England to be his bride, and still, my sister-in-law would have found some unfounded reason to berate his choice for the simple reason it was not *hers*. You must not dwell on what was said last night, my dear, for it matters not to Lord Matlock and me what has occurred privately between you and my nephew, so long as you have found love and joy with each other. To those of us who truly care for your happiness, nothing else can be of any significance."

Elizabeth was too stunned to speak.

Lady Matlock smiled as she added, "I must say, I am almost relieved Catherine did not approve of you, for if she had, I would have been forced to question Fitzwilliam's soundness of mind. You see, he and my sister-in-law have never shared the same tastes, the same opinions, or the same ideals. Yes, I am, indeed, delighted to be gaining such a lovely niece! And your marriage cannot come too soon for our family, I am afraid."

Elizabeth's expression showed her puzzlement, but Lady Matlock only continued to smile as she explained, "Thus far, Georgiana and Anne have been our only girls. I believe they found their childhood rather trying at times due to the exuberance of their male cousins and their overactive imaginations. To be always teased by such spirited young men can be an experience, to say the least."

Elizabeth imagined Darcy and Colonel Fitzwilliam as boys and smiled. Lady Matlock continued, "Both young ladies were rather shy, so I daresay they found themselves easy targets for mischief. It was all in good fun, mind you, and Fitzwilliam, excellent brother that he was, never allowed their pranks to get out of hand. He was always attuned to Georgiana's feelings. I am convinced someday he will make an exceptional father, as well." She squeezed Elizabeth's hand.

"Yes," Elizabeth replied, "I have often thought so."

"Lord Matlock and I have three sons, you know. My eldest, and my husband's heir, is Harold. He is currently at our estate in the country, seeing to some affairs but will soon join us for Christmas. You met Richard the other day, and my youngest, Ethan, is in his final year at Cambridge. He is to take orders soon and will also join us at the end of the week."

Elizabeth laughed. "I confess I am quite envious. I have no brothers, only four sisters."

"Oh! Better and better," exclaimed Lady Matlock with genuine enthusiasm. "I can hardly wait to see Richard's face when he finally finds himself outnumbered and, I daresay, outwitted by so many ladies! But you did mention your sisters the other day, did you not?"

"Yes, I did. We are all as different as night and day. Though we certainly have engaged in our own share of teasing and mischief—and still do when the moment strikes us—we do happen to love one another dearly."

"Of course you do, my dear. I believe they are all here now, are they not?"

Elizabeth nodded. "Yes, my elder sister, Jane, informed me this morning they were not going out and could all be found in one of the drawing rooms with my mother."

"Then I should like it very much if you would introduce us, Elizabeth. Let us go down now and join them. Perhaps you can ring for tea?" She rose and offered Elizabeth her arm.

Elizabeth felt a tingle of trepidation as she linked her arm with that of Darcy's aunt. "As you wish… Aunt, but I must caution you. Several of my sisters are young still, and their manners in company can be a bit wanting, particularly when in the presence of a handsome young man in a red coat." She smiled meaningfully. "You may wish to keep Colonel Fitzwilliam's profession a secret; otherwise, he may never have any peace so long as Kitty and Lydia remain in Town."

Lady Matlock laughed. "Excellent! I daresay Richard would deserve it, too! Oh, no, my dear. We must leave your younger sisters in no doubt of his noble profession. It is about time my most troublesome son receives his just desserts for teasing poor Georgiana and Anne so mercilessly all these years!"

When Lord Matlock and Darcy, who was now refreshed, shaved, and presentably attired, went in search of the ladies an hour or so later, they found them all ensconced in the music room. It was a sight Darcy would not soon forget. Georgiana sat at the pianoforte as she chatted with Kitty and Lydia, her serious expression from the previous night now replaced by a happy smile as she played a lively duet with Mary, who also seemed to be enjoying herself. Elizabeth, whose disposition could only have been described as wretched before he had parted from her not five hours earlier, was now smiling and laughing with Jane. Jane was seated next to his aunt, who appeared to be taking an inordinate amount of pleasure in her conversation with Mrs. Bennet. He was astounded, to say the least.

He turned toward his uncle and, leaning in so he would not be overheard by any of the ladies, inquired, "Exactly how much brandy did I consume this morning, Uncle?"

Lord Matlock looked at him for a moment before clapping him on the back and erupting into hearty laughter.

Darcy grinned. *Yes, perhaps all will yet be well.*

Mr. Bennet entered the room then, carrying a long, slender package, and made his way over to Darcy with great enthusiasm. "Ah, Darcy! Just the man I have been looking for," he said with a wide smile. "I have just this morning acquired an excellent new hunting rifle. Come and have a look. I daresay the craftsmanship is superior to many in Mr. Bingley's collection, and the gunsmith has assured me that the accuracy is unparalleled."

Darcy's smile was rapidly replaced by a look of undisguised panic.

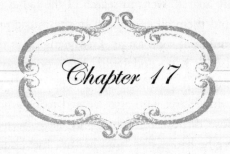

Chapter 17

"OH, ELIZABETH!" GEORGIANA EXCLAIMED WITH PLEASURE. "You look so beautiful in that color. Fitzwilliam will not be able to take his eyes off of you. Shall you wear it to the theatre tonight, do you think?"

"It is a beautiful gown, but I am not yet sure. I must confess to loving the burgundy best of all. What do you think, Jane?"

"I believe Miss Darcy is correct, Lizzy. The dark green one becomes you very well. Though the burgundy is very elegant and flattering, as well, I think it would be better suited for a ballroom rather than the theatre."

They were interrupted then by Mrs. Bennet as she bustled into Elizabeth's dressing room. "Oh, girls! If I do say so myself, that is the perfect dress for the theatre tonight! Mark my words, Lizzy, it is just the thing to keep Mr. Darcy's eyes turned toward you all evening, for you know there will be many pretty young ladies with large fortunes and expensive gowns hoping to capture the interest of a rich gentleman. You would not want Mr. Darcy changing his mind about you before your wedding takes place. Much can happen in two days, you know, and I always say you can never be too careful."

Jane smiled and gave her sister a knowing look; then, placing a quick kiss upon her cheek, she left them to begin her own toilette.

Elizabeth rolled her eyes and suppressed a smile as she ran her hand over the exquisite deep emerald silk of her new gown. "Mama, if Mr. Darcy has not changed his mind by now, I doubt very much he will do so by Saturday."

Georgiana, however, was genuinely troubled by their mother's statement. "Oh, no, Mrs. Bennet, you need not worry yourself over such a thing. I assure you, my brother loves Elizabeth very much. He has been nothing but caring and attentive whenever I have seen them together. Indeed, if you had only witnessed the tenderness and intimacy that exists between them, especially on Sunday last, I am certain your mind would now be completely at ease." Then, with a gasp, Georgiana's hand flew to her mouth as she sent a panicked glance to Elizabeth before casting her eyes downward, clearly mortified, not only by what her well-intentioned words had certainly implied, but also by what she had alluded to.

She need not have worried, for Mrs. Bennet, lost in her own musings, merely shrugged and said, "Oh, well then, I daresay I shall rest easier knowing Lizzy will at least be able to keep him interested until after the wedding takes place." She gave her daughter a critical look and made a minor adjustment to the ribbon on the bodice of her gown. "Hmm…" she mused, "I do believe this neckline is particularly flattering to your bosom, Lizzy, and I must agree, the color is perfect for you. Yes, you shall wear it tonight with the emerald necklace and earrings Mr. Darcy was so generous to present to you the other day. And do not be late. I hardly think it would please your future husband to be kept waiting." Mrs. Bennet then left Elizabeth to Georgiana's society in order to oversee Jane's preparations for the evening.

Elizabeth leaned against the door, closed her eyes, and expelled a long, slow breath. Georgiana looked contrite as she sat, perched upon the edge of the small sofa in the sitting room, staring at her lap in misery. Elizabeth approached her, and Georgiana reluctantly raised her eyes, now swimming with unshed tears. "Oh, Elizabeth, can you ever forgive me?" she whispered. "It was very wrong of me to have said such a thing to your mother just now. I never should have mentioned any of it at all. What you and Fitzwilliam choose to do when you are alone together—*oh, no,*" she gasped. "I certainly did not mean to say that! Please, please forgive me. It is none of my business, any of it, and I ought not to speak of such things. Fitzwilliam would be appalled by my lack of decorum. I can only imagine what you must think of me for speaking so."

Frowning, Elizabeth sat beside her and gathered her hands in her own. "I believe I am more concerned at the moment with your opinion of me," she said. "I had no idea you had reached this particular conclusion about your brother and me, Georgiana, but perhaps I should not be so surprised. We have done a rather poor job of keeping our affection for each other a secret from the rest of the world. As you well know, your aunt had much to say on the subject, and indeed, I am very sorry you were forced to bear witness to my shame. I am sure it must have been distressing for you, to say nothing of the shock of seeing your brother comforting me in such a familiar way. I am afraid that, in our distress, both of us were not entirely aware of our actions or their possible repercussions. I very much hope you will tell me if you are still troubled by what you have seen, my dear. I would never wish to be the cause of any pain or discomfort to you, nor, do I believe, would your brother."

Georgiana averted her eyes. "I am fine, Elizabeth, truly. You need not worry yourself over me."

"Come, Georgiana. We are to be sisters. You need not feel as though you cannot speak to me as such. I promise, you have no reason to fear that I shall pass judgment on you or your feelings, even if you believe what you are feeling may occasion *me* pain or discomfort."

Georgiana fussed with the trim on her shawl. "I… very well, then. I will not pretend it did not bother me when I first figured out that you and Fitzwilliam have been… *intimate* with each other."

Both ladies blushed, and Georgiana said, "Forgive me, Elizabeth. As I have said, I know very well it is none of my concern."

Elizabeth cleared her throat and inclined her head.

They sat in companionable silence for a time before Georgiana spoke again. Though her voice was subdued, Elizabeth could sense an underlying agitation. "Elizabeth, I once knew a man who told me he loved me. He told me he wanted to marry me, but it turned out he did not. He only wanted my fortune and… and my virtue. He never wanted *me*. He was someone I had known and trusted my entire life, yet he used my affection for him to try to convince me to… *to be with him*. I did not want to, not before we were married, and he knew it, yet he continually tried to persuade me otherwise, all the while claiming to be in love with me. He said if I loved him I would… *show him*." A tear ran down her cheek, and she hung her head.

Elizabeth's eyes widened at this admission. "Georgiana, do you mean to tell me this young man has… has compromised you in some way?"

Georgiana took a shaky breath. "Yes," she answered, "I mean no. Not entirely. It is not as bad as that." She rose and paced the length of the room several times, reminding Elizabeth very much of Darcy. "I thought I loved him, Elizabeth! I thought I knew my own mind. I thought I knew *him*, but it turned out I did not. I knew nothing. I almost ruined my life and my reputation, and I brought Fitzwilliam and Richard a great deal of pain and mortification. And even though I had hurt them—even though I had disappointed them—they were both still so very kind and loving toward me, as though none of it was my fault.

"Later, my brother told me, any man who is unwilling to respect my wishes—any man who will try to talk me into an elopement, or take my virtue before we are married by the church, or make me do anything I am not comfortable with—is no gentleman. He told me a true gentleman will never demand such things from a woman he truly esteems and loves before she is ready to give them willingly, before their marriage has been sanctioned by the church. Knowing this, can you not understand why I cannot help but be troubled by Fitzwilliam's familiarity with you?"

"Georgiana, have you spoken to your brother of your feelings?" Elizabeth asked.

Georgiana shrugged. "I have not. He did approach me the following day and on several occasions since, but I was not yet comfortable discussing my feelings about his… his indiscretions. I made up an excuse so I could leave him quickly, before he could mention it. He has since been very busy with various matters of business, and I have taken precautions so we would not be alone together. I have spent quite a bit of time wondering how my brother could ever have done this to you. I do not want you to think I believe any of the wretched things my Aunt Catherine has accused you of, not even for a moment, Elizabeth. I know you could never behave in such a disgraceful manner as she would have me believe. She is only upset that Fitzwilliam is not to marry Anne, but she was so horrible to you! You did nothing to deserve her abominable treatment. I am no longer naïve. I know very well that none of this would ever have happened, had my brother not taken advantage of your innocence and your affection for him in a moment of weakness and… and… *seduced you.*" Her last words were barely above a whisper.

Elizabeth inhaled sharply. "Oh, Georgiana, is that what you think?"

She nodded and looked away.

"I assure you that is not the case." Elizabeth forced their eyes to meet and said, "This is, by no means, easy for me, but I must endeavor to correct this mistaken impression you have formed about your brother. While I will admit he may have been very… persuasive in his manner of expressing his affection for me on more than one occasion, I cannot allow you to think him capable of unscrupulously misleading me into doing something I objected to. His goodness and his moral principles would never allow such deception, such duplicity."

Georgiana stared at her. "I know you love him, Elizabeth, and he you, but how can you say that after what he has done? What made you think you could trust him? Even though he is my brother, and the very best of men, he is still a man."

Elizabeth smiled. "I knew enough of his character to know I *could* trust him. By the time we had shared our love with each other, Georgiana, your brother had long since professed his strong feelings for me many times over and had already asked me to become his wife. I would never have accepted your brother under any circumstances unless I loved him deeply."

Georgiana lowered her eyes and said, "I do understand how easy it is, Elizabeth, to forget propriety when your feelings are so overwrought with another, but you must see how my brother has placed your reputation in jeopardy because of his unwillingness to follow his own code of honor. I can hardly believe he would consciously do such a thing—go against everything he told me—yet, I have daily proof of it before me. I feel as though he has let me down, and because of it, I will never again be able to trust another man. He has made everything worse."

Elizabeth walked to her and said, "Do not allow one terrible experience with one wicked man to influence your judgment of others who are truly good. There are many good men in the world, Georgiana, your brother being an excellent example. I know you are feeling inclined to lay all the blame upon him for our current unhappy situation with your aunt, but that is unfair. The truth is we are both to blame, my dear. You should realize by now, he is guilty of doing nothing more than allowing the strength of his emotions for me to cloud his better judgment. My conduct, I am ashamed to say, has been no better. He has done nothing that I did not allow purely out of the love I have for him. Please do not judge him based upon this indiscretion alone. It would do neither of you any credit."

Georgiana was silent for a long while as she considered Elizabeth's words. "I suppose Fitzwilliam has always been very different from George. Even when they were children, they did not always see eye to eye." She sighed. "I know you are correct, Elizabeth. George's motives with me have always been selfish and self-serving, while Fitzwilliam's are born solely out of his strong love and admiration for you." She gave Elizabeth a small smile. "Thank you for finally making me see the difference."

"George?" Elizabeth inquired with a frown. "Is that the name of the young man you knew?"

"Yes," she said, blushing, "George Wickham. He was the son of my father's steward. He and Fitzwilliam were always very close when they were younger. They attended Cambridge together but did not continue their acquaintance after that. I now suspect it was because of George's nefarious habits."

Elizabeth paled and felt as though she would be sick. "George Wickham!" she gasped. *No wonder Fitzwilliam was so affected by his presence in Hertfordshire! It is a wonder he did not kill him that day in Meryton!*

Georgiana hesitated. "Do you know of him, Elizabeth?"

Elizabeth slowly nodded, too horrified to speak.

"I was at Ramsgate for the summer with my companion, Mrs. Younge, in whose character my brother and I were both deceived," Georgiana explained. "Fitzwilliam surprised me the day before I was to leave for Gretna Green with George. He was furious and demanded I end my engagement. I could not grieve him, Elizabeth. Fitzwilliam has raised me alone since I was a little girl. It was not long until George's true nature revealed itself to me in any case. I am truly ashamed."

"No. You have no reason to feel ashamed, Georgiana. You were very young at the time. Mr. Wickham preyed upon your innocence and your trusting nature. You cannot be held accountable for what he tried to do. Believe me, I am well acquainted with Mr. Wickham and his… *expectations* of young ladies." Georgiana was startled by the bitterness in her voice.

They spent the next half hour in earnest conversation about Mr. Wickham until it was time for them to part and dress for their evening at the theatre, each lady feeling a little easier for having confided in the other and feeling a genuine bond of sisterly friendship that would only continue to grow deeper with time.

Colonel Fitzwilliam peered into the drawing room, praying he would find his cousin alone, and slipped into the room.

Darcy, who was standing by the window, turned at the sound of the door clicking shut. He could not help but laugh at the picture his cousin presented. He found it diverting to see Colonel Richard Fitzwilliam, one of the bravest men in Her Majesty's Army, reduced to a state of senseless fright every time he entered Darcy House. "Fear not, Fitzwilliam. The two youngest Miss Bennets have removed to Gracechurch Street for the evening. You are safe, for tonight anyway."

"Thank God!" he exclaimed as he threw himself into a nearby chair. "How on earth did you happen to manage that feat?"

"Actually, you have Mr. Bennet to thank. It seems he has decided to take pity on you." Darcy handed him a glass of wine as they waited for Jane, Elizabeth, and Georgiana to join them. Bingley would be meeting them at the theatre.

"Well then, I shall do so when next I see him." They sipped their wine in companionable silence. "I understand my parents paid you a visit earlier in the week." Darcy nodded. "I would like to offer my support to you and Miss Bennet, as well. From what I have seen of her, she is an excellent woman. I believe, Cousin, that had I met her first, second son or not, I would have been quite unwilling to relinquish such a treasure to any man, to say nothing of the likes of you."

Darcy smiled. "Believe me, Fitzwilliam, when I say there is no other woman like Elizabeth. You can have no idea what she is to me, no idea at all. I have been completely at her mercy from nearly the very first moment of our acquaintance, yet I was too proud to acknowledge it for far too many weeks. She had absolutely no idea of my regard, which, I will admit, when I finally realized it, pained me considerably. When I now think of what I would have missed had I not declared myself and continued to stubbornly resist her beauty and her wit, it frightens me to no end. I am determined to spend every moment of my life leaving her in no doubt of my affection."

Colonel Fitzwilliam laughed. "Yes, I noticed as much the other afternoon. I do hope you realize we are not blind, Darcy. Your affection for Miss Bennet is quite transparent to all who have had the pleasure of seeing you together. No one could ever doubt your deep attachment to her, but I assume you also realize it could very easily be misconstrued by gossips and naysayers. I hope you will restrain your eagerness for her society when we are out in company tonight. As your marriage has yet to be sanctioned by the church, I doubt very much you will wish to call attention to Miss Bennet and yourself in any way that may assist in lending credibility to Aunt Catherine's slander. Be very careful with her, Cousin. There is far more at stake here than just Miss Bennet's reputation."

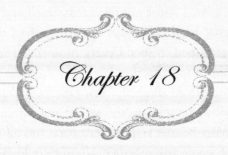

Chapter 18

With a scowl, Darcy promised his cousin he would be on his best behavior for the evening, but his word proved difficult to keep once he saw Elizabeth wearing her new emerald gown. He had found himself paying the modiste and her staff a personal visit earlier in the week, and it was far from sociable. Indeed, Mrs. Duval had been so apologetic and so regretful of the treatment Elizabeth had received that she had promised the completion by Thursday of at least three of the gowns Elizabeth had ordered, including the one she would wear for her wedding. They had all arrived earlier in the day with Mrs. Duval's compliments, accompanied by two of her most trusted assistants to see to any necessary adjustments that might have had to be made. Elizabeth had spent the bulk of the afternoon closeted in her rooms with Jane and Georgiana, trying them on.

Darcy thought she looked stunning in the dark green silk creation she had chosen to wear that evening. It was elegant and tasteful while showing off her curves in a most flattering manner, making him conscious of the fact that he had not been alone with her for days. It took every ounce of restraint he possessed not to pull her into his arms and press his lips to her mouth.

The emerald and diamond necklace he had given her was beautifully displayed against her creamy breasts. He swallowed hard and repressed a powerful urge to reach out his hand and caress her, to take both soft globes in his mouth and make her moan with pleasure. *God, but I want her! How am I ever going to make it through this damned evening without touching her?* Darcy could already tell he would fail miserably and, terrified he would soon take to acting upon his forbidden impulses, ran a shaky hand through his hair.

Darcy's eyes bored into her with a searing heat that reached all the way to her inner depths, causing Elizabeth to flush each time she met his gaze.

Throughout the evening Darcy struggled to remain a gentleman, keeping the physical contact between Elizabeth and him to a minimum, but by the commencement of the second act, he was almost at his wits' end. Throughout the entire first act he had not been able to tear his gaze from her at all. He had found himself mesmerized by the small smile that played across her lips and the sparkle in her eyes as she watched the actors perform on stage. He observed the steady rise and fall of her breasts as she breathed and the way her tresses bounced when she laughed. She was sitting in the corner of the box, to his right, and, deducing that very little would be discerned by anyone else in their party in the darkened interior of the theatre, he slowly slid his fingertips along the contour of Elizabeth's leg.

He felt her body tense. She closed her eyes, and Darcy repeated the action, watching her lips part and her breathing become more rapid. He felt an immediate tightening in his trousers as he observed the swell of her breast, and his own breathing increased. Impulsively, he took her hand and placed it in his lap, over his arousal. Her eyes flew open, and he began to stroke the length of her arm with agonizing slowness.

Finally, Elizabeth turned her head and met Darcy's intense gaze. She felt a deep pull within her and an insistent throbbing between her legs, which made her long to run her fingers over his erection. It suddenly seemed far too long since she had last felt his touch, but this was not the place to act upon such desire. She swallowed hard and fought it, finally succeeding in pulling her arm from Darcy's grasp. He seemed unwilling to relinquish her easily, giving in only after Colonel Fitzwilliam leaned forward in his seat and pointedly cleared his throat.

Against his better judgment, Darcy continued to try his hand at coercing Elizabeth throughout the remainder of the play.

Shortly before the play was to end, she had finally had more than she felt she could possibly bear, and rose from her seat under the pretense of getting some much-needed fresh air. She brushed past Bingley and Jane on her way out of the box. They hardly noticed.

Not half a minute later, she heard Darcy's voice call to her. She was but halfway down the grand staircase and stopped to wait for him. He was carrying her new fur pelisse and gloves, as well as his own coat, gloves, and hat. When they reached the entrance, he eased the pelisse to her shoulders, and his fingertips lingered. With Darcy's hot breath upon her neck, Elizabeth began to fasten the clasps, and a feeling of unease descended upon her. She found herself thinking of Georgiana and the conversation they had earlier in the afternoon. Her discomfort with the situation increased. Elizabeth knew that, though they appeared to be quite alone at the moment, they were still very much in public, in a crowded London theatre full of people who would be descending upon them in a matter of minutes. It was too much for her, and she found herself pulling away from him just as his lips brushed her cheek.

Darcy drew close to her once more and murmured in her ear, "You are so beautiful tonight, my love. I hardly know how I have managed to keep my hands from you this evening. You have been driving me to distraction ever since I first saw you in the drawing room." The soft timbre of his voice sent shivers down her spine.

"I believe we are currently in the middle of a theatre, Mr. Darcy," she said with only a shadow of her usual archness. "From what I knew of you in Hertfordshire, sir, I would have expected the master of Pemberley to be well practiced in the art of self-control by now."

Darcy laughed, his breath stirring the curls upon the nape of her neck, and said, "I believe that was only when you first knew me, Miss Bennet, for it has been many, many weeks now since you have managed to drive away all remaining fragments of that self-control I had once so prided myself upon." He then gently directed her gaze to where their images were reflected in the panes of a large window. "Look at you, Elizabeth. Have you ever seen any woman looking as beautiful as you are this evening? My God, but I have missed having you in my bed."

He had placed his hands upon her waist and was leaning forward to allow his lips the pleasure of kissing her neck when she withdrew from him again, her face flushed scarlet. She hurriedly walked toward the window and put distance between them. "Fitzwilliam," she implored, "please, I beg you would not. Not here."

He only continued to look at her with that same fire in his eyes. It was as though he had not heard one word she had said to him, and it angered her enough to say, in a low voice, "I remember a time, sir, when you almost murdered a man who had dared to speak disrespectfully of me. I would dearly wish to know what has changed so much since that day to have made it acceptable for you to behave thus with me in the middle of a public theatre? Have your aunt's words already faded from your memory? Have the remnants of my reputation come to mean so little that you would risk causing a scandal here?" She gestured to their surroundings. Darcy instantly paled.

His shock, however, very soon gave way to growing indignation. Wrapping his hand around her upper arm, he escorted her from the building and out into the street, where he ordered their carriage. They stood without speaking until it came. No sooner had they seated themselves inside and closed the door than Darcy drew the shades and spoke, his voice shaking. "You dare to compare my conduct with the disgusting behavior of that… that despicable blackguard?"

Elizabeth visibly swallowed and turned aside her head. He leaned forward and grasped her chin in a somewhat rougher fashion than he had intended, and directed her face toward his. Elizabeth flinched, and after several seconds, Darcy released her. He slumped back against the interior of the coach to run the back of his hand across his pursed lips. "Is that truly what you think of me tonight, Elizabeth? That I have so little respect for you that I would act upon the same self-serving, loathsome impulses George Wickham possesses?"

"No," she said with no little vehemence, "of course, you are *nothing* like him. You could *never* be like him." A lone tear rolled down her cheek then, soon to be followed by another. She wiped them away. "Forgive me. I should never have spoken so. You are the last person who deserves such an unfeeling and unjust reproach for what I, of all people, should well know to have been simply a passionate response to the love you have for me. I do not know what is wrong with me tonight. Perhaps I am only too aware that we have not had a moment to ourselves in several days, but that can hardly compare with the fact that I am… not proud of our conduct this evening, and I am afraid my disapproval must also extend to several other, rather specific, unguarded moments we have spent in each other's company while we have been in London, as well."

She laid her head back against the seat and closed her eyes. "To this day, Fitzwilliam, I have no idea what Mr. Wickham said to you to make you lose control like that. Perhaps it is best that I never know, but after what has transpired this afternoon, I can imagine only too well what it probably was, and it is, perhaps that, more than anything else, which has me feeling so very much unlike myself tonight."

Darcy stared at her with growing concern. "What do you mean 'after what has transpired this afternoon,' Elizabeth?" When she did not immediately answer him, he reached across the coach and placed his hand upon her knee. "Elizabeth, did something happen this afternoon that I should know about?"

Elizabeth took a deep breath and nodded. "Georgiana has revealed to me that she is aware that you and I have anticipated our wedding vows. It was not my intention to confirm or deny it, but the mention of such a subject quickly led to other questions she has had regarding trust and broken promises. She also shared something with me that was both very personal and extremely difficult for her. To be honest, I was stunned."

Darcy could hardly believe his sister would have mentioned such a thing to anyone—even to Elizabeth—but he had to know for certain what he thought and what she had actually heard were, indeed, the same thing. "Did she tell you about Wi… about Ramsgate?" he asked.

Elizabeth nodded. "She told me everything. I am certain you, more than anyone, are well aware that Wickham's treachery has greatly affected her self-confidence and her trust of others—of gentlemen in particular. A great deal of her distress this week has been owing to her belief that you, the one person she had felt she could trust implicitly not to behave in a similar manner had, in all actuality, seduced me, thus jeopardizing my reputation and causing all of our recent difficulties with Lady Catherine. I, of course, informed her that is far from the truth. I do believe I finally managed to convince her of it by the time we parted to dress for the theatre, but it does not lessen the guilt and mortification I must bear for our thoughtlessness and our total want of propriety while in company with others—your sister, especially. You must admit, Fitzwilliam, we have been far from discreet about hiding our gestures of intimacy toward each other since I have arrived in London. Even in Hertfordshire, there were times when we were less than careful."

Darcy only looked at her, unable to say anything, his distress written on his face. "I am worried your sister is not the only one who knows for certain of our indiscretions," Elizabeth admitted. "I am terrified to think of what my family would say if they were to find out, and I am very much afraid of the whole of London hearing that Mr. Darcy of Pemberley, who could have married any woman in the first circles of society, has chosen to marry, instead, a fortuneless country upstart whom he has taken as his… as his *mistress*." She whispered the last word, tears welling up in her eyes.

Darcy scoffed. "That is absurd, Elizabeth."

"Is it?" she asked. "Lady Catherine said very much the same thing to you, did she not?"

His face paled. "Is this what you have been thinking all evening? Every time I touched you, was I making you feel as though you are my mistress?" She said nothing, only averted her eyes. Darcy crossed over to the other side of the carriage to sit beside her and cradled her face in his hands. Elizabeth swallowed. *Yet another breach of propriety.*

"Elizabeth, please," he pleaded. "Have I truly made you feel this way tonight?"

She closed her eyes and shook her head. "No. At least not at first. It was not until we were in the lobby that I had begun to feel… oh, what is the point?" she asked tiredly. "The damage has already been done, has it not?"

Darcy's voice was soft and regretful. "It was never my intention to draw attention to us or to cause a scandal; you know it was not. I have missed you, Elizabeth. The last four days have been more than difficult for me. Even though we have shared the same house and have seen each other daily, I have not had a moment alone with you, and it has been driving me mad. I have been praying for an opportunity to express my love and devotion to you beyond mere looks of longing from across the room or a chaste kiss upon your hand. Perhaps my box was not the best venue for such a show of affection, but I believed you would have felt much the same after being unable to have so much as a moment to ourselves."

"Fitzwilliam," she said gently, "by no means do I object to you expressing your love for me. It has always been something I have welcomed and cherished, but I must now ask that we at least try to refrain from being so unguarded with our affections when we are not in the privacy of our own home and within the sanctuary of our own family party. We have only to wait two days, and we shall be husband and wife. I realize it has been difficult; it has been so for me, as well, but please, we must at least consider Georgiana and her feelings, not merely our own."

Darcy colored. "I suppose I had hoped any speculation about us would simply disappear upon the arrival of our wedding day. I have been completely irresponsible in more ways than just one." He raised her hand to his lips and bestowed a lingering kiss upon it as he caressed a curl at the nape of her neck. "I will endeavor to control myself when I am in your presence, my love. My uncle"—and here, he had the decency to blush—"has also alluded to our familiarity on occasion but has pledged his support and that of my aunt no matter what occurs. I confess his reassurance in this quarter may have lulled me into a false sense of security. The earl is a very powerful man, and he is truly taken with you, you know."

Elizabeth flushed, as well, and raised her hand to his cheek. A slow smile warmed Darcy's features. "Do you have any idea how exquisite you look this evening?" he murmured as his lips caressed her palm.

Elizabeth leaned toward him and placed a kiss upon his lips. "Indeed," she whispered, "I would not know, Fitzwilliam, for I have been far too preoccupied with the handsome gentleman before me to notice."

Chapter 19

DARCY RAISED THE SHADES AND RESUMED HIS PROPER PLACE ON the other side of the carriage just before the play ended and the patrons began to file out of the theatre and into the street. Rather than leaving Bingley, Jane, Georgiana, and Colonel Fitzwilliam to wander about in search of Elizabeth and him, Darcy waded into the fray to find them. After being accosted by numerous acquaintances inquiring about the identity of his beautiful companion and wondering where she had disappeared to, he finally returned to the coach with the rest of their party. While Bingley ordered his own carriage and assisted the ladies, Colonel Fitzwilliam took his cousin aside. "Is all well, Darcy?" he asked with a furrowed brow.

"Yes, Fitzwilliam, perfectly well. Elizabeth only required a bit of fresh air."

The Colonel then raised his brow, and Darcy sighed. "Very well. I fear I have kept my word very poorly this evening, and believe me, Elizabeth has already had much to say on the subject. Fear not. I believe I have finally learned my lesson and will attempt to behave myself until Saturday. After that, I cannot be held accountable for my behavior, and you will just have to accustom yourself to my having an extremely pretty wife whose fine eyes may tempt me to act as I would not otherwise in polite company. But, as I promised Elizabeth, I shall endeavor to show my affection for her only when we are within our own family circle, and not until after our wedding. Will that do, Fitzwilliam?"

The Colonel laughed and slapped him on the back. "Well enough, Darcy, well enough. I suppose I shall just have to overlook your offenses, so long as you promise not to hide yourself and your lovely wife away from the rest of us."

Darcy gave his cousin a wide smile as they made to climb into his carriage. "Follow Mr. Bingley's carriage to Grosvenor Street, Foster." With a sharp rap upon the roof of the carriage, they were off.

The two carriages pulled up in front of Mr. Hurst's house on Grosvenor Street, and the ladies within were immediately handed down to the safekeeping of the gentlemen. They all made their way into the house with very little ceremony and were shown into the drawing room, where they were received by the Hursts and Miss Bingley, who, much to that particular lady's vexation, were unable to join them at the theatre due to a prior engagement.

After about ten minutes of perfunctory conversation, Mr. Hurst stood and addressed his wife. "I say, Louisa, those blasted Saundersons hardly fed us properly when we dined with them this afternoon, and I have been starving now for a good five or six hours since. I say we dispense with this chatter and eat. What say you, Bingley?"

Bingley, as could be expected, remained speechless, but Mrs. Hurst rolled her eyes and steered her husband and his empty wine glass in the direction of the dining room. Bingley escorted Jane, and Darcy was about to offer Elizabeth his arm when he found it suddenly seized by Caroline Bingley instead. She immediately engaged him in meaningless banter as she dragged him with some effort toward the dining room, leaving Elizabeth staring after them. Every attempt Darcy made to return to her was met with fierce resistance by Miss Bingley, and so he could only look back at his betrothed. While she followed on Colonel Fitzwilliam's arm with Georgiana, she smiled, and her brow arched.

Dinner was the usual affair—usual meaning Elizabeth found herself placed as far from Darcy as she had become accustomed to during her visits at Netherfield.

Darcy, as ever, found very little pleasure in the seating arrangements. Elizabeth made a valiant effort to lighten his dark mood by casting playful looks in his direction from the opposite end of the table. Being seated next to Caroline Bingley was hardly to Darcy's liking, particularly after the serious tone of the earlier discussion he and Elizabeth had in the coach outside of the theatre. Though it now appeared she had discovered an ample diversion in their current circumstances, he still had no idea what she was truly thinking at the moment, and it bothered him.

When the gentlemen separated from the ladies after supper, Darcy, for the first time in a long while, found himself hesitating. He had no wish to separate himself any longer from Elizabeth, and from what he could see from her frequent glances, neither did she wish it. There was, however, very little he could do about it, and when Colonel Fitzwilliam clasped him firmly on the shoulder on his way to the study, he reluctantly followed, determined to return in a timely fashion to Elizabeth's side, whether his host was willing or not.

The ladies soon settled themselves in the drawing room. Mrs. Hurst sat by complacently while Miss Bingley made a show of fawning over Georgiana. Jane and Elizabeth were simply ignored and left to their own devices. Elizabeth, who had grown quite used to their rude behavior in Hertfordshire, found this all rather amusing, but Georgiana found much to distress her and tried her best to include her future sisters in her conversation with Bingley's sisters. Finally, after Miss Darcy had cast many uncomfortable glances at Elizabeth and Jane, Mrs. Hurst said to Elizabeth, "Miss Bennet, I do believe we are very soon to be wishing you joy. When will the happy event take place, do you think?"

Resisting the urge to glance at Miss Bingley, Elizabeth replied, "I am to marry Mr. Darcy on Saturday." The slightest smile of satisfaction curved her lips as she heard Miss Bingley choke on her meringue, the remnants of which landed on the finely woven carpet at her sister's feet.

Mrs. Hurst leaned over to pat her sister on the back and continued as though nothing untoward had occurred. "Oh, so soon? Will you be staying in Town after the ceremony or removing immediately to Pemberley?"

"I believe Mr. Darcy plans on remaining in London for some time."

Caroline Bingley had, by this time, recovered sufficiently to add, "What a treat for you, Miss Eliza. I am certain all of Mr. Darcy's fashionable friends will be thrilled to make *your* acquaintance this Season. What a shame no one from his family will likely be in attendance at your wedding." She leaned forward and continued in a confidential tone, "Now do not worry yourself, Eliza. I am certain their absence can only mean they have yet to learn of Mr. Darcy's understanding with you. It cannot possibly be because his closest relations disapprove of you as his choice. Perhaps he has not yet seen fit to inform them of his intentions and simply plans to present your marriage as a sort of fait accompli, so to speak. That way you may be spared the embarrassment of having someone as illustrious and powerful as the esteemed Lord Matlock objecting outright to your alliance."

Jane and Georgiana wore identical expressions of incredulity. Elizabeth, however, smiled sweetly as she said, "Actually, Miss Bingley, Lord and Lady Matlock have assured me they will both be in attendance with the rest of their family. They and Colonel Fitzwilliam have been very warm and attentive ever since we had the honor of being introduced."

Miss Bingley refused to allow this information to deter her and so tried her hand again. "I suppose you shall be married from your uncle's house in *Cheapside*, Miss Eliza? I daresay Lord and Lady Matlock will find it charming, attending the wedding breakfast within full view of your uncle's warehouses." She and Mrs. Hurst could hardly keep themselves in check and, so, burst into fits of laughter.

Jane, who had not thought her two future sisters-in-law quite so bad as this, gasped. Before Elizabeth could form her biting reply, however, Georgiana had placed her hand upon her arm and forced herself to say, "Of course, Mr. and Mrs. Gardiner will be at the wedding, but Elizabeth and my brother shall be married from our house in Grosvenor Square. Our patronage in the church is very important to my brother, and since Darcy House will soon be Elizabeth's home, as well, she has graciously agreed to indulge us. As far as my uncle and aunt are concerned, they are both quite taken with Elizabeth. I do believe my uncle already considers her to be a favorite. They plan to hold a ball in honor of Elizabeth, and as my brother detests large gatherings, you can imagine he shall insist the guest list be kept to a rather smaller number of his closest friends and intimate acquaintances." She said this last part with a pointed look at Miss Bingley, who suddenly recalled something very pressing that required her immediate attention on the other side of the room.

The gentlemen rejoined them shortly thereafter. Darcy was rather relieved to find Elizabeth and Jane in rapt conversation with Georgiana. Mrs. Hurst was attending them with disinterested politeness. Miss Bingley, who had noticed him immediately from her perch on the settee at the other end of the drawing room, rose and glided toward him.

"Oh, Mr. Darcy, I do believe I owe you my congratulations, sir! I had no idea we were to lose you a mere two days from now. What a loss for all of the accomplished ladies of the *ton.* You are doing us all quite a disservice, sir. So many hearts shall surely be broken." Her sly smile repulsed him. "I do not suppose you are having second thoughts, sir? I do believe it is customary for many gentlemen to reconsider their options before taking such a fateful plunge." Miss Bingley moved in closer, gripping his arm tightly, and purred in a throaty voice that made him cringe, "You know, it is not too late to change your mind, Mr. Darcy."

Darcy disentangled himself from her grasp and directed a warm look at Elizabeth. "No, that is quite unnecessary, I assure you. You find me only too willing to make the most beautiful woman in all of London my wife."

Miss Bingley's face contorted in obvious displeasure and, before she could think better of it, blurted out, "Well, then I wonder at your wanting to marry Elizabeth Bennet."

"What?" The room stilled, and Darcy fixed her with a look of contempt so menacing that Miss Bingley actually recoiled. Convinced she may have finally crossed a fine line Darcy had drawn, she dared not do anything more than stare after him as he walked quickly away to join Elizabeth, Jane, and Georgiana, his body stiff. Colonel Fitzwilliam, who had joined them moments earlier, stood with his brows raised while Bingley, sporting a scowl that rivaled Darcy's, crossed the room in three strides and steered his offending sister out of sight and into another room at the end of the hall.

With a glance at her husband, Mrs. Hurst abandoned her chair to follow them but was halted by Mr. Hurst's stern voice. "Louisa, sit! I will have none of this in my house! Now fetch me a brandy and one for Bingley's Miss Bennet, as well. I daresay she looks as though she could use one."

All eyes shifted to Jane, who did, indeed, look pale. "I… no, that is… please, you must not worry over me. I will be fine in a moment. Really, it is nothing."

Elizabeth knelt in front of her. "Dearest Jane, do not distress yourself on my account. Truly, Miss Bingley said nothing that causes me any grief. Actually," she continued with a smile, "I confess myself rather disappointed in her scant efforts tonight. I have grown quite accustomed to receiving far more disparaging remarks from her sharp tongue." Elizabeth's eyes gleamed as she shook her head. "No, tonight she was not up to her usual high standard at all! Perhaps she is feeling suddenly unwell, or perhaps something particular has driven her to distraction?" Elizabeth turned a mischievous smile on Darcy, who raised his brow as she, Georgiana, Colonel Fitzwilliam, and Mr. Hurst erupted into laughter. It was not long until Jane joined them.

A reluctant smile broke on Darcy's face, as well. As he watched the woman he loved more than life itself, laughing along with the others, he could not help but marvel at her selfless ability to transform an unpleasant scene he knew must have brought her some degree of pain and mortification into a diversion for the benefit of her beloved sister. He doubted he would ever be able to do such a thing—find folly in an otherwise intolerable situation, laugh when he would rather have cried, even for Georgiana's sake. At that moment he felt an overwhelming urge to go to her, but not because of any physical desire. He wanted only to enfold Elizabeth in his arms and hold on to her, to place kisses in her hair and tell her how much he loved her, how much having her in his life, returning his love, meant to him.

They would be married in only two days' time, and Darcy had promised her father he would not go to her before then, but, as he continued to look upon her in the middle of the Hursts' drawing room—so beautiful, so vibrant, so strong, yet so vulnerable, one thing became undeniably certain to him—he did not relish the unhappy prospect of being unable to offer his consolation to her on that night, especially given their earlier talk in the carriage outside of the theatre.

Bingley returned to offer his sincerest apologies to a rather surprisingly jovial set of people. His sister, however, did not. Concern for Miss Bingley soon drove Louisa away, but the rest of the party spent another half hour rather pleasantly without their society before finally acknowledging the lateness of the hour.

While Darcy made his farewells to Bingley and Mr. Hurst, Colonel Fitzwilliam handed the ladies into Darcy's carriage. Colonel Fitzwilliam entered the carriage before him, and by the time the master of Pemberley joined them, he found the only option left to him was a vacancy by Elizabeth's side. He hesitated several seconds, and Elizabeth extended her hand to him and laced her fingers with his as she gave him a tired smile. Darcy glanced at the others in the carriage, but they all seemed to be suspiciously well occupied, either looking out of windows, examining gloves, or searching through reticules.

At last, Darcy seated himself beside Elizabeth, giving her hand a small squeeze as he raised it to his lips and then placed it upon his lap. He heard her quiet sigh, a sigh of exhaustion, emotional as well as physical, and felt her turn her face into his shoulder for a fleeting moment. It had been a difficult day for her—a difficult week, actually—and, without so much as a second thought, Darcy turned his head to bestow a kiss upon her temple as he allowed himself to whisper ever so softly, so only she would hear, "How I love you, my dearest, loveliest Elizabeth."

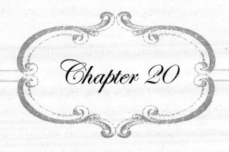

Chapter 20

Elizabeth awoke early Saturday morning to find her maid, Sonia, bustling about in preparation for her mistress's morning bath. She smiled as she threw back the counterpane and reached for her dressing gown. Despite the numerous trials of the week, this was Elizabeth's wedding day, and she was convinced nothing could spoil it.

Sonia gave her a happy, knowing look. "Good morning to you, ma'am. Your bath will be ready shortly, and a tray will be sent up to you in an hour. Mrs. Hildebrandt said it will not do to have the master see you in all your finery before you are wed, and thought it best you break your fast in your room this morning."

"Thank you, Sonia. Please tell Mrs. Hildebrandt I appreciate her thoughtfulness." The young woman nodded and slipped from the room.

When Elizabeth stepped into the steaming bath, she did so with a sigh and leaned her head back against the soft towel that had been placed on the rim of the tub. A warm feeling of relaxation and contentment settled over her, and her thoughts soon drifted to Darcy. Though their courtship had been brief and riddled with difficulties, she could assuredly say it had been a most enjoyable time for her.

Not only was Darcy a passionate, caring man who was unafraid to show her his affection, he was also considerate and generous, almost to a fault. He was more than willing to do any little thing for her comfort and pleasure, and she was truly surprised by the lengths to which he was willing to go in order to secure her happiness. She smiled to herself, recalling the day before when her mother, in her effusions over the impending nuptials the following day, had managed to work all her daughters and poor Georgiana into a fit of nerves that could have rivaled her own. Just when Elizabeth had been certain she could take no more, Darcy appeared with Mrs. Hildebrandt.

"I do not mean to intrude, Mrs. Bennet, but Mrs. Hildebrandt and I find ourselves at quite a loss over certain unresolved details for the wedding breakfast tomorrow. We were wondering whether you would be so kind as to assist us, as it is truly of the utmost importance."

He cast a meaningful glance at Elizabeth and, though his demeanor appeared to be just as serious as ever, she recognized a slight twitch at the corners of his mouth. She was certain it was discernible to no one but Georgiana and herself, and she had to turn away for a moment to hide her smile.

"Ah, but I see you are very busy at the moment. Forgive me, madam. I am certain the cook can work out some other alternative to the fish we were planning to serve. Perhaps we shall just go without? What say you, Mrs. Hildebrandt?"

The plump housekeeper then replied, in a voice that sounded suspiciously well rehearsed, "Why yes, sir, whatever you think is best. I shall tell Mrs. Richards immediately that we shall simply go without the fish."

"What do you mean, *go without*? Go without? I should say not! Where is this cook of yours, Mr. Darcy? I daresay I shall set her to rights before long! No fish for my own daughter's wedding breakfast, indeed!" She turned to Elizabeth, who had to struggle to keep her composure. "Lizzy, you shall just have to do without me, I am afraid, for I am needed immediately to organize the wedding breakfast. I cannot be bothered with these other trivialities just now," she said as she waved her handkerchief at her daughter. "Your gown is lovely, and I am sure your maid shall do an excellent job with your hair, child. You need not worry yourself over a thing, especially now that Mr. Darcy has seen fit to consult me on the business of the breakfast. Sir, you were very right to come to me."

That having been said, she ran ahead of Mrs. Hildebrandt to find the cook. The housekeeper looked back at her master, casting him a look of some trepidation, to which he only nodded. Elizabeth looked to Darcy with a raised brow, barely able to contain her amusement, and Darcy returned her look with a dazzling smile. Raising her hand to his lips, he bowed to her and quitted the room, leaving the ladies to continue their plans and preparations unencumbered.

It was not until much later in the evening that Elizabeth had finally found an opportunity to speak with Darcy alone, for, though she and her sisters had not been forced to bear her mother's excessive raptures or disapprobation throughout the course of the afternoon, she had discovered the same could not be said for Darcy.

She found him in his study, with a cup of hot tea and some biscuits, reading over some matters of estate business that he had put off to attend Mrs. Bennet. Darcy rang for a servant to bring another cup, and Elizabeth happily joined him.

With an arch smile, she said, "Though I had no doubt you were speaking the truth when you once said you would do anything in your power to ensure my happiness, sir, I confess I had not completely comprehended the lengths to which you were willing to go in order to secure it. I believe I am indebted to you, Fitzwilliam, for your selfless act earlier this afternoon."

Darcy, who was in the midst of raising his cup to his lips, returned her smile. "Yes, I believe you are, my dearest."

"So, did you enjoy your afternoon?" she asked.

Darcy laughed. "Let us just say it was an experience I am not particularly eager to repeat any time soon. I confess I had no idea fish, meats, cakes, breads, flowers, table linens, china, and whatever other details with which your mother saw fit to torture me were of such import to becoming your husband, Elizabeth."

Elizabeth bit her lip. "Was she very awful, then?"

"No. *She* was not awful. It was the endless list of details and frippery that exhausted me to no end. I believe that in all the time I have known her, I have never once seen your mother expend her efforts beyond the pursuit of eligible husbands, the gleaning of gossip, and shopping. I must say, however, when redirected to another purpose entirely, she is quite a force to behold. She is determined you shall have nothing but perfection on your wedding day, Elizabeth. I was moved by her devotion to you. It is obvious your mother cares a great deal for your happiness."

Elizabeth smiled, pleasantly surprised he would have made such an observation of her mother. "Indeed, Mama is devoted to all of us in her own unique way; however, I suspect her taking such a tremendous interest now in *me* has occurred only to such an extent because I am to marry *you*. Though I know she does love me dearly, I have never been a favorite of my mother. That is an honor that

Jane and Lydia must divide between them, and I might add, one that I have always been perfectly content to forego."

"Does that not trouble you, though?" he asked.

Elizabeth shook her head. "Not at all. I have always had an excellent relationship with my father, which has more than made up for any disinterest on my mother's part. He and I are far better suited, both in disposition and in taste. I suspect it has been harder on Kitty and Mary, though."

"Yes, perhaps."

Returning her cup to its saucer, Elizabeth inquired, "And what of your parents, Fitzwilliam? Were you closer to one more than the other?"

Darcy's answer was immediate. "My mother. Like you and your father, we shared many things in common. We would while away many hours out-of-doors, walking the paths around Pemberley, talking of books, philosophy, music, art. In the evenings, she would play the pianoforte and sing for my father. She taught me how to play, as well, though I hardly ever do now and never in company. She had a beautiful singing voice, not unlike your own. In many ways you remind me of her, Elizabeth. She had your spirit, your zest for life, your talent for talking to others, your fervent devotion to those she loved. I know she would have loved you, as well."

Elizabeth smiled sadly. "You must miss her very much."

"I do. She died when I was but twelve. I was devastated, as was my father. Regrettably, Georgiana has no memory of her."

"She must have passed away, then, when Georgiana was but a very small girl."

Darcy looked away and swallowed. "When she was only a few days old," he said softly. He got up and walked to the window, raking his hand through his hair, and then walked back to the desk.

"Georgiana looked very much like my mother, and my father adored her, doted on her. He devoted many hours to her amusement and did all he could to encourage a bond between us, but for the first year of her life, I could hardly bear to do more than look upon her. I found it too painful. I blamed her for my mother's death."

"But you are both very close now," she added.

"Yes. Yes, we are," he murmured. "Not long after Georgiana had reached her second year, she fell ill with fever. She was not expected to live. Late one night, I went to the nursery where the doctor was tending her with my father. Her tiny body looked so frail and lifeless. It was then, while watching my father pray for the life of his only daughter—the daughter my mother had desired so much that she had been prepared to die for her—when I suddenly realized just how important my baby sister had become to me. At that moment I dropped to my knees and made a promise to God: If he allowed Georgiana to live, I would, from that day forward, be the elder brother she deserved. Regrettably, I have not always succeeded in keeping that promise."

Elizabeth had no doubt Darcy was alluding to Ramsgate. Without a word, she reached out to him and took his hand. He gave hers a squeeze and then pulled her to her feet, touching his forehead to hers as he stroked the softness of her cheek. "Enough," he said softly. "It was not my intention to burden you with my painful memories of the past. Tomorrow we are to be wed, and then we shall begin our life together, one that shall be built on nothing but our love and happiness. No sorrow, no pain, only joy from this moment forward."

"You know, Fitzwilliam, that sounds suspiciously like my own philosophy. I heartily believe in thinking only of the past as its remembrance gives us pleasure."

Darcy's lips grazed her hair. "So it does."

Elizabeth kissed him before laying her head against his chest and drawing his body closer. The soft thu-thump of his heart soothed her. "Then it is settled," she sighed. "We shall be the happiest couple in the world."

Darcy could hear the lightness in her tone and the conviction in her voice, and smiled.

"Ma'am?" Sonia's voice roused Elizabeth from her bittersweet reverie. "Ma'am, forgive my intrusion, but you must make haste if we are to have you dressed and ready in only a few hours."

"Yes, thank you, Sonia," she said as she rose from the tub to dress for the day. *My wedding day*, she thought with a smile.

As Darcy and Bingley stood in the church awaiting Elizabeth's arrival, the latter leaned in close to his friend and whispered, "I say, Darcy, you look as though you are going to your death. Smile, man. It is your wedding day, after all, not your funeral."

Twisting his signet ring, Darcy replied, "Bingley, you know how I detest being in front of a crowd. I cannot help but feel as though I am on display."

Bingley chuckled. "I would hardly call a handful of your closest relatives, the Bennets, and Mr. and Mrs. Gardiner a crowd, Darcy."

"Perhaps," Darcy conceded as he shrugged, "but you cannot deny that I am certainly on display at the moment." He ran the back of his hand across his mouth in apparent agitation, then, leaning toward his friend, he said in a low voice, "I must confess, Bingley, I had given very little thought to any of this beyond being wed to the woman I love. I cannot thank you enough for standing up with me."

"You are most welcome, Darcy. Fear not. It shall soon be over. Then you will have three months in which to recover before you must journey to Hertfordshire to bear witness to my own happiness." Darcy rolled his eyes, an indulgent smile upon his lips, as with a wide grin, Bingley slapped him on the back.

After a few moments of awkward silence, Darcy's gaze darted to the door of the church before falling upon the dozen or so relations murmuring in the pews. His brow furrowed, and he said, "Bingley, I cannot help but notice the absence of your sisters and Hurst. I thought they had intended to be present today. I hope they are well."

Bingley gave his friend a wink and said, "I suspect they are all in excellent health, though Caroline is, no doubt, mourning your loss, or rather, her own, with all the dignity and grace of a truly accomplished lady."

Darcy shrugged. "No doubt."

"To be honest," Bingley continued, "you have Hurst to thank. He did not trust Caroline to hold her tongue and behave herself, and I must admit I cannot but share his opinion. He forbade them to attend today. Of course, Louisa cried and carried on, trying her utmost to change his mind, but he held firm, declaring that the future Mrs. Darcy deserved to celebrate her wedding day with those of her friends who sincerely wish to share in her happiness, not disparage her good name."

A smile turned up the corners of Darcy's mouth. "I cannot but agree, as well. I shall have to thank your brother-in-law properly when next we meet." Properly, of course, meaning a case of the finest brandy from Pemberley's cellars.

Their attention was then called to the door at the entrance to the church as it opened to admit Jane, who walked toward the altar with a serene smile. It was not difficult to ascertain the direction of Bingley's thoughts as he watched her approach. By the expression on his face, Darcy expected he was, even at that moment, rethinking the length of his engagement.

It seemed like an eternity had passed before Elizabeth appeared, but when she finally began her slow promenade down the aisle on her father's arm, Darcy's breath caught, and he felt a distinct lump form in his throat. Never before had he seen her looking more lovely and more desirable than she was at that moment. She wore an exquisite gown made entirely of snowy white silk. Beautifully draped, the garment flowed to the short train trailing behind her. The cut was simple and sophisticated, and accentuated her curves. The flattering neckline showed her beauty to its full advantage without being too revealing. There was no ornamentation on the dress beyond some intricate embroidery and pearl beadwork along the bodice and hem of her gown. To Mrs. Bennet's vexation, not a drop of lace was to be seen, but it needed no further embellishment. Adorning Elizabeth's neck was a beautiful pearl and diamond necklace, a companion piece to her engagement ring. Her hair was swept up and arranged in an elegant style; her locks fastened in place by dozens of pearl hairpins of various sizes, all gleaming in the early morning light of the church. Matching pearl-drop earrings dangled from her ears, and rather than the traditional wedding bonnet, a long length of Belgian lace, procured by her Aunt Gardiner at her mother's insistence, covered her head.

To Darcy, she looked like royalty. He could hardly contain the joy he felt knowing she was just moments away from becoming his wife. He forgot himself for a moment and started to go to her, but his eagerness was immediately checked by his uncle's chuckle. Darcy flushed with heat, and when Elizabeth finally reached his side, he saw her eyes sparkling with amusement. As her father placed her hand in his, she gave him a breathtaking smile. Unable to resist her, Darcy returned it with a smile of his own and silently uttered a prayer of thanks for his excellent fortune at having found her.

The minister called them to attention by clearing his throat to begin the ceremony, and Darcy reluctantly released her hand. While Elizabeth seemingly made an effort to attend to everything the elderly gentleman said, Darcy found himself hard-pressed to focus his attention on anything beyond the beautiful woman before him. He was startled back to cognizance when he heard the minister say, "Fitzwilliam Darcy, wilt thou have this Woman to thy wedded Wife, to live together after God's ordinance in the holy estate of Matrimony? Wilt thou love her, comfort her, honor, and keep her in sickness and in health, and, forsaking all others, keep thee only unto her, so long as ye both shall live?"

Darcy gazed at Elizabeth and, in a voice brimming with such intensity of feeling that it could not but move her, and many others, as well, replied, "I will."

From the pew where she stood with her husband, Mrs. Bennet smirked with satisfaction. She was vastly pleased by the match her second-eldest daughter had made for herself. Darcy's interest in Elizabeth had come as nothing short of a shock to her. That the refined and reticent master of Pemberley was not only drawn to, but actually seemed to *prefer*, the wild ways and wry wit of her least favorite daughter to the superior beauty and serene countenance of her eldest, was a concept Mrs. Bennet still found rather difficult to grasp. Watching now, however, as that same daughter stood at the altar, pledging her obedience to her wealthy bridegroom, she was forced to concede that Elizabeth looked every inch the mistress of Pemberley.

Indeed, Mr. Bennet had been reluctant to part with so many hundreds of pounds for her gown and trousseau, but, as far as Mrs. Bennet was concerned, it was money well spent, if for no reason other than to gloat over the approving looks and knowing smiles that graced the distinguished faces of certain members of the peerage who happened to be in attendance. In any case, no one could deny that Darcy was completely smitten with his bride, whose beauty on that day, her mother was forced to concede, rivaled that of her own dear Jane.

Elizabeth finished reciting her vows, and upon receiving an encouraging nod from the minister, Darcy took her left hand in his and placed the simple gold wedding band upon her finger, which announced to all who saw it that he and Elizabeth were now man and wife. As their eyes met, a warm, affectionate smile passed between them. Elizabeth looked radiant, and Darcy beamed with uncontainable happiness. They were married! Elizabeth was his wife! Never again would he have to part with her. She was his, now and forever. At that moment, he wanted nothing more than to kiss her tempting lips and whisk her away to the ends of the earth, but the ceremony was not yet over.

Three-quarters of an hour later they were in Darcy's coach and on their way back to Darcy House for the wedding breakfast. Elizabeth laid her head against his shoulder as they sat side by side, and a small, contented laugh escaped her lips. Darcy smiled as he held her hand tightly upon his lap, his gaze fixed upon the gleaming gold band she now wore on her left hand. Slowly, he turned his head to place a kiss upon her hair and murmured, "I take it you are well, Mrs. Darcy?"

Elizabeth laughed again. "Yes, extremely well, Mr. Darcy."

He placed another kiss upon her temple. "I am very glad to hear it. I want you to know I will do everything in my power to ensure your happiness, Elizabeth. I shall deny you nothing that will bring you pleasure. You need only ask."

Elizabeth withdrew her head from his shoulder and turned so she could look upon his face. The love and devotion she saw in his eyes was overwhelming, and for a moment, she was too overcome to speak. Holding his intense gaze, she drew closer to him and swallowed several times. "Kiss me then, Fitzwilliam," she whispered, and without any further encouragement, he did just that.

The wedding breakfast had been proclaimed a monumental success by all in attendance, and to Mrs. Bennet's immense delight, Lord and Lady Matlock had been impressed by all the attention she had paid to even the most minute of details. Even Darcy had to agree that Elizabeth's mother had quite outdone herself, though her resulting success had been at the expense of his staff, who had suffered immensely under the strain of her command.

As a special surprise to Darcy, Mr. Bennet announced the removal of his entire family party to the Gardiners' house on Gracechurch Street for the remainder of their stay in London, which would conclude in two weeks' time. Lord and Lady Matlock invited Georgiana to stay with them in Berkeley Square, as well, and after some further consultation between the two families, an invitation to Matlock House was also extended to Jane, Mary, Kitty, and Lydia so the five young ladies might continue to benefit from one another's society. Colonel Fitzwilliam made a valiant attempt to disguise his horror at such a prospect, but there was very little he could do about it, since he did not have a house of his own to which he might escape the effusive, not to mention persistent, admiration of Elizabeth's two youngest sisters. Only out of complete desperation did he plead his case to his cousin for temporary asylum at Darcy House.

As could be expected, his request was met with hearty laughter. "You must be desperate, indeed, to make such an outrageous request of me on my wedding night, Fitzwilliam. But I am afraid I must disappoint you, Cousin, as I have no plans whatsoever of entertaining the likes of you when I now have a beautiful new wife to distract me with her considerable charms."

"Be not alarmed, Darcy," Colonel Fitzwilliam countered in a tone that begged him to reconsider, "I assure you I will be no bother at all. As a soldier in Her Majesty's Army, I am quite used to amusing myself. I shall not interfere with you and your lovely bride."

Darcy could not but laugh again. "It pains me to say it, Fitzwilliam, but I am afraid you will just have to bear the Miss Bennets' visit with fortitude. After all, is that not what they teach you soldiers in the army?"

Colonel Fitzwilliam grumbled something incoherent that Darcy could not quite make out, but laughed at all the same, and before he could be set upon once again by Lydia, quickly moved to quit the room.

It was not until late in the evening that all their guests finally departed Darcy House, leaving the newly married couple completely to themselves but for the servants. The door had barely shut upon Mr. Bennet, who, Darcy suspected, had purposely stayed to such a late hour only to inflict some form of final punishment upon his son-in-law for the liberties he had taken before his marriage to his favorite daughter, when the clock struck nine o'clock.

Without preamble, Darcy pulled Elizabeth into an intimate embrace, claiming her lips with a passionate kiss that left her clinging to him, breathless and wanting more of the same. He was only too happy to oblige her by trailing his lips along the delicate curve of her neck, across her shoulders, to the ample swell of her breasts as they teased him from beyond the neckline of her gown. Not until his attentions produced a moan from his wife did Darcy's senses finally return, and he discovered they were still standing in the middle of the front hall on full display.

Gathering Elizabeth in his arms, he held her for several moments, willing his rapid breathing to slow. He placed a kiss upon her curls and inhaled her scent. "My wife," he whispered, his voice full of feeling.

Elizabeth gave him a mischievous smile as her fingers toyed with his cravat. "Is there nothing you would care to show me in your study, Mr. Darcy?"

He stared at her a moment in incomprehension before a rakish smile overspread his face. "I should say not. Tonight, Mrs. Darcy, I shall ravish you properly—in our bed in the master's chambers, where you belong."

She giggled, and lifting her easily in his strong arms, he raced up the staircase and down the corridor leading to his private rooms, pausing only long enough to push open the door and kick it closed again with a thrust of his foot. It was with great embarrassment that they were then met by Darcy's valet, Mr. Stevens, who had been waiting to attend his master.

Without releasing his wife or tearing his gaze from her crimson countenance, Darcy dismissed his rather perturbed valet with strict orders not to return on the morrow unless summoned. Darcy then instructed him to relay a similar message to Sonia, who was, undoubtedly, awaiting Elizabeth in the mistress's chamber. With what dignity remained in his possession, Mr. Stevens hastened from the room.

Darcy carried his blushing bride to the bed and laid her upon it, reclaiming her mouth with a tenderness that sent delicious shivers through her body. Elizabeth deepened their kisses and coiled her fingers into his hair. She pressed herself against her husband's strong body and felt his arousal grow even harder against her.

With a moan, Darcy buried his face in her neck and ran his tongue along her flesh while his hands busied themselves with her breasts. Through the silk of her gown, he felt her nipples become hard and took to rolling them between his fingers, eliciting a gasp and then a low moan from Elizabeth. Disentangling her fingers from his hair, she explored his upper body. When she reached his waist, she lingered there, caressing his waist and hips. Darcy rolled onto his back, bringing Elizabeth with him, and kissed her with feeling as she kilted her skirts above her knees and straddled him.

Darcy released her and ran his fingers over her stockinged legs with a featherlight touch until he reached her garters. Elizabeth arched back her neck, enjoying the sensation of his hands as they caressed her. He unfastened her garters and eased her silk stockings from her legs before continuing his exploration, onward to her hips and then to her derrière, which he massaged and kneaded as she rocked herself against him. Her breathing increased with each movement, and she felt deeply satisfied when she heard her husband's gasp of pleasure.

Darcy's hands slid upward along her back to the many intricate fastenings of her gown. Elizabeth leaned forward and claimed his mouth with hers, their tongues performing an intimate dance. Many, many minutes passed before he finally managed to undo the very last button, tugged gently at the delicate material, and freed his wife's shoulders from the confines of her gown. His mouth descended to her newly exposed skin while his hands moved onward to release her breasts, and further still, until Elizabeth's dress pooled around her hips. She helped him with her corset, chemise, and petticoats, and soon, Darcy beheld her in all her splendor as she sat astride him, her body glowing in the moonlight that filtered down upon them from the windows on either side of the bed.

He gasped at the sheer beauty of her, moved beyond words as he savored the sight of her curves and the passion in her eyes as she returned his intense gaze.

She leaned forward to work the knots of his cravat free, and then the buttons on his tailcoat, his waistcoat, and his shirt. Elizabeth eased the articles from her husband's body, allowing her hands to linger upon his flesh, caressing the smooth plains that had been hidden from her sight. She swallowed and lowered her lips to his, teasing them apart with her tongue.

Darcy moaned against her as her hands blazed a path of fire from his shoulders all the way down his torso to his waist, stopping only when she reached the buttons on his trousers. Elizabeth took her time, releasing each one slowly, taking care to caress his straining erection with one hand as she worked each button free, making Darcy writhe beneath her. "Oh, God, Lizzy, yes," he panted against her lips before recapturing her mouth in an ardent kiss.

Elizabeth's heart quickened. It was the first time he had ever referred to her as simply "Lizzy," and in such an intimate setting, it had an intense effect on her. She returned his passionate kisses, her desire for him flaring while both her hands worked to pull his trousers down his legs.

Darcy lifted her from his lap to remove them himself, as well as any other remaining articles of his clothing. When he returned to the bed and began to move toward her, she surprised him by pushing him back down so he could lie, once again, upon his back.

Starting with his neck and moving downward to his chest, Elizabeth began to cover his body with deep, sensual kisses. When she reached his abdomen, she felt him stiffen, though whether in anticipation or trepidation, she was not yet certain. She raised her head, hoping to gauge his wishes, and found him watching her intently, his eyes filled with desire, his breathing heavy and ragged. When she ran her tongue over her lips, she saw him swallow hard and close his eyes. When he opened them again, he silently formed her name.

With a seductive smile, Elizabeth lowered her head, keeping her gaze fixed upon his face. When he felt the softness of her cheek graze his arousal, his body shuddered, his eyes closed, and a moan escaped from his lips. His moans became louder as he felt the tip of her tongue touch him tentatively. When her warm mouth finally encircled him, taking him in while the velvet of her tongue caressed his length, he lost all coherent thought, abandoning himself completely to the overwhelming sensations she was exciting in every fiber of his being.

It was not long before Darcy's moans became cries of ecstasy. Overwrought with desire, he slowly opened his eyes to see Elizabeth's curls, with so many tiny pearl hairpins intertwined throughout, outlined against his pale flesh as she moved over him. Suddenly, it was too much, and he called out for her in his urgency.

Before he reached his peak, however, Darcy suddenly disengaged himself from her mouth and, pulling her toward him, captured her lips with his in a fierce kiss that demanded her very essence. He ran his hands over her body, stroking her in all the ways he knew would bring her pleasure. His fingers soon found their way between her thighs, and as he began to massage her most sensitive flesh, she cried out for him. That cry and the exquisite wetness within her proved his undoing. Her body, as well as her voice, beckoned to him, and he could no longer resist the call of either.

Taking care not to be unduly rough with her, Darcy eased Elizabeth onto her back and covered her with his body. Between ragged breaths, he managed to pant, "Forgive me, my love, but I can wait no longer for you," and in the next instant, buried himself deep within her, expelling a long, shuddering cry as he entered.

Elizabeth, too, could not help but sigh with pleasure and, as he began to move within her, wrapped her legs tightly around him, pulling him farther within her depths. She met his every thrust with raised hips, moving with him as though they were both one and the same. As the heat of their embrace began to build to an almost intolerable pitch, she could feel the delicious warmth coming. Her muscles tensed, and her back arched, and Darcy drove himself into her, ever deeper, ever faster, until they were both suddenly overtaken by earth-shattering waves of ecstasy.

So powerful was their joining, it took a long while before either was able to return from whence it was they had journeyed together. Fearing his weight was growing oppressive, Darcy rolled onto his side, taking Elizabeth with him without disengaging from her body. He held her securely and rested his forehead against hers, still struggling to regulate his rapid breathing. He kissed her deeply, entwining his fingers into her hair, disturbing the last few remaining hairpins that had chanced to survive their lovemaking. When he released her lips, he buried his face in her neck and let out a long, shuddering sigh as she stroked his cheek. "There is truly no woman like you, Elizabeth."

Darcy raised his head, and Elizabeth gazed into his eyes, so full of his love for her, and could not help but smile. "So you have discovered," she whispered. He kissed her again, tenderly, and they spent the rest of their wedding night engaged in numerous activities meant to reassure each other of their fervent devotion.

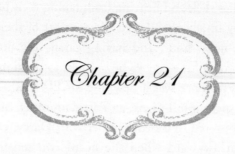

Chapter 21

Needless to say, the newly married Mr. and Mrs. Fitzwilliam Darcy did not rise at their usual early hour the following morning. Having been intimately engaged in passionate occupations throughout the course of the night, sleep had no claim on them until the very first rays of dawn began to show themselves through the windows. Nestled together in an intimate embrace, with Darcy's chest pressed firmly against Elizabeth's back, they finally allowed themselves to succumb to exhaustion.

Some time after nine o'clock, Darcy awoke, still cradling Elizabeth in his arms. He inhaled deeply of her scent, which permeated his pillow, his counterpane, his entire body. He found the sight of her, with her tousled mane of curls and her creamy skin, intoxicating, and, no longer able to resist the feel of her body snuggled against his, Darcy feathered gentle kisses upon the woman sleeping so soundly in his arms. After kissing, caressing, and stroking Elizabeth into a state of desire, he made her his own once more, spilling his seed into her as he gasped her name against the curve of her neck. Then they slept again. Every few hours they would awaken, teasing, tasting, making love to one another, sometimes with exquisite care, sometimes with wild abandon.

Afterward, both would collapse, breathless, their limbs entangled and their bodies slick and heaving from taking their pleasure.

When they finally abandoned the comfort of their bed, it was well past the noon hour, and having eaten very little the night before, Darcy rang for a tray to be brought to them in their sitting room. This experience was a new one for Elizabeth, who, having never before spent a full night, an entire morning, and part of an afternoon, cloistered in a bedchamber with Darcy, could not but feel somewhat awkward when she heard two servants enter the outer room.

There, they found a tray ladened with an assortment of delicacies. They partook of the bounty before them at a leisurely pace, Darcy hand-feeding her pieces of succulent fruit and Elizabeth teasing him with kisses upon his neck while he enjoyed a particularly heavenly chocolate torte. The dessert was soon abandoned in favor of far more satisfying fare, namely his wife, and they spent another hour or so unaware of anything beyond each other.

They lay spent, Elizabeth stroking her husband's chest while he toyed with one of her long curls. Then he tilted his head closer to her and placed a kiss upon the top of her head. "What should you like to do this evening, Mrs. Darcy?" he asked in a lazy, contented voice.

She was thoughtful for a moment before responding with a laugh. "I believe, Mr. Darcy, that I should very much like to take a hot bath."

"Mmm. An excellent idea," he said. He kissed her again and then reluctantly rose. "Shall we use mine, then, or would you prefer we use the one in your rooms?" he asked as he slipped into his robe.

Elizabeth stared at him. "*We?* Do you mean to say that you intend to join me, sir?"

Darcy nodded.

"In my bath?" she asked, her tone incredulous and her brow raised nearly to her hairline.

"Yes," he said, but then noticed her frown. "Surely this does not bother you?"

"I am surprised, that is all," Elizabeth stammered. "I have never before *shared* my bath, Fitzwilliam."

He returned to her and placed a kiss upon her lips as his hand caressed the softness of her cheek. "I am very relieved to hear it," he said with a low growl and a roguish gleam in his eye. He kissed her again, this time more deeply, drawing forth a long sigh of satisfaction from Elizabeth after he released her. "Come, my wife," he said, "and I shall attend you."

The days immediately following the wedding were amongst the happiest Darcy and Elizabeth had ever known. The couple found great enjoyment being in one another's society, spending an inordinate amount of time abovestairs in the master's chambers, enraptured with one another. Quite unused to seeing the very proper and otherwise conventional master of Pemberley flouting even the most minuscule customs of propriety, the staff of Darcy House soon found themselves unprepared for the unguarded and rather amorous behavior they caught him engaging in with his pretty new wife in public locations throughout the house, including, but not limited to, stolen kisses and intimate embraces in the hallway abovestairs, in the conservatory, in the master's study, in the breakfast parlor, in the music room, and in the library.

Not at all eager to embrace the prospect of receiving callers at Darcy House so soon after having installed his lovely bride to her rightful place within, the master gave strict instructions to Mrs. Hildebrandt and the rest of his staff that he and Mrs. Darcy were not at home to visitors, and therefore, under no circumstances, save for the gravest of family emergencies, were they to be disturbed by company until well into the new year. If left solely to Darcy, the couple would easily have remained sequestered for many weeks, nay, many months on end, however impractical that may have proven to have been.

While content to remain exclusively in her husband's society, Elizabeth could not, in all good conscience, forego celebrating the Christmas holidays with her family so long as they chose to remain in London. Therefore, on the twenty-fourth of December, it was with no small degree of difficulty she finally managed to persuade her uncooperative and surprisingly petulant husband to dress for dinner and order their carriage to deliver them to Gracechurch Street. There, they would pass the evening in the most agreeable company of her aunt and uncle, father and eldest sister, and, for Darcy, at least, the almost unbearably trying company of her mother and three younger sisters.

As could be expected, dining once again with the Bennets was a lively affair, made even more so by the addition of Bingley, Georgiana, and the Gardiners' four young children, all under the age of eight, whose excellent manners, incidentally, Darcy was not the least bit surprised to see far surpassed those of their elder cousin Lydia. Even after several days under the solicitous instruction and care of Lady Matlock, Lydia still appeared to be the same wild, flirtatious young woman she had been before; perhaps made even more so since Colonel Fitzwilliam was installed under the same roof, leading her to fancy herself enamored with him at all hours of the day and well into the night. Upon hearing her regale her mother with accounts of her outlandish escapades and machinations, all designed and executed at the expense of ensnaring the colonel, Darcy winced and fervently prayed that his cousin would not hold his outright denial for asylum in Darcy House against him. Indeed, his conscience was so guilt ridden that, should Colonel Fitzwilliam happen to show up on the doorstep later that very night begging his assistance, Darcy swore to himself he would permit his poor cousin occupancy for the duration of the Bennets' stay in Town, even if it should be another month complete; though nothing, he suspected, would make up for the very great imposition of being the object of Lydia Bennet's attentions.

Though they were a large party, Mrs. Gardiner chose to keep the dinner informal by leaving her guests to select their own seating arrangements, thus ensuring all in attendance were happily situated and at ease with their dinner partners. While Elizabeth was more than pleased to sit with her new sister to her right, Darcy was not so happy to have to relinquish the chair to her left to Mr. Bennet, who made a show of claiming the honor of his daughter's company on the occasion. Fearing he would be left conversing with Mrs. Bennet, Mary Bennet, or, worse still, with an exuberant Kitty or Lydia, Darcy seized the opportunity of sitting beside Mr. Gardiner, with Jane to his left. With Bingley seated on her left, Darcy could hardly expect his sister-in-law to be an attentive dinner companion, but it hardly mattered, as he had found Elizabeth's uncle far from wanting in that respect whenever he had been in company with him. Throughout the meal, they had intelligent discourse on all manner of subjects, oftentimes including Mrs. Gardiner in their discussions, who, to Darcy's immense pleasure, seemed to be particularly knowledgeable and well informed on all aspects of her husband's business affairs and political interests.

The entire party attended church services together at the cathedral located in the same area of town in which the Gardiners lived. Darcy was thankful for this arrangement, as it afforded Elizabeth and him some much-desired privacy—far more, he knew, than they would have received had they chosen to attend his own church near their neighborhood in Grosvenor Square, where many people knew him by sight, rather than by name and reputation alone. The service was very beautiful, and, not for the first time, Darcy found himself watching his wife, whose warm smile and glistening eyes were an indication of how moved she was by the miraculous spirit of the season. Darcy squeezed her hand and held fast to her until it was time to quit the church. Even then, he found himself willing to release her only until they had reached the privacy of their carriage, where he promptly took her in his arms and held her as the coach swayed and rocked over the cobbled streets on its way back to their Mayfair neighborhood.

By the time they arrived home, it was very late, and Elizabeth wanted nothing more than to retire to the warmth and comfort of Darcy's arms. She quickly dressed for bed and joined him in his room, slipping beneath the counterpane to be enveloped by her husband's embrace. She sighed in contentment as his lips caressed her curls. "How I have longed to have you to myself all evening," he murmured against her hair. "You looked beautiful tonight in your crimson gown. I daresay you must have done it on purpose to torture me."

Elizabeth let out a soft laugh as she snuggled against his chest. "Yes, I see you have finally figured it out, Fitzwilliam! No, my vanity will never again be satisfied with my being considered only *tolerable.* Heaven forbid you should once again find me *'not handsome enough to tempt you'!* As the wife of the formidable Mr. Darcy of Pemberley, it would be most unpardonable on my part. And you are now well aware that I loathe to be a cause of disappointment to you, my dearest husband."

"You delight in teasing me, do you? Shall those wretched words never cease to haunt me, Elizabeth?" he asked with a rueful smile. Then, in a more serious tone, he said, "It was extremely ill-mannered of me to ever utter such an untruth. Though it is hardly an excuse, I fear I was far from being in a good humor that evening. I am afraid I was prepared to say anything to have Bingley leave me in peace, even at the risk of wounding the most beautiful young lady at the assembly." His fingers skimmed over her shoulder, sending shivers of desire through Elizabeth. "I do not believe I have ever regretted saying anything more in my life than I have those words. Will you never forgive me?"

"My love"—she laughed lightly—"I hardly think I would have married you one week ago had I not already done so." She tilted her head up to him in order to look upon his face. "Truly, Fitzwilliam, it has long been forgot; however, as your wife, I must reserve the right to tease you about it on occasion."

"Apparently, it has not been long forgot, but very well, my lovely wife, if you insist, *I* must then reserve the right to do *this* on occasion." He then leaned in to kiss her. "Do you object, Mrs. Darcy?" he whispered.

She swallowed and, with heavily lidded eyes, shook her head. "Who am I to object to something that brings us both such pleasure?"

"Elizabeth," he said in a ragged voice, his eyes filled with desire, "you cannot possibly know the true extent of what loving you has done to me. You have become everything to me, Elizabeth—*everything.*"

He kissed her again, teasing her lips apart with his tongue so he could taste all the delights of her mouth as he clasped her body firmly against his. *"Everything,"* he breathed, over and over again. *"Everything,"* as he slowly eased her back onto the pillows and covered her body with his. *"Everything,"* as he tasted and tantalized her in all the ways he knew would bring her pleasure, and finally, a softly gasped, *"Lizzy,"* as he skillfully brought them both over the edge of their passion, the familiar, dizzying waves of ecstasy washing over them in a release so poignant, so powerful, it would cost them every remaining ounce of energy they possessed between them.

Elizabeth awoke the following morning to find Darcy observing her with an expression of contentment. She stretched and laid her hand upon his cheek, which, having not yet been shaven, felt delightfully abrasive. "Merry Christmas, Fitzwilliam," she purred.

Darcy caressed her lips with his own. "Merry Christmas, my sweetest Elizabeth," he murmured happily. Before he could return his lips to hers for another kiss, however, she gently pushed him away and sat up.

"I almost forgot! Wait right here, and do not leave before I return." And with that, she threw back the counterpane, wrapped herself in her discarded dressing gown, and hurried to the door that joined her husband's rooms with hers. She returned in a moment with a small, neatly wrapped box and handed it to Darcy with a look of delight as she climbed back under the covers.

"What is this?" he asked.

"It is a present, my dearest," she replied, barely managing to contain her pleasure.

"Elizabeth, there is no need for you to give me any gifts."

"Yes, I know, but I wanted to give you this gift. You have been so wonderful to me, and I merely wished to do something special for you in return. Now open it, Fitzwilliam, before Christmas is over and the New Year is upon us!"

Darcy smiled and began to remove the thick paper surrounding the box. He lifted the lid to find several gentlemen's handkerchiefs, all embroidered with his monogram. He removed them and was about to compliment her on the fine quality of her workmanship, when he beheld a beautifully painted miniature of his beloved wife staring up at him, a glint of mischief in her eyes, which the artist had captured to perfection. "Elizabeth! This is absolutely exquisite. It is exactly what I have most desired, after having been so fortunate as to acquire the original, of course," he said with a grin. "Thank you. I shall carry it with me and treasure it always."

Elizabeth beamed. "You are very welcome. I was hoping you would."

Darcy ran his finger over the glass covering the miniature, caressing with tenderness the tiny version of his wife. "It is truly an excellent likeness of you. Did you sit for it while you have been in London?"

Elizabeth smiled. "No, I had it framed in London. I sat for it when I was still in Hertfordshire."

"Hertfordshire? May I ask the name of the artist?"

"Bennet," she replied.

It was not what Darcy had expected to hear. "Bennet?"

"My sister Kitty has many talents aside from that of chasing after poor, unsuspecting officers with Lydia. She was very pleased to do it and took great pleasure in the knowledge that it would be my gift to you. I believe she has never before concentrated so much of her effort on one tiny painting!"

"It is a small masterpiece. I had no idea Katherine was so gifted. She would benefit greatly from having a London master, do not you think?"

"That she would, indeed; however, my parents hardly have the means to support such an endeavor."

Darcy looked at her with a twinkle in his eye. "And are you not the mistress of Pemberley, Mrs. Darcy? Surely, we can well afford to have your sister stay with us in Town and forward her education."

Elizabeth kissed him soundly. "You are truly a generous man, Fitzwilliam."

He laughed. "Yes, I certainly am!" He removed himself from her embrace and left the bed to procure a small, elegantly wrapped parcel from his own dressing room. When he returned, he presented it to Elizabeth with a flourish and resumed his place beside her under the counterpane.

Without ceremony, she eagerly tore off the wrapping, exclaiming with pleasure at the delicately painted porcelain box she cradled in her hands.

Darcy lifted the hinged lid, and a beautiful melody began to fill the room. Elizabeth smiled as he explained, "It is a waltz. It is still considered quite scandalous in England, but I assure you it is very popular in Austria. A gentleman and a lady twirl and glide across the dance floor, holding one another quite close. It is very beautiful to watch but, I daresay, highly inappropriate." He smiled as he gave her a penetrating look of longing. "I am determined to dance with you someday while I hold you in my arms, Elizabeth. No doubt, it will bring me immense pleasure."

She placed the music box upon the nightstand and wrapped her arms around his neck. "Well, until then, sir, perhaps you will allow me to bring you immense pleasure in some other way?"

"I would by no means wish to suspend any pleasure of yours, Mrs. Darcy."

Christmas day at the Fitzwilliams' home in Berkeley Square was, most unfortunately, a far cry from the pleasurable evening Darcy and Elizabeth had spent with her family in Gracechurch Street the night before. Though Elizabeth did experience many enjoyable moments conversing with Georgiana, Lord and Lady Matlock, Colonel Fitzwilliam, and his brothers, she found very little pleasure in the society of Lady Catherine de Bourgh, who also happened to be in attendance with her daughter, Anne.

Contrary to Elizabeth's expectations, Darcy's cousin proved to be quite the opposite of her mother—slight and frail, extremely pale, and almost sickly in appearance. She spoke very little to anyone, or rather, Lady Catherine did not permit her to voice more than a few syllables before interrupting. Elizabeth noticed Miss de Bourgh's sickly pallor took on a crimson hue, not only whenever her mother treated her in such an unfeeling and controlling manner, but also whenever she happened to attempt to malign Elizabeth and even Darcy, for what she deemed his inappropriate choice of wife. Though she was a young woman of very large fortune and the sole heiress to Rosings Park, which Elizabeth had understood from Mr. Collins's accounts to be a very grand estate, Elizabeth could not help but feel pity for Miss de Bourgh. In spite of her obvious wealth, her life seemed to hold little in the way of pleasure.

It was evident by the dark scowl he wore for most of the day that Darcy was by no means enjoying himself. Lord and Lady Matlock did their utmost to deflect Lady Catherine's bitter expression and scathing remarks from their intended target—her new niece—but, as that great lady was not a woman used to being gainsaid, they were not entirely successful in their endeavors.

There was one moment, however, that brought Elizabeth unexpected comfort. Anne de Bourgh, who was forever under the constant observation and scrutiny of her imperious mother, had taken great pains to secure a moment alone with her cousin's new wife, with the assistance of Georgiana and Lady Matlock. They found themselves in a small parlor abovestairs, and though a bit awkward at first, the meeting did not remain so for long as Anne, who had confessed to not being in the best of health, proclaimed her sincere delight upon having learned of Darcy's marriage.

"My dear Mrs. Darcy," she said in a demure voice, "I am thrilled for you both. I have long hoped Fitzwilliam would find a woman who would make him truly happy, as I have always known he and I have never shared my mother's misdirected opinion that *we* could find felicity with each other. We are both of such a taciturn, unsocial nature and, therefore, in desperate need of marital companions who will bring us some liveliness." She bowed her head then and said, with some emotion, "Do you think you could ever find it within your heart to forgive me for my mother's unjust treatment of you, Mrs. Darcy? I have been greatly distressed since I first learnt of it and have been increasingly more so after witnessing her abominable behavior toward you today, as well."

Taking pity upon her, Elizabeth touched the back of Miss de Bourgh's hands, which were clasped tightly upon her lap. "Miss de Bourgh, I can hardly hold you accountable for your mother's ill treatment of me. Please, think upon it no longer. I should dearly like for us to be friends."

Miss de Bourgh raised her head and looked upon the new

Mrs. Darcy with such an expression of appreciation and relief that Elizabeth had to smile. "Thank you. I should like that very much. I have had very little opportunity to form many friendships of my own choosing, and I believe your society would be a most enjoyable change of venue for me."

The two ladies, unfortunately, were to have only a few more minutes of each other's company before they were interrupted by Georgiana, who informed them that Lady Catherine was beginning to grow anxious over Anne's whereabouts. They parted, however, with the plan of corresponding with each other through Lady Matlock, so as not to invoke the wrath of Lady Catherine. Elizabeth remained abovestairs after Georgiana had led Anne back to her mother. She was relieved to have found Miss de Bourgh to be the complete opposite of Lady Catherine. She smiled as she recalled the sincerity and kindness of her address and the happiness she had shown when Elizabeth had offered her friendship.

There was a knock upon the door then, and without waiting for a reply, Lady Matlock stepped into the room with a warm smile. "So, my dear, I understand you and Anne are to become good friends?"

Elizabeth returned her smile and nodded. "Yes. I must confess I am relieved to find her extremely amiable and kind. I was happy to make her acquaintance. Though I never doubted Fitzwilliam's assurances his cousin would not be offended by his choosing me, I could not help but worry over meeting Miss de Bourgh, particularly after her mother had made such a strong impression upon me!"

Lady Matlock approached her. "You astound me, Elizabeth, with your ability to laugh over such shocking recollections. However do you manage it?"

Elizabeth shrugged and said, "I cannot say, but I have always found it is far better to laugh than to cry in some situations—one of the rare bits of knowledge I gleaned from my mother! Very often she would say or do something mortally embarrassing, which would bring a blush to my face; however, rather than crying over it, I would simply think instead of something to make myself laugh. I daresay the same philosophy shall help me greatly when moving in London society. I hear the ladies of the *ton* can be extremely formidable!"

Lady Matlock laughed. "Yes, to be sure they can. You do realize, I hope, that Henry and I will always value and appreciate you, Elizabeth. You have brought such joy to Fitzwilliam. He has known so much sorrow and loneliness since the passing of his dear parents that we cannot help but love you, as well. Whether Catherine comes to accept you or not, we shall strive to protect you from her cruelty."

Lady Matlock directed her to a small sofa across the room, and Elizabeth said, "I can almost feel sorry for her. She must have suffered cruelly at one time in order to have so very few scruples about making others feel wretched."

They sat for several minutes until Lady Matlock shook her head and said, "You are an insightful young woman, Elizabeth." She then gave her a meaningful look and reached for her hands. "I am going to share something with you, something I believe may better help you to understand my sister-in-law. You see, Catherine has suffered a disappointment in her past, and I am afraid it has had a lasting effect on her. Did you know she is the elder sister of Fitzwilliam's mother, Anne?"

"Yes, I have been given to understand that. She is Lord Matlock's elder sister, is she not?"

Lady Matlock nodded. "What you will not know, for I doubt very much even my nephew is aware of this, is when Catherine and Anne were hardly more than girls, they were introduced to Sir Lewis de Bourgh, who was considerably older than they. Though he found both sisters to be beautiful, he immediately became enchanted by Anne's wit and vivacity. He wished to marry her, but Anne did not return his regard. Sir Lewis then applied to her father, but he would not hear of it, as Anne was his particular favorite, not to mention still quite young—especially for a man nearly fifteen years her senior. Sir Lewis vowed to wait for her until she was of a more acceptable age to receive his suit, but was devastated when she became engaged not two years later to George Darcy, who was much younger and utterly devoted to Anne in much the same way her son is devoted to you, my dear. Catherine, also, was discontented with the match, as it was long suspected she was in love with George. After Anne's marriage, Sir Lewis settled on Catherine instead, though Henry has often wondered whether she accepted him more for his title and connections than for the man himself.

"It was not a happy union, made even less so by the undisguised bliss Anne and George had found together and refused to hide from society. It was obvious Sir Lewis still desired her, though he was no longer quite so open about it, at least not unless he had been drinking. When Fitzwilliam was born, Sir Lewis felt it as a personal blow. Not long afterward, Catherine gave birth to a little girl, and though she protested vehemently, her husband insisted on naming her after Catherine's sister. It made Catherine bitter, a bitterness that rules over her to this very day."

Elizabeth raised her hand to her lips, and Lady Matlock continued, "Sir Lewis doted on his daughter as he surely would have doted on her namesake. He had never doted on his wife, and Catherine continued to grow increasingly angry over his inattention whenever they were in company. In the meantime, Anne Darcy had suffered several failed pregnancies, which left her vulnerable to bouts of illness. Finally, when Georgiana was born, Anne's body was simply too weak to continue to sustain her life. When word of her failing health reached Rosings, Sir Lewis was beside himself and determined to go to her, despite the evident jealousy and displeasure of his wife, who flatly refused to visit her sister. They argued, and he left in the middle of the night for Pemberley. He had not ridden five miles beyond Rosings when he was thrown from his horse. His injuries were fatal."

"How awful!" Elizabeth exclaimed. "Poor Miss de Bourgh, to be left solely to the care of such a resentful parent, and Lady Catherine, to be left alone with a daughter who would always remind her of her husband's steadfast devotion to another woman. Though I cannot help but feel a certain sympathy for Sir Lewis de Bourgh for falling hopelessly in love with a woman who could not return his regard, I can hardly agree with his decision to marry poor Lady Catherine in her stead. Of what could he have been thinking, I wonder?"

Lady Matlock smiled. "I hardly know, but I see you have already begun to take pity upon Catherine."

Elizabeth was thoughtful for many moments. "It is not so easy to forgive her for saying such hurtful things aimed purposefully to wound, but I do pity her. How can I not when I am married to such an extraordinary man of whose regard I have daily proof? It makes me wonder, though, why Lady Catherine would ever wish to promote a union between her daughter and the son of her sister."

"I believe it would have given her a certain perverse satisfaction to see her sister's beloved son, whom I imagine she cannot help but favor, as he is so very much like his excellent father, bound to her own daughter. I believe she viewed the idea of a union between them as a sort of victory for herself, in the sense that she would have gained access to a portion of what she felt would have rightfully been hers had George Darcy only returned her regard: Pemberley." Lady Matlock hesitated a moment. "I can only hope she does not carry her displeasure regarding your marriage beyond our family circle. I would hate to see her abuse you, Elizabeth, and make it difficult to establish yourself in society."

Elizabeth frowned. "I have no doubt she will abuse me to all Fitzwilliam's relations, but would she truly be so unscrupulous, do you think, to relate her malicious rumors to those outside of her family circle?"

Lady Matlock smiled sadly. "For your sake, and for Anne's, I would like to think Catherine above such machinations; however, when one is bitter and used to behaving bitterly, I cannot so easily discount such unfeeling behavior."

They were joined shortly thereafter by Darcy. "Lady Matlock, you have been keeping my wife to yourself this last hour. It is most ungenerous of you."

Both ladies smiled and made to stand, but just as Elizabeth was about to reach him, she felt light-headed. She grabbed a chair to steady herself, but not before she was observed by Darcy, who was at her side immediately. Putting his arms about her, he asked, "Elizabeth, dearest, you are unwell?" Lady Matlock observed her with a mixture of concern and curiosity.

"No. I believe I am fine now. I felt a little dizzy a moment ago, but it has passed. Perhaps I am tired, Fitzwilliam. We were out very late last night, and I did not get much sleep."

"Yes, perhaps, my dear." It was Lady Matlock who spoke. "Why do you not lie down for a while? Fitzwilliam, you can take her to the blue room. I believe there is a fire in the grate. I will send a pot of tea, which I have found to be particularly soothing when I have experienced similar symptoms."

"Thank you, Aunt, but, if you do not mind, I believe I would prefer to return home now."

Lady Matlock smiled kindly. "Of course, my dear. Go home and rest yourself in the comfort of your own rooms, and perhaps, we might meet later this week for tea."

Elizabeth offered her a warm smile. "I would like that very much. I truly enjoy your company. In the few short weeks I have known you, you have made me feel very welcome. I cannot thank you enough for all you have done for me."

"You are very welcome." She embraced her new niece then and, with a meaningful look, said, "Take particularly good care of yourself, Elizabeth, and should you need anything, anything at all, I sincerely hope you will not hesitate to approach me."

Darcy thanked his aunt and, still very much concerned over his wife's spell of dizziness, closely attended her until they reached the privacy of their carriage, where he could finally take her into his arms and hold her.

Elizabeth surrendered herself quite willingly to the solicitous care of her husband, ever thankful for his unparalleled devotion.

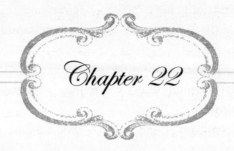

Chapter 22

THE DARCYS REMAINED QUIETLY AT HOME UNTIL THE following Saturday, when Elizabeth's family was to leave London. They met for an elegant breakfast at the home of Lord and Lady Matlock—the Bennets, the Gardiners, the Darcys, and Bingley. As a special treat for their two eldest nieces, Mr. and Mrs. Gardiner invited Jane to extend her stay in Town and to reside with them in Gracechurch Street, ensuring she would meet often with her beloved Bingley without the well-intentioned interference they had been receiving daily from Mrs. Bennet. This was met with great pleasure by everyone, especially Bingley, who felt an overwhelming sense of gratitude to the Gardiners, both for their invitation and their guarantee of constant admittance to their home.

The following Monday saw Lady Matlock, Mrs. Gardiner, Jane, and Georgiana calling on Elizabeth. Unfortunately, Darcy happened to be in the middle of attempting to persuade his wife to return with him to their room for an amorous interlude when the ladies were announced. To his further annoyance, Elizabeth invited them all to stay for luncheon, and afterward, she and Georgiana took great delight in entertaining everyone with lively duets. Their entire visit, which spanned from late morning until nearly tea time, drove Darcy practically mad.

By the time the ladies finally left, Elizabeth could hardly hold her laughter in check.

Darcy was far from sharing her amusement. "Madam, if I did not know better, I would believe you to have arranged the events of this day solely to vex me."

"Really, Fitzwilliam"—she smiled—"you do have a remarkable imagination!"

Darcy sat upon the couch and sulked.

"You should have seen the expression on your face when I invited your aunt to stay to luncheon," she said with a giggle. "You looked positively wretched, my dear."

"Elizabeth, it is hardly a laughing matter. A man could come to great harm by repressing his ardent desire for his wife."

"Oh! Is that so?" she asked with a slightly raised brow, failing miserably at assuming a more serious countenance.

"Well," Darcy mumbled with no small degree of ill humor, "it certainly felt that way today."

Elizabeth smiled seductively and positioned herself on his lap, her fingers exploring his shoulders, snaking their way around his neck and toying with his impeccably tied cravat. "My poor, poor husband. How selfish and unfeeling a wife I have been to you. While *I* have passed a delightful afternoon in the company of our most excellent relations, *you* have sacrificed your physical well-being for *my* pleasure. How shall I ever make it up to you, Mr. Darcy?"

Her impertinence could not but please him. Indeed, he had always reveled in her teasing. "I hardly know, Mrs. Darcy," he pouted, "but I daresay it will require a very significant amount of time to accomplish."

"Well, then, my dear," she said, "I do believe we should begin immediately, if we are to be on time for supper."

To Darcy, who had been more than willing to oblige her at any given moment throughout the duration of the afternoon, this was all the invitation he required, and he entwined his fingers somewhat roughly in Elizabeth's hair, disturbing the many jeweled hairpins that held it securely in place, scattering them upon the couch and on the carpet. His mouth met hers in a desperate kiss that revealed every ounce of his pent-up desire. Elizabeth felt his hands upon her body—touching, stroking, kneading, demanding—claiming every inch of her as his own. It seemed as if he could not get enough of her, and it thrilled her to see the potent hunger in his eyes when he finally released her lips to draw a deep, staggering breath.

In one smooth motion, Darcy was on his feet and striding toward the door, which he promptly closed and locked before returning to gather her in his arms. They were in the music room, and to Elizabeth's surprise, instead of reclining with her upon the couch or the carpet, he carried her to the pianoforte, where he seated her, not upon the bench, but upon the instrument itself. He raised her skirts and pulled her forward to sit upon the edge, spreading wide her thighs. His breathing was rapid. Without ceremony, he wrapped one arm about her hips as he pushed two fingers into her depths and then withdrew them, brushing over her folds as he did so. Elizabeth shuddered as he raised the fingers to his lips and inserted them into his mouth, his eyes holding hers with a quiet ferocity she had not yet seen. When he spoke, his voice was rough, hoarse with emotion, raw with his need. "Lie back now, Elizabeth. I wish to taste more of you." She gasped at his boldness but readily complied when she felt pleasure wash over her as he bathed her most sensitive flesh repeatedly with his tongue. She was soon crying out for him as the tension coiled tighter and tighter until, finally, she arched her back, and her release was upon her.

Though satisfied by his wife's powerful reaction to such attention, Darcy was hardly sated, and without further warning, he released his straining arousal from his breeches and was upon her, sliding her farther back upon the instrument as he covered her body completely with his. He entered her with one deep, powerful thrust that tore a cry of pleasure from each of them.

His movements were frenzied, passionate, and it did not take long before he was driving Elizabeth, once more, to the brink of ultimate release. She wrapped her legs about his hips and met him stroke for stroke, raising her hips to meet him with a determination that matched his.

It was more than he could bear. "Lizzy, oh God," he moaned with urgency before he filled her with a fiery explosion of such intensity it wracked his body for many long moments.

Elizabeth reached her pleasure just seconds later, gasping his name.

Later that night, as she lay in her husband's arms in the privacy of their rooms, Elizabeth could not but think upon their passionate escapade in the music room late that afternoon. She could not say what had shocked her more—having her husband make love to her in such a public room of the house, and in broad daylight no less, or her having allowed it in the first place. She found it thrilling, however, beyond a doubt, and as she drifted off to sleep, she found herself wondering whether the heavy desk in the library or perhaps the sturdy sideboard in the breakfast parlor might not prove to be equally enjoyable as the pianoforte.

The following day saw Darcy escorting his wife back to Mrs. Duval's shoppe on Bond Street. If asked, it was an experience she would have been happy to forego. However, her husband had been adamant, pointing out that the acquisition of a mere eight new gowns would hardly carry the mistress of Pemberley through the Season. Elizabeth was forced to concede, albeit reluctantly, that he was correct.

When the tiny bell on the shoppe door tinkled, announcing the Darcys' arrival to all within, the bustling atmosphere altered dramatically. Dozens of eyes fixed themselves upon the handsome couple, several sets of which were accompanied by pale complexions and rounded mouths that suddenly felt as dry as a desert.

Elizabeth, who was not feeling quite as comfortable as she would have wished under the circumstances, forced herself to swallow down any misgivings when she saw an elegant older woman rush forth to greet them. "Mr. Darcy," she said in a warm voice, "what a pleasure to see you. Please allow me to offer you my sincerest congratulations on your marriage." She turned kind eyes upon Elizabeth and smiled with sincerity.

"Thank you, Mrs. Duval. I believe you have not yet had the pleasure of making my wife's acquaintance." Then, bestowing an affectionate smile upon Elizabeth, which he made very certain would not go unnoticed by any of those in attendance, Darcy performed the proper introductions. "Mrs. Darcy will be purchasing a significant number of gowns for her Season in Town. I trust that the utmost attention and courtesy will be extended to her by your staff. Whatever my wife wants, Mrs. Duval, I am determined she shall have. No expense shall be spared."

Mrs. Duval understood him perfectly. "I assure you, Mr. Darcy, I have every intention of seeing to Mrs. Darcy personally." Then, to Elizabeth, she said, "Indeed, ma'am, you shall want for nothing while you are a guest in my shoppe. This way, if you please."

Darcy nodded curtly as Mrs. Duval shot several disapproving looks in the direction of her eavesdropping assistants. He felt no small degree of satisfaction as he watched the meddling women avert their eyes and lower their heads, properly chagrined. With the barest hint of a smile, he escorted his wife toward a private salon, where she would soon be shown nothing but the most fashionable styles and the most elegant fabrics and adornments. Darcy took great pleasure in observing the startled faces of the modiste and her assistants as they realized the master of Pemberley, against all previously established expectations regarding husbandly duty, meant to attend his wife on her shopping excursion, and with no intention of going away.

After four tedious hours sitting in idle repose, reading the paper, drinking tea, and eating biscuits while Elizabeth selected patterns and silk, Darcy had grown weary. If left to her own devices, he had no doubt Elizabeth would have ordered only the barest number of gowns allowable, and not the thirty or so he had insisted upon. In his opinion, thirty was a minimal number of gowns for the new mistress of Pemberley. Darcy's own mother had needed at least twice that number for her social obligations in Town each Season, but he did not wish to push his luck. They could always return another day when Elizabeth had a more thorough grasp of her new position in society and what would be required of her as his wife.

When they rose to leave not an hour later, Darcy was more than ready to return to the comfort and privacy of their Grosvenor Square home. Again, many eyes turned toward them, and he made a pointed show of raising Elizabeth's hand to his lips as they made their way to the entrance to the shoppe, his gaze caressing her with a look of complete adoration, which Elizabeth returned with equal feeling. Though he had always taken great care to avoid drawing attention to himself in the past, Darcy had to admit he felt a significant amount of satisfaction in making it clear to the busybodies and gossips in attendance that afternoon that he not only valued and esteemed his bride, but that he loved her. *Let them talk about that*, he thought, with no small degree of vindication.

Out of the corner of his eye, Darcy happened to glimpse none other than Caroline Bingley as she stood with her friend Cecelia Hayward, both staring with wide eyes and raised brows at his display of devotion. In a sudden fit of irritation, he cast a cold, haughty glare in Miss Bingley's direction as he escorted Elizabeth from the shoppe. Miss Bingley's face, which had only moments before been envious, turned pale as she realized, with horror written on her face, that Darcy had just publicly cut her.

Darcy slid his arms around Elizabeth's waist and placed a kiss upon the curve of her neck. "You are utterly intoxicating, Mrs. Darcy. I daresay I shall be the envy of every man in Haymarket Square this evening."

His warm breath felt delightful against her skin. "Mmm… and I the envy of every lady, sir."

Darcy raised his brow and, with the barest hint of a smile, said, "You flatter me, Elizabeth. No one shall even notice me with you at my side, ladies included. They will be far too busy speculating about the identity of the enchanting temptress on my arm and wondering why it is she would ever be with me in the first place."

She gave him an impertinent look. "Well, I would imagine that would be quite clear. After all, I am only after your money, Mr. Darcy."

He laughed heartily. "Yes, undoubtedly, my dear. Come, or we will be late."

It seemed Darcy had been correct, for no sooner had they entered the opera house in Haymarket Square than Elizabeth witnessed an endless sea of fashionably attired necks straining to better observe them. There appeared to be an infinite number of private conversations whispered behind lace fans and gloved hands, as well as an abundance of less discreet commentary, all with regard to the mystery of her identity, the attractiveness of her person, and the simple, yet elegant, style of her dress. Elizabeth steeled herself against the intense scrutiny of the London *ton* and held her head a little higher. She felt her husband's free hand cover hers in a gesture of reassurance, his fingers linking with hers. She turned to look at him, flashing him a smile of gratitude, which he returned. To her very great relief, Darcy ignored all the curious glances and pointed looks they received and continued to lead her up the staircase to their private box, where they met the Gardiners, Lord and Lady Matlock, and Jane and Bingley.

"Well, well, my dear Mrs. Darcy," said Lord Matlock with a wink, "I believe you have succeeded in drawing the interest of quite a crowd tonight."

Elizabeth observed him archly as she replied, "How naïve of me, your lordship, for I have been under the impression these people were here to see a performance of *The Magic Flute*."

"No, no"—he laughed—"*that* is just an added attraction, my dear lady. Is it not, gentlemen?" Mr. Gardiner and Bingley concurred with warm smiles.

Darcy observed his wife openly and with admiration. "Indeed, Uncle. Though I cannot profess myself capable of speaking for the rest of the parties in attendance, I can heartily assure you I will find it very difficult to focus my attention elsewhere this evening." He gave Elizabeth a slow, seductive smile that made her blush becomingly.

Bingley could not but laugh at his once-taciturn friend. "We are already well aware of *that*, Darcy! I declare, until I leased Netherfield and we made the fortuitous acquaintance of the Bennets, I had never known you to possess such an agreeable humor! Of course, one would be a simpleton, indeed, not to find the society of such beautiful ladies anything but completely engaging." Here, he looked with love upon his dear Jane, who gave him a smile full of appreciation and affection.

"Here, here!" exclaimed Mr. Gardiner and Lord Matlock, both with indulgent smiles upon their faces.

True to his word, Darcy did almost nothing but stare at his wife for most of the evening. Indeed, Elizabeth was stunning in her elegant dove-gray silk, which seemed to shimmer with every movement of her body. He admired the way Sonia had arranged her hair, with what appeared to be one long, delicate, curling branch of sterling silver leaves entwined throughout her gorgeous mass of curls. The contrast between the color of her hair and the highlights of the silver was eye-catching. If his life had depended upon it, Darcy could not have imagined tearing himself away from the picture of enticing elegance before him.

At one point in the performance, Elizabeth turned her gaze upon him, and their eyes held for several long moments. She reached for his hand, and as the music soared, Darcy found himself leaning in, his gaze now upon her lips, and before either of them knew what they were about, Darcy surrendered every claim to rational thought and kissed her. He heard a loud gasp of shock, though whether it had come from Elizabeth or from some other source, he could not determine, for Elizabeth had immediately turned away, and as he glanced around him in the dim interior of the opera house, he noticed many curious pairs of eyes turned upon him in wonder, amusement, and censure.

"Whoever is that beautiful creature who has so enchanted your nephew, Catherine, that he would abandon all sense of propriety in full company?" asked the all-powerful Lady Malcolm, who happened to be sharing a box with several other notable dowagers across the way.

Lady Catherine de Bourgh sniffed. "She is of no consequence."

Lady Malcolm raised her brow. "Really?" she inquired dryly. "Well, I never would have guessed, as she seems to be most comfortably installed with your brother and sister-in-law, not to mention that Darcy has not taken his eyes from her all night. Humph. Nobody of consequence, indeed."

"Yes," chimed the agreeable Lady Sowersby, "I have noticed that myself. Come, Catherine! Indulge us and tell us her name."

Lady Catherine huffed and, in her most disagreeable tone of voice, said, "She *was* known as Miss Elizabeth Bennet of Hertfordshire."

Lady Sowersby and Lady Malcolm exchanged knowing looks and smiled to themselves.

"So are we to understand that the highly coveted and ever-elusive master of Pemberley has found someone who has enticed him to the altar at last?" asked Lady Sowersby, barely able to conceal her enthusiasm.

Lady Catherine snorted. "You do not know the half of it, Eleanor!"

Lady Malcolm appraised her shrewdly. "If my eyes have not deceived me, Catherine, your nephew has fallen in love with this pretty, young woman, leaving you with no prospective bridegroom for Anne and a bitter taste in your mouth."

"Fallen in love with her!" she spat. "What has love to do with anything? She has drawn him in and has ruined any chance Anne has of finding happiness. Just look what she has done to him! She is penniless and unconnected, yet he can hardly attend to anything but her!" She gestured furiously at Darcy, who was, at that very moment, speaking in Elizabeth's ear, an intimate smile playing across his lips. His wife turned to him with a smile that echoed his and laughed at whatever he had said; then she rested her hand upon his upper arm and laid her head against his shoulder for a few moments. Darcy pressed a kiss to her temple and closed his eyes. In a gesture of obvious devotion, Elizabeth lifted his hand to her lips, bestowing a kiss upon his knuckles. Lady Sowersby sighed at their touching, yet highly improper display.

"Yes," countered Lady Malcolm, her voice dripping with sarcasm, "God forbid the poor man ever finds himself happy in life." She turned toward Lady Catherine. "I daresay your favorite nephew is far better off as he is now, Catherine—married to an agreeable young woman who obviously cares a great deal for his society, rather than being constantly pursued by the countless others who care only for his prominent position *in* it."

"And a love match at that," sighed Lady Sowersby. "Just like that of his dear parents. It is precisely like a fairy tale, is it not?"

Lady Catherine only scowled, choosing not to respond, and they soon turned their attention back to the performance on stage.

Chapter 23

"Forgive me, Bingley. I realize I should not have allowed my temper to get the better of me, but considering the circumstances, I am afraid it could not be helped. I had it on good authority your sister had been responsible for regaling her friends with her distorted prejudices regarding Elizabeth's situation and the nature of my attentions to her during the course of our courtship. She was hardly discreet, as several of Mrs. Duval's assistants were speaking most improperly of the hateful gossip Caroline had imparted to Cecelia Hayward in their presence."

Darcy rose from the mahogany desk in his study to stand before the window, clearly agitated. "To this day, Elizabeth has not spoken of it to me, but Georgiana immediately informed me she had witnessed firsthand the very great pain and mortification Elizabeth experienced that day in Bond Street. Your sister's bitterness led the staff to treat Elizabeth with rudeness and contempt. In light of that fact and the unpleasant scene that unfolded at Hurst's home shortly before my wedding day, I can no longer pretend your sister's behavior toward my wife is anything other than calculating and spiteful. I will not stand idly by and allow my wife to be harassed and humiliated, Bingley."

Bingley ran his hands over his face and sighed. "No, of course not, Darcy, nor will I allow it. Do not forget that Elizabeth and I shall soon become brother and sister." Bingley walked several paces. "Damn! I had a strong suspicion Caroline had purposely withheld some sort of pertinent information regarding her encounter with you in Bond Street the other day. Now I have a much better understanding as to why. Thank you for enlightening me."

Darcy walked to the sideboard and poured two glasses of brandy. He handed one to Bingley, which his friend gratefully accepted, then resumed his original station behind his desk. "Bingley, as a testament to the strength of our friendship—and assuming it is also what you wish—I would, of course, be willing to acknowledge your sister in society. However, unless she is able to treat Elizabeth with the respect and civility that is her due as my wife, I regret to say she will no longer be welcome in my home. In *any* of my homes," he added pointedly.

To Darcy's surprise, his friend laughed. "Do you mean to tell me we might actually manage to pass a fortnight at Pemberley in relative peace, then? Without fear of Caroline's constant raptures on the evenness of your writing or the length of your correspondence?"

Darcy joined him, a chuckle escaping his lips. "Or the many accomplishments of a truly refined lady or the extensive size of my library or the superiority of Madame Harnois's blancmange as opposed to that of the Hursts' *equally* capable French cook? Yes, I see your point, Bingley."

Both men took long, satisfying drinks from their glasses, each clearly occupied by his own thoughts. *Hmm,* Darcy mused, *I daresay if Caroline Bingley refuses to treat Elizabeth with civility, then this may very well be the first year I will not be required to take the precaution of locking the door to the master's chambers while I am within—or without, for that matter. Of course, with a wife as lovely and tempting as Elizabeth, perhaps I shall continue to do so in any case.*

Bingley gave him a sly grin. "I was just thinking, Darcy, that perhaps you should not be too hasty in your reconciliation with Caroline. You know, this could be just the thing she needs to humble her once and for all. I would be very interested to see how my high-and-mighty sister would react to being reminded that your wife is the granddaughter of a gentleman, something Caroline, with her dowry of twenty thousand pounds, cannot claim herself. Our grandfather, you will recall, was in trade."

Darcy returned his self-satisfied smile. "You know, Bingley, being well acquainted with your sister and her inability to hold her tongue and her temper when in company, I daresay the possibility of seeing her humbled in society may yet be realized." Eying his friend's empty glass, Darcy asked, "Would you care for another, Bingley?"

Bingley nodded and offered his glass to his host. "I don't mind if I do, Darcy! I don't mind if I do!"

Elizabeth was walking in Hyde Park on a particularly mild winter morning with Jane and her Aunt Gardiner when she felt a wave of light-headedness overtake her. She stumbled, managing to catch Jane's arm, but her vision was soon obscured by encroaching darkness, and she collapsed, unconscious, upon the ground. She awoke moments later to the concerned face of her aunt hovering over her as she lay with her head cradled upon Jane's lap.

"Oh, Lizzy! Thank goodness you have come back to us!" It was Jane's worried voice she heard first, and in an effort to reassure her, Elizabeth reached for her hand and held it, returning the slight pressure Jane applied. She attempted to rise, but her aunt urged her to lie still.

"Lizzy, my dear, how are you feeling? Can you remember what happened?" asked her aunt, whose composure was remarkably collected.

"I hardly know. I remember feeling warm and light-headed, and then everything began to grow dark, but I can recall nothing beyond that."

Mrs. Gardiner laid the back of her hand upon Elizabeth's forehead and then her cheek. "You fainted, Elizabeth. Tell me, have you been feeling unwell lately?"

"No, not at all, except I have felt a little light-headed on other occasions, but only when I happen to rise quickly from my chair or from my bed in the morning."

Her aunt gave her an appraising look. "Were you ill this morning, or any other mornings?"

Elizabeth answered in the negative.

"Have you felt unusually tired at all?"

"Yes, now that you mention it, I have, but I suspect that is due only to my not getting enough sleep lately."

They spoke some more while Elizabeth rested, and after the passing of another few minutes, she was well able to rise to her feet with Jane's assistance and to think of returning to Grosvenor Square for some light refreshment.

Though the reality of her fainting had frightened her to some degree, she no longer felt she was in any danger of repeating the act, and, as she had felt recovered enough to walk on her own two legs to the carriage, she could hardly comprehend why her aunt wished her to exercise such caution once she had safely returned to her own home. She was standing in the drawing room, arguing the matter further, when Darcy came upon them. Upon hearing his wife proclaim herself to be perfectly fine *now*, his brow furrowed.

"May I inquire as to what you are arguing about so vehemently with your aunt, Mrs. Darcy?"

Elizabeth rolled her eyes. "I would prefer you would not, sir, as there is no need to mention the matter any further. As you can see with your own eyes, I am perfectly well, and that is all that matters."

Mrs. Gardiner spoke up. "Yes, Lizzy, but it could very easily happen again. You have said yourself you have been having bouts of light-headedness for some time now. Do you not think this is an indication you ought to take greater care?" She turned to Darcy and said pointedly, "Lizzy fainted this morning in Hyde Park, Mr. Darcy."

His brows shot up, his concern evident. "You fainted, Elizabeth? Why on earth would you ever wish to keep this from me? Do not you think I should be made aware of such information? I am your husband, Elizabeth. What if something were to happen to you? I would hardly know what to do for you!"

"This," she said with exasperation as she threw her hands in the air and dropped herself into the nearest chair, "is precisely why I have not informed you, Fitzwilliam. I am sure whatever is ailing me will soon pass, and then I shall be the same as I have always been."

Mrs. Gardiner, however, observed her newly married niece with no small amount of amusement. "I would certainly not count on *that*, if I were you, my dear. At least not for some time," she proclaimed.

Darcy gaped at her, his alarm palpable, while Elizabeth leaned forward in her chair and laughed. "Surely there can be nothing seriously wrong with me, Aunt?"

Her aunt only smiled and shook her head, glancing from

Elizabeth to her worried husband and back again. Suddenly, the eyes of her nieces lit up with pleasure as a happy possibility for Elizabeth's situation made itself known, but Darcy, who clearly had not interpreted Mrs. Gardiner's implication as it had been intended, only continued to grow more concerned for his wife. Eager to enlighten him and to ease his mind, Elizabeth rose with no little alacrity and hastened to where he stood but, before she could do more than take his hand in hers, her head began to spin again. Darcy caught her in his arms just as she fainted.

Doctor Carter closed the door to Elizabeth's bedchamber and entered her sitting room, where Darcy had been pacing in constant agitation for the last three quarters of an hour. Clearing his throat, the doctor said, "Other than a minor bump on her head, most likely from her fall in Hyde Park, your wife is perfectly healthy, Mr. Darcy. With any luck, everything will go smoothly, and there will hardly be any reason to worry for many months to come, but you had better accustom yourself to pacing, sir. You will find it to be the only thing you will be able to do once Mrs. Darcy's time finally comes."

Judging from the expression of alarm on his face, it was clear Darcy had no better understanding of Doctor Carter's words than he had of Mrs. Gardiner's. "I thought you just declared Mrs. Darcy to be in perfect health?" he asked.

The doctor observed him for a moment. "Mr. Darcy," he said evenly, "may I inquire as to what knowledge you may have of your wife's current condition?"

"I assure you, I have not the slightest knowledge of her condition. She has fainted twice today and has informed me she has been feeling faint periodically since Christmas. Surely that cannot be an indication of good health."

Doctor Carter chuckled. "Sir, perhaps you should speak with your wife at this time. I assure you, Mrs. Darcy is feeling quite well—she *is* quite well—and is most likely anxious to inform you of her condition herself. If you find you are in any further need of my services, it will be my pleasure to attend you. Please feel free to summon me at any hour, day or night." He placed his hat upon his head and said briskly, "Good day to you, sir," before taking his leave.

Still ill at ease over the state of Elizabeth's health, not to mention puzzled, he thanked the doctor, bid him a hasty farewell, and strode to the door to his wife's bedchamber. He breathed deeply and ran his hands over his face several times before he finally turned the handle and entered. Elizabeth appeared to be lying peacefully upon the bed, wearing her nightshift and dressing gown. She smiled at him from the midst of a large pile of pillows and beckoned him to join her. He was at her side almost immediately.

"How are you feeling, my love?" he inquired, feathering a kiss upon her forehead as well as the hand he clasped almost violently in his. "Are you comfortable? Can I get you anything?"

Elizabeth shook her head. "Have you spoken with Doctor Carter, Fitzwilliam?"

Darcy simply nodded and looked away, not trusting himself to speak.

"And?" she asked.

Her husband remained silent.

Elizabeth could not understand his solemn reaction—his complete lack of enthusiasm—to such wonderful, nay, such miraculous, news. Her smile faltered and then faded completely.

"You are not pleased, then," she whispered, a crushing burden of disappointment weighing upon her heart.

Darcy turned to look at her, a wealth of emotions flooding his eyes. He somehow managed to keep his composure as he muttered, "I wish only for you to be well, my love. That is truly the only thing that matters."

She stared at him for a moment before she finally understood what he might be thinking. "Fitzwilliam," she asked, her voice quiet, tentative, "you do understand that I am going to have a child and not apoplexy?"

He stared at her, his mouth literally falling open. "*A child?* You mean to tell me you are not… that you are only… that is to say…"

Darcy finally abandoned his attempts at verbal communication in favor of running the back of his hand over his mouth for several moments. Elizabeth watched with growing amusement as his agitation seemed to increase to what she suspected to be an almost intolerable proportion. At long last, he blurted out, "You are *with child*? Elizabeth, you are completely certain of this?"

Elizabeth stroked his cheek with her fingers and smoothed a stray curl from his furrowed brow. "Yes," she assured him. "Of course, we will not know for certain until the baby quickens, but Doctor Carter is fairly sure I am, though only in the very early stages, and I believe my aunt also shares his opinion."

Relief flooded his features and Darcy placed a kiss upon her temple before he buried his face in her hair. "Thank God," he murmured, his voice strained with emotion.

Elizabeth held him close. "My dearest," she said, her tone soft and soothing, "I promise you, all is well. Doctor Carter has assured me many women experience similar symptoms and go through their confinements with very little or no difficulty at all. He does not anticipate my confinement to be any different and believes we shall have a healthy son or daughter to bring to Pemberley sometime in the middle of September."

Darcy raised his head and cradled her face in his hands, searching her eyes for a long while. "Elizabeth," he began, his voice quiet and filled with hesitation, "does it not frighten you? Even a little? Are you not scared?"

Suspecting he had been thinking of his mother, she shook her head and smiled. "No. I feel only happiness. This precious new life has begun from our love, Fitzwilliam. It is an extraordinary gift we have given one another, is it not?"

Not trusting himself to answer, Darcy responded in the only other way he knew, and leaned in to caress her lips so tenderly with his own that Elizabeth shivered before he had barely touched her. As the tension of the last several hours drained away, he began to relax with her, deepening his kisses until he felt her body responding to his touch. It was not what he had planned after such an emotionally draining afternoon, especially when he was still uncertain of whether or not the doctor had imposed any limitations upon her. Reluctantly, Darcy pulled away and shifted his position so he could recline beside her on the bed. He removed his boots and covered them both with the counterpane. Elizabeth snuggled against him as he enfolded her in his arms, placing several kisses in her hair as he diligently proceeded to remove each pin. They lay quietly together for a long time, so long that both had begun to wonder whether the other had succumbed to slumber, but then Elizabeth heard Darcy ask, "Elizabeth, am I truly to become a father?"

Elizabeth shifted so she could look upon his face and smiled. "Yes, my dearest, you are going to be an excellent father."

Darcy closed his eyes and tightened his arms around the woman he loved.

Elizabeth could see the corners of his mouth turn up in the barest hint of a pleased smile. "I love you, Elizabeth, more than I could ever express to you with mere words."

Elizabeth's smile grew wider. "As I love you, Fitzwilliam." They soon drifted off to sleep, their repose being sound and filled with contentment, dreaming of the new life that had begun from their love.

Chapter 24

The Darcys were at breakfast several mornings later when the post arrived. A delighted smile spread across Elizabeth's face as she plucked from the elegant silver tray held by one of the servants a thick letter addressed to her in a familiar hand. "What brings you so much pleasure, Mrs. Darcy?" her husband inquired.

"It is a letter from Charlotte."

"Ah, yes. Miss Lucas. And what news does she send from Hertfordshire?"

Elizabeth broke the seal and began to read. "Oh dear," she said after a few minutes. "She writes that her anticipated wedding to my odious cousin will take place at the end of next week. She says it is her dearest wish that we might attend." She laid aside the missive and bit her lip as her husband scowled.

He studied her before he spoke, his voice tinged with barely concealed bitterness and a hauteur she had not heard from him for some time. "You cannot tell me you wish to bear witness to your intimate friend pledging her obedience to that ridiculous excuse for a man, Elizabeth?"

Elizabeth sighed. "Fitzwilliam, Charlotte and I have been the closest of friends since we were young girls. I do confess I am extremely loath to see her consign herself to such a fate—to enter into a marriage where there is little chance of any real affection or respect—especially with such a man, but however I happen to disagree with her choice, Charlotte has asked this of me, and out of respect for our friendship, I feel obligated to accept her invitation. Indeed, I realize it makes very little sense, especially since our paths are not likely to cross again for some time—if ever—but I know what it would mean to Charlotte. She mentions she has written to Jane, as well. Perhaps she and I could travel together with Mr. Bingley in his carriage. That way you would not have to attend an event I know would bring you nothing but vexation and grief."

He stared at her with incredulity. "How, in all that is holy, can you honestly believe I would allow you to travel all the way to Hertfordshire without me, Elizabeth, so soon after our own marriage, especially now that you believe you are with child?"

"All the way to Hertfordshire?" She laughed. "It is but half a day's journey. And Jane and Charles would be with me, so I would hardly be alone or unprotected." Her eyes developed an impish gleam. "Of course, I would greatly prefer your company to that of Mr. Bingley, Fitzwilliam. Excellent man though he is, I cannot but find your society far superior to that of any other man of my acquaintance, my future brother included."

Darcy rolled his eyes and pretended to consider her request, all the while knowing he could not bear to part with her or deny her anything he knew would bring her pleasure. Sighing, he nodded his acquiescence and grumbled, "Of course I will accompany you, Elizabeth. Though it will give me absolutely no pleasure to be once again in company with Mr. Collins, I would not wish to deprive you of sharing in your friend's joy on her wedding day.

When would you care to leave? Are you certain you are feeling well enough to make such a journey?"

"I assure you, my love, I am quite well. As for our departure, it shall, of course, depend upon any obligations you may have, but I was hoping to be able to spend at least a few days with Charlotte and our families before the wedding. I cannot think of when she and I may be able to meet again."

Darcy pursed his lips. "I would have suggested you meet in Hunsford during my yearly pilgrimage to Rosings; however, I highly doubt that to be a possibility in our immediate future, if ever."

She rose then and, situating herself upon Darcy's lap, kissed his frowning mouth. She meant it as a passing gesture, one with which to reassure him before broaching the uncomfortable subject of his aunt Catherine, but her husband seemed to have other ideas; he captured her mouth in what quickly became an ardent kiss before she could even begin her speech. When their lips finally separated, Darcy buried his face in the curve of her neck, breathing deeply while his arms held her close. "My love," Elizabeth began but was soon silenced by his muffled words.

"Pray, do not mention that woman, Elizabeth. I care not to discuss her abhorrent behavior at this time. Only know that I cannot so easily forgive her for her disrespect of you."

Elizabeth acknowledged his words by gently running her fingers through his hair and holding him a little tighter against her breast. "As you wish," was all she replied.

The trip to Hertfordshire was uneventful. Bingley, Jane, Darcy, and Elizabeth all left London in Darcy's carriage late Tuesday morning, stopping only for a light luncheon at an inn along the way, so they, as well as the servants and horses, might rest themselves. They arrived at Longbourn at teatime, much to Darcy's consternation, as he had been most persistent in his insistence that they first stop at Netherfield so their party might refresh themselves somewhat after a rather tiresome journey.

He was especially concerned with Elizabeth's comfort, worrying himself over her current state and trying to gauge whether or not she was fatigued by their journey, but Elizabeth was not of a mind to acquiesce to any particular demands to rest herself, stating she had managed to fall asleep for a while in the carriage and felt perfectly well enough to dine with her parents and sisters. Though Darcy remained skeptical, he reluctantly let it go, as she had agreed to his proposal that they stay with Bingley at Netherfield, rather than at Longbourn with her family.

Elizabeth had given in to this arrangement mostly for the sake of her husband, whom she knew would be far more inclined to be open in his cordiality to the neighborhood should he not have to share the same roof with her mother so soon after they had just parted company in Town.

Though she very much wished to accompany her brother and sister to Hertfordshire, it was decided between them that Georgiana would remain in London under the protection of Lord and Lady Matlock until their return. Neither Darcy or Elizabeth wished to risk having her meet accidentally with Wickham, should he still be in the vicinity. They soon saw their judgment proven quite sound, for, when they dined several evenings later at Lucas Lodge, many of the officers, Wickham included, happened to be among those in attendance.

For Darcy, it was a doubly trying evening as he found himself thrown into the rather unsavory company of his father's former favorite as well as his aunt's officious clergyman. As could be expected, he bore the insincere flattery of the latter with less than civil forbearance; the former, who leered at him with a smirk throughout the course of the entire evening, he found far more difficult to treat with indifference. Darcy found himself glaring at the man for the duration of the night, particularly when he noticed Wickham's gaze sweeping over Elizabeth's elegantly dressed figure. As a precaution, Darcy strayed little from her side.

The party, for the most part, was a merry one, especially with the two youngest Miss Bennets in attendance. They flirted with all the officers and called upon Mary to play lively airs so they might dance with them, as well. Both girls, but Lydia in particular, had become intimate with Colonel Forster's young wife, Harriet, who just happened to be close, both in age and temperament, to Lydia. At one point, their laughter was so effusive it actually drew Mr. Bennet's notice from his conversation with Colonel Forster, who, rather than sharing Mr. Bennet's sentiments on the silliness of the young ladies, commented, instead, on his pleasure in seeing such liveliness in females, as he found it to be a welcome diversion from the oftentimes grave responsibilities he carried as a soldier in a time of war.

Toward the end of the evening, in an effort to get some much-needed fresh air and a few moments to herself, Elizabeth slipped away while Darcy was engaged in conversation with Colonel Forster and her father. She had not enjoyed above two minutes of solitude on the terrace located just outside the drawing room, when she overheard a disturbing conversation being conducted in hushed voices by Lydia and a gentleman whose voice she could not quite identify. Appalled by her sister's total want of propriety and decorum, Elizabeth advanced several feet toward a manicured hedge and discovered her youngest sister in a most disgraceful and compromising situation with none other than Mr. Wickham.

"Lydia!" she cried, "you will return to the house immediately!"

The lovers jerked back in obvious surprise. Lydia hastily covered her exposed bosom, which Wickham had been fondling just moments before, and wrapped her arms around his shoulders. "La, Lizzy! Just because you are now shackled to such a dour man, it does not give you the right to spoil all the fun for the rest of us. You are hardly in charge of me just because you are now a married woman. I shall continue to do what I please with my dear Wickham, never mind what you say."

Rage flowed through Elizabeth's veins at Wickham's nonchalance. "Come now, my pet," he said in a voice that made her feel ill, "be a good girl and run along inside while I have a word with your sister. I will join you shortly."

With a look of resentment toward her sister, Lydia kissed Wickham full on the lips before flouncing through the French doors, slamming them behind her. Elizabeth turned to follow her but found herself detained by Wickham, who was quick to circle around her, blocking her way to the house. "Well, well, Miss Elizabeth," he said with his usual air of insincerity, "or rather, I should say, *Mrs. Darcy.* I see we are destined to meet again, though I must confess to have been rather shocked when I heard from your sister that Darcy had actually deigned to marry you. Quite out of character for one in his station, I assure you, but I do suppose being caught in a compromising position by a clergyman must carry *some* weight with his conscience."

Elizabeth turned her head away, but he only laughed. "You must have made it quite impossible for Darcy to refuse you, Mrs. Darcy." He ogled her figure in a repugnant manner that brought a rush of heat to her cheeks. Seeing her agitation obviously excited him. Wickham's breathing became shallow and he raised his hand to touch the swell of flesh at the neckline of her gown. As in her aunt's drawing room, Elizabeth attempted to strike him, but again, she found her wrists captured by his strong grip. He laughed. "I see not much has changed, Elizabeth. I still find you undeniably fetching, in spite of the fact your temper leads you to hasty actions you may soon find yourself sorry for… or not."

Her eyes widened as he drew her against his body. She began to struggle in an attempt to extricate herself from his grasp, his evident arousal pressing against her stomach. "Mr. Wickham!" she exclaimed. "I beg you to reconsider your actions, sir! Surely you know my husband will happily kill you for such an insult, as would his cousin, Colonel Fitzwilliam!"

This seemed to sober him somewhat, for he scanned the area around them, his gaze darting to the doors leading back into the house. He soon returned it to her figure, however, and tightening his grip so it was especially painful for her, he said hoarsely, "You do make an excellent point, madam; however…"

Elizabeth held her breath, praying for some opportunity to escape. Wickham was, by now, holding her far too tightly for her to be able to free herself, and realizing this, her stomach lurched.

"Tell me," he demanded as he lowered his head close enough for her to smell the brandy on his breath, "did you scream and fight when your husband first insulted you, or did you dutifully submit to his will when he took possession of you?" Elizabeth gasped, and with one swift motion, Wickham pressed his mouth to hers in a brutal kiss as he shoved her body back against the wall of the house.

She fought against him with every ounce of strength she could muster as he continued to take possession of her mouth, his lower body undulating against her hips. Just as Elizabeth thought she would become physically ill, he released her, grasping the base of her neck with one hand while he ran the fingers of his free hand along one side of her face.

"Not a word, my dear Mrs. Darcy, not a word," he panted. "I just wanted to have a little taste of what Darcy delights in every night, although he cannot possibly appreciate such a feisty little chit in the manner he should." Upon seeing the fear in her eyes, he murmured, "Be not alarmed, my dear. I doubt our paths shall cross again after tonight, but if they should, I daresay your loveliness shall most likely force me to claim some further basis for my comparison between you and, well, let us just say, one other young lady of my *intimate* acquaintance." With one last, hungry look, Wickham released her and disappeared into the night.

Elizabeth slid to the ground, her legs finally giving way beneath her, and, holding her face in her hands, she cried for some time. Not long after she ceased, she heard lively music being played in the drawing room. Attempting some semblance of composure, she wiped the tears from her cheeks and stood, but not before hearing her husband's voice raised in alarm as he questioned her sisters about her whereabouts.

In the next instant, Darcy threw open the French doors and strode out onto the terrace, where he found Elizabeth doubled over near the hedge, emptying the contents of her stomach. He looked at her in horror as he took in her tear-stained cheeks and swollen lips. She raised her handkerchief to her mouth, and he gasped at the angry bruises beginning to encircle both wrists.

Elizabeth found she could not meet his eyes, which held just as much pain and anguish as she suspected her own did, and felt herself sway as another wave of nausea washed over her, fear of her husband's reaction to what had just occurred gripping her.

Darcy shut the door and, closing the distance between them, enfolded Elizabeth in his arms, where she finally collapsed, a few unshed tears escaping from her eyes. She clung to him, terrified to release him for fear of what she would see in his eyes when she pulled away.

He held her just as tightly, whispering endearments and stroking her back, all the while struggling to keep his alarm at bay, lest he add to Elizabeth's distress. There was no doubt in his mind her discomposure had something to do with George Wickham, who Darcy noticed was conspicuously absent from the drawing room only moments earlier.

Elizabeth soon calmed, though Darcy continued to soothe her with his touch and gentle words for many minutes to follow. He was afraid to ask what she had been forced to endure at the hands of that… *man* and remained silent on the subject for as long as he dared before his fear for her well-being finally got the better of him. Pulling her from his breast, he said, in a tight voice, "Elizabeth, dearest, you must tell me what he has done."

She glanced at him before averting her gaze and, placing a shaking hand over her eyes, said, "I… he has not done the absolute worst. At least not to me."

He stared at her, his eyes fearful as he brushed a stray curl from her face with a trembling hand. "Are you certain?" he whispered.

She nodded. "Forgive me, but I cannot be concerned solely with myself right now." She took a deep breath and told him of how she had discovered Lydia in an amorous encounter with

Wickham only moments before. "After all that has occurred in the last several months, I cannot believe she is blind to the true nature of such a man! He told me our paths are not likely to cross again after tonight, but he alluded to the eventuality of… something, though I hardly know what. I cannot fathom what might be in his mind, but I am concerned. And what of Lydia? She cannot possibly marry someone like him, yet Lord only knows the liberties she has allowed him. It is in every way horrible!"

Darcy took her hands in his, his anger rising as he traced his finger along her bruised wrists. "I must speak with your father and Colonel Forster immediately, and you must come into the house. You are freezing with only a shawl." He looked at her, his steady gaze boring into her. "Are you certain you are not… *injured* any more than what I can see, Elizabeth?" He nearly choked on the words.

Elizabeth noticed then that his eyes were glistening. She offered him a weak smile and cradled his face in her hands. "I am not injured," she said softly, "I am only feeling unbelievably foolish for having gotten myself into such a dangerous predicament in the first place; though, if I had not come out for some air, I never would have discovered Lydia's partiality to him, and God knows what would have happened to her, that is, if it has not already taken place."

Darcy drew her against him and placed a kiss upon her hair, thanking God she had not been seriously hurt or worse. He reluctantly released her, and lacing his fingers with hers, he bestowed another gentle kiss upon her temple before leading her around to the other side of the house, where they entered through another set of French doors. To Darcy's relief, they found themselves ensconced in a comfortable parlor, mercilessly devoid of any members of the Lucas family or their guests. He settled Elizabeth in a chair by the low-burning fire and removed his tailcoat, wrapping it around her shoulders.

Elizabeth closed her eyes, inhaling his scent as it lingered on the fibers of the fabric, allowing its soothing effects to wash over her senses. After a few moments, she felt some of her agitation fade, and she was able to relax, if only a little.

Darcy added several logs to the fire, and very soon the entire room was bathed in a glowing warmth. He walked to where Elizabeth sat and knelt before her, taking both her chilled hands between his. Rather than raising them to his lips, however, he lowered his head and laid it to rest upon her lap, closing his eyes and willing himself to rein in the powerful emotions churning in his breast.

Elizabeth kissed his curls and laid her cheek against their softness. Both gave and received comfort in equal measure. They remained thus for some time before they were intruded upon.

Mr. Bennet had roamed the house in search of his favorite daughter, only to find her hidden away in the small parlor and engaged in an intimate embrace of sort with her husband. The elder gentleman could easily see all was not well between them, and after hesitating a minute, he cleared his throat. Elizabeth raised her head, and Darcy rose to his feet, but rather than turning to face the intruder, he strode to the window, where he remained for several minutes with his back to the room, his hand passing repeatedly over his eyes. Elizabeth, her father noted, wiped at tears that were glistening upon her cheeks.

"Lizzy, my child," he asked with concern as he approached her, "what is wrong? Have you quarreled?"

Elizabeth shook her head, not yet trusting herself enough to speak, and glanced at Darcy, who was still staring out into the darkness.

Mr. Bennet turned to his son-in-law. "Darcy, what has happened? If it involves my Lizzy, I will not rest until I know."

Without so much as a backward glance, Darcy spoke in a controlled voice punctuated by ill-concealed anger. "Then perhaps you should invite your youngest daughter and Colonel Forster to join us. I am certain they would be most interested to hear what has taken place tonight."

Mr. Bennet gaped at him. He was just about to demand Darcy reveal all, but upon seeing the pained, pleading look from his daughter, he simply nodded and left them. He returned moments later, leading Lydia by the arm with Colonel Forster close behind. Darcy strode to the door and closed it firmly, a scowl upon his face as he returned to his place near the window. From there, he glared at Lydia with distaste.

"Lord, Lizzy!" she exclaimed. "You look positively wretched! It is no wonder your husband looks so cross." Then, looking around her, she asked, "Where has Wickham got to? Lord! He is not still waiting for me on the terrace, is he?"

Mr. Bennet's eyebrows shot skyward.

Elizabeth turned aside her head at her sister's lack of shame.

It was all Darcy could do not to throttle the ignorant girl. "Lydia," he said, his voice low and dangerous, "Mr. Wickham has left, perhaps forever, and you would do well to forget you ever had any dealings with him."

Lydia gasped. "What? Why?" She rounded on Elizabeth. "Lizzy! You did not send Wickham away, did you?"

Elizabeth rose from her chair, walked to where Darcy stood, and took up her own vigil at the window.

"Why could you not simply allow me to be with the man I love?" Lydia whined. "It is so unfair, Lizzy! You and Jane always get to have all the fun, and I have none!" she exclaimed and ended with a pout.

One glance at his son-in-law made Mr. Bennet see how

perilously close that gentleman was to unleashing his temper. He knew he had better act, and he had better do it quickly. "Lydia!" he admonished, and rather more harshly than he was accustomed to doing, "Is this true? Have you been meeting with Mr. Wickham?"

Lydia lifted her chin. "Of course, I have, Papa, for we are in love, and Wickham says when he has enough money saved up we are to go away together."

Mr. Bennet's face paled. "What did you say?" he asked, his voice deadly.

Lydia huffed. "Lord, does not anyone listen to what I say?"

"Oh, for God's sake, enough!" he hollered. "You will go out of this room now and return to the drawing room, where you will await me with your mother and sisters!"

She made to protest, but her father, who very rarely ever raised his voice to any of his daughters, did so again. Lydia retreated with haste, slamming the door behind her.

With a grim expression, Darcy regaled the two gentlemen with the events that had taken place that evening. To say Mr. Bennet's anger upon hearing of the disgraceful and willful antics of his youngest daughter was severe would have been a gross understatement, but it was almost nothing in comparison to the deep distress he received when he learned of that same gentleman having forcefully taken similar liberties with his favorite daughter.

As far as Lydia was concerned, Darcy wanted very much to believe she would be properly chagrined by the exposure of her thoughtless actions. He would also have liked to believe she would feel a deep and abiding concern for the disgraceful treatment Elizabeth had been forced to endure at the hands of her lover, but, judging from her petulant and selfish attitude, he dared not even hope for such an outcome.

Colonel Forster's countenance was fierce. He immediately took the blame for Wickham's nefarious actions upon himself, proclaiming he had failed in his duty as a commanding officer, which should have included his keeping a close watch upon the unscrupulous lieutenant—especially after the incident with Darcy in Meryton several months prior. Shortly after Darcy finished relating the disturbing particulars, the colonel departed Lucas Lodge with his officers, hoping to catch Wickham before he could flee Hertfordshire, where he would very likely leave behind numerous unpaid bills with his creditors and, no doubt, several debts of honor involving their daughters.

Darcy, who had become even more agitated after watching his wife struggle to keep her composure while he informed her father of Wickham's abominable treatment, expressed his intention of accompanying the colonel and his men. He was finally dissuaded from doing so by his father-in-law, who impressed upon him the probability of such rashness adding greatly to Elizabeth's heightened distress. One look at his wife decided him. He would not leave her.

Chapter 25

The evening was soon at an end for the Bennet family. Darcy's blood boiled with the barely contained fury he felt toward the outrages Wickham had perpetrated against Elizabeth. He marveled at his ability to project some modicum of control over his roiling emotions as he tended to his wife and ordered the carriages. Mr. Bennet, with the assistance of Bingley, urged the rest of his family to offer their appreciation to Sir William and Lady Lucas and take their leave.

Once seated in the carriage, Darcy flouted propriety, taking Elizabeth onto his lap and cradling her in his arms as she buried her head in the crook of his neck. Confused and knowing only that something unsavory had occurred involving Elizabeth, Lydia, and Wickham, Bingley indulged his friend and stared out of the window in silence until they arrived at Netherfield. Once they had gained the sanctuary of the house, Bingley grabbed Darcy by the shoulder and inquired about the situation. Darcy glanced at the sleeping woman in his arms and, after a moment of indecision, consented to join Bingley in his study once he saw Elizabeth settled for the night.

When he pushed open the door to his wife's bedchamber, Darcy saw that Sonia was waiting to assist her mistress, but he dismissed her, not wanting any hands other than his to touch her again that night. He undressed her with tenderness, and though she did awaken, he continued his ministrations, tucking her beneath the counterpane while speaking soft words of devotion and love, and stroking her face until she finally seemed to succumb to what he hoped would be a peaceful slumber.

Darcy swallowed down the lump in his throat and joined Bingley, who handed him a glass of brandy as he waited for him to begin his tale. Darcy began pacing almost immediately, draining his glass in several large gulps and offering it without comment to be refilled. His friend complied and watched with concern on his face as Darcy took up his customary position at the window, looking out into the darkness as he drank without tasting.

When he finally spoke, his voice was low and dangerous. "That blackguard dared to touch my wife; he dared to *kiss* my wife, my beautiful wife, who carries *my* child, *my heir*, in her womb as we speak. She has never done anything to deserve such abhorrent treatment from anyone, much less the likes of George Wickham," he spat. "I have sworn before God to protect Elizabeth, but instead, she has been the recipient of such perverse, repulsive acts of degradation forced upon her by that… that unscrupulous *animal* whom I was once ignorant and naïve enough to call my friend!"

He drained his glass and hurled it into the fire, where it shattered into dozens of pieces. Catching sight of Bingley's shocked expression and distrusting his own emotions, Darcy turned his back to him again, laying his forehead against the cold windowpane. It did little to soothe his temper. "This is no one's fault but my own," he continued in a defeated voice full of self-admonishment. "If I had only kept my emotions and desire for Elizabeth in check that day several months ago in Meryton, none of this would ever have happened. Wickham singled her out, not for her beauty and vivacity, but because he recognized my admiration for her, just as I am certain he has chosen to seduce Lydia for the same reason—simply because she is Elizabeth's youngest sister, and ruining her would surely be just one more way of revenging himself upon me. She is, without a doubt, one of the most easily led, ridiculous girls in all of England, Bingley, but Lydia Bennet hardly deserves to receive *this* for her ignorance and indecorum! Damn him! Damn him to *hell* for carrying this vendetta so bloody far!"

He felt Bingley's hand grip his shoulder. "What do you wish to do, Darcy?" he asked.

Darcy let out a bitter, rueful laugh and, through gritted teeth, said, "I want to kill the bloody bastard, Bingley! I want to squeeze every ounce of breath from his disgraceful body so he will never hurt another member of my family again as long as I live!"

Bingley let out a long breath. "Dueling is illegal, my friend, and murder, I am afraid, is not an option I would endorse in this particular instance, no matter how appealing it may appear at the moment."

Darcy slammed his fist against the window frame and hollered, "He has forced himself upon my *wife*, for God's sake! He has compromised *two* of my sisters, both under the age of sixteen! It is well within my right, both as a husband and a brother, to run him through without so much as a second thought to his miserable existence!"

"Yes, Darcy," Bingley said, "but you can hardly expect such a dishonorable blackguard to play fairly when so much is at stake, my friend. And then there is Elizabeth. It would grieve her beyond everything imaginable should Wickham harm you or, worse, kill you in a duel. You cannot expect her to go through that agony, Darcy—that senseless heartbreak—especially if what you say is true and she is, indeed, carrying your child."

Bingley sighed and shook his head. "I know you wish to do this because you are thinking of them, Darcy—because you wish to protect them, and because right now, you hold yourself accountable for failing to do so in this particular instance—but you must truly think of them, my friend, before you decide to react with impetuosity and rashness. The consequences for such actions could be devastating and irreversible, and I doubt very much Elizabeth would appreciate your placing yourself in such jeopardy simply to rid the world of one dishonorable man. Your wife is hopelessly in love with you, you know, in part because you are a man who has always conducted himself with honor and decorum. You can never be anything less."

Darcy walked to the nearest chair, where he finally allowed himself to collapse, exhausted both physically and emotionally. He could not keep from thinking of his Elizabeth, whom he felt, in his heart, he had failed to protect, just as he had failed to protect Georgiana at Ramsgate. Holding his head in his hands, his shoulders began to shake uncontrollably as the lump in his throat, which he had been fighting against so ineffectually, finally succeeded in forcing its way into his mouth. He felt a warm hand reach out to him, then another, enveloping him in a secure embrace, but, rather than Bingley's strong grasp, this touch was one of tenderness, love, and complete devotion. Darcy clung to the one person who he knew, beyond a doubt, would offer it.

"Charles is right, you know," she said quietly. "Georgiana and I would never wish for you to risk your life for the sake of ridding us of such a man, Fitzwilliam, nor would any other member of our family, be they Bennets, Darcys, or Fitzwilliams. I daresay we shall all survive this ordeal without such an impressive display of gallantry, my dear. Too many people depend upon you, my love, and you are far too precious for me to allow you to risk our future together in exchange for some reckless solution to this series of unfortunate dealings with Mr. Wickham. No one is worth that kind of contemplation and sacrifice, especially *that* man."

Elizabeth held his head against her breast, clad only in the silk nightshift she had not bothered to change out of or cover, before following the sound of her husband's anguished voice, raised in anger, to Bingley's study.

The warm, smoothness of Elizabeth's flesh, her tender endearments, her soft kisses, the soothing rhythm of her heartbeat, all became a balm for Darcy's soul. Drawing a shaky breath, he pulled her onto his lap and rested his forehead against hers, closing his eyes as she wiped away the last of his tears. He had never been one to show such a display of weakness and vulnerability—to give way to tears and grief in front of another, no matter what the cause—and he was embarrassed that Elizabeth had borne witness to his utter loss of self-control. He entwined his fingers within her hair and breathed deeply, drawing comfort from her closeness. Her lavender scent almost always had a calming effect on him, although, on many occasions, it was enough of a stimulant to arouse him profoundly. On this night, though, he simply reveled in her consolatory presence.

Darcy sighed against her lips as she brushed them over his. "I love you, Fitzwilliam, so very much," she whispered as she smoothed her fingers over his hair and stroked the line of his jaw. "Let us think no more on this tonight, my love. Come with me, and we will lose ourselves in each other."

Bingley had slipped from the room the moment Elizabeth entered. Darcy opened his eyes and pulled his head back just enough to search hers. They were wonderful, dark, liquid pools in which he could easily drown, and he marveled, not for the first time, at Elizabeth's ability to find strength and courage in the face of such adversity. Without a doubt, this woman was the true mistress of Pemberley, and he thanked God, once again, for his good fortune—not only for allowing him to find her, but for allowing him to recognize her worth enough to overcome his misplaced pride and haughty reserve in order to earn her love and devotion. He returned her kiss and then placed another on her forehead. "My love, I am so very sorry I was not there to protect you from him tonight."

"Shhh, Fitzwilliam, we are not to speak of it any more tonight, and, indeed, my love, I am in earnest about this," Elizabeth whispered as she feathered a kiss upon his furrowed brow. She removed herself from his lap and extended her hand. He raised it to his lips to bestow a kiss upon her palm, her wrist, and each finger before lifting it farther still, to cradle against his cheek.

She caressed him, feeling the slight growth of his beard, and tugged against the hand that held her captive. "Come, my dearest, and we will endeavor to make happier memories of tonight." Without further thought, he followed her into the hall, up the staircase, and to her bedchamber. Elizabeth pushed the door closed and led Darcy to the bed, the very same bed where he had first made her his own not so many weeks before. He closed his eyes against the world as she began to work the intricate knots of his cravat free, his breathing deep and even.

"Elizabeth," he rasped, "you need not do this."

"Hush," she whispered. "I want to." She pulled the length of silk from around his throat and began to unfasten the buttons on his tailcoat, his waistcoat, and his shirt. She removed each item and dropped them to the floor with very little formality.

Elizabeth turned her attention to the expanse of her husband's chest, now fully revealed to her discerning eyes and gentle hands. Darcy shuddered when he felt her fingers exploring the contours of his torso. She lowered her mouth to his flesh and placed sensual kisses along his neck and shoulders, gradually, unhurriedly, making her way lower. When she reached his waist, her hands made quick work of the buttons on his trousers as she dipped the tip of her tongue into the slight depression on his stomach. She slid the fabric from his hips, and before Darcy could form a coherent thought, Elizabeth had knelt down to caress his arousal with her lips, her tongue drawing slow, wet circles over his flesh.

A low moan escaped from the back of his throat as Elizabeth's warm mouth enveloped him fully. His fingers tangled in her thick mass of curls. It was almost effortless for Darcy to lose himself in her—in her eyes, in her body, in her very existence. It had always been so. Even in the lonely, confusing weeks that preceded their courtship, when even a chaste kiss upon her hand was never an option, Darcy had adopted a nightly ritual of escaping the trials and tribulations of his mundane existence by submersing himself in private musings and forbidden fantasies about the only woman he had fallen in love with.

Elizabeth's fingertips brushed his hips and his thighs. The glorious curls crowning her head tickled his flesh. The sensations she elicited were potent, almost overpowering in their intensity, and Darcy began to fear for his self-control as he surrendered to the bliss of her ministrations. He opened his eyes, and his breath caught as he was overtaken by the exhilaration of watching his wife, still clad in her nightshift, kneeling before him in such a manner. He groaned as a wave of raw passion swept through him. Elizabeth's eyes turned up to meet his, and in an instant, Darcy pulled her to her feet, his mouth devouring her lips as his hands traveled over her body, leaving her skin hot and tingling, as though she were on fire. He struggled to untie her shift, his fingers fumbling with the ribbons, until, with a sound of frustration, Elizabeth nudged aside his hands and released them herself. She took a step back, and their eyes locked as the shift fell away to reveal her curves, pooling in a puddle of ivory upon the floor.

Darcy closed his eyes, fighting for command of his body, which, at that moment, desperately wanted to ravish this bewitching seductress. Elizabeth must have sensed his urgency, because she reached out and entwined her fingers with his, which were trembling with his efforts. He gripped her hand tightly, as though afraid she would somehow slip away from him. He felt her full breasts brush against his chest as she leaned toward him, pushing him back upon the bed, and inhaled sharply.

Elizabeth climbed atop him, dragging her body along his frame, moaning as his arousal brushed against her. She was about to take him into her, when Darcy rolled them over, showering her lips and face with kisses while his hands found their way to her breasts, his thumbs teasing her nipples, sending shivers of pleasure coursing through her. His hands continued to roam over her curves, exploring, tantalizing her flesh. When Elizabeth moaned his name, Darcy let out a strangled sob of longing, alerting her to the urgency of his need.

"Fitzwilliam," she gasped, "I need you. I need to feel you. *Please. Now.*"

Her words, spoken so quietly, yet with a commanding insistence that only served to further inflame his desire for her, penetrated the last fragments of Darcy's self-restraint, granting his body permission to take action over the more tender sentiments of his heart and mind. He slid into her depths with a shuddering cry that drew forth an identical response from Elizabeth as their bodies began to move together in a rhythm that heightened the intensity of his pleasure. His movements soon grew frenzied.

It was not long before Elizabeth was soaring toward her completion.

Darcy felt her muscles tightening around him as he buried himself within her, time and again, deeper and deeper, until, finally, with a loud cry, he suddenly felt one of the most powerful releases he had ever experienced.

They did not speak, but lay together, hands and bodies entwined, rapid breathing slowing, frantic heartbeats calming, the silent reassurance of the other's presence enveloping them. Darcy bestowed a lingering kiss upon his wife's forehead as he closed his eyes, exhaustion finally claiming them at last.

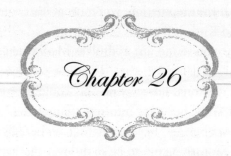

Chapter 26

"Lydia, you are insufferable! Surely, you must see the danger and impropriety of indulging in such disgraceful behavior with a dangerous scoundrel! You permitted him to take outrageous liberties with you that many respectable married women will not even allow their husbands, and you were in public! Have you no shame at all?" Elizabeth found Lydia's refusal to see the error of her ways regarding her scandalous conduct with Wickham the night before infuriating. To further inflame her anger, Lydia merely turned her back to her sister and sulked.

Jane's approach was more sedate. "Lydia, you must understand that with your lack of fortune, your virtue and reputation are all you have to recommend you to a respectable gentleman. You cannot continue to conduct yourself in such a degrading manner with a man like Mr. Wickham. Surely you must know by now he cannot be respectable if he insists on taking advantage of you in such a way and encourages you to bestow your favors upon him. Your scandalous behavior not only reflects poorly upon your own reputation as a respectable young lady, but that of your dear sisters, as well. By indulging in such sinful behavior, especially with a man of questionable character, you are greatly lessening the probability of Mary and Kitty making prudent marriages. Even if you are not concerned with your reputation, you must at least consider those of poor Mary and Kitty."

"Lord, Jane, you sound just as droll as Mary when she is reading from Fordyce!" exclaimed Lydia. "I cannot see how I have done anything so very wrong. I daresay no one would have been the wiser had Lizzy not stuck her nose into my affairs last night instead of minding her own business like she ought. I am heartily disappointed in you, Lizzy, for turning out to be so disloyal and hypocritical!"

Elizabeth stared at her with incredulity. "Whatever do you mean by saying I am hypocritical? That is hardly a term I would associate with myself in any case, particularly in such an instance as this! And certainly, Lydia, you must know my loyalty must lie with preserving the respectability of my family, not with the utter degradation of it!"

"Lord!" Lydia snorted. "That is certainly rich coming from you, pretending to be so high and mighty now that you are a married woman. But admit it, Lizzy, you cannot, in all honesty, say you appreciated Mr. Collins's bothersome interference in *your* amorous encounters in the garden with Mr. Darcy. I would have thought that, after all the scandalous things he told Sir William about *your* behavior before *you* were married, that you would have had far more compassion for me and my dear Wickham. Do not deny it, Lizzy, for everyone in Meryton knows you surrendered your virtue to Mr. Darcy long before you exchanged your vows with him in church."

"How dare you, you insolent, ungrateful little—"

Elizabeth's uncharacteristic shouts resonated throughout her father's house, startling servants and sending members of the family rushing toward Lydia's bedchamber with surprising alacrity. The first to reach them was Darcy. He threw open the door with a thud and entered the room with an expression of alarm. He was stunned to see his elegantly dressed wife lunging toward her youngest sister while Jane struggled to hold her at bay. Lydia was in the midst of hollering something especially appalling in reference to the size of Darcy's fortune and Elizabeth's willingness to bed him before they were married. Darcy's jaw dropped open.

"I swear I shall strangle you for your vulgarity, Lydia!" Elizabeth yelled as she finally succeeded in shoving Jane out of the way. Lydia jumped back, and Darcy bolted forward, seizing his wife around her waist. With very little effort, he managed to carry her flailing form to the other side of the apartment. "Unhand me this instant, Fitzwilliam!" she commanded. "I must throttle my impudent sister before I regain my senses!"

Lydia stuck out her tongue and laughed. "Ha! I'd like to see you try, Lizzy!"

In an effort to escape, Elizabeth elbowed Darcy in the ribs, hard. Rather than gaining her freedom, however, she succeeded only in ensuring her continued captivity, for her husband responded to her act of aggression against his person by throwing her over his shoulder and carrying her, kicking and screaming, out of the room. They passed an incredulous Mr. Bennet on the stairs, who very wisely gave them a wide berth, his look of complete astonishment soon giving way to amusement as he watched the staid master of Pemberley struggle with his daughter.

Darcy stalked into the first room he encountered, which happened to be his father-in-law's library, and slammed the door behind him. He turned the key and then pulled it from the lock. Only then did he release his wife. He deposited her onto a chair by the fire and stood before her, his breathing hard, his hands curled into fists upon his hips. "Pardon my language, madam, but what the *hell* was that display abovestairs?" he demanded. "You are the mistress of Pemberley and *with child*! You are not to conduct yourself in such a disgraceful manner!"

He began to pace, one hand raking through his hair. "For God's sake, Elizabeth! What if you had injured yourself or the baby? And over what? Some ignorant piece of idle nonsense your sister spews forth from her accursed mouth?" He made an inarticulate sound of disgust and threw himself into the chair next to the one she was occupying. Rubbing his aching ribs, he growled, "You need not have taken your fury out on me, Mrs. Darcy. It was most underhanded of you, not to mention unsportsmanlike. I shall expect far more respectful treatment from you in the foreseeable future, madam, effective immediately."

Elizabeth, her arms crossed over her breast, merely scowled before turning away her head. After several long minutes of uncomfortable silence, she ventured a glance at Darcy, who was still staring at her. Several more minutes passed in much the same manner before she finally forced herself to say, with some small degree of contrition, "I am sorry I injured you, Fitzwilliam. It was certainly not my intention. I hardly know what has come over me this morning, except to say I have simply not felt like my normal self as of late." She expelled a breath of air and drummed her fingers upon the arm of the chair. "My aunt Gardiner mentioned to me that sometimes a woman may experience some inexplicable alterations in her mood and temperament when she is expecting a child."

Rising from his chair, Darcy rolled his eyes and mumbled, "Apparently," in a particularly bitter tone as he walked over to the nearest window, where he stared at the road for some time. Before long, there was a knock upon the door. Lost in his own contemplations and forgetting for the moment he was not in his study in Town, Darcy called out, "Come."

Elizabeth raised a speculative brow.

He was startled back into reality, however, when he heard Mr. Bennet's amused voice say from the other side of the door, "How gracious of you, Darcy, to grant me admittance to my own sanctuary! However, I currently find myself unable to take you up on your generosity, as you seem to have taken it upon yourself to lock me out of my library, sir!"

Darcy strode to the door, inserted the key, and turned the lock. His face was flushed by the time his father-in-law entered and appraised him with a look not dissimilar to the one Elizabeth was currently leveling at him. "Forgive me, sir. I seem to have forgotten myself. I hope my actions have not unduly offended you," he mumbled, properly humbled.

Mr. Bennet raised a brow. "No, not at all, sir, not at all." With a pointed look at his daughter, he said wryly, "I daresay you have quite a bit on your plate at the moment, Darcy. My Lizzy, when provoked, can truly be a fearsome sight, can she not?"

Darcy hazarded a glance at his wife, who appeared to be far from amused by her father's comment. "Yes, sir," he said dryly, "quite fearsome." Then, with a flicker of a smile and a wink at Elizabeth, he said, "However, I believe she is now *my* Lizzy, and I would not give her back again for all her fearsome behavior this morning."

Elizabeth rolled her eyes, and Mr. Bennet chuckled. "Wisely said, young man, wisely said." He turned toward his daughter then, his manner grave. "Now, Mrs. Darcy, I can imagine I need not tell you how thoroughly disappointed I am with your behavior. I understand your fury with Lydia for behaving in such a scandalous manner with Mr. Wickham, my dear. Indeed, I would like nothing better than to get my hands on that scoundrel and throttle him to within an inch of his life; however, such conduct as you have shown this morning toward your sister, no matter what disgraceful bit of vulgarity she may have uttered in order to get a rise out of you, is quite unbefitting of a lady, especially a lady of your current standing in society. I do not doubt your husband has already communicated his displeasure on the subject, so I will not bore you with any further commentary, except to say I never want to see such an appalling display in my house again."

"Yes, sir," Elizabeth replied.

Mr. Bennet turned to his son-in-law. "The question of what is to be done remains. Lydia has certainly been compromised, though how thoroughly is still to be determined. In any case, I am afraid we have little choice. Wickham must be found and made to marry her. There is nothing else to be done."

Elizabeth paled. "No, Papa!" she cried. "You cannot sentence poor Lydia to a life with that scoundrel! Do you not remember what Fitzwilliam told you he is capable of all those weeks ago? Or what he attempted only last night with me? Having such a man forever among us, bound to our family for all eternity, shall bring us nothing but hardship and wretchedness of the most acute kind. The honorable institution of matrimony will never inspire him to abandon his nefarious ways. If anything, Lydia's silliness and ignorance will only serve as a catalyst for even greater acts of desperation and deplorability." She leapt from her chair. "I will not have my excellent husband imposed upon by such a man, to have creditors come to him to settle Mr. Wickham's debts, or irate fathers who wish restitution for his debts of honor with their daughters. Oh, thoughtless, thoughtless Lydia, to involve herself with such a man! No, Papa, I absolutely will not have my husband imposed upon any further by that *barbarian*!"

The vehement strength of her opposition greatly alarmed Darcy, but he could not, in all honesty, say he was surprised by it. He looked from Elizabeth to his father-in-law before saying, "Mr. Bennet, I must agree with my wife. From the very first moment he arrived in Meryton, Wickham singled out Elizabeth for the sole purpose of revenging himself upon me for an assortment of imagined wrongdoings he feels he has suffered at my hands. He has chosen to prey on Lydia for similar reasons. If you do succeed in forcing a marriage between them, which will undoubtedly cost a very large sum of money, in any case, he will see to it that her existence is one of misery and degradation. If I may offer a suggestion, I feel our best course of action here is to wait and see if there are any consequences. God willing, there will be none to speak of, and in turn, I would be willing to contribute several thousand pounds to enhance Lydia's dowry, as well as those of Katherine and Mary. I also believe all three girls would benefit greatly from enrollment in a reputable school for young women I happen to know of in London. Katherine would be able to study art with a master; Mary, music; and in Lydia's case, I believe having such an opportunity would bring about maturity, restraint, and a healthy measure of decorum, which she is currently lacking. Of course, Elizabeth and I would be willing to finance the tuition for all three girls."

Mr. Bennet closed his eyes and steepled his fingers as he sat behind his desk. He hardly knew how to respond to his son-in-law's generous offer. Indeed, it appeared Darcy was willing to step in and take charge of an unsavory situation he had allowed to become so out of hand. He had been remiss in his duty as a father in many ways, but never more so than now, with Lydia. If they were lucky, they might escape a scandal, seeing that it was Elizabeth who had come upon her youngest sister in an amorous embrace with Wickham and not one of their neighbors or, God forbid, another officer of the militia. The elder gentleman took a deep breath and expelled it slowly. Perhaps all might yet be well, but for how long? While Mary had devoted much of her time to reading and practicing her music, Kitty and Lydia's existences were ones of dissipation and idleness. No, Darcy was correct. Both girls were in dire need of discipline and guidance, and this, Mr. Bennet was well aware, they had not received, nor were they ever likely to receive, at home.

He sighed and ran his hands over his face. "I thank you for your very kind, very generous offer to my family, Darcy."

Darcy inclined his head. "Your family is also my family, sir. Elizabeth's sisters are now my own, and therefore, they are entitled to my protection just as much as she is. I take my responsibility to the members of my family very seriously, Mr. Bennet."

"Yes, and it speaks well of you, Son. I hope, however, you will not be unduly offended if I defer my acceptance or declination of your kind offer for a day or two. I would appreciate some time to fully consider the matter and all its implications."

Elizabeth gawked at him. "But Papa, how can you not accept Fitzwilliam's offer? Cannot you see that it is in everyone's best interest? Such an opportunity can only lead to advantages my sisters will never have available to them otherwise. Would you have them remain always at Longbourn, idle and ignorant?"

Before her father could respond, however, Darcy said, "Mr. Bennet, take all the time you require. We will be remaining in Hertfordshire until we can be certain of Wickham's whereabouts. God willing, Colonel Forster and his men will be able to locate him within the next few days, and of course, we will be better able to decide on a course of action then." He turned toward his wife and squeezed her hand. "Come, Elizabeth. I believe your father might appreciate having his library to himself. Perhaps we can take a turn in the garden before luncheon is served?" And with that, he led a very perplexed, not to mention irritated Elizabeth out into the hall.

They retrieved their coats in silence and left the house to walk in one of the gardens. "Fitzwilliam, I hardly understand why my father would need to think over such a generous offer. Would it not be to the advantage of our entire family? He must be well aware he could never afford to do so much for them. He has not your income or your influence in society." Elizabeth folded her arms.

"Yes," Darcy answered, "he is, Elizabeth. He is well aware of the differences in our financial situations, and it is a matter of some delicacy. How do you think you would feel if you were in his position? Your father is very upset over Lydia's outrageous behavior, and he must, undoubtedly, be laying a healthy portion of the blame for her failings on his own shoulders. Please do not be too hard on him, my love. Just be patient, and give him the time he requires. In essence, I have offered to assume responsibility for all your sisters, as though he has not done an adequate job. It was not my intention to cause your father any further pain or humiliation, and most definitely not to imply that he has not been a good father to you, but I fear that is precisely what my making such an offer may have accomplished. That is not something to be taken lightly. I hope he will understand that I meant him no disrespect. I only wish to help redirect your sisters to a more propitious path."

Elizabeth stopped and turned to face him. "I am sure he understands that you wish only to help us. You are truly the best man I know, Fitzwilliam, and I love you all the more because you possess such selfless goodness." She wrapped her arms around his waist and leaned in to give him a kiss. "I only hope my father will see fit to accept your offer, for all of our sakes."

Darcy hugged her closer. "Your father is an intelligent, sensible man, Elizabeth. He knows what is best for his family." Then smiling, he said, "He allowed you to marry me, did he not?"

Elizabeth laughed. "Yes, but that hardly signifies! As much as I love my father and do not wish to occasion him any pain or disappointment, I would have married you without his consent, in any case. We would have been forced to wait only until next year, when I would have become of age. I love you that much, Fitzwilliam. Indeed, after knowing you, my dearest, I am certain no other man could ever make me happy."

Darcy rested his forehead against hers. "Elizabeth, you cannot know what it means to have you for my wife. Waking every morning with you in my arms is happiness like none I have ever known. I thank God every day that I have you to love me." He kissed her then, with great feeling, and they remained thus engaged until Bingley's arrival called them back into the house.

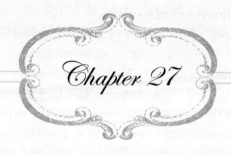

Chapter 27

On the day Charlotte Lucas became Charlotte Collins, it came as no surprise to the inhabitants of Longbourn that Mrs. Bennet declared herself unequal to the task of feigning a pleasure she could not feel. Indeed, the knowledge that Charlotte, and not one of her own daughters, would usurp her place as mistress of that estate after the death of her husband brought her no comfort. To make matters infinitely worse, it had recently been brought to her attention that Lydia, who was by far her favorite child, had been discovered in a compromising position with George Wickham. Normally, this would not have been the cause of much agitation and distress to Mrs. Bennet, for she would have looked upon the prospect of having another daughter married as nothing short of a fortuitous act of providence; however, the unhappy reality that the prospective bridegroom had seemingly fled the area without so much as a hint of his whereabouts, left her in high dudgeon and with a fit of nerves that amazed even her husband.

"Oh, Mr. Bennet! You must find him and *make* them marry," she cried, her distress extreme, "for soon everyone will hear of it, and then what will become of us all?" She blotted her eyes with her damp handkerchief and continued. "I simply do not understand it! Lydia was always such an obedient, respectful girl. Never any trouble at all—and so popular with all of the officers, too. Surely, there must be one of *them*, at least, who would happily marry her if Wickham is not found!"

Darcy rolled his eyes and walked to the window to stand beside his wife, who laid a hand upon his arm in a gesture of assuagement. He gave her a searching look before raising her hand to his lips, caressing her fingers with an almost reverent kiss. It was truly beyond his abilities to understand how Elizabeth and Jane could have been born to a woman as impractical as his mother-in-law, and he found himself suddenly wishing they could depart for London on the following day, as they had originally planned. In light of all that had occurred, however, Darcy had decided to remain in Hertfordshire until Colonel Forster and his men determined Wickham was most definitely not in the area. In his opinion, such news could not come soon enough.

Elizabeth's spirits had been low since her encounter with Wickham, and it concerned him. At her insistence, Mrs. Bennet had not been made aware of Wickham's assault, and it was obvious to Darcy that Elizabeth's state of mind was far from improved by her mother's obtuse comments. He longed to take her away from the unpleasantness of the last few days and from the added stress of reliving the painful event in the antagonistic company of her youngest sister.

If he was honest with himself, Darcy knew he was really longing to take her not to London, but to Pemberley, where he felt fairly confident his wife would soon find many ways to raise her spirits as they submersed themselves in their new life together.

Mr. Bennet's dry voice, tinged with anger, rang out from across the room. "My dear, if anyone should hear of your daughter's indiscretion, I am certain it will be by your own mouth, as the only people who are aware of Lydia's shameful conduct currently occupy this room." He then made a sweeping motion with his arm, indicating Darcy, Elizabeth, Jane, and Bingley. Colonel Forster was the only absent party. Darcy cringed. He would not put it past Mrs. Bennet and her loose tongue to advertise the scandal any more than he would Lydia herself. He briefly wondered where his sister-in-law was at the moment, as he had hardly seen her since they returned from the wedding breakfast at Lucas Lodge. Lydia, due to her shameful behavior at that house not two nights prior, had not been permitted to attend. It was now nearly teatime.

Just then, the front door to the house opened, and Lydia's loud voice could be heard ringing throughout the front hall. Her father strode to the door and summoned her into the drawing room. Lydia immediately took in the grave faces collected there and her mother's incessant wailing, and rolled her eyes. "Lord," she muttered, "you are a dreary lot."

"And why should we not be?" cried Mrs. Bennet. "Mr. Wickham has gone from the country, perhaps never to return!"

With a huff, Lydia threw herself upon one of the sofas. "Oh, Lord! Wherever did you get that notion, Mama? I daresay you ought not to put stock in anything Mr. Darcy and Lizzy have to say on the subject, for they cannot possibly know anything of my dear Wickham," she said as she readjusted a bit of lace on her gown. "Indeed, Wickham shall return for me. He must only have some very pressing matters of business, I am sure, for he dearly loves me, as I do him, and we shall be married sooner or later." Here, she shrugged. "It hardly signifies to me when our wedding shall take place, for I know I shall someday be Mrs. George Wickham." Then she laughed. "Lord, how droll that sounds!"

Elizabeth had heard all she could possibly bear, and with a sound of disgust, she hastened from the room, slamming the door behind her. Darcy made to follow her, but Jane placed a steady hand upon his arm and shook her head. "I will gladly see to my sister, sir. Do not trouble yourself."

Darcy relented, only to pace before the window and quit the room himself not five minutes later. Shutting the door behind him, he stood in the hall before he discerned the sound of Jane's voice coming from abovestairs. Not wishing to intrude upon a private moment between the two sisters, he had just taken a seat to await them when he heard the distinctive sounds of retching, followed again by Jane's soothing voice. Taking the stairs two at a time, he soon came upon both ladies seated upon the floor of the nearest water closet.

"Elizabeth!" he exclaimed as he stood over the pale form of his wife and watched her lay her head upon Jane's lap.

"I am well," she whispered.

He knelt before her and stroked her clammy brow. "You are not well. I shall call for a doctor."

"No. There is nothing Mr. Jones will be able to do for me, Fitzwilliam. Indeed, this is perfectly natural."

Darcy studied her with an incredulous expression. "*This* is perfectly natural? You cannot be serious."

Elizabeth closed her eyes and swallowed several times. "Jane," she implored.

Jane colored and, without looking at her brother-in-law, said, "I believe it is to be expected for a married woman in my sister's condition, sir."

Taking her meaning at last, Darcy could find nothing to say other than a simple, "Ah," as he twisted his signet ring.

They were joined then, and quite unexpectedly, by Bingley. "So this is where you all have got to. I was—good God!" he exclaimed as he beheld Elizabeth's pale face.

Embarrassed to have Bingley come upon her in such a state, Elizabeth attempted to rise; however, such an action only served to exacerbate her nausea, and she promptly found herself doubled over the basin yet again. Darcy insinuated himself between Jane and Elizabeth, moving to support his wife as she continued to empty the contents of her stomach. Knowing her sister was in good hands, and understanding how uncomfortable Elizabeth must feel having Bingley seeing her thus, Jane took the opportunity to lead him away.

It was some minutes before Elizabeth's situation improved. With a groan, she leaned back upon Darcy, whose outstretched arms enfolded her, securing her against his chest. Wishing to distract his wife from her discomfort, he kissed her temple and said, "Though your sister's cavalier attitude with regard to her behavior certainly causes me to feel ill, I had no idea it was appalling enough to actually inspire the contents of one's stomach to revolt. I now see I stand corrected. Perhaps I should exercise caution, as well? What think you, my dearest?"

Elizabeth closed her eyes and swallowed hard, wiping the back of her trembling hand across her mouth. "I think you choose the most outrageous moments to display your sense of humor, Fitzwilliam," she said in a weak voice but with the hint of a smile upon her lips.

He kissed her temple once more. "Forgive me. I could not resist," he said. "I realize I should not tease you so when you are in such a state, especially when this particular state of affliction is due, in part, to my own, ah, very explicit attentions to you. Tell me, are you feeling any better?" he asked, brushing several curls away from her face.

"Yes," she replied, "although, I fear if I move much I shall begin again."

"Then here we shall remain until you are feeling completely recovered." He shifted his weight so they were both a bit more comfortable. Darcy bestowed a kiss upon her head and closed his eyes. They remained thus until well after supper had been announced, and then only to remove to Netherfield so they might spend the rest of the evening in quiet solitude, away from the tiresome ranting of Mrs. Bennet and her favorite daughter.

Kitty made her way to the breakfast parlor the next morning with a small, secretive smirk upon her lips. Her father dismissed it as foolishness, which he had long known to run rampant under his roof, but then a quarter of an hour passed without any sign of Lydia. Mrs. Bennet seemed to be the only one willing to remark upon her favorite daughter's absence. "Kitty," she said, "you must go upstairs at once and tell your sister to hurry herself along. There is much to be done today. When Lizzy arrives, I will go into Meryton to sit with my sister Phillips, and you girls shall accompany me."

Mr. Bennet, without raising his eyes from his newspaper, said firmly, "You will do nothing of the sort, Mrs. Bennet. I will not have anyone in this house speak so much as one word about your youngest daughter's behavior. Since she has not the sense nor the humility to recognize the disgrace she has brought upon herself or her family, she will no longer be permitted into society until she can prove to me she has spent the day in a productive manner, which, I suspect, will not be for some time. The same will apply to you, as well, Kitty."

Kitty pouted and protested, and even went so far as to cry, but to no avail. Her father would not be swayed. Darcy, Elizabeth, and Bingley's arrival was announced, and with a few further words of admonishment, accompanied by a stern look or two from Mr. Bennet, the subject was soon dropped.

Another half hour passed by rather awkwardly, and still, Lydia did not appear. "Oh, where is that child?" cried Mrs. Bennet. "Kitty, run upstairs and fetch your sister. I must speak to her at once."

At this, Kitty's pouting mouth slowly transformed itself into a flicker of a smug smile. Blotting the corners of her lips with her napkin, she replied, "I am afraid I cannot, Mama."

Her mother gaped at her, and Mr. Bennet raised his eyebrows. "What do you mean you will not?" cried Mrs. Bennet. "I demand you fetch her at once, and do not venture to speak to me so, insolent girl!"

To this, Kitty replied, "I did not say I *would not*, Mama—only that I *cannot*, for Lydia is not to be found in her room this morning."

This statement caught Mr. Bennet's full attention, as well as that of every other person in the room, and his wife exclaimed, "What do you mean she is not in her room?! Where else would she possibly be found at such an hour?"

Kitty remained silent until her father's patience had reached its limits. "Katherine! Explain yourself! Do you know where your sister is?"

She nodded, but any trace of amusement was now erased from her face. "Yes, sir."

With some hesitation and downcast eyes, she surrendered to her father a folded missive written in Lydia's flowing hand. Mr. Bennet read it and paled. "Good God," he whispered as he handed the note to Darcy with a shaking hand. His son-in-law read it and, with a sound of disgust, thrust the missive toward his wife.

"Whatever does it say?" demanded Mrs. Bennet. "Is it from

my dearest girl? Do not keep me in suspense! What does she have to say?"

Darcy glanced at Mr. Bennet, who sat stock still, holding his head between his hands. "Pray, enlighten your mother, Elizabeth, and read aloud what your sister had to say," Darcy said with barely concealed contempt as he rose and strode to the window. She cleared her throat and, in an unsteady voice, complied.

Dear Kitty,

You will laugh when you awaken in the morning and find me gone, and if you cannot guess with whom, you are a simpleton, indeed, for there is but one man whom I love.

My dear Wickham asks that you conceal my absence as long as you can, and I confess, I am in complete agreement with him, for it will be such a good joke, will it not, when Lizzy and her droll Mr. Darcy hear that he has come for me at last, just as I knew he would, and in the dead of night, too? Is it not the most romantic thing you have ever heard? You must tell me how they both looked when next you see me, for Wickham and I would dearly love a good laugh at their expense. Tell Mama I will write if I can—though I am certain, as a married woman, that my husband shall engage me in far more pleasurable activities—and that she has my leave to inform the neighborhood of my impending marriage. I remain your loving sister,

L. B.

Mrs. Bennet's shrieks easily overshadowed Jane's and Mary's horrified gasps. Mr. Bennet removed to his library, Darcy and Bingley hard on his heels. Elizabeth made to follow, but Darcy caught her hand and stopped her, his eyes communicating that her presence would not be allowed for this particular meeting. The door to the library closed upon her, and she found herself quite alone.

Mrs. Bennet, overcome with distress, retired to her room with the assistance of her faithful housekeeper. Kitty was left to her own devices, worrying over the blame she would shoulder for Lydia's rash elopement. Since Elizabeth had taken up an agitated vigil outside her father's library, it was left to Jane and Mary to attend their mother.

To Elizabeth, half the day seemed to pass before the gentlemen emerged, but in fact, it had been no more than three-quarters of an hour. When the door finally opened, she sprang from her chair and looked in expectation from her father's grave face to that of her husband's. With a nod from Mr. Bennet, Darcy led her by the hand to a small parlor and closed the door. Elizabeth gripped his hands and waited in silence for him to begin.

In a low voice he said, "Surely you must realize Wickham has not taken your sister to Scotland, Elizabeth. It is my belief they are most likely gone to London, and I have told your father as much. It may still be within our power to recover her, but we must act quickly. Colonel Fitzwilliam has many contacts there whom I believe can greatly benefit us in our search." He scowled. "Having grown up with Wickham, I have knowledge of his habits and tendencies. From what I have witnessed in Hertfordshire, he has altered little, but much for the worse. With any luck, we will be able to locate them within a matter of a few days, though I would not hold out hope for your sister's virtue, if it is, indeed, still intact."

Elizabeth looked away; she had no hope on that score. Darcy began to draw circles upon her palms with his thumbs. "Bingley has agreed to stay behind and look after you and your family while your father and I search for them in London. We shall depart within the hour."

Elizabeth could hardly credit these last words. "You mean to say you are leaving me here?" she asked.

"I see very few options before us, Elizabeth. I had rather thought you would prefer to remain with your family at this time. Certainly, your mother and sisters will be in need of you."

"And you will not?" she asked.

Darcy averted his eyes. "That is not what I meant; you know it is not, but London is not safe. There is nothing you could possibly do there to aid your sister. You would do better to stay here with your family."

Elizabeth stared at him. "And is this what you truly wish?" she asked, her voice strained.

"Of course not," he answered quickly, "but I cannot see my way to bringing you with me. There is nothing for you to do in London that would not put you at risk. You know Wickham is not to be underestimated."

"There is everything for me to do in London!" she cried. "Will you not need my comfort after enduring God-only-knows-what for the sake of my family?" She caught his face in her hands and forced him to meet her eyes. "Even if I spend day after day alone with none but the servants for company, it shall be far preferable to having to spend my nights without you. Indeed, Fitzwilliam, I want no distance between us. I am going with you. You are my husband, my life. My place is with you."

He considered her words for a long moment before placing

his hand upon her cheek and nodding once. "As you wish," he said, "but I will not have you venturing out alone. You will not so much as leave the house for any reason without my protection, do you understand?"

Elizabeth brushed her lips upon his hand. "You have my word. I will do nothing you do not think is best. I wish only for us to remain together."

"Let us inform your father, then, and be off. We have not another moment to lose."

The trip to London passed silently, and as Darcy's carriage rolled through the streets of their Mayfair neighborhood and on to Darcy House, Elizabeth felt herself relax, if only a little. They were now home and would, hopefully, within several short hours, meet with Colonel Fitzwilliam, to whom Darcy had dispatched an express just moments before they left Hertfordshire. She only prayed it had reached him and he would be available to meet with them that evening.

She need not have worried on that account, for they had no sooner set foot in the front door than they were informed by Mrs. Hildebrandt that the colonel had been awaiting their arrival in Darcy's study for the last hour.

Darcy bade his father-in-law proceed without him then pulled aside his anxious wife. "I know you wish to attend this conversation, Elizabeth, but your resting yourself is more important. I will not have you placing yourself or our unborn babe at risk."

Over her vehement protests, he continued, "No. I will not hear another word. I beg you would rest. It would greatly ease my mind to know you are taking every precaution. Please, dearest, do this one thing for me, and I promise I will keep nothing from you."

Elizabeth addressed him with narrowed eyes. "You promise, no matter what happens, to tell me all?" she demanded.

"You have my word."

She sighed. "Very well, Fitzwilliam. I will try to rest for one hour, but I cannot promise I shall be successful."

"That is all I ask."

He brushed his lips against hers, and she returned the gesture before saying, "I expect you to come to me as soon as your plans are decided." Then, with a parting glance, she turned and left him.

Darcy watched his wife retreat up the staircase and out of sight before he made his way with haste to his study, where he found Colonel Fitzwilliam in deep discussion with Mr. Bennet.

"Darcy," he said, "I was just telling your father-in-law that I have dispatched eight of my most loyal men to search for Wickham and Miss Lydia; however, I do believe our best bet might be to venture to Mrs. Younge's. What think you? Surely, she must have some idea of the blackguard's whereabouts."

Darcy poured three glasses of brandy and handed them around. "I agree, though he has other acquaintances in Town, as well, who may prove useful to us."

The colonel nodded and drank slowly from his glass before saying, "We must prepare ourselves. I do not expect to find them tonight. Her virtue—"

"Her virtue is likely no longer an issue," said Mr. Bennet with disgust. "Forgive me, Colonel, but I can have no illusions that my youngest daughter will be returned to me whole. Not after their conduct the other night, and certainly not after what that scoundrel dared to attempt with my Lizzy." He swallowed the rest of his brandy and slammed his glass upon Darcy's desk. He settled his angry gaze upon his son-in-law and, in a voice of deadly calm, said, "I want them found, and I want him to suffer. I hardly care what means are employed to achieve this, so long as it is brought about. I care very little for charges of desertion or for his debts to area merchants. He has insulted two of my daughters, and I intend to see him punished, once and for all."

Mr. Bennet tore his gaze from his son-in-law and took several steps toward the fire. Leaning his forearms upon the mantle, he took a deep breath and said, "You warned me, Darcy, of the very great danger that scoundrel posed to my family, yet I failed to heed your words of caution, even after all that had transpired in Meryton. You showed me you were more than willing to assume responsibility for Elizabeth's protection, and I confess, I was quite content to allow you that honor. It now appears to have been the one sensible decision I have made where my daughters are concerned." Mr. Bennet laughed ruefully and passed his hand over his eyes. Then, cursing softly, he said, "If I had only bothered to follow your example and exert myself with the rest. There is no excuse for my neglect. The fault for Lydia's brashness and impetuosity lies on no man's shoulders but my own, and for once, I am feeling the full weight of it, as I certainly ought." And with that, the elder gentleman excused himself and quitted the room.

Darcy strode to the nearest window and stood with his back to the room. Colonel Fitzwilliam exhaled slowly and fixed his cousin with a look of grave concern. "What is this about Wickham insulting your wife, Darcy? Is it true?" he asked.

Darcy nodded. "He laid his hands upon her, as well as his vile mouth."

"But no more?"

"No more!" Darcy spat, his temper immediately rising. "Is that act alone not enough to make a husband wish to see that bastard hang? He assaulted and terrified my wife! He threatened to force himself upon her should they meet again! She is with child! And even if she was not, I cannot allow further harm to come to her at his hands. No, when we capture Wickham, I will see him punished, as I should have last summer at Ramsgate. I know not how but, as God is my witness, Fitzwilliam, this time he will pay for his crimes."

Colonel Fitzwilliam slowly nodded. "Then there is much to be done. I do not expect to hear from my men until the morrow, unless there is some unforeseen development tonight. Do you think Mr. Bennet intends to challenge him?"

Darcy shrugged and raked his hands through his hair. "I know not, but surely we must discourage such a measure. He is upset, and rightly so, but his family will suffer acutely if he is not successful. Though Lydia is hardly a favorite of his, the same cannot be said for Elizabeth. She has not recovered her spirits since that villain accosted her, and I am certain her feelings have not escaped Mr. Bennet's notice. If it were up to me, I would have pursued him and put a bullet through his worthless heart in Hertfordshire, but I hardly think Elizabeth would condone such an act." Darcy sat down behind his desk and held his head in his hands. "Indeed, I know for a fact she would not. Whatever we do, Fitzwilliam, we must take great care. Wickham must be punished, and the less Elizabeth knows of it, the better. I do not wish to distress her further."

Colonel Fitzwilliam traced the rim of his glass. "You do not intend to force a marriage then, Cousin?"

Darcy snorted. "My sister-in-law cannot marry that blackguard. I will pay to increase her dowry if need be or hide her away in the countryside until after her confinement if it comes to that, but her father and I are in agreement—Lydia cannot be shackled to that piece of filth for the rest of her life. God knows, as do you and I, whatever Wickham would do to her would hardly be pleasant. Nor will I have that scoundrel associated with my wife in any way."

"Fair enough," Fitzwilliam said, glancing at the mantle clock. "It is now nearly supper hour. When would you care to pay a call upon Mrs. Younge?"

"With that woman, the element of surprise is our best advantage. We could dine within the hour and then pay her a visit tonight after Elizabeth retires." Darcy drained his glass. "How does Georgiana?"

"She is well, though she is anxious for your return. I have yet to inform her that you and Elizabeth are in Town. I have yet to inform anyone. I did not know if you would wish it, under the circumstances."

Darcy shook his head and sighed. "No. Not yet. Although I know her society would be good for Elizabeth, I cannot help but wish to protect my sister from this business. To hear that Wickham has succeeded with Lydia, when it was very nearly herself, she may not take the news at all well."

"Georgiana is stronger than you think. Did you not tell me she confided in your wife of her own volition?" Darcy nodded and Colonel Fitzwilliam continued, "Well then, I see no harm in bringing Georgiana home to Darcy House in a few days. She and Elizabeth will, no doubt, find comfort in each other's society. To be honest, Elizabeth may need the distraction, for there is no telling how many hours you will be called away during the next week or so, and I doubt you will want her to venture out with Wickham still at large."

Darcy grunted in acquiescence, and the two gentlemen retired shortly thereafter to freshen themselves before dinner.

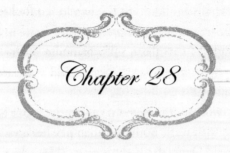

Chapter 28

It was close to midnight when Darcy and Colonel Fitzwilliam knocked upon the door of a somewhat respectable-looking boarding house in an unrespectable section of Town. Four of the colonel's most trustworthy officers accompanied them.

The look of surprised horror on the face of the middle-aged woman who opened the door was, to the gentlemen, promising. They pushed their way into the front parlor before she could protest, and closed the door behind them. "Mrs. Younge," Colonel Fitzwilliam said, "I trust you know why we have come."

In addition to being Georgiana's former governess, Mrs. Younge held the notoriety of being a trusted associate of George Wickham. As such, she had been little inclined to talk, and several hours later, Darcy wanted nothing more than to have her out of his sight. It had taken close to thirty pounds of his money to finally coax her to reveal that both miscreants had been granted admittance to her home, but had been turned out several hours later after their boisterous interlude abovestairs escalated into a heated argument, in which several personal effects of some value were destroyed. She admitted that Lydia, who she claimed Wickham had referred to as Lizzy in a moment of fury, had initially seemed willing—even happy—to be with him, but, upon quitting the establishment, had appeared utterly terrified. Darcy left the house in a foul temper and promised Mrs. Younge further payment should she discover any information regarding either party's whereabouts. That the woman had been most adamant Wickham had referred to Lydia by his wife's name brought him nothing but unease.

The next several days passed slowly and uneventfully, both to the relief and frustration of those involved. Colonel Fitzwilliam was a constant visitor at Darcy House—dropping in at all hours of the day and night to meet privately with Darcy and Mr. Bennet in Darcy's study and, oftentimes, with Mr. Gardiner, when that gentleman's business would allow it. Though Elizabeth was kept abreast of nearly all of their dealings, she could not help feeling that her husband was keeping something pertinent from her, though she could not imagine precisely what. On top of that was the added hardship of being left to her own devices day after day while the gentlemen conferred and came and went as required. Though she had come to accept this probability in theory before she had left Hertfordshire, upon arriving in London, Elizabeth soon found she was not in the least prepared to be alone with her troubling thoughts and wrenching worries for the majority of the day.

After the visit to Mrs. Younge's, Darcy had decided against sending for Georgiana. He could not trust the woman to refrain from showing up on his doorstep, and though Mrs. Gardiner visited Darcy House as often as her time would allow, she still had a household to run and several young children to care for, which left little time to devote to her niece. Elizabeth tried to hide her disappointment as best she could, but it was becoming increasingly difficult to do when, on most days, she found very little reprieve from the inner turmoil of her active mind.

In an effort to divert her focus from dark thoughts, Elizabeth immersed herself in learning the management of her new household. Though she had some limited experience assisting her mother in the task, she was not prepared for the large amounts of money and the wide disbursement of funds she suddenly found at her disposal. She devoted many tedious hours to poring over the books with Mrs. Hildebrandt, struggling to perfect her understanding of the operation of her husband's London household. Under the housekeeper's instruction, Elizabeth persevered in her endeavor until satisfied she had finally acquired enough knowledge of the management of Darcy House to do an effective job without supervision.

In the moments when she was not working closely with Mrs. Hildebrandt or attempting to conceal her anxiety behind a book while awaiting some word or scrap of news, however small and insignificant, regarding her sister's whereabouts, Elizabeth took to wandering the cold, empty courtyard of Darcy House. It was the only form of exercise out-of-doors Darcy would permit her, even accompanied by him. She had been walking for some time amongst the barren beds, dry fountains, and statues; her thoughts turned toward the disreputable situation her youngest sister had brought upon herself—and all her family—with Wickham.

During their last days at Longbourn, there had been several painful instances where Lydia had accused Elizabeth of behaving in very much the same disgraceful manner, regarding her own conduct with Darcy. It disturbed her, so much so, that she could not stop herself from thinking back, time and again, to her relationship with the man who was now her beloved husband.

She recalled the past events since she and Darcy had met and, with a sudden epiphany, realized that, though she could not, in all honesty, discount Lydia's accusations, there still remained one very significant difference in their circumstances: Darcy had been in love with her—ardently, passionately, unfailingly in love with her—and that, Elizabeth was finally forced to concede, made all the difference in their situations, at least where it mattered most—to her.

She was lost in her own thoughts, so much so, that she failed to hear the soft click of the French doors to the courtyard, nor the sound of purposeful footfalls.

Not wishing to startle her, Darcy stopped several feet away before calling her name. Elizabeth turned to face him, and he noticed the troubled look in her eyes. He was about to speak, to ask her why she appeared to be in such a state of wretchedness, but then thought better of it. Instead, he closed the distance between them and embraced her. Finally, without removing from his arms, Elizabeth said, "Thank you for loving me so, Fitzwilliam, despite every obstacle we have been forced to overcome."

Darcy knew the last few weeks had been difficult for her, and for this reason in particular, it pained him that they had yet to find Lydia. They had been in London for nearly a week, and still, there was no sign of her, no word, nor any leads to follow. He was fast losing hope for her recovery, as were Mr. Bennet and Mr. Gardiner. He answered her not with words but by holding her more tightly. Elizabeth sighed and, after a time, pulled away and busied herself with adjusting her pelisse.

Darcy cleared his throat and said, "My aunt and uncle have extended an invitation to dine in Berkeley Square tomorrow evening. It seems they are no longer ignorant of our presence in Town. I took the liberty of accepting the invitation, but I have not shared with them any information regarding your sister's alleged elopement. I believe we could both use an evening in the company of family. My sister, I hear, is desirous to see you." He dropped his voice. "You should never have been made to suffer this alone, Elizabeth. I fear I have not done my duty by you these last few days. Can you ever forgive me for neglecting you so?"

Elizabeth stared at him before lowering her gaze. "There is nothing for me to forgive. I did not expect you to be constantly by my side, Fitzwilliam. You are here to search for my sister. Of course her untenable situation must have first claim on you. I would not have it any other way."

"But I would," he said. "It should not be so. You should not have been left to your own devices at such a time as this. You have endured more in the last few weeks than should be expected of a gently bred woman, and I feel as though I have abandoned you in favor of one whom I can hardly esteem. I am sorry, Elizabeth. I do not mean to pain you further, but neither can I lie to you."

Elizabeth shook her head and took several steps from him, pressing her fingers to her eyes. "No. If only Lydia had not run away from home. If only my mother had not been so indulgent. If only my father would have taken the trouble to check her wild behavior, rather than contenting himself to simply laugh at it, then, perhaps we would have been spared such worry and humiliation, but it was not to be."

Darcy extended his hand to her and pulled her close. "If you wish, I will send word to my aunt that we are unable to attend her dinner. I understand that her dear friends, Lady Malcolm and Lady Sowersby, are to be present, as well. They are both very kind, but I can understand if you do not wish to go through such an ordeal at present."

"No, Fitzwilliam. You are correct in thinking some familial society will do us both good. Are my father and the Gardiners invited, as well?"

"Yes, though your father has declined. I believe he will remove to Gracechurch Street for the evening. I am not yet certain whether the Gardiners will attend, but I can only assume that, under the circumstances, they may decline, as well. Richard and my other cousins will, of course, be in attendance, as will Georgiana. My uncle has informed me that Lady Catherine and my cousin Anne have since returned to Rosings and do not plan to return to Town for some time."

She nodded. *At least I will not have to bear that woman's scorn and disapprobation*, she thought with some relief.

Darcy guided her to the house, and they retired to the privacy of their apartment. He rested with his wife, stroking her back until he was certain she had finally fallen asleep; then he rose and returned to his study, where he found Colonel Fitzwilliam frowning over a note that had only recently arrived from one of his men. Darcy looked at him with anticipation, but Richard only shook his head. "There is no news. I have only been informed that Mrs. Younge has been out now for several hours. Three of my men are following her at a discreet distance. She appears to be making calls. They will send word if they discover anything."

Darcy cursed under his breath. "We must find them. I can no longer countenance seeing Elizabeth in such low spirits. This is supposed to be a happy time for her; she should be enjoying her new position as my wife and the prospect of motherhood, yet she is close to tears each hour of the day and separated from me because of this business with her sister. I will not have it. Discover them. Do whatever you must, promise whatever you must; I will pay for it, but Lydia must be found. Elizabeth and I cannot live as we wish until she is recovered. After that, I shall remove both Elizabeth and Georgiana to Pemberley, the Season be hanged. I can no longer abide this insufferable situation."

The Darcys dined at Berkeley Square the following evening. Elizabeth had somehow managed to rally her spirits, if for no reason other than to conceal her family's unhappy situation. Though Lady Matlock may have discerned something in her manner that gave her a cause for concern, both Lady Malcolm and Lady Sowersby were unaware of it. They found themselves immediately taken with the new Mrs. Darcy. Elizabeth was, to them, all that was charming and lovely. Darcy was as enchanted and attentive as ever, if somewhat concerned for her state of mind, and while Lady Malcolm and his nearest relations could easily tease him for it, Lady Sowersby, who had never married and who was ever the romantic, could find nothing but pleasure in his solicitous and tender attentions to his beautiful new bride.

Halfway through the meal, a message arrived for Colonel Fitzwilliam, who quickly excused himself from the table. Many minutes passed, and he failed to return, leaving at least two persons in the party anxious over his lengthy absence. After receiving numerous glances from Elizabeth, Darcy also excused himself. He eventually located his cousin in his uncle's study. "What news, Fitzwilliam?" he asked without ceremony, shutting the door behind him.

The colonel's countenance was grave. "My men have located a young woman whom they believe may be Miss Lydia. It is not promising. She is currently residing in Madame Tremont's house. Do you know of it?"

Darcy's eyes grew wide. "In a brothel? I cannot believe this," he gasped, shaking his head. "Is it known whether or not she came to be there willingly?"

Fitzwilliam exhaled loudly. "I believe it unlikely Miss Lydia would have agreed to enter such an establishment of her own volition. It is my guess that Wickham probably sold her into servitude. He is no doubt low on funds and most likely growing desperate."

Darcy ran his hands over his eyes. "Good God. This will kill Elizabeth. I cannot have her learn of this. We must leave at once and recover Lydia. God only knows what may befall her in such an establishment. We have not a moment to lose."

"I agree, Darcy. I have dispatched my orders to my men. We will be moving within the hour, but you must know you cannot possibly accompany us."

"Why ever not? She is my sister-in-law. She is *my* responsibility. *Wickham* is my responsibility. Surely, I must be the one to go."

Fitzwilliam gaped at him. "You cannot be serious! Do you have any idea what it will look like if you were to go? To a brothel? You, who have only just exchanged your sacred vows before God—and with a woman whom Lady Catherine would happily tout in public as your mistress if given leave to do so? Can you not imagine the talk such an action will inspire amongst the *ton*? The repercussions to Elizabeth's reception in society alone would be devastating, to say nothing of your gaining a reputation as a philanderer."

Darcy, who had been pacing, threw himself into the nearest chair and growled in frustration. "What the bloody hell am I supposed to do, then? Elizabeth will want me to retrieve her sister, as well I should!"

"But not at this cost, Darcy! There will be enough talk already. You will do well to leave this to me. Miss Lydia knows me—well enough to understand I would not harm her in any way. I am confident she will feel safe enough to leave with me. In fact"—he smiled grimly—"I would wager a great deal that she will jump at the chance—especially if I am wearing my red coat."

Darcy looked at him sharply, and Colonel Fitzwilliam moved

to lay a hand upon his cousin's tense shoulder. "Forgive me. That was poorly done. If it is, indeed, Miss Lydia, Darcy, I shall return her to her family tonight. Shall I bring her to Darcy House, or would you rather I deliver her to the Gardiners?"

Darcy ran the back of his hand over his lips. "No, bring her to Grosvenor Square. The Gardiners have young children. They should not be subjected to such scandal."

"Very well. What will you tell Elizabeth?"

Darcy sighed. "I hardly know. I do not want to raise her hopes if it is not Lydia. In any case, the news will be distressing, to say the least. I will make our excuses to your parents in a short while. They shall not suspect anything untoward. Elizabeth is not quite herself, in any case, and I daresay my aunt has discerned as much. Then I suppose I shall wait at Darcy House for word from you. What of Wickham?"

Colonel Fitzwilliam shook his head. "I have received no word of Wickham, but when I do, you shall be the first to know."

It was nearly eleven o'clock that night when Colonel Fitzwilliam was ushered into the dimly lit back foyer of Darcy House, bearing Lydia Bennet in his arms. Elizabeth had been on edge ever since her husband had reluctantly told her Richard's men had discovered the location of a young woman who may or may not be Lydia. Elizabeth raced down the stairs when she heard Darcy's voice mingled with that of his cousin, barely managing to fasten her dressing gown about her waist as she went. She gasped when she beheld Lydia, who appeared listless, battered, and bruised. Holding back tears, Elizabeth instructed the colonel to carry her sister to one of the family apartments abovestairs. One of his men went off to summon the doctor; another, Mr. Bennet, who had not yet returned from Gracechurch Street.

Elizabeth saw to her sister's comfort as best she could, assisting one of the maids with bathing her, dressing her, and tending to her battered face, which felt feverish to the touch. All the while, Elizabeth spoke to Lydia in a low, soothing voice full of tenderness and unrestrained affection. After Lydia was settled beneath the counterpane, and even when the doctor finally arrived, Elizabeth pointedly refused to leave Lydia. Indeed, even after her father had appeared by his daughter's bedside and insisted Elizabeth rest, she would not. She was determined to stay beside her youngest sister until she was well—be it hours or days.

Darcy looked on with concern for his sister-in-law, as well as his wife. Since this was to be his wife's stubborn decision, and since he had very little success in swaying her from it, Darcy saw nothing else to do but emulate it. If Elizabeth would not leave her sister, neither would he leave Elizabeth. The fact that he felt she was putting her own health at risk, as well as that of their unborn child, by refusing to look after herself, disturbed him. In vain did he and Mr. Bennet attempt to persuade her to retire and rest in the comfort of her own rooms. Not until the following evening, when Elizabeth finally succumbed to exhaustion—falling asleep in a chair by Lydia's bed—was Darcy able to remove her to their bed for the night. Though she stirred and attempted to rise and return to her sister several times while Darcy eased her gown, corset, and chemise from her body, somehow, he hardly knew how, he had managed to calm her agitation, cradling her in his arms until she drifted into a heavy slumber. He did not dare leave her side, not even after the sun had risen high into the cold, gray sky.

Another week would pass before her family could be reassured of any improvement in Lydia, and before Colonel Fitzwilliam would finally receive word from his men with regard to George Wickham's whereabouts. It was a frigid night when the cousins departed Darcy House with eight trustworthy officers, all of whom shared the distinction of having female members of their acquaintance affronted by Wickham in one unscrupulous manner or another.

The two unmarked carriages that transported the ten men rolled up to a run-down house in one of the seedier parts of London. There was a commotion coming from within—angry voices and the sound of breaking glass. Colonel Fitzwilliam took the lead, banging upon the door with a heavy fist. A frightened young girl of no more than twelve peered through a dirty window several seconds later. Upon seeing the blur of red coats assembled on her father's steps, she threw open the door and beckoned them to enter, practically pulling Colonel Fitzwilliam by his sleeve. "Please! You must stop 'im! 'E is out of 'is mind with rage!"

"Who?" prompted the colonel.

"My Papa! Please! 'E says 'e's gonna kill 'im! My Papa can't go ta jail! 'Tis just my ma, my sister, an' me. 'Ow'll we ever live?" She dragged the colonel up a narrow staircase and into a dimly lit hall, with Darcy and the other men hard on their heels. The sound of raised voices alerted them to Wickham's unmistakable presence in the room just beyond. All ten men drew their weapons and entered to the appalling sight of George Wickham gasping for air while suspended against the far wall of the small parlor by the hands of an irate man, much in the same manner Darcy had held him not many months before against the side of the milliner's shoppe in Meryton, his hands closed around the scoundrel's throat.

Colonel Fitzwilliam advanced and ordered the man, who

was slowly choking Wickham to death, to cease and desist. Unsurprisingly—or not—the man refused to release his captive. "This bloody bastard laid 'is 'ands on me eldest girl, 'e did! I ain' goin' ta let 'im go fer nothin'! Not until the life is squeezed from 'is miserable body! Do with me wha' ya will after, but I ain' lettin' 'im go 'til 'e's good an' dead!"

It was Darcy who approached the angry man and, with a cold look of hatred directed at Wickham, cocked his pistol and extended it without ceremony to the irate father, who grinned. "I see ya 'ave a grievance with this 'ere fine gentleman, as well, ya rotten piece o' filth," the man continued with renewed vigor. "Perhaps 'e'd like ta do the 'onors instead?" Then he addressed Darcy, his eyes—and his hands—never leaving Wickham. "What'd 'e do ta ya? Did 'e 'urt one o' yer precious girls, too?"

Darcy leveled an icy glare at Wickham and muttered in a voice devoid of any feeling, "Two of my sisters… and my wife." Then suddenly, Darcy's hands gripped Wickham's throat as the man stepped back with a sadistic smirk.

"I do believe this 'ere gentleman'll kill ya righ' good, 'e will. An' all the better fer me."

The terror in Wickham's eyes was now palpable. Darcy leaned in and, in a voice shaking with barely checked fury, said, "You touched my wife, George. You laid your filthy hands upon her and insulted her in a most vile and reprehensible manner. She has not been the same since, and it has made me very, very angry. So angry, in fact, I do believe I would now like to see you dead. I care not how or by whose hands. I only know it will not be by mine. I will not risk my wife's displeasure by dirtying my hands with your blood, no matter how sorely I am tempted."

He threw Wickham toward the knot of red coats clustered

around them, all gripping pistols and sabers, and watched as Wickham soiled himself while his hands massaged his bruised windpipe. Tears streamed from his eyes. "Have mercy on me, gentlemen! I am certain we can reach some sort of agreement here," he rasped, but it was too late. Eight men seized him and dragged him, screaming, from the house.

Darcy fought for control while Colonel Fitzwilliam addressed the man in front of them. "You need not fear for your family, sir, I can promise you. Every man in this room tonight has been wronged by that blackguard, and they are anxious for retribution. He will not be found." The man nodded.

Darcy, finally feeling in better control of himself, asked, "Pray, how is your daughter, Mr…?"

"Browning, sir. She's a righ' mess, but she's strong. It ain' nothin' she won' recover from eventually. The dirty blackguard hadn' the time ta do 'is worst, by God, but tha' don' mean I didn' wanna kill 'im in any case."

Darcy gritted his teeth. "No. I share your sentiments completely." He noticed the young girl peering around the side of the door then and reached into his coat pocket. He extracted his purse and handed it to Mr. Browning. "For your daughters, sir, and for your trouble. It is not nearly enough, but if it helps in any way to ease their suffering after this horrible event, please accept it with my gratitude. If it were not for the commotion here tonight, my cousin's men would never have discovered that scoundrel. I thank you for your assistance, though I am exceedingly sorry for the cause. If you will allow it, I would send for my physician so he can tend to your daughter."

Mr. Browning accepted the purse and nodded. "She's with me wife now, but I thank ya fer yer kindness." As they moved toward the door, Mr. Browning extended his hand to Darcy and said, "Yer a good man fer doin' wha' ya done 'ere tonigh'. I 'ope yer wife and sisters'll be alrigh'. I don' need ta know yer name. It ain' necessary. Ya can be sure I won' be talkin' to no one 'bout any o' this."

All three men shook hands and parted ways—Darcy home to Elizabeth, and Colonel Fitzwilliam into the night with his men to deal George Wickham his last and most fateful hand.

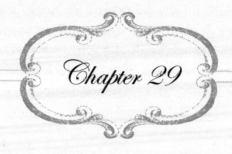

Chapter 29

During the weeks that followed, Lydia recuperated at Darcy House and slowly regained her strength, though her personality, once so brash and energetic, was now much subdued. Whether it was the compassionate friend she found in Georgiana, the nurturing and reassurance she received from Elizabeth and her father, or the unassuming kindness shown to her by Darcy, despite the trouble she had caused him, Lydia had begun to change for the better. In such an environment, where genuine affection, respect, and rational conversation reigned, it was easy for her to see the vast contrast between a Fitzwilliam Darcy and a George Wickham.

Lydia found Darcy's concern genuine and his desire to please her while she remained a guest in his home, sincere. Gradually, to her chagrin, dull Mr. Darcy no longer seemed so very dull after all, but rather all that was generous, compassionate, and considerate to a fault. Nothing, however, swayed Lydia's opinion quite so much as witnessing an unguarded moment of intimacy he shared with her sister.

While in Hertfordshire, Lydia had heard the gossip about Elizabeth and the master of Pemberley, and had even spread some of it herself, for no reason other than to have some fun at their expense. Lydia had never completely comprehended the serious harm in such gossip, and much like her mother, neither could she fathom the interest such a rich, handsome, serious man like Darcy could ever have in her impertinent sister. Even though she had never desired his attentions herself, Lydia had thought it would have been a very good joke if Darcy had taken a fancy to her, the youngest of all her sisters. After noticing his attention drawn almost exclusively to Elizabeth, however, Lydia was quick to decide that such pointed attention must be the result of a strong physical lust on Darcy's part, and her sister's interest in the master of Pemberley nothing more than a desire to obtain status and wealth—enough for a marriage of convenience, as was more common in society than not, but certainly nothing deeper.

After witnessing her taciturn brother-in-law engaged in an amorous encounter with his wife during a stolen moment when they had likely believed themselves to be alone, however, Lydia was forced to admit there was far more between them than mere physical desire and the pursuit of worldly riches. The words Darcy had uttered, and the fervency and sincerity with which they were spoken; the way his lips claimed her sister's as his hands traveled tenderly, almost reverently, over her body; the way Elizabeth responded to him—unreservedly and with her entire self—would forever leave an indelible mark on Lydia. She was forced to recognize and acknowledge the differences between the way Darcy coaxed, nurtured, and caressed his willing wife, who obviously loved him, and how Wickham had simply flirted with, demanded, and then taken from Lydia that which, in spite of her earlier boldness, she had been more than a little reluctant to surrender to him when the time was at hand.

It became obvious to her that Darcy worshiped her sister—that he loved Elizabeth from his heart—and, from that moment, Lydia was determined she would settle for nothing less than a similar adoration and respect for herself. Never again would she make the same grievous mistakes she had only so recently made—mistakes that had very nearly cost her far more than her virtue, as irretrievable as that now was to her. She would comport herself with dignity and decorum and earn the respect and love of an honorable, passionate man like her brother-in-law, or she would never again give herself to any man.

As a result of her newfound respect for Darcy's character and, more specifically, his passionate nature with her sister, Lydia's interactions with the master of Pemberley became reserved and almost deferential. Darcy's ardent feelings for Elizabeth seemed to humanize him far more effectively than any kindness toward Lydia ever could, and because of his open displays of admiration for his wife, Lydia's estimation of Elizabeth also increased.

Away from the constant petting and giddy effusions of her mother, Lydia began to develop a true bond with and an admiration for her second-eldest sister, which became stronger and more remarkable the more it was fed and nurtured. With Elizabeth and even with Georgiana—whose support had proven her to be a true friend, and who also happened to be the same age—Lydia was able to speak of many things she felt she could not at home. It was to Elizabeth that Lydia eventually related the details of the horrible nightmare she had endured with Wickham. She held nothing back—not even the fact that Wickham had plotted to ruin, not only her own reputation, but Elizabeth's, as well, and for no reason other than it would have been the most effective way to cause Darcy the deepest pain and suffering. Lydia also revealed to her sister the exchange that had taken place at Mrs. Younge's, when Wickham had referred to her by Elizabeth's name in a moment of unrestrained lust.

They had spent an exhausting afternoon reliving Lydia's terrifying experiences, and it was not until early in the evening that Elizabeth finally left her sister's room so they both might rest for a while before supper was served. Elizabeth retired to her own rooms, her head pounding. She hardly knew what to do, for it was only now—after all that had come to pass, and in spite of his imposing himself upon her at the Lucas's—Elizabeth fully admitted to herself she had grossly underestimated Wickham's malicious intent, as well as his frightening propensity for exacting revenge upon her husband. She felt she had been an ignorant fool to have erred so greatly in her assessment of the danger to herself and her family, and thanked God that Colonel Fitzwilliam had managed to find Lydia before Wickham's hateful wrath had claimed far more than her sister's virtue. Indeed, Lydia very nearly *had* been lost to them forever.

For more than an hour, Elizabeth sat at her dressing table and stared, unseeing, at her reflection in the elegant mirror that adorned it. She was close to tears and dropped her head into her hands. Darcy found her thus when he entered to dress for supper.

He approached her with trepidation and laid a hand upon her shoulder. "Elizabeth, are you well?" he asked.

She nodded, grasped his hand, and gave it a squeeze as she wiped the moisture from her eyes with her other. She lifted her head, and their eyes met in the mirror. "Will you not tell me what has become of Mr. Wickham?" she asked.

Darcy started. He had not been prepared to receive such an inquiry and averted his eyes. "Why do you wish to hear of his fate?" he asked. "Surely nothing can be gained by your knowing."

"No," she agreed, "but then, it might just bring me a certain peace I have not felt in a long while, do not you think?"

Darcy shrugged and glanced at the floor. Elizabeth took a deep breath and said, "I spoke with Lydia today at some length. She told me in great detail about Mr. Wickham and his cruelty to her, as well as his determination to hurt you irrevocably through me. It sounded very much as though he intended to do me great harm. You must have known this, yet you never saw fit to tell me of it."

"No," he said, his voice hoarse as he released her and strode to the window, where he looked out over the darkened square. "I did not see the need of alarming you. It is of little consequence now, in any case. Lydia has been recovered, she is well, and Wickham is gone. He is no longer a threat to us… nor to anyone."

Elizabeth rose and joined him. "Did you kill him?" she asked in a trembling voice.

Darcy shook his head. "I knew you would not want me to act in such a violent manner, even for the crimes he committed against your family," he murmured. "I will never forget the horrified look on your beautiful face, nor my tortured thoughts that day in Meryton after I nearly strangled him to death with my bare hands. Though I was again tempted to do just that when I came face-to-face with him, I could not bear your disappointment in me."

Elizabeth laid her hand upon his arm as she contemplated his words. It was not long before she inquired, "What happened to him, then, Fitzwilliam? Surely Mr. Wickham did not simply disappear into the night like an apparition. I am not so naïve as to believe some form of retribution was not exacted for his crimes."

Darcy was silent for a long while. "There was a duel," he finally admitted, "and eight angry officers—friends, or brothers, rather, of Richard's—who demanded satisfaction for crimes Wickham had perpetrated against ladies of their acquaintance: sisters, wives, lovers. I understand he was made to face each man in turn until each had exacted punishment upon Wickham's person, one wound at a time. Fitzwilliam informed me that, though there were no serious injuries to his officers, Wickham did not survive. It is not common knowledge. Duels are illegal. There is far too much at stake."

"Oh," she said, tightening her hand upon her husband's arm.

"I did not wish to further distress you by burdening you with such particulars. It is why I never told you. A husband does not usually share such things with his wife."

At this, a wry smile flickered across Elizabeth's lips. "I believe, Fitzwilliam, much has already passed between us that does not usually pass between a husband and a wife in this proper society of ours. I would not wish for that to change in any way, even after hearing of the awful things you have just related. I value our honesty, our forthrightness, our intimacy far too much for that."

Darcy turned his head and met her eyes. "As do I. Should I continue to worry over you, Elizabeth?" he asked as he slipped his arms around her waist. "It would pain me to know I may have upset you further by what I have just related."

Elizabeth closed her eyes and shook her head. "No. Not anymore. I can hardly explain it, but I feel better now."

Darcy breathed a sigh, and though he told himself he would have to wait to determine whether they would prove true, he was heartened to see, before even a full day had passed, several telling signs that indicated that the same teasing woman he had married would soon be restored to her former impertinent self.

Not a week later, Lord and Lady Matlock came to call. They were most anxious to discuss the ball they had determined to hold in

Darcy's and Elizabeth's honor. Though Lady Matlock felt such a celebration was now long overdue, Darcy and Elizabeth could not bring themselves to echo her sentiments. It was decided, however, it would be held in two weeks' time, and though Darcy wanted no part of a large assembly, his aunt insisted as she stressed the necessity of including many, if not all, of the most prominent families and notable personages of the *ton* for her new niece's official introduction into London.

As Georgiana was not yet out, and considering the ordeal Lydia had recently overcome, Darcy was adamant that neither of his sisters would attend the ball. Georgiana was disappointed to have to miss Elizabeth's debut, but to everyone's surprise, Lydia did not appear distressed by the prospect of spending the evening quietly at home. Elizabeth and Darcy had discussed the merits of treating Lydia—who seemed to be earnest in her endeavor to improve herself—much as they would any young lady who was not yet out. Anticipating fierce resistance from Elizabeth's youngest sister—especially after they had made it clear the unrestrained freedom she had enjoyed at Longbourn would not be permitted at Darcy House—the couple barely managed to contain their surprise when Lydia not only accepted, but adhered to, their restrictions.

And adhere to them she did, for the more Lydia heard Georgiana speak of her own coming out—which Darcy's sister had never done before her newfound friendship with Lydia—the more Lydia gave thought to the possibility society might yet come to consider her to be a worthy young woman, much like her two eldest sisters. She was determined to learn to comport herself with dignity and grace, and make Darcy and Elizabeth proud of her efforts in the meantime.

Jane and Bingley returned the following week in order to attend the ball with the Gardiners, whom Lord and Lady Matlock had grown to like very much. As Elizabeth's nearest and dearest relations, they would be given the distinction of standing with Darcy's family in the receiving line. As Mr. Bennet did not care to make the trip from Hertfordshire—he had returned to Longbourn just two weeks earlier—neither he, his wife, or their two remaining daughters were expected to attend, much to Kitty's consternation and Mrs. Bennet's displeasure. Darcy, who had long dreaded his mother-in-law's introduction to the illustrious London *ton*, breathed a sigh at the news. It did not go unnoticed by his wife. Elizabeth gave him a disapproving look and pinched his arm, though her false display of ire was belied by the teasing smile that quirked the corners of her mouth.

As could be expected, the ladies passed much time at the modiste and other such shoppes in preparation for the upcoming affair. Though Darcy could not confess to a fondness for shopping, he did accompany his wife and sisters to Bond Street, if for no reason other than to ensure Elizabeth received the proper deference and attention owed to her as his wife. Satisfied by her positive reception, he excused himself for an hour or so to peruse the nearby bookseller and, on impulse, a local jeweler, whose stunning variety of unique items happened to catch his eye.

Rather than waiting for the evening of the ball to present his recently acquired purchase to Elizabeth, Darcy chose to do it that very night after they had retired to their rooms. Elizabeth sat brushing her hair and, unable to resist the urge to perform the task himself, he offered to assist her.

Elizabeth sighed as she surrendered her brush to his hands. She watched him in the mirror, a soft smile of contentment upon her lips as she enjoyed his gentle ministrations. Afterward, as Darcy placed the brush upon the dressing table, he retrieved a prettily wrapped box from one of the drawers and laid it before her with a smile.

"And to what, my dearest, do I owe such a lovely surprise?" she asked with a grin, touched by his unexpected gesture.

"I did not think I needed a reason to present my wife with a token of my love," he said, his eyes sparkling.

Elizabeth laughed. "I daresay you do not. It is, however, quite unnecessary. You know I have no need for trinkets, Fitzwilliam. You are enough. Mmm… more than enough," she added as Darcy swept her hair aside and leaned in to nuzzle the curve of her neck.

"Do not question your good fortune, my love," he murmured. "Open the box. I believe you will approve." He moved his mouth to her pulse and sucked lightly, then trailed the tip of his tongue along her shoulders, moving the fabric of her nightshift aside as he went.

"Fitzwilliam," Elizabeth moaned, "if you expect me to open this gift, you must cease your attentions, for I cannot… possibly… ooh," she gasped, "concentrate on anything… beyond… your exquisite touch."

With a grin, Darcy placed a kiss upon the nape of her neck and straightened as he nudged the box closer to her. "By all means, Mrs. Darcy," he said with mock severity, "I would not wish to distract you from your purpose."

"Incorrigible," she murmured as she tore the paper from the box and lifted the lid. Inside was a beautiful arrangement of what appeared to be strand upon strand of delicate flower-and-leaf–shaped diamonds, amethysts, and emeralds. Elizabeth had never before seen anything so unique, and she gasped at the sheer beauty of such items. She lifted them from the box and examined them closely in the candlelight. "Fitzwilliam," she whispered, "I hardly know what to say. They are stunning—so delicate and lovely."

Darcy could not contain his smile at her obvious pleasure. "I thought so, as well. You will look quite elegant with them entwined in your hair or perhaps even attached to one of your gowns. You might consider approaching Mrs. Duval about that possibility. I am certain she would enjoy accommodating you."

After several moments of running her fingers over the precious stones, Elizabeth replaced them in the box with great care and turned her head to kiss his cheek. "Thank you. I am speechless."

Darcy laughed as he took her hands and tugged her to her feet. "I never thought I would see the day when my impertinent wife would be rendered speechless."

Elizabeth buried her fingers in his hair and smiled against his lips. "Oh? So I am impertinent, am I, Mr. Darcy?"

"Oh, yes," he murmured as his eyes darkened with a look that made Elizabeth's heartbeat quicken. "The most impertinent woman I have ever known. Whatever shall I do with you, Mrs. Darcy?" he mused.

"I am certain, sir," she said breathlessly, "you will think of something." She smiled as she felt his arousal press against her stomach.

Darcy's lips quirked into a rakish grin. "Ah. It seems I already have."

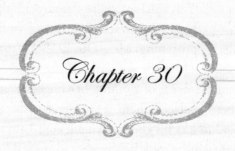

Chapter 30

For Elizabeth, the evening of Lord and Lady Matlock's ball was filled with equal parts anticipation and dread. She took extra care with her appearance, knowing full well she would be under close scrutiny from hundreds of pairs of discerning eyes, not only for her success in securing Fitzwilliam Darcy of Pemberley for her husband, but for actually going so far as to capture his heart, as well.

Sonia was just putting the finishing touches on her mistress's hair when Darcy entered Elizabeth's apartment. She was seated at her dressing table and watched his reflection in the large beveled mirror as he approached. A smile graced his lips as he gazed upon her with open adoration. She returned it, beaming at him. Sonia tucked the last of Elizabeth's curls in place and made a minor adjustment to the strands of tiny gems she had entwined in her mistress's hair; then she stepped back so the master of Pemberley could better admire his wife.

Elizabeth turned her head from side to side and beamed. "Sonia, you have outdone yourself. I believe I have never before felt so lovely as I do tonight, not even on my wedding day. Thank you."

Sonia bowed her head. "Thank you, ma'am. I am honored you approve."

Darcy gave the young woman an appreciative smile. "Yes, Sonia. I daresay Mrs. Darcy is nothing short of breathtaking this evening; though, I must also point out that this is not an uncommon occurrence while in your capable hands."

"Thank you, sir," she answered with a blush, then, addressing her mistress, asked, "Will you require anything else, ma'am?"

Elizabeth shook her head. "No, that will be all, Sonia, thank you. Do not bother to wait up for me. I believe we will not be returning until very late."

"Very good, ma'am," Sonia replied as she curtsied and turned to leave.

The door had barely closed before Darcy had taken Elizabeth in his arms. "You look absolutely beautiful, Elizabeth," he whispered against her ear. "Wearing the jewels in your hair is a lovely touch, but that gown—it becomes you, my love, in ways I never dared imagine. You are stunning."

Elizabeth kissed him and rested her coiffed head upon his shoulder as she encircled his waist with her arms. "It is completely your own doing, you know," she said, her voice carrying an impish inflection. "I have never before owned such an exquisite gown. It is beyond beautiful. Yellow is, by far, my favorite color, and I know I shall cherish such a gift for many Seasons to come. I hardly care whether or not it is deemed acceptable to be seen wearing the same gown more than once. I know London fashions change quickly, but, as the mistress of Pemberley, I believe I shall do as I like. Thank you, Fitzwilliam."

Feathering a kiss upon the top of her head, Darcy smiled at her independent spirit and held her tighter. "I daresay you shall, and you are most welcome. I remember your sister once saying you have always wished to own such a gown—pale yellow silk the color of sunlight, a gown that would brighten the mood in even the darkest room. Tonight, Elizabeth, you will turn every head with your brilliance, and all of London will see precisely why I fell in love with you."

Elizabeth raised her head, and their eyes met. "You are so wonderful to me. Sometimes I cannot help feeling I do not deserve you."

Darcy fingered a rebellious curl at the nape of her neck as his other hand caressed her bare shoulder. "No," he said, his voice serious. "You deserve a man far better than I, but I fear you are stuck with me for the remainder of our life together. You shall just have to make the most of it."

His words and seriousness caused her to stiffen. Elizabeth placed her hand upon his cheek, and her eyes searched his. "I would never have it any other way. It is you I want. You I need. I love you. Do not ever forget that or take it lightly. You are the most important aspect of my life. You and this child I carry. I could never do without you, Fitzwilliam. Indeed, it troubles me to hear you speak so."

Darcy closed his eyes, and just as he had done not so very long ago when they were alone together in the library at Netherfield, he turned his lips into her palm and kissed her. "I could never take your love lightly, Elizabeth. You have become more necessary to me than the air I breathe. I would be but a shell of a man without you to lighten my dark moods."

The clock upon the mantle chimed seven times. Elizabeth stood on the tips of her slippered toes and kissed her husband's cheek. "We had best depart if we are to be at your uncle's on time, my dear," she whispered as her eyes took on a mischievous gleam. "This is a joyous night, Fitzwilliam, and from what I understand, there is to be a waltz. What better way to celebrate our marriage than to dance with each other in our arms? Will that not be wonderful? It is something you have longed to do, is it not, my handsome husband?"

Darcy grinned. "Yes. I believe nothing shall give me greater pleasure tonight. Richard insists it is my uncle's idea of a gift to us. Since he has witnessed my scandalous behavior toward you whenever my senses have become overwrought by your presence, I believe he views this as a perfect opportunity for me to appear in full company and hold you close without risking your respectability overmuch." He smiled and caressed the length of her gloved arms. "I confess I am very much looking forward to it."

And so he was, for when they arrived at Matlock House not a half hour later, Darcy found it difficult to stand sedately beside his wife in the receiving line—as was expected of him—to greet his aunt's guests as they arrived. He was ever conscious of Elizabeth's sweet fragrance and the feel of her body as he placed his hand upon the small of her back. His gaze was forever darting to and lingering upon the ample swell of her breasts, made even more enticing now that she was several months into her pregnancy. As expected, his actions did not go unnoticed by his uncle, who repeatedly cleared his throat while he attempted to hide his smile.

By the time the dancing began, Darcy was eager to lead Elizabeth to the center of the ballroom to open the festivities. He had been correct—every eye was, indeed, turned upon her, though not all in admiration, Miss Bingley's narrowed slits included. Though Darcy's blood still boiled whenever he thought of her ill treatment of Elizabeth, for the sake of his long-standing friendship with Bingley, he had asked his aunt to extend an invitation to both his friend's sisters. To his relief, Elizabeth bore it all—the crowd, as well as Miss Bingley's odious presence—with grace and dignity, her elegance, her wit, and her impeccable manners serving as further proof of her suitability as his wife.

The ball was a crush, and Darcy, though anxious for Elizabeth's acceptance in society, found himself growing irritated by the attention she was receiving from the other men in attendance.

Elizabeth's dance card was soon filled with the names of unknown gentlemen eager to become acquainted with the enchanting Mrs. Darcy of Pemberley.

Darcy could only watch as his wife was led through the dance by partner after partner, each of whom seemed to be captivated by her beauty and vivacity. Elizabeth was his. He did not wish to share her.

"You know, Darcy, if you are not careful, that scowl will become a permanent part of your countenance."

Darcy only grunted in response to his cousin's teasing remark. His gaze never wavered from Elizabeth as she danced with the handsome and accursedly agreeable Lord Abernathy, a good friend of his cousin Harold. The young man, several years Darcy's junior, seemed to be mesmerized by her lively discourse, as well as her pleasing figure. Darcy took a sip of wine and asked dryly, "What do you think would happen if I were to call Abernathy out for making my wife smile? Am I well within my rights as a jealous husband, or should I wait until he does something a bit more untoward?"

Colonel Fitzwilliam laughed. "Really, Darcy, this is a switch! I believe I have never before seen you thus. Usually, it is the other way around, and you are the one to inspire feelings of jealousy, but rather in handsome young ladies. It is about time you received a taste of your own medicine."

"A taste of my own medicine, is it? Fitzwilliam, you imply I sought such favor from all of those fortune hunters and their matchmaking mamas. I assure you, I did not, and I believe you are well acquainted with that fact," he said stiffly.

His cousin clapped him on the back and said, "Precisely, Darcy. Is it Elizabeth's fault so many men find her as irresistible as you do? What would you have her do? She cannot refuse to dance with them and still be able to dance with you later, though you are her husband. I am afraid this indulgence is necessary in securing your wife's place in society, and let me just add that it is working. They seem to love her."

"Yes, well, I will not deny that the gentlemen are certainly charmed; however, at the first sign of love, I shall be forced to remove her to Pemberley, where, I might add, I would happily remain for the rest of my days."

"You are insufferable, Cousin! I would gladly trade my commission to gain at least a portion of the happiness you have found with Elizabeth. Indeed, you can have nothing to repine."

Here, Darcy gave his cousin a look of warning, which only served to make the colonel laugh. "Darcy, you must face the music, old man—your wife is a highly desirable woman. It is a curse you will simply have to live with, but, apparently, it is a cross you will not have to bear alone." He motioned then to Bingley, who was standing on the opposite side of the room, watching Jane go down the dance with the eldest son of an earl. The look of displeasure upon his face rivaled Darcy's. Colonel Fitzwilliam grinned.

The dance ended, and Lord Abernathy escorted Mrs. Darcy back to the safekeeping of her husband, whose hand immediately went to the small of her back. "Thank you for returning my wife, Abernathy. I am most obliged to you. I daresay most of the other gentlemen in attendance this evening—if, indeed, they can be referred to as such—simply chose to keep her to themselves between sets."

Elizabeth glanced sharply at him. Darcy's haughty mask was firmly in place, as it had been when they had first met in Hertfordshire so many months ago, but then he focused his penetrating eyes upon her, and she could see something else—vulnerability. She was very soon reminded, however, that while she had danced every dance thus far, her husband had not, but not, Elizabeth knew, for want of willing young ladies to partner him. Indeed, whenever she had looked up from among her own attentive partners, searching for a glimpse of him, Elizabeth had not had to look far to observe Darcy's stormy, protective gaze upon her, nor the many feminine eyes turned wistfully—and not so innocently—upon her handsome husband.

While Darcy engaged in small talk with Lord Abernathy and Colonel Fitzwilliam, his gaze all the while darting to his wife, Elizabeth formed a resolution and, when there was a pause in the conversation, intervened. "If you would excuse us, gentlemen, I would like a word with my husband before the next set is to begin."

The two gentlemen bowed to her, and Elizabeth curtsied. She cast a meaningful look at Darcy, and they extracted themselves from the throng to search for a place where they might have a few moments of privacy. When his wife led him out of the ballroom and toward the family wing, where guests were certainly not allowed, Darcy expelled a lengthy breath. *Surely this cannot be a good sign*, he thought grimly as he began to fidget with his signet ring. Elizabeth placed her hand over his and stilled his action. Darcy swallowed.

They finally reached a small parlor—the very same parlor, he noted, where Elizabeth and Anne had met secretly at Christmas. Darcy reluctantly entered, and when he saw Elizabeth close and then lock the door behind them, he closed his eyes and braced himself for the chastisement he knew was coming. It did not, however, come. Rather than harsh words of reprimand for his display of jealousy, his ears received his wife's soft lips as she bestowed a kiss upon his lobe. Darcy's eyes widened. *What on earth could she be about?* "Elizabeth, what—" he began, his voice hoarse. Her gloved fingers silenced his words.

"Shhh," she whispered. "I thought, perhaps, you might be in need of some reassurance and also a reminder of where my affections lie." Her gaze caressed him as her tongue darted out to wet her lips.

Darcy's eyes searched hers, and upon receiving confirmation of her words by way of her lips caressing his hungry mouth, a low, inarticulate sound tore from the back of his throat. In the next instant, he clutched Elizabeth almost violently, his lips hard upon hers as his hands roamed possessively over her body.

Elizabeth gasped at Darcy's powerful reaction, her initial surprise soon replaced by a potent desire as he unfastened the top buttons at the back of her gown to free her breasts. With a groan, he took one breast in his mouth and suckled her. While one of Darcy's hands pleasured her other breast, toying with her nipple and eliciting the most delightful sensations in Elizabeth's body, his other hand had unfastened the buttons on the fall of his silk breeches. Not until he raised her skirts past her hips and she felt the heat of his potency against her naked flesh, did Elizabeth fully comprehend the ferocity of her husband's need.

Darcy lifted her in his arms, his lips pressing the curve of her neck. "Elizabeth," he gasped, "I need you—I need you desperately!" Then, with urgency, he pressed her back against the wall and drove his hard length into her with a shuddering cry. Elizabeth clung to him as he possessed her.

His fevered urgency sent a thrill through her that served only to push her own desire to new heights. Far sooner than she had anticipated, Elizabeth felt the beginning of her release. Her muscles tightened around Darcy's arousal, and as Darcy could not stop himself from moaning words of passion and desire in her ear, she soon surrendered to the feelings of bliss that coursed through her body.

For Darcy, who had watched his Elizabeth laugh and dance with countless handsome and engaging men for half the night, whose feral need to possess her, to mark her as his and his alone was driving him mad, it was the point of no return. In the next moment, he found his completion with a violent thrust and a primal groan as he spilled his seed into her.

Darcy's legs gave way, and he quickly maneuvered to support his wife as he sank to his knees, his breathing rapid, his heart pounding furiously within his breast. He clasped Elizabeth to him as he struggled to regulate his breathing.

After several minutes of silence, she laughed softly. "I believe, sir, it is safe to assume we have missed the Supper Dance."

Darcy smiled and kissed her, teasing her lips apart with his tongue. When he pulled away, he leaned his forehead against hers. "I am sorry," he said. "It was not my intention to forego any of my dances with you tonight."

She raised a hand and stroked his cheek. "I know," she said, "but you were hardly in a frame of mind fit for dancing. Please tell me you are better now."

Darcy kissed her again, his lips a soft caress. "I am, thank you… although, I believe I owe you an apology. I never should have treated you thus, especially in the middle of a ball given in our honor. I hope I have not hurt you in any way."

Elizabeth smiled. "I believe I am hardly complaining, Fitzwilliam."

"No," he said, "however, we will very likely be missed soon, and I would not wish for the truth as to why we were absent from the Supper Dance to become generally known."

"No, I would imagine not." Elizabeth grinned and rose, straightening her gown and checking her appearance in a mirror upon the wall while Darcy made himself presentable. When he had done, he refastened the buttons on her gown, and she ran her hands through his hair, coaxing his curls back into place. "There," she declared. "Now you look every inch the handsome gentleman once again."

Darcy frowned and made to run his hand through his hair to dispel some of the agitation he felt at her words. Elizabeth stopped him before he could cause any damage and gave him a questioning look. "You must think me an insecure beast to take advantage of you in such a way," he muttered.

Elizabeth caught his face between her gloved hands and forced his eyes to meet hers. "No," she said in a gentle voice. "I think only that my husband, whom I love more than any other on this earth, must love me to distraction. Believe it or not, Fitzwilliam, though your jealousy is not something I can condone, it is something I can, *and do*, understand. You have nothing to fear, my love. There is nothing that could ever make me turn from you." To emphasize her point, she kissed him with no small degree of feeling. "Come," she finally said as she laid her hand upon her waist, now slightly thickened from pregnancy, "I am hungry, and I daresay so is this little one of ours."

Darcy gathered her in his arms, his hand caressing her stomach. "Of course, Mrs. Darcy," he said with a small, pleased smile. "Let us find something with which to tempt you both. You must keep up your strength. I would not have you starve on my account."

Elizabeth smiled and smoothed a curl from his forehead. "I know not of our child, Fitzwilliam, but I do believe I have quite enough to tempt me right here. I doubt I would ever starve with you to care for me." She sighed. "I do love you so, my dearest. Never question it."

Darcy swallowed and ran his fingers over the softness of her cheek, his voice hardly more than a whisper. "For as long as I live, Elizabeth, I never shall."

The rest of the evening passed without incident. Other than an appraising look, a pointed cough, and a raised brow from Lord Matlock when Darcy and Elizabeth finally made an appearance at supper, their cheeks flushed and their skin glowing, no mention was made of their absence. It was generally noted, however, that Darcy's sour demeanor seemed to have improved significantly. Rather than scowling at the many remaining gentlemen who were fortunate enough to partner his wife for the second half of the night, he focused his undivided attention upon her alone, his mouth turned up in the barest hint of a private smile whenever their eyes met as she went down the dance.

Elizabeth made sure their eyes met often.

Between sets, Lady Matlock took Elizabeth around to all of the notable dowagers and other esteemed guests in attendance. When questioned, Elizabeth spoke easily of her family and of her father's estate in Hertfordshire, of her interest in books, philosophy, and music, and, to those who had the audacity to inquire, of her fondness for her husband. She happened to be speaking with Lady Sowersby and Lady Malcolm, both of whom had fast become her avid champions, when Jane and Bingley joined them and, shortly thereafter, the Gardiners. It was not long before their group was engaged in a lively discourse, to the very great satisfaction of Lady

Matlock. It was obvious the two dowagers were equally as impressed by Jane as they had been by Elizabeth, and pleased, as well, by the intelligence and elegant manners of their Cheapside relations.

Through it all, Darcy stood beside Elizabeth with his hands clasped behind his back. He was itching to reach out and caress her, to feel the curve of her waist through the buttery yellow silk of her gown. He did not dare attempt it, not after the pointed look his uncle had given him at supper. Instead, he put forth a valiant effort and focused his attention upon the conversation at hand. He could not help but smile at his wife's keen wit and easy manners while in the company of two such exalted persons as Lady Malcolm and Lady Sowersby. Darcy was extremely pleased to see Lady Malcolm, who was well known throughout the first circles for her biting sarcasm and discerning intellect, delighted to have found in the new Mrs. Darcy an equally discerning and witty companion.

His smile increased when the first strains of a waltz floated through the room, and as the conversation between the ladies did not wane, Darcy cleared his throat. "Pardon my interruption, but I do believe, Mrs. Darcy, you have promised this particular dance to me," he said as he fought to conceal the grin that was threatening to overspread his features.

Lady Sowersby smiled indulgently. Lady Malcolm, however, gave him a wry look and said, "Upon my word, Fitzwilliam, I have never before seen you thus. This newfound eagerness for the dance is extraordinary, or perhaps it is your eagerness for the company of your pretty young wife that makes you so willing to partake of an act that has never before afforded you much pleasure?"

To Elizabeth's delight, Darcy blushed as he answered, "What you say is quite true, your ladyship. I believe I had only to find the perfect partner to transform the act from an odious chore to an unrivalled pleasure." Then, with a sly glance at Elizabeth and a rakish grin, he added, "Now, if you will be so kind as to excuse us, I have long desired to dance while holding my wife in my arms, and I am loath to pass up the opportunity to do so now." Elizabeth colored and then laughed, her pleasure in her husband's affection apparent to all.

Bingley, who had been standing beside his friend, coughed behind his hand. Then, upon seeing Darcy leading his wife to the center of the room, he offered his own arm to his beloved Jane. She accepted with a smile and a blush that became her. They were then joined by the Gardiners, Lord and Lady Matlock, and many other daring couples whose mornings had lately been employed in learning the art of the scandalous waltz for just such an occasion.

As Darcy guided his wife around the ballroom, one hand clasping hers while the other held fast to her waist, Elizabeth could not recall a time when she had ever enjoyed dancing more. She and Jane had practiced all week with their willing partners, and now, as Elizabeth admired her sister's beauty as Bingley led her through the dance, a look of absolute bliss upon both their faces, the mistress of Pemberley could hardly contain her smile.

Her gaze then drifted to her own partner, whose eyes were alight with happiness. Never before had she seen him looking so pleased, so relaxed while in company—especially in a ballroom. In fact, as Darcy gazed upon her with a look of delight, Elizabeth wondered if he had quite forgotten they were being observed. He held her a little tighter and pulled her a bit closer than propriety would have allowed—even during such a dance—and Elizabeth gave him an arch smile, knowing full well it was because he found her irresistible. "If you hold me any closer, Mr. Darcy, I do believe there shall be a scandal!" she teased.

Darcy loosened his hold, but only slightly. "Forgive me, Mrs. Darcy," he said, a sheepish smile quirking the corners of his mouth, "but I find I am still feeling a bit possessive. Indeed, madam, you can have no idea how intoxicating you look at this moment, or how many other men are admiring you as I hold you in my arms."

Elizabeth's voice softened as she continued to smile upon him. "You are correct, Fitzwilliam, for my eyes are only for you, my handsome husband, and, as I am certain you have noticed, there are just as many sets of fine eyes fixed upon your stately figure."

"Perhaps, but my admiration is for you alone, Elizabeth." His eyes darkened, and he leaned in closer. "Do you think it is too early to make our excuses to my aunt and uncle?"

"Fitzwilliam, you are incorrigible," she laughed, suspecting he was half serious and half in jest. "You know very well we cannot. Besides, I have not yet had my dance with your cousin Harold."

"Hang Harold," Darcy growled. "I am tired of sharing you. How will I be able to stand the sight of you with another man after having danced a waltz with you? Besides, my thoughts at this moment are hardly conducive to gentlemanly behavior."

Elizabeth wisely made no reply, but when the dance ended and all the couples applauded, she allowed Darcy to lead her away to one of the balconies. The crisp air was refreshing, and as they were quite alone, Darcy took the opportunity to steal a kiss. "Are you certain I cannot convince you to retire for the night, Elizabeth?" he asked in a low voice as his fingertips lingered along the edging at her neckline.

Elizabeth slapped his hand away and smiled. "No. I am by no means tired. You forget, sir, that you made me take a nap this afternoon."

"Yes," he said, "and I daresay you are in need of another." He began to drag the tip of his nose along the curve of her neck. Elizabeth closed her eyes and reveled in the sensations that coursed through her. Darcy boldly continued on, his lips moving to caress the swell of flesh just above her neckline. He dipped the tip of his tongue between her breasts, which elicited a gasp of pleasure from her.

In an effort to steady herself, Elizabeth moved her hands to Darcy's shoulders. "Fitzwilliam," she protested, "we cannot. Not here. Someone might see. We must stop," she insisted, though somewhat weakly.

"Very well," he said, his tone petulant as he gave her one last kiss and offered her his arm. "But I demand the last dance of the evening."

Elizabeth smoothed her gown and smiled as she took his proffered arm. "I would never have it any other way, Mr. Darcy. You shall always have the last dance of the evening."

Chapter 31

The month of March arrived in much the same manner as that of a hungry lion—ferocious and unpredictable. The Darcys found themselves overwhelmed by countless social obligations, many of which the couple would have been perfectly content to forego. Nevertheless, at the urging of Lord and Lady Matlock, they steeled themselves and accepted the invitations with a sigh of resignation. There were still many within the exalted ranks of the *ton* who had not yet had an opportunity to make the acquaintance of the new Mrs. Darcy and, thus, were hesitant to accept the descriptions circulating about her being a witty and intelligent lady, rather than a clever fortune hunter who had used her arts and allurements to seduce the ever-vigilant master of Pemberley.

Throughout it all, Elizabeth bore with finesse the tedium of attending such events. To those who had come to know her well, it was no surprise to see her charming many of the naysayers with her easy, unaffected manners, her intelligent repartee, and her reputed beauty. Her affection for her husband—and his for her—was apparent to all who saw them together, and except for a handful of bitter mamas and their petulant daughters, who had long had their sights set on the highly coveted gentleman from

Derbyshire, Elizabeth's introduction to most of those who moved within the higher circles of London society was declared a success.

As the first day of spring approached, so did Jane's wedding to Bingley. It was with great relief and a lightness of spirit that the inhabitants of Darcy House quitted London and headed for Hertfordshire once again. The trip was easier going than the one they had made previously. Elizabeth was now far enough along in her pregnancy to be feeling quite well all of the time. She no longer experienced bouts of nausea, fits of light-headedness, exhaustion, or much discomfort of any kind, to the immense relief of her husband.

Darcy had always admired her slender waist and inviting curves, but with the onset of Elizabeth's pregnancy, he was surprised to find even more to admire in his wife's figure. The knowledge that she was carrying his child in her womb was enough to send a flood of warmth through him, but the added inducement of seeing the slight bulge of Elizabeth's increasing waist, her widening hips, and the more pronounced swell of her breasts was enough to drive him to distraction. She seemed to glow from within and, to Darcy's very great pleasure, had an almost insatiable desire to lie with him at all hours of the day. He was always willing to oblige her.

Rather than sitting beside his wife on the carriage ride to Hertfordshire, Darcy found himself occupying the seat opposite her. Georgiana had never been able to ride backward in a coach for more than a few miles, and as Elizabeth had recently discovered that facing any direction other than forward agitated the heir of Pemberley and, thus, the contents of her stomach, Darcy was forced to endure a long, agonizing ride in which his eyes were constantly focused upon his wife's most intoxicating attributes.

To her amusement, Elizabeth caught him staring at her

bouncing breasts many times as the carriage rocked and swayed over the bumpy roads. Darcy's lips would part, and his tongue would dart out to moisten them; his eyes would flare, and then, just as quickly, he would avert them, crossing and recrossing his legs as he stared out of the window with a heavy sigh or an occasional quiet groan, his desire for Elizabeth apparent.

Elizabeth smiled at his obvious vexation. She passed the time by chatting with Georgiana and Lydia—who remained with them still—and, to add fuel to an already blazing inferno, Elizabeth further amused herself by attempting to draw her suffering husband into whatever conversation happened to be at hand, but with little success. From the dark, penetrating looks he sent from across the coach, she was left in little doubt that he had no desire whatsoever to engage in any such act with her, but rather a different act altogether, and one that did not require words.

Indeed, once they had arrived at a small inn where they had determined to stop and water the horses, it had taken all of Elizabeth's powers of persuasion to convince Darcy that demanding a room for a mere hour would very likely give rise to talk, to say nothing of the reactions they would receive from their impressionable, young traveling companions.

"I hardly care what anyone will say," he whispered urgently as he leaned in close. His hot breath against her neck caused her to stumble as they followed Georgiana and Lydia while the innkeeper's wife led them to a private parlor abovestairs. He placed his hand upon the small of her back to steady her and stroked his thumb in a lazy, circular motion. "I daresay our sisters shall think only that you need to rest. Elizabeth, I am begging you! I will never survive this torturous ride to Hertfordshire without first burying myself within you, teasing woman."

Elizabeth blushed at his uttering such words in public and shook her head, causing the curls framing her face to bob. A slight smile of satisfaction quirked her lips. "I am afraid you will just have to wait, Mr. Darcy, but," she murmured seductively, "I can safely promise you that the reward you will receive for your patience shall be well worth the effort of your restraint."

They entered a modestly furnished but pleasant private dining parlor and took a seat at the table. The proximity of their two sisters restricted their continuing with such a topic, but the master and mistress of Pemberley were now seated close enough for Darcy to place his hand upon Elizabeth's leg—quite unnoticed—and caress the length of her thigh with his fingertips. If, in the course of conversation, she happened to falter somewhat or drop her fork during the meal, wisely, no one ventured any comment.

True to her word, after their arrival at Netherfield Park, Elizabeth did indeed reward the master of Pemberley most handsomely for his saintly patience. After exchanging the required pleasantries with their host and hostess, Elizabeth led Darcy upstairs to what they had now come affectionately to think of as their own room in Bingley's house. The following hour or so was spent expressing their fervent passion for each other—several times—and, though Darcy and Elizabeth tried to be discreet about their chosen activity, they found it difficult not to voice at least some of the pleasure they were giving—and receiving—from each other's society.

After resting and bathing, the entire party dressed for dinner. Mr. and Mrs. Bennet, Mary, Kitty, and Jane, who had returned from Town the previous week with the Gardiners, would be joining them that evening for a family dinner. As it seemed to be taking Elizabeth far longer to complete her toilette than it had taken Darcy to perform his ablutions, he informed her of his intention to pass a quarter of an hour or so in the billiard room with Bingley and made his way toward the main staircase. On his way, he met Lydia.

He bowed to her and said, "You look lovely, Lydia. Is that not one of the gowns Georgiana urged you to purchase? The color suits you very well."

Lydia smiled at such a generous compliment from her brother-in-law. "Thank you, Mr. Darcy. I received the gown just yesterday from Bond Street. I have another for Jane's wedding and also for the ball Mr. Bingley will hold in her honor tomorrow night."

Darcy smiled. "I am glad to hear it. According to your mother, a lady can never have enough gowns."

Lydia's expression grew serious, and she said, "I have been wondering, Mr. Darcy…"

Darcy waited, then inclined his head and raised one brow.

"I have been wondering if I might speak to you of something very particular?" she asked. Seeing her brother-in-law, again, incline his head, she forged on, this time in a rush. "I have been talking to Georgiana about it, you see, and she said she thinks it a very good idea, and that I should ask you and Lizzy—especially you—but I am afraid I cannot possibly tell you unless it is in some place more private. I could not bear it if anyone else were to overhear. Especially Miss Bingley. She can be an awful, gossiping shrew, you know, and—" Her hand flew to her mouth. "Oh, Lord! Forgive me. I know I should not have spoken so. And I have been doing so well, too. Lizzy would be very disappointed in me."

A smile threatened to turn up the corners of Darcy's mouth, and he cleared his throat to regain his composure. "No, indeed, you should not, but I do hope you know you may always speak with me of anything you like, Lydia. And, if you prefer, Elizabeth need not hear of this slip of the tongue. It can remain just between us."

Lydia gave him a small smile, and he escorted her to a well-lit parlor, which happened to be fortuitously empty. They took a seat upon two chairs by the fire, and Darcy waited for her to begin.

"Mr. Darcy, I… I suppose I will have to return to Longbourn tonight," she said.

"Yes, I suppose so. Was that not what you and your parents had discussed while you remained in London?"

"It was, but I was wondering if… actually, hoping that, perhaps, well… you and Lizzy might consent to keep me? At least for a little while longer, I mean. Certainly not forever."

Though Lydia had certainly become more relaxed within his household since the first weeks of her recovery, Darcy had thought she would now be eager to return to her own home. Mrs. Bennet had been impatient for her youngest daughter's return to Longbourn, but Darcy had taken it upon himself to speak to Mr. Bennet on the subject and had managed to persuade his father-in-law to allow Lydia to extend her period of convalescence in London, much for Elizabeth's peace of mind, as well as to ensure Lydia did not suffer any further ill effects from her experience. He observed her closely for a few moments and tapped his finger against his lips. "Longbourn is your home. You do not wish to resume living with your parents?"

Lydia dropped her gaze to her lap. "It is not that. I am afraid to return to Longbourn, Mr. Darcy. I have not behaved very well at all. Everyone must know of my running away and how very bad I have been. I am sure Mama and Kitty have spoken of it to the entire neighborhood by now, to say nothing of Mary and her tiresome sermonizing."

"No," he said. "No one knows the truth of what really happened, Lydia. After we read your letter, your mother took to her room immediately, and your sisters were instructed never to speak of your absence. Colonel Fitzwilliam and his men were very discreet when making their inquiries in Town, and though, perhaps we should have done so, your father and I decided it was best not to inform Colonel Forster of what had transpired. We were all very careful, including your mother. There has been no talk of this in London, and there shall be no talk of it here. You need not worry yourself. If anyone asks, you need only say you were visiting your sister in Town. After all, it is the truth, is it not?"

Lydia nodded slowly. "It is," she said. "I have stayed with you and Lizzy now these two months. It was far more than I deserve, I know, especially considering all the trouble I have caused you. I know Lizzy was very frightened for me, and she did not look after herself as she should. The danger to her was so very great. Wickham wanted to do terrible things to her, you know."

"I was there to care for Elizabeth while she cared for you. I would not have allowed her to make herself ill, and I would not have allowed Wickham to harm her in any way. I am only sorry I failed to do the same for you," he said. "You are my sister now, and I did not do enough to protect you from him."

Lydia swallowed. "He was a very bad man. Lizzy and Jane tried to warn me, and so did you, but I did not want to listen to the truth. I know how lucky I am, Mr. Darcy. I am so very sorry I caused so much trouble, especially while Lizzy is expecting a baby. If you want, I will go home to Longbourn tonight. I have since learned many things about conducting myself as a proper lady from observing Lizzy and Georgiana. Perhaps I will never be as good as they are, or Jane, but I promise you I shall never stop trying."

Darcy was reminded very much of how Georgiana had sounded after Ramsgate. He reached out and touched the back of Lydia's hand. "I believe your parents would be disappointed not to have you with them while you are here, and, indeed, Kitty and Mary, as well. But I will speak with Elizabeth of your wish to stay with us, and if she agrees, and if you feel you would still prefer to remain with us for a while, you may accompany us when we leave for Pemberley after your sister's wedding to Mr. Bingley—with your parents' consent, of course."

Lydia's pleasure was evident in her smile. "Thank you, Mr. Darcy. Lizzy was correct—you truly are the best man in the world."

Dinner was a pleasant affair. For Elizabeth, it was the first time while dining in the company of Miss Bingley and the Hursts that she found herself seated next to her husband. It was clear by observing Miss Bingley's scowling countenance that she had no hand in the arrangement of the place cards, nor did she appear to take any pleasure in her own placement, which saw her seated between Mr. Hurst and Kitty, and across from Mr. and Mrs. Bennet.

It did not, however, stop her from eying Elizabeth with distaste each time she noticed Darcy turn toward his wife with a small smile or a private look. On several occasions, Miss Bingley was almost positive she had witnessed him slipping his hand beneath the table to caress his wife's leg, *though surely,* she thought with abject horror, *that could not possibly be the case!*

Miss Bingley's anger only grew as the evening wore on. She knew nothing could be gained and everything lost by maintaining the contempt she harbored for the new mistress of Pemberley, but she could not seem to curb her deep resentment. She had been disgusted months ago when Darcy had shown the first signs of burgeoning interest in Elizabeth and, later, was shocked and insulted when he had actually chosen to make the reputed local beauty his wife—an upstart country miss with little breeding and no elegance, so different from herself, whose superiority as an accomplished lady and dowry of twenty thousand pounds should have been his obvious choice.

The fact that Darcy had cut Miss Bingley in Bond Street shortly after his marriage made her stiffen in indignation. He could not possibly have been moved to act in such an offensive and demeaning manner toward her without the influence and manipulation of his wife. She obviously held a great deal of sway over him, though Miss Bingley could hardly understand why, especially after noticing how Elizabeth's fashionable gown seemed to fit her somewhat unfashionably, a clear indication she was not quite as slender as when they had all first known her. This, Miss Bingley decided, could only be to her advantage, and she would certainly use it to turn Darcy's attention from Elizabeth and toward herself.

"Pray, Eliza, might I persuade you to follow my example and take a turn about the room? It is so refreshing after sitting for so long in one attitude."

Her brow raised, Elizabeth glanced at Darcy, whose equal surprise at having heard words very nearly identical to those uttered by the same woman many months prior showed clearly upon his face. The entire room seemed to quiet, much as it had six months earlier, as all eyes became fixed upon the two ladies.

"Thank you, Miss Bingley, but I will decline. I am feeling a little tired, and if everyone will be so kind as to excuse me, I do believe

I will retire." Elizabeth knew precisely what her calculating hostess was about and smiled ruefully to herself. She would not fall victim to whatever scheme Miss Bingley had devised. She was not in the mood.

Elizabeth rose, and Darcy with her. "I shall join you, as well. I believe we have both had a long day."

Miss Bingley made a slight sound of protest, but her brother's amicable voice overpowered hers. He rose and said, "I am very sorry to be losing your company so soon this evening, but perhaps you will consent to a ride in the morning, Darcy? I am in desperate need of a good gallop—that is, if Elizabeth is feeling well enough to spare you. I cannot pretend to know anything of the particulars in these delicate matters, being a man and all, but..." His words died on his lips when he caught sight of the look of exasperation upon Darcy's face. Striding toward them, his cheeks flaming, Bingley took both of Elizabeth's hands in his and, under the pretense of giving her a brotherly peck on her cheek, whispered, "I certainly know how to put my foot in it, do I not, Lizzy? Please forgive my blunder. Darcy told me of your delightful news when you were last in Hertfordshire. I certainly did not mean to speak out of turn."

Elizabeth had to laugh at his flustered demeanor and hastened to save him from further distress. "I beg you would think no more of it, Charles. My aunt and Jane know, in any case, as do Georgiana, Lydia, and several of Fitzwilliam's discerning relations. I daresay the others appear to be none the wiser." With a smile, Elizabeth inclined her head toward her parents and remaining sisters, all of whom were presently engaged in their own conversations and paying no mind to hers. "Tomorrow I will share our happy news with the rest of my family. There, that being said, you are now at liberty to be completely at ease."

Elizabeth squeezed Bingley's hands and bid the room, in

general, a good night. She and Darcy then made their way to their rooms at a leisurely pace, their arms linked. "Though I can overlook Bingley's misstep, I can hardly account for Miss Bingley. What on earth could she have been about, do you think?" Darcy asked dryly, repressing a teasing smile.

"I believe, my dear," Elizabeth answered in a tone that was half amusement, half irritation, "you know very well what she was about. She saw only my increasing size and wished to draw attention to the distinct differences in our figures, much as she did when she attempted it the first time I was a guest here."

Darcy laughed and pulled her into a close embrace. "Yes, and with much success, I might add, though none of it in her favor. In my eyes, your figure was by far superior to hers, and as for how I now feel, you are well aware I take nothing but the utmost pleasure in your increasing figure and the reason responsible for it." He trailed one finger along her neckline with agonizing slowness. "Your breasts alone are inducement enough to lock you away and have my way with you," he murmured. "You are stunning, even more so now that you shall be a mother. It is all I can do to remain in control around you, for your body seems to rob me of every gentlemanly instinct I possess."

Elizabeth closed her eyes and sighed as Darcy's hand slipped lower to caress her breast. He drew slow circles through the fabric of her gown with his palm, and she moaned softly. "Mmm… as wonderful as this feels, you know we cannot continue here. Someone may come upon us at any moment."

"Indeed," he whispered against her neck. "What say you to the library, then? Surely no one will come upon us there."

"No one but my father," she laughed. "Whatever is wrong with our own rooms, Fitzwilliam?"

Darcy sighed and embraced her as he rested his forehead against hers. Transferring his hands to her back, he admitted, "Nothing at all, but I have always had a certain fantasy, if you will, of seducing you in Bingley's library. The delightful image of you in all your maidenly innocence, succumbing to my powers of persuasion, dominated my every waking moment while you were staying here nursing Jane shortly after I had first arrived in Hertfordshire."

Elizabeth pulled back her head and looked into his eyes as a slow smile played upon her lips. "I had no idea. I thought only that you did not wish for me to intrude upon your privacy, which I confess to doing just to provoke your ire. After all, I believed you had done the same to me at the time."

He stroked a stray curl from her cheek. "Hardly. Though I knew it to be wrong, not to mention dangerous, I confess to seeking you out whenever the opportunity arose. I could not seem to help myself. I was purposely throwing myself in your way—tempting fate, if you will—and wishing for I know not what to happen between us, but, at the very least, desperately hoping to spend some time in your company without anyone else to observe my open admiration. As you well know, it quickly turned into ardent love." He sighed. "As you can see, Mrs. Darcy, very little has changed."

"Oh, no. I would have to disagree with that, Mr. Darcy," she said archly. "You see, I now have a much better understanding of your taciturn nature, and I have come to discover you are not the least bit proud or disagreeable. No, my dear husband, I now find your society to be infinitely satisfying. Never would I provoke your ire, sir, at least not for my own amusement. In fact," she said, "where you are now concerned, I find my desires to be quite the opposite of what they once were."

"How very fortunate, then, for me," he murmured against her

lips as his hands stroked her hips and the softness of her derrière. "Let us retire to our room before I take possession of you right here in the middle of Bingley's hall." They did retire and spent half the night in amorous occupation, completely oblivious that every word they had uttered had been overheard.

After Darcy and Elizabeth had quit the drawing room, Miss Bingley had passed several minutes in a fit of pique before she finally resolved to retire herself, certain that the following morning would provide another opportunity for her to expose Elizabeth to possible censure. As she made her way toward her apartment, she heard lowered voices. Realizing too late precisely who it was and what they were engaged in, Miss Bingley stopped dead in her tracks, her eyes wide as her mouth literally dropped open.

Her first impulse was to give them a severe scolding; her next, to run; but then, and quite against her will, she found herself studying them, listening to them. She knew she was infringing upon their privacy—nay, on their intimacy—but, try as she would, she could not seem to tear herself away from the picture they presented. It was at that moment Miss Bingley finally understood it was not some passing infatuation on his part that had forced Darcy to sacrifice himself and all his wealth and consequence to the woman in his arms. Darcy was truly in love with his wife, and even more astounding to Miss Bingley was the realization that Elizabeth returned his love.

As Miss Bingley made her way to her room, she thought back to the time when she had first made the acquaintance of Elizabeth Bennet. None of Netherfield Park's inhabitants had thought her anything extraordinary, Darcy included, but Miss Bingley soon recalled that the master of Pemberley had not passed three evenings in her company before he had declared her eyes to be especially fine and her face rather beautiful. If Elizabeth had been aware of it, she had never given any indication of such knowledge. As a matter of fact, she had always acted as though Darcy was no different than her stodgy Uncle Phillips.

Contrary to Darcy's position in society, his great estate, his exceptional looks, his fine clothes, and his wealth, Elizabeth had never treated him with any preference she did not extend to any other person of her acquaintance. If anything, she treated him with less. She had never fawned over him, deferred to him, or gone out of her way to please him, nor, Miss Bingley thought ruefully, did she have to. Elizabeth had succeeded in catching Darcy's eye with no exertion on her part, but could it have been her open manner, her compassionate nature, and her witty intelligence that had captivated him? Miss Bingley was forced to concede that may have been the case.

She laughed scornfully over the unfairness of the situation. After all those years of trying to win Darcy with her flattery, elegant manners, and constant attention, Miss Bingley now thought it bitterly ironic that the master of Pemberley had never really wanted to be flattered and catered to, but, rather, treated as a simple man with simple tastes, and on equal terms with others. She could kick herself. So blinded was she by what Darcy had represented in terms of status and riches, it had never even occurred to her that he may have wanted to be appreciated and sought for who he was, not for what he had. She now saw with perfect clarity that Darcy had been drawn to Elizabeth in the first place because she had dared to treat him as no other woman ever had—or would, for that matter—and she had accomplished it all with great impertinence. In the end, Darcy had cared not and, in the meantime, had slowly grown to love her for it.

The final piece fell into place, and Miss Bingley knew the only thing left for her now was to come to terms with the fact that, no matter what she did—or would ever do—Darcy would never, ever choose her over Elizabeth. He loved Elizabeth, that much was now obvious, and Elizabeth returned his love, valued him, esteemed him. Miss Bingley had never been in love with Darcy. She had only been infatuated with what he could offer her as her husband—status, wealth, and the distinction of being mistress of a very great estate.

She breathed deeply and raised her hand to her now aching head. Darcy and Elizabeth would become her family in just two days' time. Family or not, Miss Bingley knew if she could not conduct herself with civility when addressing Elizabeth, it would only be a matter of time before Darcy would no longer invite her to Pemberley or perhaps even refuse to acknowledge her. She knew it would be far worse than it had been that day in Bond Street, for if Darcy happened to snub her again, there would certainly be no healing such a breach. She would never be welcomed among those of his circle. She would never find herself a wealthy husband. She would never be able to show her face in society again.

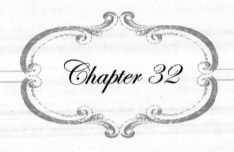

Chapter 32

Darcy kissed Elizabeth's cheek, and her eyes fluttered open. "Your nose is cold!" she admonished with a laugh. "That was hardly a gentlemanly way to wake a lady."

Darcy smirked and eased his fully dressed body onto her unclothed form as she lay beneath the warm counterpane. He buried his hands in her hair and his face in her neck, causing her to retreat farther under the covers with a small squeal. His guessed his cheeks must be cold as well.

Darcy grinned and murmured in her ear, "I cannot recall you behaving as a lady last night, nor any other night, now that I come to think of it, and I do believe I can also recall several afternoons quite recently where your comportment has been questionable."

Elizabeth gasped in mock indignation. "Are you saying you disapprove of my behavior, sir? I assure you, I am *very* much a lady."

"Disapprove?" he asked as he raised his head. "Certainly not. I have nothing but the utmost approval and respect for everything you do, my alluring wife. I will even go so far as to say it has been many months now I have considered you to be the most accomplished lady of my acquaintance, for a multitude of reasons that I shall be only too happy to enumerate for you."

With a slow, languorous smile, Elizabeth slipped her arms around his neck and fingered his cravat. "Such flattering words, sir! But I am afraid I must confess to having a very attentive instructor. He has been most diligent, you see, in his duties to the constant improvement of my mind. However, it may be time for another, more thorough, lesson." Then, quirking her brow, she inquired with an air of seduction, "Do you, Mr. Darcy, happen to know of anyone to whom I might turn for such attentive instruction?"

Darcy grinned as he ran one finger across her full lips. "I believe I happen to know of just such an instructor, and I daresay, madam, he is at your disposal."

By the time they had bathed, dressed, and made their way downstairs for breakfast, it was quite late, and though Darcy had already been up for several hours—he had met Bingley quite early for a ride across the neighboring fields—Elizabeth could hardly contain her embarrassment at the lateness of the hour, especially when she saw that Georgiana, Miss Bingley, and Mrs. Hurst had already finished their morning meal. They were about to rise when Elizabeth and Darcy joined them at the table.

Everyone exchanged pleasantries, and then silence settled over the table as those who had not yet finished continued to eat. Miss Bingley chose to remain and, so, sat quietly clearing her throat and smoothing her gown. After much pause, she ventured to speak. "I trust you slept well, Mrs. Darcy, and are rested and refreshed after your journey yesterday?" Her addressing Elizabeth in such a civil manner caused the others at the table to turn their heads toward her. Her tone and her expression held no hint of the jealousy and contempt she was well known to harbor toward the mistress of Pemberley. It was remarkably out of character for her to address Elizabeth as anything other than Elizabeth, and it did not go unnoticed by those in attendance, either. Darcy's eyes narrowed.

Elizabeth stared at Miss Bingley for several seconds before she managed to find her voice. "Yes, I thank you. I slept very well, indeed."

Miss Bingley offered her a strained smile before she turned her attention to Darcy. "And you, sir? Did you sleep soundly, as well?"

"I did, thank you, Miss Bingley."

"I am glad to hear it." She offered Darcy a similar version of the same smile, though decidedly more sincere, before she astonished the group further by addressing Elizabeth once more. "I know there is nothing quite like being in one's own home, but I do hope you are both comfortable here at Netherfield. I shall trust you to notify me of anything particular you may require, Mrs. Darcy. We have an excellent staff here. You may rest assured they would be more than happy to see to your every need."

Throughout the entire exchange between Miss Bingley and Elizabeth, Georgiana, Bingley, Darcy, and Mr. and Mrs. Hurst could do nothing but stare in wide-eyed astonishment.

"Thank you again, Miss Bingley," Elizabeth said in what she sincerely hoped was a calm, pleasant voice. "I am well acquainted with the efficiency of your excellent staff. I am certain, however, such attention on your part is hardly necessary. I would not wish to put you to any trouble."

Miss Bingley straightened her shoulders and sniffed. "Nonsense," she said dryly but with civility. "We are to be family, Mrs. Darcy. I assure you, it will be no trouble at all. It would be my pleasure." She cleared her throat once more and rose from her seat. "If you will excuse me, I must see to several last-minute preparations for tonight's ball. I would like everything to be perfect for Jane and Charles."

Mrs. Hurst also rose and followed her sister, leaving behind a table full of incredulous people. It was Mr. Hurst, however, who finally broke the silence. "Who was that woman, and what the deuce did she do with our Caroline?"

Georgiana choked on her tea while Bingley merely shook his head and stammered, "I hardly know."

Elizabeth and Georgiana ventured to Longbourn after breakfast, leaving the gentlemen to themselves for several hours. Though Elizabeth was excited about the prospect of becoming a mother, she dreaded her own mother's reaction to her news. She had tried, in vain, to persuade Georgiana to remain at Netherfield, but her sister-in-law would not hear of it. Unfortunately, Mrs. Bennet's joy, as well as her advice on such an occasion, was not to be underestimated.

"Oh! I knew how it would be!" she cried. "You must take after me, Lizzy, for I was with child in no time at all after my marriage to your father. You have done your duty to your husband very well, indeed. Now, if you can just give him a son, then I am sure Mr. Darcy would not mind in the least if you were to tell him you do not wish to do it again."

Elizabeth was grateful Georgiana was, at that precise moment, engaged in earnest conversation with Lydia and Mary on the other side of the room, especially after she heard her father add dryly, "I would certainly not count on *that*, my dear, if I were you." He then retreated behind his paper with a throat-clearing and did not emerge until the end of the visit. Elizabeth blushed.

Upon their return to Netherfield, Elizabeth and Georgiana were astounded to see Miss Bingley's earlier civility—though whether forced or sincere, they had yet to determine—had survived the course of several hours. Their hostess made a concerted effort at small talk without insulting or disparaging Elizabeth even once, showing the mistress of Pemberley every courtesy in her power. Georgiana made a point of observing Miss Bingley carefully, and upon noticing her staring at Darcy and Elizabeth with what could only be described as an unfathomable expression upon her face, she became even more bewildered by her behavior. Georgiana could detect nothing malicious or calculating in Miss Bingley's manner, however, so only exchanged a confused look with her brother.

Even Darcy could not find fault with Miss Bingley's conduct, though it did continue to baffle him, as well. He could hardly credit this sudden change in his friend's sister, but it did not necessarily follow that he did not appreciate the effort it certainly must have cost her.

By the time the hour of the ball arrived, the house had become flooded with guests, all of whom were eager to enjoy what promised to be a delightful evening. To the four-and-twenty families who resided in the neighborhood were added the many friends and family members who had come from various distances to attend the wedding. Among them was a Mr. Brewster, a young man of three-and-twenty who was to perform the office of standing up with Bingley. He was quiet and seemed somewhat reserved, but very agreeable all the same. His handsome looks and reported income of three thousand a year immediately captured the interest of all the young ladies in attendance, but very much like another taciturn gentleman before him, he had very soon settled his eyes on only one.

"Miss Lydia," said Bingley, "allow me to present my very good friend, Mr. John Brewster of Scarborough. Brewster, this is Miss Lydia Bennet, my dear Jane's youngest sister."

Mr. Brewster bowed to her. "The pleasure is mine, Miss Lydia, and if you are not otherwise engaged, might I request the honor of dancing the next with you?"

Lydia smiled and inclined her head. "Thank you, sir. I am not engaged."

He offered her his arm, and they made their way to the center of the room. "You reside in Scarborough, then, Mr. Brewster?" she asked.

"Yes, but my family is originally from Brighton. It is where I passed most of my youth."

"Brighton, you say? How wonderful! You must tell me all about it, sir, for I have always longed to go to Brighton."

Mr. Brewster could not help but smile at her enthusiasm. The music began, and they proceeded down the dance in happy conversation.

Later that night, Darcy paced the length of Bingley's study. "All I am saying, Bingley, is you should have consulted with either Mr. Bennet or myself before you took it upon yourself to make the introduction. Lydia is still recovering from what can only be described as a nightmare. She has told me she is reluctant to remain here with her own family because she fears society's censure, although, I confess, I am somewhat relieved to hear it. She has changed in the last two months, much for the better. She is no longer thoughtless and wild, thank God. Elizabeth and Georgiana have been an excellent influence on her, quite the opposite of her own mother, I must say."

Bingley took a long sip of port and sighed. "I cannot disagree with you, Darcy, and perhaps I should have first approached her father—especially considering the circumstances of late—but John Brewster is a very great friend. I have known him nearly half my life, and I can say with all honesty he is one of the most respectable gentlemen of my acquaintance. His intentions are honorable. He certainly will not take advantage of Miss Lydia."

"No. Perhaps not, but what if they form an attachment? What if Lydia one day feels compelled to confide in him her ordeal with Wickham? Is he the type of man who might abandon her and destroy all her hopes after his honor has become engaged? I hate to admit it, but even the most honorable man would be a fool not to think twice before offering for her after hearing such a confession."

Bingley stared at him. "You are behaving much like a mother hen trying to protect her chick, Darcy. They have danced only two dances together. I hardly think that constitutes an offer of marriage."

"Yes, they danced two dances but spent the remainder of the night in conversation. Other than you, Mr. Bennet, Mr. Gardiner, and myself, Lydia danced not one single dance with any other gentleman—not that it would have been prudent, in any case, but you must remember how fond she is of dancing." With a loud exhalation, he raked his hands through his hair and muttered, "Forgive me, Bingley, but I cannot like it. It makes me uneasy."

Bingley chuckled. "I truly feel for you, my friend. You now find yourself in the unsavory position of caring for two very young, very impressionable, and very pretty ladies who, for all intents and purposes, are not yet out, and you are feeling the full weight of it."

With a grin, he raised his glass. "For the sake of your sanity, Darcy, I do sincerely hope Elizabeth will give you a son."

Darcy closed his eyes and massaged the bridge of his nose. Finally, with a heavy sigh, he muttered, "Yes. I cannot but agree."

The wedding the following day was all that was elegant and delightful. It came as no surprise that Jane, a very beautiful woman, made an equally beautiful bride. While Elizabeth's wedding gown had been declared exquisite by all who had attended her wedding to Darcy, it was almost deceptively simple in comparison to Jane's, which was much closer to what society had come to anticipate from the blushing bride of a gentleman of no insignificant means. Nearly every inch of Jane's glorious silk gown was covered in imported Belgian lace, and though not quite to Elizabeth's personal taste, the gown her dearest Jane had chosen—or, more appropriately, her mother—certainly succeeded in flattering the new Mrs. Bingley's elegant figure, to which Mr. Bingley's steadfast gazes and dreamy expressions were a constant testament.

The wedding breakfast was held at Netherfield, where the bride and groom were to spend their wedding night before leaving to tour some of England's southern regions. Out of respect for the newly married couple, the many guests and relations who had arrived the day before and had spent the night—the Darcys included—soon made their farewells to the newlyweds and departed.

Mrs. Bennet was quite put out that Darcy would not consent to stay for a fortnight or two at Longbourn. She had been informed by her husband just that morning that Lydia was to travel to London with the Darcys and then on to Derbyshire, where she would remain for the next two months at least. Mrs. Bennet attempted to persuade her second-eldest daughter to use her influence with her husband, but to no avail. In fact, Elizabeth took great pleasure informing her mother that, in this particular instance, Darcy would not be swayed. He was anxious to return to his beloved Pemberley, where he had not set foot for the better part of a year. He was also looking forward to introducing Elizabeth to what was now her home, and extremely desirous of doing it before she could no longer be expected to make such an arduous trip. Assuming the weather was fit for travel, it would likely take them two or three days to reach Derbyshire, even from London. Darcy and Georgiana could barely contain their enthusiasm.

The Darcys and Lydia spent the following week in Town, taking their leave of the Gardiners, the Fitzwilliams, and certain close acquaintances, packing their trunks, and closing up Darcy House before finally departing for Derbyshire. The journey was long, tedious, and exhausting. Once again, Darcy found himself sitting opposite Elizabeth, but managed to force himself to pass the time more constructively by reading, which he did with only an occasional glance of longing directed toward his wife. Elizabeth chatted with her sisters while she attempted to work on some embroidery, which proved rather challenging while she sat in a constantly rocking carriage. She gave it up after their first day on the road in favor of a new book of sonnets Darcy had procured for her while in London. Georgiana was ill once, but not seriously so, forcing the party to stop earlier than expected for the day. By that time, Darcy had been more than ready to alight from the confines of the carriage and whisk his enticing wife away to the privacy of their adjoining rooms.

After three full days of traveling, they arrived at Pemberley. Darcy instructed the driver to stop the coach at a certain spot where the house could be viewed to particular advantage by all within, and Elizabeth's head reeled as she beheld the splendor of Pemberley House for the first time. Never before had she seen a house more happily situated or for which nature had done more.

"Lord, Lizzy!" Lydia laughed. "To think you are now mistress of all this!"

Elizabeth smiled at Darcy, who had been observing her reaction to her new home. He leaned forward to grasp her hand and asked, "Do you approve, Elizabeth?"

Elizabeth gave a soft, delighted laugh and said, "Oh, yes. Very much. I believe there are very few who would not approve."

"Perhaps," he said as his gaze caressed her with a look of love and just a hint of mischief, "but your good opinion is so rarely bestowed and, therefore, more worth the earning."

She laughed aloud and swatted his arm. "You are incorrigible," she chided.

Lydia and Georgiana smiled, and Darcy laughed. "Welcome home, Mrs. Darcy," he said. In the next instant, he rapped upon the roof of the carriage, and the driver urged the horses forward once again. They were soon well on their way to the house, where Elizabeth would now pass the rest of her days, most agreeably, she suspected, as mistress of a very grand estate.

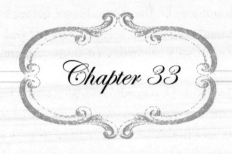

Chapter 33

To Elizabeth, and no doubt to those before her who had received the pleasure of setting foot in Pemberley House, the building's interior did not disappoint. Very much like their beautiful home in Grosvenor Square, the house—even with its imposing scale and obvious grandeur—reflected the refined elegance and partiality for comfort she had come to expect from her husband.

The main foyer, which held an outrageous number of servants assembled to welcome their master and new mistress home, was massive. It took Elizabeth several moments to overcome her awe and collect herself so she could properly address everyone before her. It was not difficult to see that they had been waiting eagerly—and with more than a little trepidation—to finally glimpse the lady who, it was rumored, had captured their master's heart. Elizabeth greeted them warmly, and her easy manners earned genuine smiles from many.

Amongst them was a kind-looking elderly lady whom Darcy introduced to Elizabeth as Pemberley's long-time housekeeper. Though not at all similar in appearance to the plump Mrs. Hildebrandt, Mrs. Reynolds had a motherly look about her all the same. It was apparent to the new Mrs. Darcy, who had observed the warm manner with which they had greeted each other, there existed a great fondness between the slender lady and Pemberley's master that transcended the bounds of the traditional roles of master and servant.

After making the necessary introductions, Darcy—with a smile that tugged at the corners of his mouth—escorted his wife to their private apartments. As they walked arm in arm through Pemberley's splendid halls, visions of Elizabeth as she reclined upon the enormous bed in the master's chambers pervaded his thoughts. It took some effort on Darcy's part to keep his eagerness in check and, thus, his dignity intact before the servants. So overjoyed was he to finally have Elizabeth with him at Pemberley, where he had long pictured her at his side, even before he had declared himself to her, that Darcy found it nearly impossible to restrain himself from sweeping her up in his arms and taking the stairs two at a time. Instead, he contented himself with bestowing several passionate and private looks upon his wife, which communicated to her his mood on the occasion.

They reached the mistress's chamber first, and as Elizabeth moved about the elegant apartment, Darcy's heart overflowed with happiness. He studied her with great satisfaction and pleasure as her eyes took in all that was now hers. It was by no small feat he had managed to force himself to remain in one spot rather than following her throughout the rooms like a calf-eyed young pup. The awed expression upon his wife's face, in Darcy's opinion, rendered her utterly enchanting. When Elizabeth finally turned to give him a breathtaking smile, he stepped forward to place his hand upon the small of her back as he offered comments on certain objects and furnishings, and encouraged her to make any changes she might wish. After restraining himself for a full five minutes, Darcy finally gave in to the impulse to gather Elizabeth in his arms and kiss her. What began as an innocent embrace soon flared into an expressive display of passion as Darcy's hands began to roam over his wife's body.

Far too soon—and much to his irritation—there came a knock upon the sitting room door, and Darcy tore his lips from those of his wife with a sound of frustration. He rested his forehead against hers and attempted to subdue his desire. After a few moments, he kissed her once more before stepping away. "Enter."

Blushing, Georgiana appeared from behind the closed door, cleared her throat, and said, "Forgive my intrusion, Fitzwilliam, but I thought you and Elizabeth would like to know that supper will be served in an hour."

"Thank you, Georgiana. Will you and Lydia not rest yourselves until then in your rooms? Our journey today was rather taxing. I would not wish for either of you to tire yourselves unduly."

Georgiana giggled. "I believe we shall both rest quietly until we must go down to dinner. You need not concern yourself with entertaining us, Brother. We have become quite capable of amusing ourselves in your absence."

Darcy gave her a stern look and she left quickly, her mirth barely in check. Scowling, Darcy took Elizabeth in his arms and said, "I do believe my sister has been just as much influenced by Lydia as Lydia has been by her these past months. I am yet uncertain whether I approve of her newfound impertinence."

A smile graced Elizabeth's lips as she slid her hands to his shoulders and beyond to bury her fingers within his thick curls. "I am very surprised to hear *that*, for I have long been under the impression that you approve of impertinent young women and hold them in nothing but the highest esteem. I believe I have even heard you, on occasion, pronounce one such lady to be uniformly charming."

"You, my dearest, are the only woman whose impertinence and teasing I have ever found charming," he growled as he captured her lips with his. "I cannot but approve of the way you tease me, for if you did not, I fear I would be far too serious and ill-humored far too much of the time."

She returned his kiss with some feeling. "Mmm… I cannot argue with that. I can recall just such a time, though not with as much clarity as I once might have, and although I found you equally as handsome then as I do now, I would not wish to have you so serious and grave again. You see, sir, you are utterly irresistible when you smile."

Darcy did smile then, and tugged Elizabeth toward the door that led from her rooms to the master's chambers. "Then I would have it no other way. Come, Elizabeth. You must be terribly tired after your journey. Perhaps you should rest yourself." His tone was teasing.

Elizabeth laughed at his blatant attempt to seduce her so soon after their arrival, and her eyes sparkled with mischief. "I assure you, Fitzwilliam, I am not the least bit tired; however, I might be persuaded to partake of some *exercise* if you would consent to join me."

A wide smile overspread Darcy's features as he led her into his apartment and kicked the door closed with his foot.

Elizabeth's first week at Pemberley, while enjoyable, passed far too quickly for her liking. After the rigors of traveling for so many days—which included all the amenities being confined to what coaches and country inns could possibly afford—she rejoiced at being able to retire each night to the comfort of her own bed, or rather, the incomparable luxury of her husband's. Her sleep being sound, Elizabeth rose early each morning to partake of a quick breakfast before she would steal away from the house with Darcy. As Derbyshire was so far north, its inhabitants were still experiencing the chill of winter, but the two lovers cared not. They wandered the grounds for hours, oftentimes losing themselves in the pleasure being at Pemberley afforded them. Elizabeth was so happy to be out-of-doors with just Darcy to accompany her.

Darcy was elated to finally have Elizabeth with him at his ancestral home, which meant almost as much to him as the woman he loved. Not even a blizzard, he suspected, could deter him from showing his wife as much of the grounds and surrounding woods as could be seen on foot without her becoming unduly fatigued.

The following week demanded that Darcy return to his duties as Pemberley's master, which entailed lengthy talks with his steward, daily rides to survey the estate, and meeting with tenants to resolve any concerns or disputes. Added to this list were many frequent and detailed exchanges with his solicitors, both in London and abroad. Elizabeth filled the hours of her husband's absence by familiarizing herself with the layout of the house, learning the names of the staff, and acquainting herself with the inner workings of the household. She soon found she had much to learn, and just as the running of Longbourn could hardly approach the complexity of Darcy House in London, so Darcy House and its operation paled in comparison to that of Pemberley.

Mrs. Reynolds had been in service with the family since Darcy had been a lad of four years, and while Elizabeth could easily tell that the elderly woman was a very warm, amiable lady, Pemberley's mistress soon found herself adding patience to the housekeeper's endless list of attributes, as well. Mrs. Reynolds was of great assistance to Elizabeth as she applied herself to her new responsibilities. Indeed, the kindly housekeeper spent a great deal of time assisting her in any way she could and, at Elizabeth's prodding, even went so far as to regale her new mistress with boyhood tales of Darcy and Colonel Fitzwilliam. As a result, Elizabeth took great delight in teasing her husband over his youthful antics. This form of torment always led a petulant Darcy to grumble about having a few choice words of chastisement for the elderly woman.

The months passed, and soon spring turned to summer. With the warmer season came the added responsibility of overseeing the fields after the spring planting, which would take up much of Darcy's time. It was not uncommon for the master of Pemberley to depart shortly after breakfast, not to return until an hour or so before supper was served. Though Elizabeth would have preferred to spend her days in the company of her husband, it was not within her power to do so. As difficult as this adjustment was for Pemberley's new mistress, she soon found much contentment and satisfaction in the society of her two younger sisters who, under her steady guidance and womanly assurance, were fast becoming promising young ladies. Pemberley's master could not be more pleased.

Though Darcy had initially experienced some trepidation when he had first learned of Elizabeth's pregnancy, it had quickly given way to delight at the prospect of becoming a father. As Elizabeth's slender body slowly increased, Darcy's joy became such that he did not feel the least bit inclined to dwell upon the moment when his wife would have to give birth. By the time August arrived, however, Elizabeth's size had increased to substantial proportions, forcing Darcy to finally give thought to the niggling fears he had, until that time, successfully managed to push to the back of his mind. With each passing day, he began to experience more concern for his wife, especially as he could not help noticing how she now found certain tasks, such as walking out for any distance or ascending the stairs to her room, to be more of a challenge. Darcy became on edge for Elizabeth's safety and, as a result, took great pains to ensure someone was there to watch over her on those occasions when he was unable to accompany her. Though this precaution did go a long way in appeasing Darcy's worry over her immediate safety and comfort, it did very little to free his mind from dwelling on the dangers Elizabeth would very soon face with the birth of their child.

He remembered all too well his mother's ordeal when she had been expecting Georgiana and, even more vividly, the long, arduous birth and heart-wrenching sorrow that had followed. Though Elizabeth was not experiencing any difficulties other than those that all healthy young women who are fast approaching their confinement have in common, Darcy's anxiety for her multiplied. For Elizabeth's sake, he attempted to conceal his unease as best he could, but it did not take long for his astute wife to notice her husband's agitation.

Elizabeth sensed Darcy's anxiety growing daily and, knowing him so well, had her suspicions regarding the cause. She became especially concerned when she noticed his distraction was such that he had resumed his old practice of staring at her from across the room, much as he had done in Hertfordshire, to the exclusion of anyone else who might also be in their company at the time. Elizabeth had asked him, on several occasions, to confide in her, to share the source of his disquiet, but Darcy simply looked at her, shook his head, and kissed her as he assured her all was well and that he was tired or distracted. Elizabeth did not believe him for a moment, and one night, as she sat at the pianoforte and played a particularly moving love song, she happened to glance up to find his gaze fixed upon her with such a look of anguish it caused her fingers to fumble upon the keys. Their eyes locked, and then Darcy quickly turned aside his head and swallowed thickly. Elizabeth turned her attention back to her music with a frown.

At the end of her song, Darcy rose and strode from the room without so much as a word or even a look to her. Elizabeth followed him to his study. Without knocking, she entered to find him standing before a large window as he looked out into the darkness. His forearm rested against one of the window's panes, his other hand on his hip.

"Was my performance so lacking you felt the need to flee without so much as a word to me?" she asked.

Her words were teasing, but there was a seriousness to her tone that caused him to shift uncomfortably. "Nothing is wrong with your performance, I assure you," he said in a low, almost painfully quiet voice. "I am only distracted tonight, that is all."

She crossed the room to stand beside him and placed her hand upon his arm. "Allow me to say, Fitzwilliam, that your assurances in this quarter have come to mean very little. Will you not finally speak to me of this thing that has been weighing upon you so heavily that you would persist in concealing it from me rather than confess?"

Darcy shook his head. "In this instance, I am afraid there is nothing that can be gained from my speaking of it. Indeed, I cannot."

Elizabeth stroked her hand over his arm and asked, "You cannot, or you will not?"

He swallowed hard then. "Elizabeth, do not ask this of me," he said, his voice hoarse. "It is not my wish to cause you distress."

She stared at him, her exasperation and concern at his stubbornness evident. "Fitzwilliam, you cannot possibly cause me more distress by speaking with me than you already have by your refusing to do so. By your failing to confide in me, my agitation shall only continue to increase. Can you not see this?"

She squeezed his arm gently, and Darcy ran one hand over his tired eyes. A full minute passed before he inquired, "Are you certain you truly wish to know?"

"I do," she said, her voice earnest. "Please, speak to me."

He sighed and, after a few moments, began to speak in a pained voice, his gaze fixed upon some imaginary point as he continued to stare out into the darkness. "Whenever I close my eyes each night, whenever I think of you during the day—which, as you must know has always been constantly—I cannot help but be reminded of the very great danger I know you shall soon have to face. In vain I have struggled to think of happier thoughts, but I cannot seem to stop myself from dwelling upon the worst. I fear for you, Elizabeth, I fear for our unborn child, and, selfish as it is, I fear for myself. There is no possible way I can continue to exist if you do not. I cannot put it any plainer than that."

Elizabeth, thankful to have her suspicions confirmed at last, said, "Fitzwilliam, indeed, you need not trouble yourself with such thoughts. You know I shall never leave you, and certainly not like that."

Darcy turned then and faced her, his eyes tortured. "But you and I *cannot* know that, Elizabeth. Not for certain."

"No," she said. "No one can ever know anything for certain. We can only put our faith in God and hope for the best. Fitzwilliam, my mother bore five healthy daughters, and she survived each birth with no complications whatsoever. My pregnancy, from what I understand, is much like hers. In any case, you have seen for yourself and heard the doctors' reassurances that nothing untoward has occurred to give rise to any worry." She paused for a moment before adding, "I am not your mother, my dearest. I am myself. Though you were quite young then, you must recognize some difference in our circumstances. Can you not?"

He pulled her into his arms. "I can," he admitted. "I know you are not her, Elizabeth, but it is because of her that I cannot help but to think in such a manner. Believe me when I say I do not wish to dwell upon such wretched possibilities."

"Then do not," she commanded softly. "Do not think any longer of such things. Only have faith in me when I say to you all will be well." He said nothing in response, and Elizabeth said, "Fitzwilliam, I am so very happy I am carrying your child. I want for you to be happy, as well. We have only one short month until we shall become parents. Our privacy—our entire lives—will be greatly altered by this new life growing within me. Do not waste this precious time we have alone together with such dark thoughts. Do not dwell upon what may never come to pass. Rejoice in the knowledge that I love you and our child, and all shall be well in the end."

Darcy nodded mutely and buried his face in her hair. Breathing deeply, he held onto her with a fervency and an emotion he had not dared in days. "Tell me again that you will not leave me, Elizabeth," he whispered in a pleading voice.

"Never," she promised with absolute finality. "I shall live a long, healthy life and bear you ten children, tormenting you daily with my impudence."

Darcy laughed as he hugged her tighter.

Elizabeth smiled and placed a kiss upon his cheek. "Come," she said. "It has been a long day, and I believe we are both in dire need of rest, my love. Let us retire and think no more of this."

Many hours later, Darcy lay awake, unable to find repose, but, miraculously, not due to any tormenting thoughts that might have plagued him earlier. Elizabeth had been tossing in their bed for more than two hours, attempting to find a position she could abide for longer than ten minutes. The air had grown quite hot and uncharacteristically oppressive for Derbyshire, even for August, and Darcy longed to bring her some relief, though he hardly knew how. Finally, Elizabeth sat up and dropped her head into her hands. "I feel as though I will never again sleep longer than two hours altogether. I am so hot and uncomfortable, Fitzwilliam," she whined.

Darcy sat up, as well, and rubbed her lower back. He hoped the circular motion might soothe her. "I am sorry, my love," he said as he placed a kiss upon her exposed shoulder, where he then rested his chin. "I wish there was anything I could do to make you feel better. You know I would gladly take on your discomfort myself if it meant you would be easy. Perhaps a cool bath would do much to ease your suffering? Shall I ask Sonia to draw one for you?"

"No, it is now nearly three o'clock in the morning. Certainly, Sonia is asleep, and I would not wish to wake her, but," Elizabeth said with a sly smile, "I do believe a swim in the lake would feel heavenly right now." She threw off the tangled sheets with much enthusiasm, reached for her discarded shift and dressing gown, and then slid rather awkwardly from the bed.

Darcy leapt after her, and his concern for her safety returned in full force. "Elizabeth, certainly not. You shall be seen, and it could be dangerous. Do you not recall anything of our conversation? You are now heavy with child and should not be exerting yourself thus."

"Nonsense. No one is about at this hour, and I hardly think you would allow me to go alone, in any case. The cool water shall bring me some relief, I am sure of it." She patted her bulging stomach and grinned. "If anything, I shall be more buoyant with this ample body of mine. Indeed, I am convinced it is perfectly safe."

Clearly unconvinced, but unwilling to argue with her, Darcy sighed. "Can I not persuade you to see reason?" he asked as Elizabeth fastened the belt of her dressing gown and busied herself by retrieving several towels from the edge of Darcy's large copper tub.

"None whatsoever." She smiled then arched her brow and extended her hand to him. "Come, Fitzwilliam. I suggest you make haste and dress yourself, sir. The lady of the lake beckons, and you know it is abominably rude to keep a lady waiting."

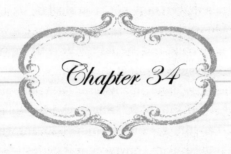

Chapter 34

With the coming of September, so came Mrs. Bennet to Derbyshire for an extended stay under her son-in-law's expansive roof. Much to the consternation of Pemberley's master and mistress, Elizabeth's mother was determined to be present for the birth of her first grandchild, whose impending arrival she did not expect until the following month. Having anticipated their wedding vows by more than a fortnight, however—and convinced their unborn child had been conceived during one of the amorous interludes preceding their marriage—Darcy and Elizabeth had decided to allow the world to believe the birth a premature one. Early births were not so uncommon, after all, and Elizabeth's labor would take place without the presence of family members and friends and, most especially, the presence of Elizabeth's mother.

It was not to be, however, for the prospect of spending several months among the grandeur and wealth of Pemberley's halls and grounds proved to be far too much of a temptation for the mistress of Longbourn to pass up, and though her husband had attempted to dissuade her from making the trip, his objections only served to make her all the more determined to go. Even after Mr. Bennet informed his wife that Longbourn's harvest would prevent his accompanying her on the two to three-day journey, and the horses would most certainly be required in the field, her resolution—and her excessive complaining—eventually won out, and in the end, her husband, now desperate for the peace and quiet her absence would afford him, sent her north to his son-in-law.

The first week of her visit was all it had promised to be. Mrs. Bennet spent the majority of her time flitting from room to room, making suggestions for various changes to the wallpaper, furniture, draperies, and floral arrangements. She even went so far as to take it upon herself to alter the menu for the evening meals. Knowing her husband to be far from pleased with the authority her mother was so brazenly assuming in his home, Elizabeth attempted to curb her behavior, but with little success. Mrs. Bennet was so full of effusions and suggestions, gossip and idle chatter, that she soon wore down her daughter, who felt more fatigued as the day of her confinement approached. That a good portion of Elizabeth's exhaustion stemmed from her mother's seemingly boundless supply of verbal energy did not go unnoticed by Pemberley's vigilant staff.

Deciding it was the only way in which Elizabeth might gain a reprieve from her mother's enthusiastic company, Mrs. Reynolds frequently insisted her mistress retire abovestairs and rest. Though she was grateful to the housekeeper for her kind solicitation, Elizabeth found she dearly missed the companionship of her sisters. Lydia had since gone off to school in London with Mary and Kitty, and Georgiana had also removed to Town. She was now living with her trusted companion, Mrs. Annesley, at Darcy House, where she would remain until Christmas. Though Darcy was always at Pemberley, every day saw him more heavily engaged as he supervised the harvest and tended to matters of estate business with his steward from dawn until dusk, and very often much later. By the time he and Elizabeth retired each night, Darcy barely managed to crawl into bed before he collapsed beside her, his arms wrapped around her as Elizabeth snuggled against the length of his exhausted body. He would find repose quickly as he caressed the enormous, kicking bulge of his wife's stomach, his other hand tangled in her mass of curls.

In the final days leading up to the birth, Elizabeth's discomfort grew to substantial proportions—and not merely all of it physical. Her mother's keen observations of her daughter's condition were growing more astute with each passing hour, and made all the worse by Mrs. Bennet loudly extolling that, had she not known better, she would be quite certain Elizabeth's time was very nearly upon her. What more could Elizabeth do besides offer her an awkward turn of her mouth and steer the conversation to any topic that might prove more successful in diverting her mother's attention from the obvious?

After experiencing several days of extreme discomfort, Elizabeth felt the first pains of her labor begin early one September morning several hours after the sun had begun its ascent over the horizon. She had been parted from her husband since dawn, as his presence was required to tend to a rather heated dispute that had been escalating between two tenants for days. Wishing to feel closer to Darcy, she chose to remain in their bed in the master's chambers, where they had passed the entirety of every night in each other's arms. The pains were nothing more than slightly uncomfortable, and Elizabeth felt a thrill travel through her at the prospect of soon holding her child in her arms. Knowing she would need her strength for the delivery and realizing it would be many hours yet until the babe would be born, she closed her eyes with the intention of resting herself. Sleep did not come easily, however, as her pains slowly advanced—both in intensity and frequency—and, with it, her anxiety at the prospect of giving birth. She knew she should alert someone to her current situation and rang for Sonia.

Sonia arrived to see her mistress breathing heavily as a wave of pain hit her. "Oh, ma'am!" she exclaimed. "I believe your time has come! I shall fetch Mrs. Reynolds at once!"

Elizabeth reached out her hand to prevent her from leaving. The young woman took it and exerted a gentle pressure. "Sonia, I wish to have Mr. Darcy informed that my pains have begun. He is currently seeing to a dispute between Mr. Roberts and Mr. Gordon. Please have someone go to him at once."

Sonia nodded. "At once, ma'am, but I shall send Mrs. Reynolds to you in the meantime. The master would never forgive me if I were to leave you alone."

Mrs. Reynolds arrived in very good time and took charge immediately, arranging Elizabeth's pillows, smoothing the bed linens, and seeing to her every comfort. The housekeeper's calm demeanor went a long way in soothing some of Elizabeth's rising panic. "It will help if you walk, Mrs. Darcy," Mrs. Reynolds advised. "Such activity has been known to hasten delivery."

Obediently, Elizabeth nodded and allowed the woman to assist her as she stood and slowly began to make her way about the apartment, wincing as her pains escalated. Sonia returned and hurried to support her mistress on her other side. Several hours passed without any news or even so much as a word from Darcy, and Elizabeth became progressively ill at ease as her pains continued to grow.

Though it had not been her intention to draw him from his duties simply to sit idly by her side to attend her, Elizabeth had imagined Darcy would have been eager to join her as soon as he was able or, at least, to send her some small missive if he found himself not yet at liberty to do so. His absence thus far caused her more anxiety than she felt she would have experienced otherwise. She found it difficult to refrain from worrying about his safety. "Mrs. Reynolds," Elizabeth finally inquired as she panted after a particularly strong contraction, "are you quite certain Mr. Darcy has been informed of my condition?"

The housekeeper squeezed her hand and smoothed back her hair. "I am, ma'am. Several footmen have been sent out to him, but as he is on the far side of the estate and currently embroiled in a very pressing matter of business, I am afraid it will be some time yet before he shall be at liberty to tear himself away."

Mrs. Reynolds did not reveal to her mistress that she had been told the dispute between the two tenants had since grown quite serious and was rumored to have escalated to such distressing proportions that, within the last half hour, the magistrate had to be sent for, as well. Darcy, per Mrs. Reynolds's instruction, had been assured Elizabeth was doing well, and therefore, the housekeeper saw no need for him to cast aside his urgent business in order to hurry home for a birth that, while being of monumental import to the entire estate, was not likely to take place for many hours yet, certainly not until well after nightfall.

At noon, Elizabeth was persuaded to partake of a light meal in her room to keep up her strength, and toward teatime, as darkness began to loom over the house, she was much relieved to hear a flurry of activity just outside in the hall. In the next instant, however, Elizabeth's heart sank as her mother, rather than her husband, entered her room, breathless and extremely vexed. "Lizzy! So it is true, then! Your time has come, I see, and a good deal early, too! Why was I not informed of it immediately? These things can be terribly trying for a young woman, as I am well aware. It is very fortunate for you that I am here to help you through it, child. I shudder to think of you being all alone with no one but the servants to assist you." Mrs. Bennet suddenly noticed Mrs. Reynolds and Sonia tending to her daughter, and she frowned.

Elizabeth groaned, and though her mother thought it merely the onset of another labor pain, Mrs. Reynolds and Sonia knew enough of their mistress to suspect it stemmed more from Elizabeth's reaction to her mother's offensive words and often overbearing presence than anything else. "Mama, I did not wish for you to be disturbed. It is not yet time for the babe to be born. I assure you, I am perfectly fine," she gasped as another contraction came upon her, and her attention was diverted elsewhere. A pointed look passed between Mrs. Reynolds and Sonia then, and with a comprehensive nod, the younger woman rose to dispatch another footman with a note for the master.

Within a half hour, Elizabeth's labor progressed rapidly, the midwife was sent for, and Pemberley's mistress was removed to the birthing room. She was now in much pain. *Where on earth is Fitzwilliam?* she wondered in panic as her mother, having repeatedly boasted of her own success at having borne her husband five healthy daughters, launched an ill-advised campaign instructing the midwife on how best to do her duty. *Surely he should have come to me by now! What could be wrong? I know very well that something must be terribly wrong!* Mrs. Bennet, even though Elizabeth knew she meant well, was far from exuding a calming influence over those present—most especially, the mistress of the house. Indeed, it was all Elizabeth could do to restrain herself from ordering her mother from the room.

"Take several deep breaths now, Mrs. Darcy," the midwife instructed in an authoritative voice. "I believe it is almost time to begin pushing, but not quite yet."

Oh, God, Fitzwilliam, where are you? Elizabeth wanted to cry, her terror steadily augmenting.

Darcy's anxiety for his wife had grown throughout the course of the day until it nearly threatened to consume him as he was forced to deal, first, with two unreasonable tenants who had threatened to do each other grievous harm over a fertile parcel of land between their properties and, then, with the magistrate and his men. Had it not been for the gravity of the situation, which his steward had assured him would have undoubtedly escalated to horrendous proportions far sooner if Darcy had failed to remain with his tenants to assert control over the situation, the master of Pemberley would have quit the scene the very moment he had received word of his wife's condition.

By the time he had been handed a second missive from Sonia, stating that Elizabeth was in need of him, Darcy knew he had already done everything within his power to defuse the hostile situation. His steward had agreed there was little left for him to do, and as the magistrate was now on hand to restore order after Mr. Roberts's violent attack against Mr. Gordon, Darcy wasted no time taking his leave of the officials. He found he could not ride fast enough or arrive soon enough, and, as he approached the front entrance of Pemberley House, Darcy barely took the trouble of reining in his lathered mount before he leapt from the saddle and took the steps two at a time. He burst through the doors and raced up the main staircase to his wife's chambers, only to find them empty. In a panic, he ripped open the door that connected her room with his, and his heart nearly stopped beating. The bed had been stripped clean and stood before him, its cold starkness taunting him from the center of the room. Dread flowed through his veins, and he ran a trembling hand across his mouth, his thoughts a wild jumble of desperation. He prayed he had not arrived too late.

Down the hall, Darcy heard his mother-in-law's abrasive voice screeching orders to someone and then a strangled cry of pain that could only have come from Elizabeth. Such sounds had never been so welcome to his ears, and he suddenly felt his strength return in full force. Darcy raced from the room, his heart pounding in his chest, and all but tore the door to the birthing room off its hinges. He was greeted by the shocked faces of Mrs. Bennet, Mrs. Reynolds, Sonia, and a surly-looking woman he could only assume was the midwife. Mrs. Bennet stepped forward and turned him unceremoniously from the room.

"Mr. Darcy, certainly this is no place for a man, sir! I shall send word to you when it is over," she said before she turned from him and retreated back into the room. The door closed behind her.

His eyes narrowed at being thus treated in his own home, Darcy forced the door open with his hand. "No. My wife has sent for me, and I intend to see her." His voice was firm, resolute, and filled with anger.

Mrs. Bennet, however, waved him off. "You most certainly shall not. As I have said, a man has no place in a birthing room. I will ask you again, sir, to leave at once. You can be of no help to Lizzy while she is in such a state. You would only be in the way, to say nothing of the impropriety of your presence during such goings-on."

Elizabeth cried out then, and Darcy's fury reached its boiling point. "Mrs. Bennet!" he hollered. "You will step aside, madam, or I shall not be responsible for my actions! I *will* see my wife, and I will see her now!" He pushed past her and strode to Elizabeth's side.

The expression of relief that flooded her features was apparent to all. "Fitzwilliam," she whispered as she held out a trembling hand.

Darcy knelt at her side, placing kisses upon the hand he grasped between his own. "I am here, my love. I am here," he said as he moved her damp curls from her face. "Forgive me. I would have been here far sooner had I only—"

Another strangled cry was issued forth from his wife. Instinctively, Darcy placed his lips upon Elizabeth's hair as she bit down upon her lower lip with such force that a drop of blood appeared. Darcy blanched and removed it with his thumb.

"Now, Mrs. Darcy," said the midwife, "at the next contraction you must push. Push as hard as you are able. Mr. Darcy, I must insist that you leave now, sir."

Darcy's expression of outrage transformed itself into one of incredulity as his attention snapped from the midwife to his wife, who had begun to protest his removal most vehemently and with such language that could hardly be construed as that befitting a lady. The midwife and Mrs. Bennet, equally mortified by such an outburst, joined forces then, insisting Darcy leave them, but Elizabeth, in her anger and determination, refused to give way. She did not wish to be parted from her husband, whose presence was all she had wished for throughout the course of the day. Another pain began, and Elizabeth gripped Darcy's hand as she bore down, hard.

Mrs. Bennet continued her protest but found herself silenced by Mrs. Reynolds, who held Elizabeth's other hand between hers. "For heaven's sake, Mrs. Bennet, let them be!" said the housekeeper. "Can you not see how they bring each other comfort?" She then turned aside her head and muttered under her breath, "How anyone can miss it, let alone her own mother, I know not. Indeed, a blind man would see their devotion."

Mrs. Bennet started at the barb Darcy's housekeeper had just flung at her. The mistress of Longbourn was about to hurl her own invective when she heard her daughter cry out, commanding her full attention; then she could only stare as her proud and imposing son-in-law moved to support his wife completely, his devotion punctuated by firm, quiet words of encouragement, comfort, and love. Upon bearing witness to such evidence of openness and unabashed affection—which she was hardly used to from her own husband—Mrs. Bennet felt her cheeks heat and retreated to the far corner of the room, her lips pursed in a thin, hard line. Not a quarter of an hour later, Elizabeth's cries gave way to tears of joy. Pemberley's new mistress, after a day of arduous labor, gave birth to a beautiful, healthy babe.

After Mrs. Reynolds and Sonia assisted her in pushing out the afterbirth, Elizabeth was cleansed, dressed in a fresh shift, and carried to the master's chambers by her husband. Forced to yield to her son-in-law's desire to hold the newest member of his household clasped to his breast while his wife was being attended to—and in his presence, no less!—Mrs. Bennet felt her vexation magnified by tenfold when she watched Darcy reclaim his child after he had seen Elizabeth settled in their own room. Ignoring all others present, he joined his wife as she reclined upon their bed, speaking quiet words of affection with a warm smile of happiness. Darcy's eyes, brimming with tenderness, moved between his wife—who had laid her head against his shoulder—and the precious charge cradled in his arms. Mrs. Bennet suddenly found herself torn between indignation that they would forget themselves in such a way while in company, and envy that they were so obviously able to do so and with an incredible amount of ease.

Unsurprisingly, Mrs. Bennet's growing irritation at being kept from her grandchild soon overcame all other feelings. In a fit of pique, she threatened to remove herself from the room and quit the house entirely if she was kept from the child even one minute longer. It was then, after exchanging a pointed look with his wife, Darcy reluctantly rose and surrendered that which, in a matter of a mere half hour, he now held so very dear to his heart.

Mrs. Bennet's sour expression softened to one of wonder and delight as she gazed upon the tiny bundle her son-in-law had transferred to her arms, and as she spoke, to everyone's surprise, her voice was soft rather than shrill, and her words comforting rather than offensive. Darcy could only watch the transformation with awe, a smile curling the corners of his mouth as he turned to his wife and lifted her outstretched fingers to his lips.

Many hours later, Darcy and Elizabeth found themselves blissfully alone. "I am so very sorry I was unable to come to you earlier than I did, Elizabeth. If the situation between Mr. Roberts and Mr. Gordon had not been so dire, I would have made my excuses immediately to attend you. Sadly, that was not the case."

Elizabeth nuzzled against the roughness of his cheek. "There is no need for you to dwell upon it, my love. I understand your responsibilities to your tenants and to Pemberley. There is no need to explain your actions to me. From what you have told me already, it sounds as though your presence there was required far more than it was here. It would have been tragic, indeed, had either Mr. Roberts or Mr. Gordon succeeded in killing the other over such a grievance, especially on this joyous day. If I recall correctly, Mrs. Gordon is soon to enter her own confinement. Surely, had you not been on hand, there existed the very great possibility their own child would never have known his father. I believe we all have much to be thankful for." Elizabeth gave him a tender smile full of love. "You are a wonderful master, and as Mrs. Reynolds has so often said, I do believe no one here at Pemberley could ask for a better one. Your son will learn much of value from you, Fitzwilliam, and indeed, he will turn out to be exactly like you: the very best of men."

Darcy pulled her closer. Even during what had, undoubtedly, been an emotional and fearful time for her, Elizabeth had still managed to understand him so well—had managed to perceive all that had been weighing upon him, the tremendous burden he had faced and was forced to carry on his shoulders that day. She had fully accepted his role as Pemberley's master—his responsibilities to his estate and to its people—with grace and an unselfish heart. His heart swelled with pride for his wife. How could it not, for Elizabeth had certainly proven herself as Pemberley's mistress on this day.

"We must think of a name for this little one," Darcy said as he gazed with tenderness at his son, who, at that moment, suckled at his mother's breast. Darcy reached out his hand and caressed the downy hair that covered his child's tiny head. It was very dark—almost black—with somewhat of a curl to it, very much like his own. His son's infant features, however, showed him to be an exact replica of his mother, save for his eyes. Even after living in the world for only a few short hours, it was apparent to all who had looked upon him that his eyes were exactly like those of his father—penetrating and expressive.

Elizabeth stroked the softness of her son's cheek with her finger, and a smile graced her lips. She could not ever remember feeling such happiness. "Yes," she said, "we do need to find a name for you, do we not, my little prince? Do you have any preference, Fitzwilliam?"

Darcy gazed upon his son, of whom he could not be more proud, and felt his heart swell to painful proportions, both for this miracle of life and for the incredible woman who had made his son's existence in the world possible. Darcy glanced at her. "What would you say to naming him after Bingley?" he asked. "I have always been fond of the name Charles, and I believe I owe him a very large debt of gratitude."

Elizabeth looked at him with a quizzical expression, and he sighed as he raked his hand through his hair. "For many years now Bingley has been a very great friend to me and an even greater friend over this past year. He made me look at myself—my principles and my life—more closely than I had ever dared to do before and perhaps even more importantly, he forced me to examine, and acknowledge the wishes and desires of my heart. I cannot help but feel that, had he never leased Netherfield, it may have taken me far longer to find you. Perhaps it would even have taken me the rest of my life. So you see, Elizabeth," he said as he fingered the gleaming gold of her wedding band, "I owe him much."

Elizabeth laid her head upon his chest and reached her free hand up and around his neck to bury her fingers in his hair. Darcy closed his eyes as he pressed soft kisses upon her curls, which were currently arranged as he liked them best—loose and flowing, spilling over her shoulders and down her back, framing her face as a painter would a masterpiece. They were reclining together in bed—their bed—their son nestled between them as he nursed, the perfect picture of familial harmony. It was very late or very early—Darcy knew not which—and he had not parted from either of them since the miraculous moment when he had watched Elizabeth give birth countless hours earlier.

"I believe Charles would do very well for this gentleman," she said as she gazed upon her son with an expression of deep adoration. "Perhaps, Charles Thomas, after my father?"

Darcy opened his eyes and smiled. "I can think of nothing more appropriate." He gazed with tenderness at the perfect little image of his wife. Their newborn son had placed his tiny hand upon his mother's breast.

He now studied Elizabeth intently with his expressive eyes, much in the same manner his father had been known to do on countless occasions in the past and would certainly continue to do in the many years still to come. "He does have your eyes, Fitzwilliam," Elizabeth said. "See how he stares at me so? You had a very similar intensity about you, you know, when we first knew each other in Hertfordshire. Even now, I often see it in you when you look upon me. I cannot help but wonder what such a look can mean in our son, though."

Darcy leaned in and tangled one of his hands in her tresses. "Can you not?" he asked.

Elizabeth slowly shook her head, and Darcy smiled and kissed her again. "I daresay my son knows when he is in the company of a breathtakingly beautiful woman. He is bewitched by you, as I have been since nearly the very first moment I laid my eyes upon you so many months ago." His hand slipped from her hair to caress her shoulder, where he lingered for several moments before sliding his fingertips along the length of her arm. Elizabeth shuddered with pleasure and turned her eyes upon him. Darcy's own grew very dark then, and as he touched his forehead to hers, his voice dropped to a murmur. "I have long suspected I could spend an entire lifetime in your company, Elizabeth, and never have enough of you."

She leaned into his touch and closed her eyes with a sigh, a small, contented smile upon her mouth. "You are incorrigible, Mr. Darcy," she teased, then asked, her tone surprisingly serious, "Shall we put this theory of yours to a test, then, do you think?"

Darcy pressed his lips to her temple, her cheek, and, finally, her lips before saying in a low, even voice full of love and conviction, "I plan to devote my life to it, Mrs. Darcy."

And, indeed, he did.

Epilogue

Four years later, Elizabeth Darcy stood in the midst of all her relations, lifelong and newly acquired, each impeccably attired and wearing a smile of joyful anticipation as the door of Pemberley's small chapel was thrown open. As the heady scent of freshly cut roses permeated the air and beams of sunlight shone through the stained glass windows, Elizabeth smiled. Her eyes sought those of her husband as he made his way toward the altar with Georgiana on one arm and Lydia on his other. His face was an inscrutable mask as he avoided meeting his wife's joyful gaze.

After placing a kiss upon the rosy, glowing cheeks of each young woman, Darcy surrendered his sisters to the keeping of their prospective bridegrooms and claimed a seat beside his wife. His eyes were suspiciously shiny, and as the minister began to speak, Elizabeth felt her husband's hand reach for hers and apply an almost painful pressure. She moved closer and placed her other hand over his, squeezing his fingers. Their eyes met and held for a long moment, and Darcy, his emotions running high, swallowed hard several times before finally mouthing a reverent, "I love you," as he brought both her gloved hands to his lips. Elizabeth smiled, her love for him showing just as clearly in her eyes on this day as it had on the morning of their own wedding.

Once she had learnt to apply herself in the proper manner, Lydia had flourished during her years away at school in London. However, while Mary and Kitty were content to return to Longbourn once their education had been completed, Lydia was not. At the invitation of her second-eldest sister and her brother-in-law, Lydia returned to Pemberley and placed herself under their guardianship indefinitely. With consideration, encouragement, and a healthy dose of patience, her discourse had become sensible, her opinions insightful, and her talents and interests far exceeded those of her past. Her most fulfilling reward for any effort now came in the form of a few kind words of praise or a warm smile, most particularly when bestowed upon her by the master of Pemberley.

Though she, Mary, and Kitty had taken to addressing Darcy as Brother, Lydia had actually come to look upon him as more of a father figure. His good opinion was important to her, and so, she had taken it upon herself to strive to please him in very much the same manner Georgiana had always done—with the intention of making him proud of her. Lydia trusted Darcy's judgment implicitly and was apt to defer to his wisdom and experience with complete faith in his desire for her welfare, paying him a consideration and a respect she had never been inclined to show her own father during her fifteen years under his roof.

To the astonishment of many, neither gentleman permitted it to become a source of strain or resentment between them. Rather than dwell upon the implications, Mr. Bennet chose instead to do what he had always done so effectively over the years: he overlooked the offense, though, this time with a heavy heart, especially on the day when Lydia traded her maiden name for that of another. Feeling, in a matter of four short years, that his son-in-law had more than earned the right to give away the admirable young lady who had once been his most troublesome daughter, Mr. Bennet gracefully ceded the honor of escorting her down the aisle to Darcy. John Brewster, who was to be the happy recipient of Lydia's fair hand, hardly cared which gentleman held the distinction of presenting his bride to him, so long as she was surrendered at the proper hour and location.

Music suddenly filled the small chapel, signaling to all within that the ceremony was now officially ended. Darcy watched in a daze as the two smiling couples, who had eyes for none but each other, turned and proceeded up the aisle arm in arm. The doors were thrown open without ceremony, and as birdsong filled the air, all four young people burst out into the perfect June morning amidst shouts of joy and wishes of glad tidings and prosperity. Beaming, Elizabeth stood and tugged on her husband's hand. The wedding breakfast would be held on a stone terrace not far from the house. A white canopy had been erected by the servants and trimmed with seasonal flowers and silk ribbon. It would be a sumptuous affair, a perfect complement to the ball that had been held the night before. Darcy placed his wife's hand in the crook of his arm and sighed.

After a rather emotional day, and well past the hour when his guests had retired for the night, Darcy stood alone in Pemberley's nursery, gazing upon his daughter, who was not quite one year.

The door creaked open so silently he failed to hear it, nor did he discern the soft footsteps of his wife as she approached in her dressing gown and slippered feet. Her heart full, Elizabeth watched him for several minutes while he traced their slumbering daughter's pudgy little cheek with his index finger. Her voice was soft when she finally called to him.

He did not turn but remained with his gaze fixed upon their precious babe. It was many moments before he spoke, his voice low after such a monumental day. "It never fails to astound me how very much Eleanor resembles you," he murmured. "She is so tiny, yet she has your eyes, your lips, your dark curls, even that little crinkle that appears between your brows when you are contemplating something you find baffling."

Just then, the young lady in question reached out one plump thumb and four fat little fingers and wrapped them around her father's finger. She ignored Darcy's attempt to extract himself and held tight, refusing to let go. She sucked on her bottom lip as she slept on.

Darcy smiled at her quiet determination. "She also seems to have inherited your willful spirit, as well," he softly laughed. With a smile of her own, Elizabeth extracted her husband's finger from her daughter's firm grasp, then watched as he slowly raked his hands through his hair, his voice no more than a whisper. "I remember Georgiana being this small as though it were yesterday."

Elizabeth's heart went out to him. She knew, perhaps better than anyone, how attached her husband was to his sister and how acutely he was feeling her loss, especially at this moment. Having raised Georgiana on his own since she had been eleven, she had, in many respects, been more of a daughter to Darcy than a sister. He had become equally as attached to Lydia in the past four years, and having to part not with one but with both on the same day had been almost too much for him to bear. Elizabeth stood on her toes and kissed his cheek. Darcy's arms instantly went around her, and she proclaimed, "It has been an emotional day, has it not?"

Darcy buried his face in Elizabeth's hair, closed his eyes, and allowed the familiar scent of lavender to wash over him, as well as the comforting presence of her softness. The combination, even after the newness of their marriage had worn off, was still instrumental in soothing his agitation. "This day, I fear, has been more difficult than I had originally anticipated," he admitted.

Elizabeth raised her head and kissed him. "My dearest," she murmured as she smoothed an unruly curl from his brow, "I can only imagine how you must feel, but I suspect it will become easier with time. This is only the first day, and though Lydia is to reside in Scarborough, Georgiana will be settled only ten miles from Pemberley. She and Mr. Blake have promised to visit us often, and I need not remind you, Fitzwilliam, in the meantime you shall have a most attentive and loving wife to lavish affection upon you. As you are well aware, sir, you will never find yourself at loose ends so long as I am here to encompass every spare second of your time." Elizabeth reassured him with another kiss and a warm look that brought him further relief.

Darcy smiled down upon her. His eyes closed once more, and with a sigh, he allowed his wife to placate him with her ministrations. Elizabeth said in a teasing voice, "You must also strive to remember that you have a family who absolutely adores you. I believe you know I refer to more than your son and daughter, my dear. You have several other sisters, you know, who love you, as well, to say nothing of an extremely attentive mother-in-law."

At this declaration, Darcy laughed. "I do hope, however," he said, "that your mother and her good intentions will remain at Longbourn with your father for some duration before coming to stay with us again. You must own that her exuberance can be trying, especially when there is a wedding at hand. And there has been more than one occasion during this visit, in spite of your father's efforts to check her, when she attempted to lay the blame for Lydia's initial desire to leave Longbourn upon my shoulders, alone. That, you must own, is hardly fair."

Elizabeth sighed. "I cannot disagree with you, but I am more inclined to believe the happiness of her favorite daughter's most fortuitous marriage to Mr. Brewster to have eclipsed any real resentment she may have once harbored toward you on that score. You know she would hardly be civil to you at all if that were the case—or to me for that matter—and she has been, for the most part, quite affectionate toward us both."

"True. I cannot argue that, in many instances, your mother has been solicitous and kind, especially where the children are concerned, but it does not necessarily follow that because of it I am willing to excuse her more vexatious behavior. In light of all that has passed, you know how it infuriates me to hear her always speaking of frippery, suitors, and marriage to Eleanor. I am convinced that, having now lost all her daughters to common sense and enlightenment, your mother is determined to make ours into the silliest creature imaginable. I will not have it. For God's sake, Elizabeth, she is but ten months old!" he shouted.

Though Eleanor slept on, young Charles, who had been sleeping on the other side of the nursery, stirred at his father's harsh tone. Elizabeth laid her hand upon Darcy's arm as she watched their son roll onto his stomach and snore softly, clutching a toy tightly in his arms. Darcy, his jaw rigid, exhaled and ran his hands across his forehead before he strode from the room.

When Elizabeth found him a few moments later, he was on the balcony just off the master's chambers. His back was to her, and his hands were braced upon the railing, clutching the iron in his fists.

His stiff posture told her all she needed to know—he was far from happy. She came to stand beside him and inquired, "What is it that is truly bothering you, Fitzwilliam? For though my mother has often incited agitation in each of us, you have hardly been yourself this day, my love."

"Forgive me," Darcy muttered, his voice barely audible, and after running the back of his hand across his mouth several times, he confessed, "All this business of courting and weddings, I believe, has finally taken its toll on me. I am not cut out for this, Elizabeth… this meeting with prospective suitors and judging correctly whether or not they are sincere in their attentions to those whom I hold most dear. I fear I am ever doubtful and suspicious, and that is very unlikely to change… ever."

"You are an elder brother, Fitzwilliam, and now a father. Indeed, it is to be expected," she replied.

"It is more than that. I remember well what befell both our sisters not so long ago, and at the hands of the same blackhearted scoundrel. However, in many senses of the word, we have been fortunate. Though it took time, Georgiana recovered and met Blake—an excellent man—and Brewster fell in love with Lydia, much in the same manner I fell in love with you. It is not every man who would overlook what either of them went through, nor excuse their actions in such events, but it is even more than that. I cannot help but worry that someday Eleanor will desire to leave our protection only to throw herself into the power of some undeserving man who could not possibly recognize or appreciate her true worth."

Elizabeth moved to rest her cheek upon Darcy's back and slipped her arms around his waist. "Are you?" she asked, "for I must say I am hardly concerned such a thing shall ever happen.

We have many years ahead of us yet to teach Eleanor how to go about choosing a young man who is truly worthy of her love and admiration. I daresay when the time comes for her to surrender her heart to the keeping of another, she shall have no trouble whatsoever in discerning whether or not he is deserving of her."

Darcy laughed ruefully. "Forgive me if I do not share your confidence. There is no way to ensure such a thing. If Georgiana so easily failed to see what a wretched mistake she was making, and then Lydia—though at the time your sister was hardly the woman she is today—I am afraid I cannot carry so much faith in my heart."

"You fail to see the common element then, Fitzwilliam."

He turned sharply. "You mean Wickham? Though he has been dead these four years, I had not thought you so naïve as to believe there are not others in the world very much like him, who would not hesitate to do just as much harm, perhaps even worse."

"I was not referring to Mr. Wickham, my dear," Elizabeth said. "I was referring to us, to our love. *That* is the common element or, rather, one not so common." Darcy stared at her, and Elizabeth sighed, clearly exasperated. Rather than lose her patience, however, she decided to take pity upon him. "Though I have no doubt Georgiana has always been a very sensible young lady, she had not a mother to speak to her or to guide her and though Lydia had the benefit of such counsel at her constant disposal, one can hardly declare either my sister or my mother to ever have been sensible at the time. Neither of our sisters had anything truly tangible to base their woeful decisions upon. It was not until they were able to see what love should be—to observe it firsthand in us, and to discuss it openly and honestly—that they were finally able to begin to experience it themselves on some vicarious level and, ultimately, to apply that knowledge they had gleaned—that recognition—to their own circumstances. Because of this, they have been able to make sensible decisions for their own greater good and that of their husbands', as well."

Watching her husband struggle with this revelation, Elizabeth sighed and extended her hand to caress his abrasive cheek. "You are truly the very best of men, Fitzwilliam. Indeed, I have yet to meet any man who could ever begin to compete with your goodness and your sense of honor. Both Georgiana and Lydia were able to recognize that in you, as well. They chose to model their ideals after you, and as a result, they are now married to two very respectable men who love them unreservedly, in spite of their youthful indiscretions. I can almost promise you Eleanor will be no different and much quicker to pick up on it, I might add, simply because she will have *me* to explain it to her."

Darcy held Elizabeth tightly. "You are correct, of course. I should have known better than to question your logic. However better I may feel, though, it still does not help knowing that someday my baby girl will leave me, even if it is for the love and admiration of the *second* best of men," he said with a slight curve of his lip.

Elizabeth laughed. "I doubt Eleanor is ready to leave you just yet, especially after the way you have taken to spoiling her."

"Then I believe I shall have to use this information to my advantage and endeavor to continue with my current course of action. Perhaps tomorrow I shall purchase a pony."

"You may purchase twenty ponies if you like, Fitzwilliam, but I am sorry to inform you that such generosity shall not ensure your daughter's continued residence at Pemberley any longer than it takes the man of her dreams to find her and sweep her off her feet. As you know, your time would be far better spent showing Eleanor the many remarkable things you can offer her as her father, such as your wealth of knowledge and strength of character, not the material objects your money can purchase for her. In any case, that is one lesson you have learnt well since the day you met me, so I am convinced you shall do an equally admirable job with our daughter."

Darcy struggled to repress a smile at her teasing words. She was right; he knew she was. Though Elizabeth had been unaware of it at the time, she had made him work hard to earn her admiration and, ultimately, her love, but in the end, the reward was well worth every bit of the initial suffering he had endured. This woman was, beyond a doubt, his most cherished treasure, and she had been generous enough to give him two others as well: their son and their daughter.

"Indeed," he said, his voice holding a hint of a teasing inflection, "it is a lesson I found forced upon me very early in our acquaintance, Mrs. Darcy. However, it only continued to prove to me your full value as a woman worthy of being pleased. Of course, I remember well that you were often impertinent to me throughout the whole business and on far too many occasions for me to recall with any degree of accuracy."

"You are incorrigible, Mr. Darcy," she replied, then ran the tip of her tongue over his smiling lips. "I believe, sir, in cases such as these, a good memory is unpardonable. Tell me, husband, why must you forever make mention of my faults?"

Darcy captured her lips in a slow, teasing kiss before he turned his attention to the curve of her neck. When his lips reached her ear and upon hearing her sigh of pleasure, he murmured, "In my opinion it is hardly a fault, you minx, as you are well aware. Though it was the teasing look in your eyes that first drew my notice, it was your impertinence and liveliness of spirit that soon captivated me.

The combination, madam, and only in you, I might add, is one I have always found irresistible."

Elizabeth smiled as he took her lobe between his teeth. His hands wandered over her curves in agonizing slowness; all the while, he drew her body closer. She allowed herself to melt into his embrace, their bodies pressed together. Her voice was hardly more than a whisper when she said, "All this time I had thought it was my intelligent discourse."

"Hardly," Darcy growled, "but that was a most pleasant inducement, as well, as was your light and pleasing figure."

"Incorrigible," she whispered again as his hands slid down her back to caress her hips.

"Lizzy," he whispered roughly. His hot breath, coupled with the name he always reserved for those moments of deepest intimacy, sent shivers of longing through her body. "Let us see if we cannot make another impertinent daughter."

Nine months later, and over the course of the ten years that followed, Elizabeth presented Darcy with three such daughters. Though each was exclaimed over and pronounced to be a local beauty, much in the same manner that their mother and aunts had been, to the astonishment of their elder brother, none of his teasing sisters was ever proclaimed by their father to possess even half so much of their mother's celebrated impertinence. In light of such a declaration, young Charles, who had inherited much of Darcy's serious mien, could not help thinking his proud father must have had very little sense in his head at the time to have so easily fallen under the spell of a pretty young woman those many years ago… even if the pretty young woman was his mother. Darcy took great pleasure in enlightening him.

About the Author

Susan Adriani has been a fan of Jane Austen's work and her beloved characters for as long as she can remember. In addition to writing, she is a freelance graphic designer and illustrator. In 2007, after contemplating the unexplored possibilities in one of Miss Austen's most celebrated novels, *Pride and Prejudice*, she began to write her first story. With encouragement from fellow Austen enthusiasts, she continued and is currently at work on her second and third books. She lives with her husband and young daughter in Connecticut.

Mr. Darcy's Obsession

~

Abigail Reynolds

The more he tries to stay away from her, the more his obsession grows...

"[Reynolds] has creatively blended a classic love story with a saucy romance novel." —Austenprose

"Developed so well that it made the age-old storyline new and fresh... Her writing gripped my attention and did not let go." —The Romance Studio

"The style and wit of Ms. Austen are compellingly replicated... spellbinding. Kudos to Ms. Reynolds!" —A Reader's Respite

What if... ELIZABETH BENNET WAS MORE UNSUITABLE FOR MR. DARCY THAN EVER...

Mr. Darcy is determined to find a more suitable bride. But then he learns that Elizabeth is living in London in reduced circumstances, after her father's death robs her of her family home...

What if... MR. DARCY CAN'T HELP HIMSELF FROM SEEKING HER OUT...

He just wants to make sure she's all right. But once he's seen her, he feels compelled to talk to her, and from there he's unable to fight the overwhelming desire to be near her, or the ever-growing mutual attraction that is between them...

What if... MR. DARCY'S INTENTIONS WERE SHOCKINGLY DISHONORABLE...

978-1-4022-4092-8 • $14.99 U.S./$17.99 CAN/£9.99 UK

Mr. Fitzwilliam Darcy:

THE LAST MAN IN THE WORLD

A *Pride and Prejudice* Variation

ABIGAIL REYNOLDS

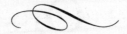

What if Elizabeth had accepted Mr. Darcy the first time he asked?

In Jane Austen's *Pride and Prejudice*, Elizabeth Bennet tells the proud Mr. Fitzwilliam Darcy that she wouldn't marry him if he were the last man in the world. But what if circumstances conspired to make her accept Darcy the first time he proposes? In this installment of Abigail Reynolds' acclaimed *Pride and Prejudice* Variations, Elizabeth agrees to marry Darcy against her better judgment, setting off a chain of events that nearly brings disaster to them both. Ultimately, Darcy and Elizabeth will have to work together on their tumultuous and passionate journey to make a success of their ill-timed marriage.

978-1-4022-2947-3
$14.99 US/$18.99 CAN/£7.99 UK

What readers are saying:

"A highly original story, immensely satisfying."

"Anyone who loves the story of Darcy and Elizabeth will love this variation."

"I was hooked from page one."

"A refreshing new look at what might have happened if..."

"Another good book to curl up with… I never wanted to put it down..."

In the Arms of Mr. Darcy

SHARON LATHAN

If only everyone could be as happy as they are…

Darcy and Elizabeth are as much in love as ever—even more so as their relationship matures. Their passion inspires everyone around them, and as winter turns to spring, romance blossoms around them.

Confirmed bachelor Richard Fitzwilliam sets his sights on a seemingly unattainable, beautiful widow; Georgiana Darcy learns to flirt outrageously; the very flighty Kitty Bennet develops her first crush, and Caroline Bingley meets her match.

But the path of true love never does run smooth, and Elizabeth and Darcy are kept busy navigating their friends and loved ones through the inevitable separations, misunderstandings, misgivings, and lovers' quarrels to reach their own happily ever afters…

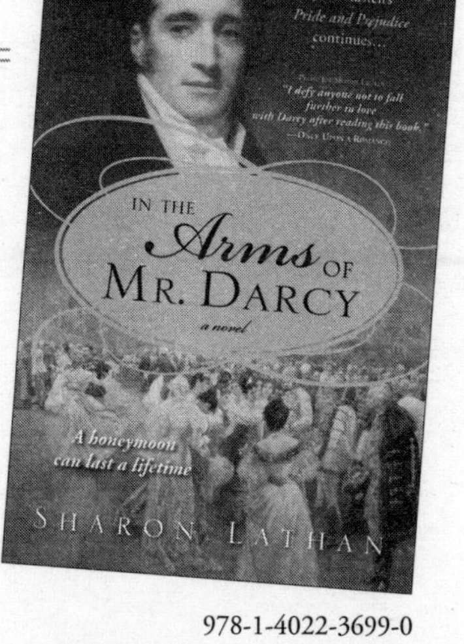

"If you love *Pride and Prejudice* sequels then this series should be on the top of your list!"
—*Royal Reviews*

"Sharon really knows how to make Regency come alive." —*Love Romance Passion*

978-1-4022-3699-0
$14.99 US/$17.99 CAN/£9.99 UK

My Dearest Mr. Darcy

Sharon Lathan

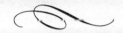

Darcy is more deeply in love with his wife than ever

As the golden summer draws to a close and the Darcys look ahead to the end of their first year of marriage, Mr. Darcy could never have imagined his love could grow even deeper with the passage of time. Elizabeth is unpredictable and lively, pulling Darcy out of his stern and serious demeanor with her teasing and temptation.

But surprising events force the Darcys to weather absence and illness, and to discover whether they can find a way to build a bond of everlasting love and desire…

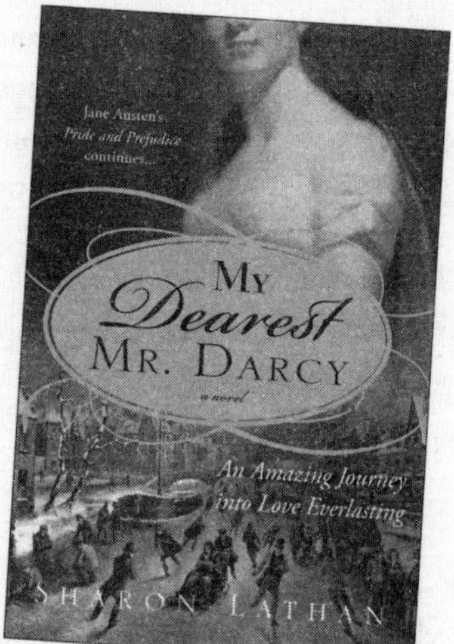

Praise for *Loving Mr. Darcy*:

"An intimately romantic sequel to Jane Austen's *Pride and Prejudice*…wonderfully colorful and fun." —*Wendy's Book Corner*

"If you want to fall in love with Mr. Darcy all over again…order yourself a copy." —*Royal Reviews*

978-1-4022-1742-5
$14.99 US/$18.99 CAN/£7.99 UK

Mr. Darcy Takes a Wife

Linda Berdoll

The #1 best-selling **Pride and Prejudice** ***sequel***

"Wild, bawdy, and utterly enjoyable." —*Booklist*

Hold on to your bonnets!

Every woman wants to be Elizabeth Bennet Darcy—beautiful, gracious, universally admired, strong, daring and outspoken—a thoroughly modern woman in crinolines. And every woman will fall madly in love with Mr. Darcy—tall, dark and handsome, a nobleman and a heartthrob whose virility is matched only by his utter devotion to his wife. Their passion is consuming and idyllic—essentially, they can't keep their hands off each other—through a sweeping tale of adventure and misadventure, human folly and numerous mysteries of parentage. This sexy, epic, hilarious, poignant and romantic sequel to *Pride and Prejudice* goes far beyond Jane Austen.

What readers are saying:

"I couldn't put it down."

"I didn't want it to end!"

"Berdoll does Jane Austen proud! ...A thoroughly delightful and engaging book."

"Delicious fun…I thoroughly enjoyed this book."

"My favorite *Pride and Prejudice* sequel so far."

978-1-4022-0273-5 • $16.95 US/ $19.99 CAN/ £9.99 UK

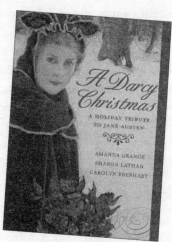